PLAY THE GAME

HANNAFORD PREP YEAR THREE

J BREE

To Laura
We are the weirdos, mister.

PROLOGUE

Harley

I'M FORCED to walk behind the sick fuck who is holding Lips at his side, pressing her into him until they're moving as one.

Every eye at Hannaford is on us, the building is holding its breath as we walk out to the waiting car. It's a statement, a public claiming, and I know that when we return to school for our junior year Lips will be treated with a whole new level of suspicious reverence. I'm going to fucking hate it, but maybe it'll keep her safe.

The BMW waiting for us is the same type my grandfather owns. It looks fucking showy, but it's the unseen elements that make it worth well over the mil mark. Bulletproof, flame retardant, and supposedly able to withstand a bombing, it's not a status symbol.

It's a vehicle built for war.

Diarmuid drops his arm from where it's slung around my shoulders to open the door and usher me in. Lips warned me about protocol and I know this is a clear move from my uncle, telling the Jackal I'm a protected player. I hate it; I hate what my life is costing everyone, but if it keeps Lips safe too, then I'll play along.

He climbs in beside me and we sit in the rearward facing seats. It's risky because I'll be facing Lips and there's no way I can look at her while the Jackal watches us both.

He watches her like he fucking owns her. He watches her like he's picking out the inches of her skin that he's going to brand with his mark to keep her chained by his side.

I fucking hate it.

The rage that grows inside my chest expands until I can't breathe and it's only the echo of her words, the rules she told me back in her room, bouncing around inside my skull that stops me from reaching forward and choking him the fuck out. My uncle sits beside me, grinning like a fucking idiot, and I try not to look back at the posturing dickhead that keeps kissing and touching my Mounty. I know he's just trying to get a rise out of me, but you know what? He's succeeding. I keep my eyes on my own hands or on the Jackal's hands.

He's gripping her knee hard enough that I know it has to be hurting her. It's her bad leg, and she's just gotten over the flare up. She ignores him, doesn't attempt to brush him off, and I know she's trying not to provoke the sick fuck. I want to kill him.

When, finally, the barren, gray wasteland of Mounts Bay looms over us, he breaks the silence in the car.

"Where are you staying this year, little Wolf? I'll check your security and make sure you are safe." He murmurs and I clench my fists. Diarmuid nudges me discreetly. I take a deep breath and force myself to unclench.

Lips hums under her breath, a habit she's picked up from Floss, and says, "Take us to the docks, Luca."

"Anything for you, princess." The dickhead says and Lips scoffs at him.

"Where are you staying?" The Jackal asks again, his voice harder. I roll my shoulders back, ready to grab the fuck if he goes for a weapon.

Lips shrugs. "Arbour is heading back up the coast and I have a few jobs lined up. I'm meeting with a friend at the docks to discuss the terms of my acceptance. You know I only take certain jobs."

He speaks through his gritted teeth. "I'm not asking what you're doing in the Bay, I'm asking where you're staying."

She pauses and then with a flat voice she says, "And I'm choosing not to provide you with that information. I told you months ago, I'm learning to stand on my own two feet. I appreciate the ride, but I'm on my own. It's me and Arbour, and any other person I choose to induct. If you wanted me to be one of yours, you should have inducted me instead of sponsoring me."

"I tried. You told me you'd rather die." He snaps.

That's news to me. I look up and meet her eyes.

I know why Floss warned me not to look at her around the Jackal; I know I can't keep the longing and the worship out of my face, and only Lips has been blind to it. I can't help but look at her now and the clenching on the Jackal's jaw lets me know he sees it for what it is.

Lips stares at me as she replies to him, "I will never be owned, and certainly not by you. I'm the Wolf."

I'm fucking flirting with danger, I know it deep in my bones, but I grin at her with the savage joy that her words rip through me. She tips her head back and laughs like a lunatic, and that's when I know she does feel fear. She's just as affected by this as I am.

The car pulls into the docks and the Jackal's hand tightens on her knee until she grunts. I lurch forward and grab his wrist, ready to choke the fucker out if I have to, and he reaches for his gun with his free hand. I hear the click of a gun to my right and tense up.

"You're hurting the little girlie, Jackal. Best you let her go." Diarmuid croons.

Luca parks the car and flings the door open, presumably to help his boss now he has a loaded gun pointed at him, but there's a beat of silence before I hear, "Boss. You'd better get out of the car."

The Jackal is sneering at Diarmuid as he wrenches his wrist out of my hand. "Pointing a gun at me? You're a fucking dead man, O'Cronin."

Diarmuid clucks at him. "Hurting a fellow member of the Twelve? You wouldn't want that getting back to the meetings, now would you? Think of what the Crow would do to you, he's been waiting a long time to take you out."

"She's mine!" he roars, grabbing her arm, and the door on his side of the car is ripped open with such force I think it will tear right off the hinges.

"Get your fucking hands off her, D'Ardo." roars the newcomer. My eyes stay glued on the Jackal until he drops her arm. He looks out the door, grimacing, and finally his face shifts into something close to wary.

I blow out a breath and yank Lips into my arms, shoving us both out of the door on the other side of the car. She's not shaking, no racing heart in her chest or shallow breathing, but I can't say I'm that as unaffected by the little spat. Once we're out, and I've run my hands over her to be sure he didn't fucking knife her without me noticing, I glance up only to find the fucking Butcher of the Bay staring back at me.

I gape back at him like an idiot. He winks at me.

Fuck me.

What the hell have I gotten myself into?

"I told you, I called for reinforcements. Illi's a good guy, the best." The Mounty whispers in my ear and then pulls away from me, stepping back into her role as the Wolf.

A good guy.

He's a cage fighter, a trained killer, his weapons of choice are his fists or a fucking meat cleaver, he shows no mercy and has no conscience, and, according to my crazy hot girlfriend, he's a good guy.

I think I'm going to have a fucking stroke.

CHAPTER ONE

S PYING on clients for the Tiger is my favorite type of work.

I'm picky about what I'll do for him. I've made it pretty fucking clear to him that I will not take out innocent witnesses just to keep his dirty clients out of prison and he's good about finding me work that is okay with my morals.

Which is how I find myself dressed like a Mounty street girl at three am outside a bar fending off sleazy, drunk assholes.

Leaning my overheated, sticky back against the brick wall staring at my phone should be a big enough indicator that I'm not currently selling but three broken fingers later and I'm still having to tell guys to fuck off. Not that I'm selling at all, it's just the best spot to find the information I'm after without attracting too much attention.

My phone vibrates silently in my hand and I cringe before opening the new text.

Right. Where the fuck are you? If you don't tell me I'm texting the group message and you can explain this shit to Avery.

Ugh. I'd told Harley not to come down until after 10am tomorrow. I wanted to finish up the job and sneak in three hours of sleep before I had to deal with the fallout of our 'chat' with the Jackal, but in typical Harley style he drove down to the Bay from his hotel on the coast early. I'd called the POA and gotten him into the townhouse in the gated community I've rented, but the barrage of text messages has only gotten worse as the night wears on.

I'll come back to the house now. I'll be 30mins.

I am not going to go back right at this second and I order an Uber to arrive in twenty minutes. I'm sure I could persuade Harley to believe there were traffic delays. The mark the Tiger had paid me fifty grand to get photos of is loitering in the gardens across the road. I know he's there for drugs, I just have to wait the dickhead out.

I'm already in the car.

Bossy fucking boys. I send him the name of the bar and glare down at all the skin I'm showing. He's either going to be a total fucking dick over it or I'll get a hot make-out session in the car. I wonder if he's boosted the car? My thighs rub together without me even realizing because I'm fucking damaged and get hot for that shit.

I keep my head ducked like I'm staring at my phone even as my eyes follow my mark. He's coming down from whatever high he's been riding and his body language is becoming more and more agitated as the night wears on. I need him to act before Harley gets here. If he makes a scene, my cover is blown and I will have to find a new vantage point and spend another night out here following the idiot around.

I hear the roaring engine first and then shouting and whistling pierces the air. I groan under my breath. When the mustang pulls up in front of me, I already know who the hell it will be, and now I have the attention of the entire damn street. It's a *fucking* nice car, a vintage muscle car that rumbles like a beast even as it idles at the curb. Matte black and silver trimmings, even to me the car looks like a wet fucking dream.

I pull my lips into my best Mounty street girl smile and trot around to the driver window. Wasted guys outside the bar start catcalling me and the other street girls start talking shit. I ignore them all for the guy smoldering in the drivers' seat.

Harley is pissed.

"I'm working so unless you want me out here again you should play the fuck along." I croon because I have to make it look like I'm giving him the sales pitch of his life.

Harley grunts but a fake smirk plasters itself across his lips and he grits out, "I can see the outline of your fucking pussy in those shorts, Mounty."

I take a shaky breath and glance down to double check that he's just being moody. Okay, I have a teeny tiny bit of a camel toe but nothing so dramatic that it's indecent or anything.

"Look, I can't leave until I get this done. This is my ninth job and I've worked my ass off since I got back so I wouldn't have to work once you got here. Please, just leave me to get this done."

He quirks an eyebrow at me and shifts in his seat to grab his wallet. The girls behind me yell out to him, trying to get his attention and cut me out of the deal. Harley's lip curls in their direction and they quieten down.

He pulls out a fifty-dollar bill and waves it at me obnoxiously. I've snapped bones tonight for less. "This gets me an hour, right? Let me take you around the corner, you can pick which one, and I can keep an eye on you while you work."

I chew on my lip for a second and then bend down to lean into the car and kiss him, dirty and raw like the street girls do.

Harley grunts as I bite his lip and he slips the money into my bra, careful not to touch me. He doesn't want to touch me like this, not when I'm dressed up to work and hating every second. It's fucking sweet. I have to remind myself of our audience and keep the kiss outrageously sexual.

It's ridiculous that I know how to do that just from growing up here.

I pull away from him and trot around the car like I'm giving him a preview of what I have to offer him. His eyes stay glued to mine.

I have to do a weird slide to get into the car because my shorts are so tight, and the smell of the warm leather seats hits me as I shut the door. I direct Harley to a good spot and he parks up, cranking the air conditioning up, a blissfully cool breeze on my overheated skin.

"Information or a hit?" Harley says.

"Photos. Nothing too dangerous really." That's a partial truth. The mark isn't a concern, but if the dealer sees me, there will be serious fallout.

"How much?" Harley murmurs, watching me as I watch my mark.

"Fifty grand. It's the smallest job, so I left it until last."

He nods and settles back in his seat, his eyes closing as he grabs my hand. I blush and try to keep my focus on the drug addict. Harley traces his thumb along my knuckles absently.

"Can we talk or will that distract you?" He murmurs, his eyes still shut.

Ugh, fuck. I sigh. "Is this about Illi or the Jackal?"

"Both of them. I know who you are. I know enough about this world to know it's not fair of me to ask you to stay the fuck away from the Jackal, but seeing him touch you and knowing how much he scares you was fucking *bad*, Mounty."

I swallow around the lump at the back of my throat. "I know. I'm... I'm taking care of it. Illi is part of that."

I grab my phone as the dealer finally shows up. The mark is directly in front of the car, across the street, but the photos I get are clear enough to show what's going down. The guy isn't subtle, but the outrageous price I'm being paid is because of how high the risk of being caught is, not because of how hard it is to find the mark scoring his dope. He's so far gone he would buy it in front of his own mother.

"How did you meet the Butcher?"

I wince. "I hate that name for him."

Harley grunts at me. "That's who he is; he fucking mutilates people."

I cut him a glare. "He also saved both our asses. He's... the same as I am. He came into this life unintentionally, but with a set of highly sought-after skills. When I told him I'd applied to Hannaford, he helped me get out, he helped me remove myself from Mounts Bay, and then he cut off all contact with me so I'd have a fucking chance at getting clear. He's a good guy."

Harley looks at me like I'm challenging his very moral system, then his eyes slide away from me and he snaps, "Fuck. We're made."

My eyes dart over to find the dealer, one of the Jackal's men

I know and who most *definitely* knows me, who is now stalking over to the car, and I move without really thinking it through. I lean forward to grab the release on Harley's seat to push it back. He inhales sharply as I climb over to kneel on the floor between his knees and crouch awkwardly under the steering wheel. His eyes widen and he swears viciously as I fumble to get his belt unbuckled and his pants undone. I can feel his dick getting hard as my hand brushes against him even as he protests.

"Mounty-" he hisses, and I cut him a look.

"I'm not going to fucking suck your dick to get out of this, but I *am* going to pretend. How are your acting skills?" I whisper and before he can answer there's a knock at the window.

I blanch a little -because, *really*, am I going to bob my head and fake this properly?- and Harley, thankfully noticing me hesitate, twists my hair around his wrist and grabs a fist full of my hair before winding the window down a few inches.

"I paid good fucking green for this slut. How about you fuck off and let me enjoy my money's worth before I get angry, dickhead?" Harley drawls, becoming the arrogant asshole from school once again.

I can't move with the grip he has on my hair, thank god. I can smell the cigarettes and weed on Reggie from where I'm crouched. He's a fucking creep and I have to hold in a repulsed shiver at his close proximity. Thankfully, the steering wheel hides most of the skin I'm showing, and he won't be able to see or recognize the scars.

"What's a guy like you doing down here, anyway? If you can afford the '67 Rector, you can afford better pussy than what the slum girls have on offer."

Harley chuckles under his breath and replies, "More expensive doesn't mean better. No one sucks like the slum girls."

Reggie waits a second and then laughs. "You can smack them around if they don't. High class girls cry if you're rough with them. Enjoy your time with her. I'll find her myself later, see if that mouth is as good as you say."

Harley grunts and rolls the window up. His tight grip loosens a little, but when I glance up at his face, he's watching Reggie leave. His hand doesn't drop away until Reggie is back in his own car and driving away. He looks fucking pissed so I try to distract him.

"You might be disappointed with this Mounty pussy. I haven't exactly been broken in like the others and I might be a shit lay."

Harley's eyes flash as he hauls me up and into his lap, awkwardly, thanks to the steering wheel. "Don't fucking compare yourself to them and, to be real fucking clear, I haven't ever been disappointed with you. I'm not gonna be either."

He sounds even more like a street kid away from Hannaford and I grin back at him even as I blush. "We'll see."

He smirks lasciviously at me. "Fuck yeah, we will."

I'm STARVING by the time we get back to the townhouse.

Harley grumbles about the weight I've lost and immediately rummages through the fridge. I hate spending money on food when I know how little I need to get by and when I stupidly mention this to Harley he snarls at me, "Well, you're fucking eating now I'm here."

With a sigh, I shove a beer at him while I make us both burgers. Harley ducks out to the car to grab his bags and dumps them unceremoniously into the living room. The place is tiny; perfect for what I need. The kitchen, dining, and living room are all one space and the two bedrooms are connected by the bathroom. The downstairs area is made up entirely by the garage which can hold two cars.

"Who's car is the 'stang?" I say, as I drop the plates on the table and grab more beer for us both. I'm not a fan of beer but I need something to soften my edges tonight. I'm still the Wolf, Lips having been put away for the summer break.

Harley takes a huge bite and groans before saying, "You need to cook more when we get back to school. Avery never makes burgers and Morrison puts fucking pineapple in them when he makes them."

I gape at him in horror, then text Blaise to express my disgust at him, forgetting it's nearly five am. He sends me a little sketch he's done of a wolf in return, simple and in blue ink. I love it.

"It's Morrison's. My dad had one and my grandfather had it scrapped after he killed him to piss me off. There's only like ten of those out there, and when I found that one Morrison bought it. I told him someday I'll buy it from him but he's a stubborn dick and transferred it into my name, anyway. So, I guess technically it's mine. Won't feel like mine until I pay for it."

Okay now I regret waking Blaise up.

I nod and try not to think about my plans for his inheritance. It'll only give me a tension headache because of how fucking tired I am. "What are you going to do after school? I've never actually asked you."

"I never thought I'd get there. I dunno. I'll go wherever everyone else does. Avery and Ash both want to go into business or some bullshit. I'll find something to do at whichever college they pick. Ma wanted to be a doctor before she met Da so maybe I'll do that for her."

I sip my beer and wince. "Doctors make bank, you'll own that car in no time."

Harley smirks at me as he takes a drink. "They don't make fifty grand in a night."

I blush. "Surgeons can, asshole. Besides, *this* is not my career path. This is making do until then."

Harley slings a casual arm across the back of my chair, pulling me into his side. I've forgotten what it's like to have him so close to me and I have to take a deep breath to relax. It's like in the weeks we've been away from each other, all the familiarity he'd managed to form that last week of school sharing my bed has been wiped away. Fuck it if I'm not the most damaged fucking option, why the hell did they pick me?

"What are you doing after school? You're coming with us, right?" He murmurs.

I clear my throat. "I'm going to conquer the world with Avery. Haven't been able to find the right college course for that just yet but we're exploring options."

I don't really want to tell him, because I still haven't told him I'm financially supporting him now, but the money I've earned during the break is being sent to Avery and put into investments so I can afford to pay for everything Harley and I need for the next two years.

Avery is a fucking genius in the stock market, so good that the inheritance she and Ash received from their mother has doubled since she gained control of the money. When she told me I immediately asked her to teach me and now, we're investing my dirty money. I'll finally have a legitimate income.

Avery is also now sending me college brochures and course ideas daily. She refuses to pick a school without my input and when I told her I'd pick whatever school gave me the best scholarship, she said she'd apply to that school with me then. No amount of arguing had managed to convince her to leave me behind and fuck it if I didn't love her more for it.

Her father had been called away for business at the last minute before their trip to Amsterdam for Joey's birthday, so they had enjoyed their trip with their father's staff instead. Avery had paid off two of the bodyguards to keep Joey away from Ash, and the twins had enjoyed the break. They had arrived back in the states two days ago and were already packing to move into the townhouse here in the Bay.

Only Blaise is stuck away from us all until school goes back in two weeks.

I am fucking worried about the cocky asshole but I have no clue about how to deal with rich, emotionally fucked, dickhead parents.

I yawn and rub my eyes. Harley kisses my temple and says, "C'mon, I'll get this cleaned up and we can go to bed."

I freeze and he scoffs at me, like my reactions are so fucking amusing.

"I've already told you, I don't have to sleep in your bed with you." He huffs at me and grabs my plate. I argue with him over the dishes until he snaps at me, "You cooked so I clean, get the fuck over it."

I move to sit at the bench, and fidget while I watch him

clean. He doesn't look at me but he has extra senses or some shit because after I've agonized over the bed situation for ten minutes and find myself jittery, he says, "Look, I get you're probably gonna have issues-"

"Why I am gonna have issues?" I snap.

He cuts me a stern look. "You've been living under the threat of rape for years and from multiple fucking sources. I'm sure that would make anyone jumpy. I'm not in a rush. The other two will take it slow, especially if you tell them why. Calm the fuck down."

I squirm and bite my nails while he washes the dishes. "I'm not scared."

"I didn't say you were. Pretty sure I said *jumpy.*"

I roll my eyes at him. "It wasn't just the Jackal that stopped me. I'm not interested in casual, never have been and never will be. I didn't want to just fuck guys."

Harley scrubs the pots in silence and I watch him while I try to figure out how the fuck to say it. When he moves on to wipe down the bench, with such thoroughness I know he's been trained well by Avery, he says, "Are you asking me if I think this is casual? Because, fuck Mounty, I'm kind of hoping you already know how serious we're all taking this."

I swallow. "Knowing something in your head is very different to letting... letting yourself really believe it. I guess, I still kind of think this is all going to blow up in my face."

Harley nods and wipes his hands before walking around the bench and gently prying my legs open to stand between them. He waits for a moment until the tension melts out of me, then I shiver as he leans down and cups my face gently, breathing the words onto my lips as he speaks. "I'm keeping you forever. I don't do this shit for anything but keeps." And then he swallows my answering sigh.

I missed this. I missed the feeling of his lips on mine and

his hands holding my face like I'm everything to him and that alone breaks the hold of the Wolf on me. I wrap my legs around his hips and pull him closer; he never fucking gets close enough to me. I wonder if I'll still feel that way when we do have sex. I shiver at the thought and moan into the kiss, sucking on his tongue for more.

Harley breaks away and groans at me, "You kiss me like you want to fucking *consume* me."

"Maybe I will." I tease, smiling and rubbing myself against his chest in a very non-Lips manner. When he groans again and pulls my hips flush with his, grinding his dick into me, I mentally high-five myself for the move. Another yawn takes over me and he chuckles.

He hooks his arms under my legs to cup my ass in his big hands, squeezing as he lifts me up and presses me against his chest. "I'll tuck you into bed, babe. I'll go take a cold shower."

I clear my throat but it doesn't stop my voice from coming out as a rasp. "Sleep in my... our bed. The other one is for Avery. We can figure out the specifics when the others get here."

CHAPTER TWO

WAKING up to Harley's hands stroking over my body is possibly the best fucking feeling in the world. The sun is streaming through the cracks in the blinds and it must be at least midday. I stretch out my back and Harley mumbles under his breath appreciatively as the move pushes my ass up towards his hand.

He strokes down my spine and gets so close to cupping my ass then moves away to start back up between my shoulders again. I grunt and open my eyes to glare at him. "Don't be a tease."

He smirks. "I'm going slow, Mounty, don't be greedy."

It might be the work of his hands, or maybe it's the decent sleep I've finally had after weeks of shit, but I turn my face into his chest and bite him. Not hard, but enough to get his attention.

"Fuck me, Mounty, you start biting me and I will bite you the fuck back." His voice rumbles and I grin at him.

He shakes his head at me. "Last night you were looking at me like you'd rather jump out of the window than touch me, and now you're grinning at me like you want to spend the day naked in this bed with me. I don't know what the fuck to do with you. I've wanted you for so fucking long, and I'm not messing this up by pushing you."

I cringe and pull away from him. "I don't mean to look at you like that. It's hard to switch between Lips and the Wolf. I don't... touch easy. This is new to me. Fuck, it took me weeks of being around Avery before I got used to her touching me all the time. The first time she hugged me I nearly jumped out of my skin. And... I don't want to talk about it, I don't want to piss you off, but before Hannaford, I was only ever touched when people were hurting me." I clear my throat to shift the lump there. Fuck me, I've caught the self-pity bug again. I change topics to try to clear the stain my confession has left in the air.

"Why didn't you tell me? If you had been wanting me for as long as you say you have, then why not just tell me?"

He groans at me and rubs his face with one of his big palms. He gives me a look from the corner of his eye and then sighs. It's weird to see him unsure of himself.

"I've never had a girlfriend or asked someone out."

I snort at him, graceful as ever. "Fuck off. I've seen you blow a load on Annabelle's face, don't start bullshitting me now, Arbour."

He smirks at me remembering the intense eye contact in the woodland area while he'd gotten off. "I'm not saying I've never fucked girls before, I'm saying I've never wanted a girl as a... permanent thing."

A permanent thing. What an eloquent way to describe what we all have now. I stare at him until he groans again and continues.

"Look, I was fucking terrified of how I felt about you. I still am, if I'm honest. My circle is small for a reason; I don't trust people and I don't like them. And then you walked into that fucking school with your head high and mouth running, and I just... I love it. I love everything you do, you draw me in and I can't get my eyes off of you. I didn't know how to talk to you without you thinking I was like every other dickhead there trying to win that fucking bet."

I nod. I've spent the weeks we've been apart stewing on this... relationship we now have, and I'm both excited and terrified by it. I like being a part of the 'family'. I don't want jealousy and relationship drama to ruin what we have. "I just don't understand how you went from wanting to rip Blaise and Ash's heads off to not giving a shit about... sharing me."

He blows out a breath and scrubs his hand over his face. "It wasn't about them being with you. It was about whether *I* would get to have you."

He pulls away and sits on the edge of the bed, like he doesn't want to look at me while he speaks. I hesitate for a second and then tuck myself against his back, my arms and legs wrapped around him. He traces the scar on my ruined leg with a finger idly.

"I thought you would only pick one of us and I couldn't deal with it not being me. We're not normal. The three of us are so fucking messed up from everything we've had to deal with and we're never going to be normal. Sharing you isn't even in the top five of weird shit we've done." He chuckles under his breath and I squeeze him.

I get the feeling this is his little declaration, like the one I made to Ash before we left school. This is him telling me he's not whole and being with him is not the easy option.

He has no reason to worry.

I don't *do* easy.

"I think it'll take all three of us to keep you safe, keep you alive. Fuck, the three of us and Floss, and maybe even then this fucking world you rule could take you out. I can't let that happen, Mounty. Sitting in that car with the Jackal proved to me that we need to get you out of here. Being stuck up the coast without you has been fucking hell."

We fall quiet while we both think about the consequences of what happened. He'd only planned to stay up there for two weeks to see his mom but I'd called his hotel to extend his stay and keep him the hell away from the Jackal. He'd fought me on it and I was forced to call Avery to talk some sense into him. Once he finally agreed, I'd sent Illi up there to watch his back. Something I will never tell Harley because it would piss him the fuck off. I know for a fact these guys have no idea of the hell that has just arrived on our doorstep. Fuck me.

Harley gets up and promises me French toast if I get some more sleep, claiming the dark circles under my eyes are still there and he won't let me out of bed until they're gone. Bossy, irresistible asshole. He takes the 'stang to the grocery store and I'm a little worried about how much food he'll bring home.

I wake an hour later to my phone pinging and I search the sheets to find it. I groan at the text. It's from Harley to the new group text that doesn't include Avery. The 'joint relationship' group. *Sweet fucking lord.* He's just fucking broadcasted my untouched status to the other two without asking me because he's an utter dick.

I hear the front door unlock and the rustling of the grocery bags. Then my phone pings with Ash's reply.

Explain. Now.

"You asshole." I yell out to him as I try to figure out how the fuck to explain this without tearing their arrogant heads off. Fucking lord.

Any guy within the Jackal's world knows they're risking

death if they touch me. I haven't left Mounts Bay for anything other than school. I haven't fucked anyone at Hannaford. Is that a good enough explanation?

I swallow and punch my pillow. I hear Harley rummaging around, putting things away and getting out supplies for my breakfast. This had better be the best fucking French toast of my *life.* His phone pings out in the kitchen as mine buzzes in my hand.

So you two haven't fucked yet? How are those blue balls of yours, Arbour?

I roll my eyes at Blaise and Harley replies.

My balls are fine, how are yours, dickhead? Just thought I'd let you both know because the Mounty is jumpy as hell about it.

That's it, I'm killing the fucker.

Ash please get Avery to start building my alibi. I'm stabbing your cousin.

Harley snorts at me, loud enough that I hear it, and calls out, "Your knife is out here, what else would you do it with?"

"I'm pretty fucking innovative when I need to be, Arbour!"

I HAVE to hold onto the photos for the Tiger for two days before I can deliver them to him in person. He's vigilant to the point of madness and refuses to use even the most secure electronic file sharing options for the work I do for him. I'm forced to load them onto an USB and text him a meetup point at the docks. The Fox is hosting his usual summer party with live music, booze, drugs, and every Mounty under the age of fifty will be there. There's nothing over the summer in the Bay bigger than this party.

I tell Harley I'll just pop in to drop the USB off and he looks at me like I've got a brain injury. So, I guess we're going to the party together. Bad idea, it will be teeming with the Jackal's men but there's no talking him out of it.

Which is how I find myself glaring at the bathroom mirror at eleven pm.

The playsuit I've got on is one of my absolute favorites. It's backless, and the top is a flowy halter-neck with a deep v. Like, so deep that you can see my belly button. The bottom half is short enough that I have to wear a thong so my underwear doesn't peek out as I move. It's sexy without showing too much ass or tits, just little glimpses. Compared to the other Mounty girls I'll look like a freaking Amish girl. The problem with the outfit is that, with my new-and-improved boobs, I have to wear some stupid fucking adhesive bra and then tape the front of the playsuit down so I'm not going to have my tits out in the warehouse.

I think Harley would have an aneurysm.

I snap a photo and send it through to Avery. She answers immediately.

Where the hell do you find these outfits? Is there a Chanel version? Also, I'm texting Harley and telling him to feed you more.

I snort at her and send her a photo of my back for good measure. She video calls me back.

"Where are you going? Has Harley seen that yet?"

I shrug. "I'm finishing my last job. Harley knows the score, you can't go to the docks without showing some skin."

Avery smirks at me and still manages to look like an evil queen while wearing her fluffy Chanel robe. "Oh, I'm sure he's positively thrilled about it. Ash just took a call from him and they're gossiping like housewives for their book club."

I snort at her and twirl to get a feel of how much movement I still have.

Avery cackles down the phone. "I just saw a nipple so unless you want Harley ripping that off of you before you make it out the door you will need more tape."

I grimace and end the call, with Avery still sounding far too amused at my expense.

Once I've taped what feels like every-fucking-thing down, I flounce out of the bathroom and stand in front of the full-length mirror in the living room. I dance around and shake my butt to make sure it's secure, I even throw in a slut drop for good measure.

I hear a strangled sort of noise and then a choking cough behind me.

Harley is sitting at the bench looking fucking devastating in his dark jeans and tight white shirt. My breath catches in my chest for a second before I see the look in his eyes as he watches me. His laptop is still on the table but the screen has been turned around so Ash and Blaise can see my outfit. Ah. They've just been watching me dance Mounty-style. Oops. I give them a little awkward wave.

"Fuck. Pick something else to wear." chokes out Blaise and Ash snorts at him.

"She can wear whatever the fuck she wants. Don't be a dick."

Harley rubs the back of his neck and grumbles, "I'd prefer it if you wore a bra though. Fuck me, I'm going to be fucking busy tonight. One of you two will pay my bail, right?"

Ash nods and waves a hand at me. "Do another one of those squat things. Slowly."

I blush and laugh at him. I go back to the bedroom and grab my phone, flicking through the songs until I find something with a decent beat to dance to. When I come back out Harley looks up at me and smirks when I start the song. He was born and bred in the Bay so he knows what's coming. The other two have no clue how Mounties party.

"No filming." I warn him sternly and he holds up his hands in a mock surrender.

It feels kind of strange to dance by myself, with three sets of eyes on me, but I've spent every summer in a party of some kind working and music lives in my soul. I shut my eyes and just let myself move with the music, not trying to be sexy or seductive, but knowing that to prim rich kids the Mounty-style will look fucking erotic.

When the song finishes, I glance up and Harley is fucking sweating.

Damn, does that make me feel good.

Blaise is gaping at me and Ash looks ready to drive the fuck down here. I shiver, and only the thick silicone of the bra stops my hard nipples from being on display. Harley's eyes darken dangerously as he watches my thighs rub together.

The knock at the door freezes me in place.

Harley glances away from me to frown at the sound and Ash swears viciously. I bend at the waist and motion for the two on the video call to stay silent, then I check the peephole. There's a giant mass of tattooed muscle and silvery-blond hair standing on the doorstep.

Sweet fucking lord.

Harley is going to have a fucking aneurysm.

I sigh and unlock the door. Before I open it, I meet Harley's eyes over my shoulder and say, as calmly as I can, "I know you disagree with me, but I swear to you, he's a good guy. I trust him. Just stay calm and hear him out. It must be important if he's here."

And then Johnny Illium, the Butcher of the Bay, or just plain Illi to me, sweeps me into a bone-crushing hug. I *do not* care that he's the most notorious cage fighter and enforcer-for-hire amongst the Twelve; I don't *do* hugs.

"Get the fuck off me, I'm not a hugger!" I gasp out and he grunts at me.

"Neither am I. That's from Odie. She told me to tell you to fucking call her, she misses listening to you bitch her out for doing things normal people do." He drops me to the floor and kicks the door shut, flicking the lock like it's his house to keep safe. Harley, honest to god, looks like he's going to kill me and then himself.

"This place is better than last year. You trying to impress your *boyfriend*?" Illi says, his voice teasing like the ass he is, and sprawls himself down into one of the dining chairs like he's a regular visitor to the townhouse. He wiggles his eyebrows at me in a way I'm sure he's hoping will piss said boyfriend off.

Harley does look fucking livid, and a little like he's going to vomit. I wince. If the Wolf is whispered about on the streets of Mounts Bay, then the Butcher is the man screamed about at parties and bars when people want to instill fear on their audience of choice.

"I thought I'd stop by to be properly introduced to the boy the Jackal is willing to risk everything to kill." He shrugs out of his leather jacket and hangs it over another seat. He sees the laptop and the open chat room and gives the guys a little mocking wave before snapping it shut. Ash is going to lose his mind.

I groan at him. "Really, Illi? You couldn't just call me?

Or warn me you were coming? We are just about to head out."

He nods along with me. "Cool. Where are we going?"

"Like fuck am I letting her go anywhere with *you*." snaps Harley and I give him what I hope is a stern look. He ignores it, and me, completely.

Illi smirks at him. "You're adorable. The Wolf doesn't need a fucking keeper, so cut your shit. I came here to tell you the Jackal offered to *triple* whatever sum you paid me. He's put a hit out on the O'Cronin kid."

I snort. "He can't. Not without answering to the Twelve."

Illi cocks his head at me. "He's put it out amongst the underlings he knows will risk the wrath it'll bring and he can easily pin the whole idea on. Not many took it up, because they know it goes against you, but there are a few who accepted."

"And you?" snarls Harley, "Are you here to kill me?"

"I turned him down." Illi says with a shrug. Well, I assume he was trying to shrug, the thick ropes of muscles that band across his shoulders make it look a little ridiculous. His fingers twitch and I know he's itching for a cigarette. I never let him smoke around me.

I know exactly what statement Illi has just made but Harley has no real experience in our world, and he's still eyeing Illi like he's an atomic bomb about to level the city. "And what is that going to cost us?" He snaps.

Illi quirks his eyebrow and swings around to give me an incredulous look. I snort and roll my eyes at him. "I'm not his *keeper* either. He can speak to you however he wants and, well, if it pisses you off, I'll only step in if I think you'll kill him. *No* killing him, Illi."

Illi glares a warning at Harley and then swings back to

me. "That's not all I'm here for, I'm afraid. The meeting will be postponed. You'll need to come back down during the fall break. I thought I'd warn you before the Crow reaches out to you."

My spine snaps straight. Meetings don't get canceled. Illi eyes Harley again, and I grit my teeth. Fucking boys!

"This is the part where I'm asking for something fucking big from you, little Wolf." Illi grimaces and stares at Harley for a beat longer.

I wave my hand at him and say, "Harley's mine. Whatever it is, won't leave this room."

Harley's eyebrows raise but he gives Illi a curt nod.

"The Vulture is dead."

Fuck.

Oh, sweet lord *fuck.*

I meet Illi's eyes and nod slowly. "So, you're mine now, too."

Harley blanches but we both ignore him. Illi scrubs a hand over his face. "I didn't intend on asking but when the Jackal approached me about your boy, he brought up Odie... I can't leave her open to anything hurting her. *Again.*"

I'm nodding before he finishes. "I know. You're mine, both of you. Between us, we'll keep her safe."

Harley looks between us and grinds out, "How does the death of that sick fuck suddenly mean you're inducting him? I thought you wanted to stay away from this world, how does taking on the Butcher keep you free?"

Illi cracks his knuckles absently but Harley watches the move carefully. "The Vulture sold my wife. Twice. I told little Wolf years ago that his death would be mine."

Harley bursts out of his chair. It's a testament to how confident Illi is of his abilities he doesn't so much as flinch. "You've killed a member of the Twelve and now you want to risk Lips by having her take you in?! Fuck. That."

I hold up a hand. "Illi and Odie are in. I should have done it years ago when you asked. I might've been able to get away from the Jackal sooner if I had."

Harley rocks back on his heels. "You've asked her before?"

If these two don't get along my life will get fucking complicated and fast. I can't even think about how much Ash and Blaise would both hate this.

Illi pauses for a second, and then sighs. "My Odie is alive because of the Wolf. If anything happened to her, there is no reason for me to continue breathing. I've asked Lips to induct me before, and I told her that even if she didn't accept, I would answer any call to arms from her."

And he had. One phone call to him back at Hannaford and he'd met us at the docks ready to throw down with the Jackal, whatever the cost. I run through the specifics of inducting him in my head and wince. "I can't pay you yet, I'm-"

"I'm a rich man. Induct me, and I'll give you a cut of my work."

I shake my head. "I'm not taking your money."

Illi stretches his legs out in front of him and laces his fingers behind his head. The move makes him look even bigger and Harley watches him warily. Illi grins at him and then fucking blows him a kiss like an ass. *Fucking hell.*

"I get it, you don't want to take on an empire. But that's why I'll offer myself to you and no one else. You won't use me. You won't betray me. You won't grow so fucking conceited that you turn into a cunt like Matteo did. You've protected Odie from the moment you met her. Offering myself to you and giving you a cut of my work is fucking *nothing* compared to what I owe you. Induct me. I will protect you and the boy, whatever the cost."

Resigned, I nod and exhale sharply. "It's forever, Illi. Just remember that this is forever."

He smiles, and it doesn't soften his fierce face at all. "So is Odie. I owe you a life-debt."

I take another deep breath. "One last thing. It's not just Harley that I'm protecting. I'm protecting my family. My best friend and... the *three* guys I'm... seeing."

Illium blinks at me and then at Harley. Then he fucking roars with laughter.

"Good! *Fuck yes!* No more abiding by Matteo's shitty fucking agendas. Done, little Wolf. Send me their details and I'll stay in touch. We'll get you the fuck away from Matteo."

CHAPTER THREE

THE VULTURE's death means the Twelve go on lockdown.

The Tiger refuses to meet at the party, texting instead to request a daytime meeting at a deli on the Main Street the following afternoon. Lots of witnesses and places to take cover. The news of Illi and Odie's inductions travels fast and I think having the Butcher answer to me makes the Tiger extra fucking twitchy.

I slip out of bed without waking Harley and leave him a note. We'd argued after Illi had left and I'd stomped off to bed to video call Avery, seething and ignoring the texts and calls from the other two. Harley had abandoned the beer he'd been drinking before Illi's surprise visit, and found my emergency bottle of whiskey. He didn't stumble to bed until he'd finished the damn thing, and I'd spent half the night positive he was going to die of liver poisoning. I should've known he'd be fine, he drinks like a freaking fish, but I'd barely managed to get any sleep.

The drop-off runs smoothly. The Tiger doesn't question me about Illi, although his usual crass jokes are absent and he keeps looking over my shoulder. There are only two members of the Twelve without inductees left and, as one of them, I'm sure that the Tiger never feels more alone than when there is a murder amongst our ranks.

It's not until I go to leave that he says quietly, "Protecting a killer isn't a smart move, Wolf."

I raise an eyebrow at him, forcing bravado I *do not* feel. "The Vulture sold skin. It's not the type of business that cultivates admiration and respect. There are thousands of people who wanted him dead. I hope you're not making assumptions, Tiger?"

He eyes me carefully before giving me a respectful nod and leaving.

I stop at a liquor store that's protected and used by the Bear to launder his dirty cash. The guy behind the counter takes one look at me and waves me on, refusing to take my money. I grab more beer and two new emergency bottles of whiskey.

I groan to myself when I think of the hungover mess in my bed. How the actual fuck do I make him understand this? Ugh.

My phone pings and I cringe as I juggle the bottles to check it.

I'm in the Bay. Can you send through your address?

I stare down at Blaise's text. I'm excited to see him, thrilled actually, but he's supposed to be in New York with his parents. His texts had been coming less frequently and sounding a lot less like him as the break goes on. I chew my lip as I send him the address and then pause for a second before texting him again.

I've just finished a job. Can you pick me up before you head there?

I find a bench to sit on and send him the details of

where I am. He must have been only a block over because two minutes later he pulls up.

The Maserati draws eyes. Too many eyes and I know this will get back to the Jackal.

I scramble over to the car and load the bottles into the back seat before climbing in. Once I get my seatbelt on I turn to greet Blaise and the words dry up in my throat. It's hard, but I do my best not to gape at him. He's got his nose piercing back in, now we're out of Hannaford, and his hair is freshly cut. He smells amazing, like he got straight into the car after his shower to come see me. The only thing wrong is the expression on his face.

He's a void.

There's no sign of my cheeky, vicious, passionate, dark rockstar. Just a blank, empty vessel, even as he pulls the car back onto the road and drives us back to the townhouse. What the ever-loving *fuck* has happened? I wait him out, but he says nothing.

"How can I fix this?" I say when I can't stand the silence any longer.

He glances over at me and his eyes are dull. "You can't. No one can."

I nod and hesitate before resting my hand on his thigh, too low to be overtly sexual, but high enough that it's more than a friendly gesture.

When we arrive at the gates I pass him the spare sensor to open them. He doesn't move to roll down his window, just stares down at the little plastic sphere like it's the answer to all of his problems. I stay quiet. Sometimes you just have to be patient and wait these things out.

"My mom's pregnant."

Huh.

Not what I expected.

"My father told me they've given up on me ever growing up. He said that they'd thought my shitty grades were a rebellion or a sign I was too spoilt and lazy to have drive, but now they know I'm just *retarded*. His exact words, not mine. They even went to a fertility specialist to make sure they would have another boy to replace me. The second he's born my father is writing me out of his estate."

The monotone sound of his voice and the complete lack of cussing has me worried. Also, I can't fix this at all. How fucked is it that we've all managed to have shitty families? Where are the decent people of the world?

"I don't even care about the money. I'm fine, I have enough of my own and I never wanted to run the business. But they're already talking about keeping my *bad influence* away from the baby. I'm going to have a brother that I'm not allowed to know because I'm too *fucking stupid* to be who my father wants me to be."

Yeah, I can't listen to this.

Not at all. Not from the guy who gave up parties and fun so he could study three nights a week to get his grades up for his miserable excuse of a father. The guy stands with his friends even if it risks his reputation and his career. The guy who goes toe to toe with Joey when he threatens someone he loves. Not the guy who charmed me, apologized to me, with playlists, poems, sketches, and sweet words. Not the guy who saved my life with his songs years before we even met.

I grab his hand until our fingers are curled together around the sensor. "Listen to me, there is plenty we can do to fix this. Not your parents or their shitty fucking attitudes, but we can make it impossible for them to keep you away from your brother. Don't even think about it anymore, I will fix it. You're not stupid. I'm the best person to judge that,

I've spent hours doing assignments with you. You're not what he wants but that doesn't make you *less* than him. I've met a lot of shitty people, Blaise, I've had to deal with a fuck-tonne of stupid, cruel, self-absorbed people and you're worth so much more than what he wants from you. You don't owe them *anything*."

His hand shakes a little in mine and then he gives me the tiniest of nods.

"No spending blood diamonds on me, Mounty. I'm not worth it."

I swallow past the lump lodged in my throat. "You're worth more than my diamonds. I'm planning on spending every single one of them on us. On our family, the one that actually counts. Even if... even if this is all a temporary thing for you guys, it's still worth it for me."

His head snaps over to me so quickly I would have startled if I weren't firmly wearing the skin of the Wolf. His eyes are wild and fierce. "This is not fucking temporary. Not for me, not for Ash or Harley, and not for you. I know we have a hell of a lot to make up for, but I'm going to do whatever it takes to do that. Don't *ever* say that shit again."

How the fuck am I supposed to walk straight after that?!

Fuck me.

Harley is asleep on the lounge chair when we get back. I help Blaise carry his bags in and we take them to *our* room, stepping over Harley's bags and dumping them in a messy pile on the floor. There isn't a whole lot of room left in the bedroom and once Ash gets here we will be in danger of bursting at the seams.

Blaise looks a little less void-like but he's still fucking morose. I give up trying to cheer him up and instead I start cooking dinner. Harley doesn't wake up with all our noise and I check to make sure the asshole hasn't choked on his own tongue.

I make Mac'n'Cheese because Blaise needs some damn comfort food and when I suggest it his lips twitch like he's thinking about smiling. I put a plate in the fridge for Harley and then I drag the blanket off our bed to wrap Blaise and I up in while we sit on the couch together and eat. Granted, I have to drop the thermostat down to ridiculous temperatures, but it's worth it when Blaise finally slings an arm around me as we eat and watch the fucking awful movie he's put on.

"What's wrong with him?" Blaise mumbles, after he's inhaled the pasta like a starving man.

I eye Harley as I grimace. "We had an argument about... a friend of mine and then he drank himself to sleep. We need to call Ash and Aves so I can tell you all at once about it. It's... about my position as the Wolf."

Blaise nods, and pulls me in closer to his body. His fingers dance over the strip of skin bared between my tank top and booty shorts. "You don't seem jumpy to me. Did Harley try to get you naked the second he got down here? I wouldn't have thought he'd be such an idiot, we all know you're good with knives."

I blush. Fucking boys. "No, he already knew, and I'm not fucking jumpy. I just needed a little time to get back to being the Mounty again and not the Wolf. This place does things to me."

Blaise nods again and dips down to kiss my throat, on

the soft skin, right under my jaw. I shiver when his tongue and teeth join the mix, his lips moving slowly down until he's nibbling on my shoulder. My head falls back as I sigh.

"Let's leave Harley out here and go to bed. We can video call the twins and you can tell us what the fuck has happened now."

I have to clear my throat twice to get the words out. "I don't want you angry at me too. Can we just go to bed and I'll face this tomorrow?"

He relents and then takes me to bed, kissing me slow and sweet, until I can't keep my eyes open anymore. I'm so fucking glad he's here and I'm not going to let the morose fucker out of my sight until I'm sure he's okay.

Sometime after midnight Harley joins us and grunts when his shins hit Blaise's bags. When he slides into the bed I roll over in Blaise's arms to face him, the glow of the alarm clock on the bedside table illuminating him enough to see the frown.

"The fuck is he doing here?" He whispers and I shrug.

"His dad's a shitty human. Are you still angry? I can't sleep with rage in the air, it gives me heartburn."

Harley grumbles under his breath then kisses me, tasting minty and clean. I kiss him back for a second before I break away. I won't let him distract me with his tongue, talented as it is. "I'm getting away from the Jackal, but I can't stop being the Wolf. It's for life. If you can't handle-"

"I can handle it, *don't* freak out on me again. I can't help that, I want to keep you safe, and let's be real, the Butcher is a demon. I'm going fucking crazy thinking about how shitty things must have been for you if you've met him. If you've become *friends* with him. But I trust you. I'm all in."

I squint at him in the dark. I wonder if these boys even know how to pronounce the word sorry, if it's ever passed their lips. Hmm. No, I've heard it once from Blaise and Harley's apologized to Avery in front of me, but I guess this is the best I'll get.

I kiss him again, just a quick peck, and fall asleep, tucked snugly between them both.

Playing house with Harley and Blaise is ridiculous and a danger to my health.

The twins have to wait another week before they can join us. Ash rages down the phone at me for an hour before I send smoke signals to Avery to get him to shut the fuck up.

Blaise is smug as fuck, and Harley thinks it's hil-fuck-ing-arious and stops taking his calls to piss him off even more.

They make a game of taunting Ash with random photos and videos of me in compromising positions. Half of them are stupid and the other half make me blush furiously and lock myself in the bathroom. I lose my cool with Blaise after he steals my phone to send fake sexts, and I break his phone against a wall in retaliation. He's fucking loaded so he barely even shrugs about the loss.

When I video call Ash later that night, he snarks at me, "Well, I didn't think you'd be texting me about your greedy, dripping pussy aching for my cock."

I gulp.

Well, maybe I'm not going to text that *now*, but I wouldn't write it off for later.

I make both of the assholes sleep on the fucking couches.

Even with the fun of hanging out and just being 'normal' for a week, I can feel the dread starting to build deep in my gut as my seventeenth birthday approaches. No amount of fun and games is going to stop the anguish from swallowing me whole.

I warn them both about what to expect, my complete inability to function, but Harley assumes he has superpowers and will be able to get me to move.

He doesn't.

I don't.

Harley holds me to his chest and promises me French toast if I get up. When that doesn't work he promises me a private Vanth Falling concert in the bedroom if I sit up and eat something. Finally, he promises me the world if I'll open my eyes.

I can't.

Not even for him.

Eventually, he gets out of bed and snaps at Blaise to watch me. The bed dips as Blaise sits down and begins to stroke my back. I want to thank him, I want to crack a joke about role reversal and me being finally being the morbid one. I can't. There's nothing left of me.

Blaise doesn't try to speak to me, just touches me gently like I'm so fucking breakable. Fuck, I guess right now I am. Then Harley's voice starts up again.

"She won't move or speak, I'm freaking the fuck out... yes, Floss... yes, come now...I don't care, just get in the fucking car and come now."

Then he stops talking. Blaise strokes the hair away from my face. Eventually he leaves me too, and I can wallow in the silence by myself.

I become aware again to the sound of Avery's sharp tones as she breathes pure ice at her cousin.

"I told you, she doesn't do birthdays at all. She functioned for Christmas because it meant something to you. She *will not* do her birthday, not even for us. Just let her have her fucking space and stop trying to fix her." I feel her lips brush my cheek.

There's murmuring by the door and then cool air washes over my body as the blankets lift and someone climbs in next to me. I don't move or speak. If the heady smell of his skin didn't tip me off, the fingers tracing patterns into my thighs are a dead giveaway that it's Ash. It's fucking hard work, but I manage to sigh.

"Shh, Mounty. We're not functioning today. Avery is going to babysit the other two and keep them busy. You and me will be nothing in here together."

I don't know how long I take, but I slowly move until my head hits his chest, and he takes it as the request it is to bundle me into his arms. I can't open my eyes or speak, but he doesn't care.

"When you're feeling better tomorrow, can you shake that perfect ass of yours for me again? I've been thinking about it non-stop and, fuck, I can't go another fucking day without seeing it in the flesh. The way your hips move, I can't wait to see how you move on my cock."

A shiver runs down my spine and he hums under his breath. "Good to know you're still alive, Mounty. Do you want to hear all about what I'm going to do to you when you're back in the land of the living? All of the things we have to look forward to?"

CHAPTER FOUR

NOBODY on this earth can make my coffee as well as Avery can.

To my utter surprise and delight, she loves the townhouse. I was sure she'd hate how tiny it is, especially since she brought more bags than the guy's combined, and we're all tripping over her shit, but having us all in one spot is all she really needs. We only get one last week together before our classes start.

We both wake up hours before the guys do so we can drink coffee and sift through the mess we're in without their pissy comments. It's fucking bliss.

"What's going to happen now the Vulture is dead?" Avery sips her coffee and nibbles delicately on her breakfast.

I eat mine like an animal, zero fucks given. "They'll run the Game again. It'll take eight or nine months before we have a new member. A lot of palms have to be greased before they can start, and the Vulture's empire needs to be assessed, divided, and dismantled."

Avery cocks her head at me. "How does that work? Who decides that?"

I sigh. "The Crow and the Jackal will go head-to-head for it, I guess. No one else has any interest in selling skin and it'll be another full-time operation to take on. The Jackal would love nothing more than adding skin to his empire. The Crow... I don't know. He'll want to take it on just so the Jackal doesn't get bigger than him but I don't see him keeping it. He's not... how do I say this... he's ruthless. He's cold, clinical, and he won't hesitate. It's what's made his empire the only rival to the Jackal, but he's not a predator. I've seen what the Jackal does to girls, I know what he'll do if he takes over the Vulture's work. I can't see the Crow selling unwilling skin. Running willing girls, hell yeah, but importing kidnapped teenagers to drug and sell off? Nope."

Avery shudders. "I wonder how much money my father has spent at those auctions."

I grimace. I don't want to think about it either, I don't want to be reminded of how much work I still have to do on the Beaumont front. I've only really made strides with the O'Cronin bunch. Having Illi around may become a blessing beyond his ability to kill.

"How's the bed sharing going? I haven't been woken in the middle of the night to the sounds of moaning so I'm assuming you haven't jumped straight into group sex."

I choke so hard on my coffee that it comes out of my fucking nose. Avery screeches with laughter and I decide I'm breaking up with *her*.

When I've mopped up the mess I croak, "Harley decided to tell the others I'm inexperienced so they've become fucking teases."

And, *fuck me*, were they good at it.

Blaise refuses to wear a shirt inside the house during the

morning and I'm fucking dying over it. Ash saw it as a challenge, to melt my brain and my damned panties, and he has taken to going for his morning run in the tiniest pair of fucking shorts I have ever seen on a man. I now fantasize about those shorts on that ass in the shower. I tell Avery to order fifty fucking pairs of them and she gags at me dramatically. Harley enjoys watching me; his eyes smoldering and intense, undressing me and fucking me with one damn look, and then when I approach him he backs off.

I think they want me to beg.

I also think I'm going to.

Avery cocks an eyebrow at me. "Well, if you want to break Ash just put on some of the lace he picked out for you. I still can't believe you didn't realize how much he wanted you back then. He insisted on picking out your damn *panties,* for Christ's sake."

I shake my head at her.

She's been giving me shit about it since the day she joined me in the bathroom and laid it all out for me. I consider it for a second and then smirk at her.

"Wanna help me get back at them? Beat them at their own game?"

She quirks an eyebrow at me over the rim of her cup. "Always, Mounty."

I lied. I'm never letting this evil queen go.

ON OUR LAST night at the townhouse, Avery declares that she's made reservations for us all to eat at a restaurant on the nice side of the city and then shepherds me into her room to get ready. It's barely three in the afternoon so I have no idea why it would take us three hours to get ready. I grumble this at her.

She clutches her stomach as she laughs at me.

It takes even longer.

Avery treats me like her own freaking doll to play with, and I just shut my eyes and let her. She tames and curls my hair into stunning, gentle waves. My makeup is simple, but with a bright red lipstick that makes my pout look lush and sexy. The red dress Avery pulls out of her wardrobe for me is sleek, stunning, and I tell her to *never* let it slip how much it cost her. It has a high neckline and from the front it looks modest, even with the skirt landing just above my knee. The show-stopper is the back, where the cutout dips low and ruches up over my ass so it looks rounded and pert. The neckline buttons at the top to look like a choker, and fuck, even I get a little excited at the look.

Avery cackles.

"Is this what you were thinking when you asked for my help?" She gloats.

I shake my ass at her and she laughs even harder. "This is better. I didn't know my ass could look this good."

There's a thump at the door and Harley grumbles at us both. "Are we going to dinner or a fucking fashion parade? I'm hungry, and if Morrison smokes anymore he's going to be useless."

I swing the door open, to find Blaise and chew him out, and Harley takes a step back at the sight of me. I smirk, even though I am having some trouble breathing at the sight of him in black slacks and a white button-up shirt.

"Jesus Christ, you're both drooling." Avery grouses as she sidles past me.

Harley smirks and steps forward to tug me into his arms. "You look like a *lady*. It's fucking weird."

I scoff at him and I'd be insulted if he wasn't looking at me like he wanted to rip the dress the fuck off of me. He hasn't even seen the best part yet. "I'm assuming Avery is taking us to some uppity place, and I can't wear a band tee and Docs there."

Harley smirks. "Blaise is still going to try."

Avery's screeching cuts through the air and we both laugh at Blaise's pissy reply. Harley's hands smooth over my ass as he leans down to kiss me. I think he was only planning for it to be a quick peck, but I open my lips to his the second they touch and I swallow his groan. Footsteps in the living room pull us apart.

"Are we still going to dinner, or are the two of you just going to fuck in the hallway?" Ash snarks and I smirk back at him.

"I'm not wasting my dress. Let's go." I pull away from Harley, and walk to the door without looking back. I hear gasps and curses, and I smile like an idiot. Avery's smug face tells me everything I need to know about their reaction to the back of my dress.

"Pretty sure you could get any of them to bend you over something right now if you wanted."

I smirk back at the guys. Blaise has joined them, and has paused in buttoning up his dress shirt to stare at me, his eyes ravenous.

"I'm hungry. Let's go eat."

Take that, assholes.

BLAISE DRIVES us in the Maserati and I sit between Ash and Harley in the back. Harley tucks his hand into mine and lets his head drop back against the headrest with his eyes closed. Ash scowls out of the window and traces patterns into the exposed skin on my thigh. When I shift in my seat he looks over at me and smirks.

"Red?" He whispers and I know exactly what he's asking.

"Nothing. I didn't want there to be lines."

Ash sucks in a breath and Harley's hand spasms in mine. I grin at Avery when she glances back at me, satisfied I've finally one-upped them in their own game.

The restaurant is ridiculously ritzy, the type of place I imagine Ash and Avery frequent because they fit right in. Blaise is at ease, but looks around with thinly veiled disgust. Harley is the only one who shares my outraged looks when we see the prices of the dishes.

"Is the lobster going to serve itself to me for that fucking price? I haven't spent that much on *groceries* for the entire fucking break."

Avery smirks at me, but Ash looks confused. "How much do groceries cost in the slums?"

Blaise cackles like a madman at the look I throw at the spoiled asshole. "I'm no longer feeding you. Also, you're on the couch tonight."

"Snap, motherfucker." Avery murmurs under her breath, mocking me the way only she can get away with.

Ash glares at her and Harley slings a smug arm around the back of my chair. I'm tempted to order the mango chicken, as a threat to Ash because I know he's allergic, but I decide not to play with fire and order a pasta dish to eat my feelings. Plus, its the only dish under a hundred dollars on the menu that *isn't* a salad.

"So, how are we all feeling about Hannaford tomorrow?" Avery asks sweetly, and Blaise throws a linen napkin at her.

"I'm glad we don't have to worry about Joey breaking down your door." Ash says, and drinks his bourbon. Yep, the spoiled, seventeen year-old asshole ordered a bourbon and no one questioned him.

"I'm going to join the state team for swimming. I'm going to apply for some scholarships for college, see if that gives me a better chance." Harley mutters. Avery meets my eyes and I give her a tiny shake of my head. I haven't told him my plans yet and I'm not going to.

"I'm getting my neck tattooed. And my hands. Oh, and I've signed up for the highest classes this year because I'm clearly fucking insane, but the Mounty has promised me she'll get me through it. If she succeeds in getting me to follow you lot to college, I'll have to get the marks to get in." Blaise says, cheerfully.

I smile at him, but the other three all stare at him with various degrees of shock on their faces. Ash recovers first. "Your father will disown you if you tattoo your hands and neck."

Oh. So, he hasn't told them all yet. Shit.

Blaise clears his throat. "Too late, he already has. Family announcement; my mom's pregnant. It's a boy. I've been cut out of the family now there's a replacement son on the way. Oh look, dinner's here."

The stunned silence continues until the waiters have left. Blaise and I tuck into our dinner happily, but it takes the others a minute to start in on theirs.

"Congrats, I guess?" Harley says, and Ash snorts at him.

"He's not the one who's fucking pregnant, and who the hell said that this is a good thing?"

Avery cocks her head. "Did your dad definitely disown you? Can I start ruining his life now?"

I smirk at her. *"We,* Aves, can *we* start ruining his life now? I have some *very* creative plans for Mr. Blaine Morrison."

Blaise looks between us. "What plans?"

"I'm going to royally, and viciously, fuck that man up."

Harley and Ash both whoop with excitement and Blaise looks vaguely concerned. Avery continues to eat her salmon delicately, pausing to say, "Are they going to name the baby Blaise, too? Just completely replace you?"

It sounds harsh as fuck, but the scorn isn't directed at Blaise. He scratches the back of his neck awkwardly. "Blaire. They're naming him Blaire."

I cringe for him. "At least it's not Eclipse?"

CHAPTER FIVE

D RIVING through the gates at Hannaford feels different this year.

Granted I'm in the front seat of the Maserati, earplugs in and singing along to the new and unreleased Vanth record like a total fucking groupie, and Blaise keeps biting his lip as he shoots me these little awed looks. Harley and the twins are in the 'Stang behind us and when both cars pull into the staff parking Blaise leaves the car idling until the song finishes.

When we finally get out Avery is there with her phone, grinning at me and when the boy's phones all ping at the same time I know she's fucking recorded my singing through the open car window.

"Ash threatened me, Lips, I was forced." She purrs and I don't believe her for a hot second.

Harley slings my bag across his shoulder and I give him a little nod. My safe and the diamonds are in there. I trust him implicitly so I don't mind him taking it, but I want him aware they're there. Fuck it, I'll probably get them to help me pick the hiding spot this year.

Blaise and Ash bicker happily while I tuck myself under Blaise's arm, still nervous about being so open about touching them. I mean, the Jackal knows about Harley and I've made it clear I'm not interested in submitting to him, but it's still fucking nerve wracking to do this. What if I paint a target on them too? *Fuck.*

Blaise notices my hesitation and curls around me protectively. I swallow roughly at the lump that forms in my throat. I'm never going to get used to being protected and cared for.

We get the same room as last year, thanks to Avery, and she pitches a fit to get the guys to leave us alone. It's nice to get settled by ourselves. School starts tomorrow and we all have to adjust to being back amongst the snakes we share the halls with.

By the time I've helped Avery unpack her shit I already miss the little bubble we'd been in at the townhouse.

Avery shoves a tub of ice cream at me and when I grumble about it she waves her own at me. We watch Ghost together after she finds out I've never seen it, and we mope about being stuck here for another two years. Okay, I mope, Avery plots on her phone and snarks at my shitty attitude.

I wake up just as pissy as I went to bed and it's only as I get dressed into my uniform that I finally remember I have something to be fucking thrilled about this year.

Three words: Thigh. High. Socks.

Junior year is going to be the fucking *best* year at the shitty snake-pit known as Hannaford Preparatory Academy. Avery laughs her ass off at me when she sees me twirling around our room in my uniform, squealing like a child at the socks pulled right up my leg.

Fuck yes!

Now if only I could convince the school board to ditch

the kitten heels and let me wear my Docs, I'd be fucking set. Avery winces at me when I suggest it to her. Traitor.

"What class do we have first? I've barely looked at my schedule." I grumble as I finally tug the kitten heels on.

Avery hums under her breath as she fusses with her already perfect hair. "We have a full school assembly first. It's a late addition, I've messaged Mr. Trevelen and the head of the school board, but haven't heard back from either of them to say what it's for."

I frown.

I'm not a fan of surprises and life just keeps throwing them my way.

The sound of our door unlocking startles me and I shoot Avery a look. She rolls her eyes. "Ash insisted on having a copy. He says it's for emergency use only and *apparently* having a locked door between him and his Mounty this morning counts as an emergency."

Ash strides into the room, Harley and Blaise following closely behind him. They all look fucking devastating in their uniforms and I swear I ruin my panties.

Ash smirks at me and calls out to his sister, "Avery, do we *really* have to have another conversation about your attitude towards my relationship with the Mounty?"

Avery shrugs sweetly. "If I come back here one day and find you with your dick out, I'll destroy you. Slowly, and with great pleasure."

Right.

I move away from the escalating Beaumont Bullshit and sling my bag over my shoulder. Blaise grins at me and gives me a quick kiss, no tongue because he's a little worried now I've armed Avery with the same type of knife I carry at all times. He's seen first-hand how sharp it is and, despite what his asshole father thinks, he's not stupid.

Harley bites his lip at the sight of my socks and hauls me into his arms, a hand cupping my face as he kisses me, walking us both to the door without breaking the kiss. It's fucking stupid, but I swoon.

He breaks away with a grin and Blaise cackles at one of Avery's snipes to her brother, trailing behind us as we head out.

Four steps.

We make it four fucking steps into the hallway before Annabelle *freaking* Summers accosts us.

"You're all fucking the Mounty *slut* now?" She spits and I clench my jaw at her.

Harley snorts at her and keeps walking, ignoring her completely. I glance back at Blaise only to find she's thrown herself at him. He's trying to, carefully, pry her arms off of him and she starts to sob dramatically. I could fucking vomit at the sight of her.

Harley drops his arm from me, ready for one of us to go deal with her, but there's no need.

Avery dumps a full cup of piping hot coffee over her head.

Annabelle screeches, scrambling away from Blaise and her pathetically fake sobs turn into gut-wrenching real ones. All of the girls in the hall freeze and gape at Avery. I mean, I kind of do too.

She stares down at Annabelle and then surveys the other girls with a detached look. Ash steps up behind her, backing her in every sense of the word.

"I'm done asking nicely. Anyone who interferes with my family from this moment onwards will be dealt with immediately and with force. I will no longer hold back and there is *nothing* I could do to any of you little bitches that I couldn't make disappear from the records. Remember that."

Avery says, her voice is glacial and I smile at her like she's my fucking soulmate. "Ash, Harley, and Blaise are off limits to you sluts. This is the only warning you're all getting."

Harley scoffs and whispers in my ear, "Stop looking at her like you want to fuck her, you'll give us all a complex."

I quirk an eyebrow at him. "If we both swung that way, we'd be fucking married by now. I would have wifed her ass last year."

He roars with laughter.

Mr Trevelen starts his welcome speech and I zone the fuck out.

The chapel is still my least favorite place at Hannaford. It's slightly more bearable to be in here now that I am firmly wedged between Avery and Ash, fingers tracing patterns into my thighs in a delicious way that makes me want to squirm. Thanks to his dirty mouth on my birthday, I now associate those patterns with the filthy things he'd whispered to me.

I was fucking starving and these bastards were parading around like French toast topped with cherry ice cream served with freshly brewed coffee.

I'm gonna break.

My attention snaps back to the stage as a woman in her late twenties walks across, her heels far too high to be a teacher. She's attractive; curvy and seductive, blonde hair with a slash of red lipstick finishing off the Monroe look. She caresses Mr. Trevelen's arm as she passes him and his feet stumble. The row of sophomores in front of us start whispering and shifting in their seats. Avery and I share a look.

The fingers on my thighs don't falter.

"Thank you for that glowing introduction, Richard. Good morning, students. As your principal has just informed you, my name is Ms. Vivienne Turner. I expect I will enjoy meeting you individually throughout this first week and teaching you all history."

Avery and I share another look before her phone comes out. Blaise angles his body so the teacher at the end of our aisle can't see what she's doing. Mr Ember is on the Jackal's payroll and we've already discussed keeping a low profile with him until we can flush out his other eyes in the school.

Ms. Turner leaves the stage, swaying her hips like she's trying to fuck the air, and Trevelen steps back up to drone on and on about his plans for the school and I let my mind wander away from his continued naivety. I need to get ahead in my studies early this year. I need to be more prepared than I was last year because there is a lot more on my plate. I have three boyfriends, I'm protecting the man who killed the Vulture, the Jackal wants Harley dead, I haven't sorted out the O'Cronins yet, the Beaumonts, and now there's the Morrisons. *Sweet lord fuck*, I may be in over my head.

When the assembly finally finishes, we leave for our morning classes together.

Avery slips her arm into mine and murmurs quietly into my ear, "I just heard back from the school board. Annabelle is here on the scholarship."

I cut her a look. A freshman nudges past us and the snarl Blaise throws at him is orgasm-inducing. "Why would they give it to her? She's barely scraping through her classes."

Avery snorts. "She wrote to them over the break and made her case to them. Told them she wanted the right education to resurrect her family business."

I roll my eyes. "Sure. She's *definitely* here for education and not for dick."

When we arrive to class for the day, having skipped the first two sessions thanks to the assembly, Blaise sulks when he finds himself on the other side of the room thanks to the alphabetical seating arrangement.

I'm at the back of our history class with Harley and the twins are directly in front of us. I don't know the girl that's seated with Blaise and that worries me. I make a note to see who the hell she is and find out what her grade average is. With all of the joint assignments we're forced to do, I need to know that she's not going to be a dead-weight.

Harley sees me eyeing her and hands me the syllabus; Avery must have gotten it early for him. He's already marked the joint assignments and where we'll split them. I smile sweetly at him. I'm sure it looks fucking stupid on my face, but he grins back.

"I have plenty of shit to keep you busy with this year." He jokes and I snort at him.

He cackles back at me and says, "We can split the children up, work out study plans and keep everyone on top. If you show me how to teach Morrison, I'll try not to rip his throat out when he's a dick to me."

I roll my eyes at him. "Maybe if you didn't talk to him like *that* he wouldn't be a dick back."

Harley shrugs. "He's always going to be a dick, Mounty; it's in every fiber of his being."

I open my mouth to snark at him, fuck knows why I'm defending Blaise because he is a total *dick*, but the door opens and our new teacher walks in like she's a stripper walking up to the pole. Christ, give me the fucking strength I need to get through this.

She smiles coyly at the male students, one by one like she's sizing them all up. Avery glances back at me with a murder in her eyes when Ms. Turner zeros in on Harley. I have two thoughts; I fucking adore that girl, and the new teacher is walking a dangerous line.

"Good morning! You all get the absolute *pleasure* of being the first students to enjoy me this year."

Blaise's snort is so loud we hear it across the room and Avery giggles at him. Ms. Turner ignores it and starts to write on the board.

"I prefer to be addressed as Ms. Vivienne. Ms. Turner sounds too old and matronly for someone of my charms."

I share another look with Avery. She sounds like a bitch in heat and it's fucking gross.

She prattles on about the *joys* and *wonders* of history in a breathy tone. I zone her the fuck out and look over the syllabus instead. I'm planning out what I'm going to tackle first when she starts handing out a pop quiz, bending low for each of the guys in the room. Ash snatches the paper out of her hand and sneers at her. When she blinks at him, shocked that he isn't panting like every other dick in the room, he hands us each a quiz.

Harley cackles. "Thanks, man."

I finish the pop quiz first, which is no surprise, but what is surprising is that Ash finishes his before Harley. I raise my brows at him and he smirks at me. The lying asshole, I knew he was smarter than he ever let on! Harley glares at him and I suddenly realize a whole new headache I'm going to be dealing with this year.

Ms. *Vivienne* walks around the room to look over the

quizzes, one by one, and I'm relieved when she smiles at Blaise and gives him a B. Thank fuck.

When she gets to our desk she rests her hip on it and crosses her arms under her tits, pushing them up so they're about to spill out of her shirt and over Harley.

Who the fuck is this bitch?

Harley stares at the whiteboard, his eyes don't even flick in her direction, and once I realize she's nothing but a fucking cradle-snatching predator on the prowl, I stare ahead as well. No point giving the bitch the attention she wants. Harley smirks and tucks his hand into mine under the desk. Avery is the only one still watching her and I know exactly what's going through her mind.

Assess.

Plan.

Destroy.

When Ms. Vivienne realizes she hasn't caught Harley's attention at all she leans across to the desk next to ours, pushing her ass into his arm. The guys across from us groan lustfully, but Harley's hand clenches in mine.

He's not like Ash.

He might not want to hurt a woman, but he's not morally against it either. If a bitch threatens him or his family, he's not going to find a peaceful resolution. He's going to deal with the fucking problem.

He wants to deal with *this* problem.

I lean into him and whisper, "Do you want me to take her out?"

Harley smirks back. "Stop flirting with me, Mounty."

When the class finally fucking ends, Ms. Vivienne calls out as we pack up. "Mr. Arbour, if you could please stay behind after the class ends. I have something to discuss with you."

My eyes snap up to her face. Avery and Harley glare towards Ms. Vivienne, and she smiles seductively back at Harley.

Fuck that.

I lean in to make a show of whispering to him, "I'll slit her throat and watch her bleed out if she touches you."

Harley smirks back at me. "I'll warn her."

WE SURVIVE the day without me having to kill anyone, but I don't get the chance to ask Harley what the hell the bitch wanted. I mention it to Avery when we get back to our room for dinner.

She sighs and flicks the coffee machine on for me. "She's a ghost. Her file is full, but it's all clean. I had someone trawl through her entire existence online and *nothing*. I thought she had to have a statutory rape hiding somewhere."

I groan as I pull my shoes off, my feet aching from the stupid heels after weeks of my comfortable Docs. Avery starts fussing with pots and pans in the kitchen, not cooking, but scrubbing maniacally. I understand her rage completely.

Which reminds me.

"The word slut is officially off-limits. If any-fucking-one calls me a Mounty slut again, I'm pulling their fingernails out with pliers." I grumble and Avery raises an eyebrow at me.

"Is that a hypothetical or is it in your skill set?"

I cut her a look. "It's in my skill set."

She tilts her head and hums under her breath. We've never discussed the specifics of what I *can* and *have* done before. I wait a minute, but when she doesn't reply I say, "Problem?"

She smirks. "Of course not, I'm just filing that information away in case a situation arises. It's good to know all the tools we have at our disposal."

I laugh at her and grab the cup of coffee she holds out to me.

CHAPTER SIX

H ARLEY TEXTS us to meet him in the dining hall for breakfast the next morning.

Avery makes us both coffees to go. She doesn't look up from her phone the whole way down, trusting me to lead her there safely with her arm tucked tight in mine. I'm so distracted by my own thoughts and worries of what the fuck the history teacher wanted with him that I don't notice the guy that steps into our path until I slam into him.

I grunt at the sharp pain that shoots up my leg and Avery, thankfully, manages to keep a firm grip of my arm to keep me upright. Her eyes make a quick assessment of whoever the fuck we've hit and then her fingers fly across the screen of her phone.

I glance up to see Darcy.

Now, I know it's not Thomas Darcy, because he was a senior last year and this guy is a good foot shorter than him, but the likeness is striking.

I mentally nickname him little Darcy.

"What can I do for you, asshole?" I snap and Avery giggles at my attitude, lapping it up.

He smirks at me and rubs his chest where I'd bumped into him. "I've been looking for you everywhere, Mounty! My brother did warn me that you're a hard girl to catch."

I roll my eyes and take a step around him, holding in the wince. Just what I need, my leg to act up.

"I just wanted to make sure you haven't been whoring over the summer break? I know that's the common occupation for girls like you and I need to know you didn't have to earn the roof over your head. I've taken over Thomas's position as bet keeper."

For. Fuck's. Sake.

I'm rendered speechless for a second over his disgusting arrogance. No matter, Avery has my back and speaks for me.

"Joey's graduated, there is no bet. Move, Darcy, before I make you disappear in a permanent sort of way." She says, sweet and dangerous.

Little Darcy has no survival instincts and his mouth just keeps running. "Just because Joey isn't here anymore, doesn't mean the bet isn't ongoing. I'm happy to clear the cobwebs out, Mounty! Maybe the time away from cock has tightened that pussy up a bit."

Deep breath in. Deep breath out...

Is what a normal person would do. Me? I break the fucker's nose with the heel of my palm and then punch him so hard in the dick I think his fucking ancestors feel it.

The squealing sound that comes out of him is magical.

Avery giggles and records the entire thing on her phone. I think about telling her to put it the fuck away because I'm going to gut the creepy fuck, but then I hear a bag drop to the floor and see the blur of dark hair and solid muscle fly past us to pin little Darcy against the wall.

"Say it again, Darcy. Proposition my girlfriend again, I

want to hear it for myself before I put you in a fucking *coma*."

I swear to god, my heart stops.

The room stops too, all of the students stop moving and talking and fucking *breathing* now there's an enraged Beaumont snarling in their presence. I have to remind my body that the Jackal doesn't own me and I can be with whoever the fuck I want, but there's still a little panic in me at Ash's words.

I just wanted more time to ourselves without the fucking gossips, and the threat of the Jackal hanging over all three of them. Fuck.

"I didn't know she was yours!" Sputters little Darcy, literally sputters because there's blood pouring out of his nose and his mouth. Avery cringes away from them, tugging my arm, but I want to see this. I want to know how Ash is going to play this.

"She's mine. She's Arbour's, and she's Morrison's, and if I find out a single dickhead has propositioned her, I will take them out. Gone. *No fucking more*." He speaks loud enough that the students watching all hear his words and I blush at the looks I'm now getting.

There are quite a few girls dumb enough to glare at me and Avery starts taking note on her phone. I roll my eyes at her. I don't have time to deal with petty teenage bullshit. Let them be jealous, fuck, I was writhing with it when I thought Annabelle had what I now do.

Ash moves a hand to grip little Darcy's throat, squeezing enough that his eyes get panicked. "My beloved sister is going to pass along the Mounty's bank details and you're going to deposit the sweep in there. It's her fucking money. If I catch you within ten feet of her again... gone, Darcy. *Gone*."

Little Darcy's phone pings and Avery gives him a sarcastic little wave. Ash drops his hands and takes a step back, swooping down to grab his bag and then he glares around the room until the captive audience scurries away.

"I had it under control." I grouse, and he snorts at me.

"Just let me defend you for once, Mounty, for Christ's sake. Besides, we needed to get word out somehow that you're our girlfriend and not just a random fuck. No better way than making someone bleed."

Avery gives him a look. "You had better not be fucking her."

Ash watches me take one wobbling step and then sighs, slinging an arm around my waist to mold me into his side. Avery tucks her arm into his on the other side but the stern look stays on her face.

"Avery, please. At some point Lips is going to want to fuck me."

Nope.

I try to pull away from him but he laughs at me, the dick, and tightens his arm.

"Lips, I'm firmly team Morrison on the v card debate." Avery says, her voice too fucking loud and we walk through the halls teeming with students.

Why? *Why*?! What have I done to deserve this?!

"You're my sister, you're supposed to be on my side!" Ash hisses back at her, pissy at her supposed betrayal.

Avery giggles and shakes her head at him like he's simple. It's nice to see it directed somewhere other than at me. "We've discussed this. It's a Battle Royale for my affections. Lips is in the lead; massively, you should really start focusing on me more. Morrison is next. Then, you and Harley are joint losers."

"What the fuck has Morrison done to get ahead?"

Avery smirks at him and I decide that death is preferable to this conversation. "You keep arguing with me over Lips, and Harley keeps shoving his tongue down her throat in my presence. Morrison at least *attempts* some form of discretion."

THE NEWS of my three-way relationship hits the dining hall before we do.

Blaise is slouched over, held up only by the wall, and Harley is frowning down at his phone as we arrive. He glances up and does a quick once over of me before sneering at Ash, "A public claiming, really? Like she doesn't already have enough on her fucking plate."

Ash's eyes grow glacial and I groan. "I've just *removed* things from her plate. Now there isn't a guy at this school that will touch her because I will personally beat the life out of them."

I shiver and pull away from him so he doesn't give me shit for reacting like he's given me flowers or some other shit normal girls like.

Blaise pushes off from the wall and tucks me under his arm. "Whatever, it's done now. Can we eat so this day can start? I already need it to fucking end."

We move into the dining hall without waiting for their answers, Blaise rubbing his cheek on the top of my head as he yawns like a damn cat.

Every eye turns to watch us.

I tense and only Blaise's arm around me stops me from pulling away from him. Avery steps up to my side and slips her arm into mine, glaring around the room until the other students avert their gaze.

"Just ignore them, Star." Blaise mumbles, and that snaps me out of my awkward nervousness. I give him my best impression of Avery's icy glare.

"What the hell kind of nickname is that?" Avery mocks and Blaise's eyes fucking twinkle. I think about thumbing them the fuck *out*.

"It's an inside joke, you wouldn't get it." He smirks and grabs a tray to fill.

Once we're seated and digging into our breakfasts, Harley's eyes flick to the door and groans. I glance over my shoulder to find *Ms. Vivienne* sauntering in. Blaise snickers under his breath and I jab him in the ribs.

"She offered to write up a *personal* recommendation letter to three different scholarship programs for me if I join her gifted students study group." Harley says, his eyes watching her warily.

"She offered that to you and not Lips? She beats you in every class, except Choir where she's beating Morrison." Ash, very helpfully, but also very dickishly, supplies.

Harley doesn't take the bait, he just raises a brow and says, "I'm aware of that, but the Mounty doesn't have a dick so I don't think she's the slut's type."

Avery holds up a palm. "I think I should warn you all. Lips has declared the word *slut* off limits. If you like your fingernails where they are, I'd choose a new word."

They all look at me and I shrug. "Pliers hurt like a bitch."

Harley smirks at me. "Is that how you're going to make her bleed over my honor, Mounty?"

I throw a napkin at his smug face. "What honor? You should take her up on it."

Avery cuts me a sharp look and I shrug, "We have nothing on her. Best case scenario she tries to touch him, and after he breaks her *fucking* hand, we own her. Worst case scenario, he has an in for scholarships."

I'm not happy about it, but I'm also not going to be possessive and pathetic about this. Either I trust him or I don't, and I wouldn't have told him I was the Wolf if I didn't trust him. Besides, she's a desperate, attention-seeking cougar. What do we have to be worried about?

Avery looks impressed. "*Ruthless.* I love it."

Harley's eyes narrow. "You're not worried about me?"

"You gonna fuck her? No? Then I'm not worried. If she gets handsy I'm confident you'll be able to figure it out. Just don't accept any drinks from the bitch."

Blaise roars with laughter over the face Harley pulls, but Avery steers the conversation into a safer direction.

CHAPTER SEVEN

W E AGREE to all meet back at our room on Friday to have an early dinner together.

I barely get to see Harley outside of class now he has his extra workload and practice with the swim team. I can tell he's starting to get twitchy about it, and after the first few weeks of being forced away from me, I find myself being backed into the bathroom for a blistering kiss. He only stops because Avery throws a serving spoon at his head. I blush profusely, but no one seems to care about my mortification. The routine is soothing for Avery, and I find it great to just hang out after another hectic week in hell.

After dinner is over and the kitchen is clean, Ash, Avery, and Harley all head off to their training sessions, and Blaise and I pull an extra study session together.

We always study until Avery gets back and death glares him into leaving with a quick kiss, which is why I'm shocked to find him lounging on my bed as I come out of the bathroom from changing out of my uniform.

I quirk an eyebrow at him and he grins at me, patting the bed playfully.

"Come on, Mounty, I've been good." He practically fucking purrs at me.

My traitorous knees tremble, but I tell them to quit. I do not need a repeat of last year, playing catch up and wading through piles of assignments last minute with him, so I prop my hands on my hips and give him my best impression of Avery's stern looks.

I'm so fucking ready to chew him out for putting the work off, but then he leans forward to strip his blazer off, popping two buttons on his shirt and letting the color of his tattoos peek out.

Sweet lord.

I cave.

I cave so fucking quickly, climbing up to lay beside him and he covers me with the hard lines of his body the second I do, like he's as desperate as I am. He stares down at me for a second and whatever it is he's looking for he finds, grinning and swooping down to take my lips.

As we kiss, deep and dirty, I slide my hands into the open collar to rub at the vibrant colors of his skin and his answering groan is *obscene*. I fucking love kissing him. The way he uses his whole body, like he needs to move against me because it's too fucking hard to stay still.

He pulls my hips flush into his and my heart stutters in my chest. I'm so fucking worked up and ready for *something* to happen. He moves his lips to kiss down my neck and I can't think anymore.

I'm fucking horny.

That's what's happening here.

They've all been teasing me and working me into a frenzy and, goddammit, someone had better fucking do something about it, or I'm going to have to deal with the problem myself.

When I tell Blaise this, groaning out the words while he sucks on the soft skin below my ear, he grinds his hips into me harder.

I can hear the laughter in his voice as he says, "I can do something about it, Star. What do you want?"

I blanch.

Well fuck, I don't know!

He chuckles under his breath at me and I give him a glare. "If you're going to be a dick about me being a clueless virgin I'm going to go have a cold shower instead."

I move to try to pull away, but he doesn't let go of my hips and the movement makes me rub against his dick. I cannot think about how big or hard he is without gulping and blushing like an idiot.

He groans at me, "Fuck, I'm not being an asshole; I'm trying to go slow. Pick something you've already done."

I blush and glare at him some more.

I watch as it clicks in his brain. He reels back. "You're not serious?"

Miraculously, my face somehow gets even hotter. I snap, "Yes, I'm fucking serious! You know I'm a virgin."

Blaise blows out a breath and reaches for his phone, his body curving over me and pressing me into the bed in an entirely too distracting type of way. "Being a virgin doesn't mean you've never fooled around before. You've never made out with a guy and gotten each other off?"

My mind flashes to the fucking insanely erotic feeling of grinding down on Harley's dick and I cough to hide my reaction. "No. I've barely done anything. Thanks for taking that so well, Jesus. Who are you calling? If you're going to fucking *tattle-*"

He presses a hand over my mouth and slides down onto the bed, maneuvering us around until my back is pressed against his chest. He pulls me until my head drops back onto his shoulder and my throat is bared, as if he's going to slit me ear to ear. It definitely should not be a turn on, but I think we all know I'm not in the ballpark of normal.

He breathes into my ear, a shiver running down my spine, "I want to make you come so fucking hard the Jackal hears you screaming my name from his little fortress. I want you so fucking wet that your come runs down my arm and I can smell you on my skin for days. You're gonna let me touch you, aren't you, Star? I want to watch you come."

Sweet merciful lord.

Who fucking taught him to talk like *that*?!

He doesn't move his hand away from my mouth so I'm forced to nod to answer him.

He mumbles happily into my shoulder as he licks and sucks his way along the skin there, tracing the little scars I have with his tongue until I'm squirming. I pant desperately through my nose when his free hand edges under my shirt and finds nothing but skin.

I decide I'm never fucking wearing a bra again.

His hand cups one of my boobs and squeezes, his groan smothered in the back of my neck sending ripples of pleasure down my spine. Thank the good lord I've been eating again and there's something for him to hold onto because I think I could come just from this.

"Fuck me." He groans, rolling my nipples between his calloused fingertips.

He grunts again when I grind my ass into his dick, and he moves the hand from my mouth for long enough to get the shirt off of me and flip me onto my back, then he keeps me quiet by kissing me like he's dying.

Fuck. Me.

I barely notice him tear my pants off. I'm too busy

trying to get his stupid shirt off without just ripping the buttons off and eventually he takes pity on me. He takes off his pants as well, leaving only his boxers, and my mouth waters at the sight of him.

Fuuuuuuck.

I'm struck dumb for a minute and when my brain decides to work again I'm smug that he seems just as affected. He runs his hands up my stomach and over my tits.

"Where the fuck have you been hiding these?" He groans and I scoff at him.

"They come and go."

He leans down to bite my earlobe and growls, "Well don't fucking let them go again."

Bossy asshole but, fuck, that's hot.

I can't think of a witty retort and he kisses me again, biting at my lips and sucking until I'm fucking gone for him. His hands work their way lower and lower until they hit my panties.

My heart stutters, but I'm still so fucking desperate that I don't think twice about moaning into his kiss.

His fingers curve over the lace of my panties and he grunts when he can feel how wet I am already. He pulls away and mumbles something into the skin of my neck as he sucks on the skin there, but there is no way I can focus enough to grasp the words, not when he's marking up the skin on my neck and sliding his fingers through the mess I've already made.

He's barely even started.

I decide that I can't wait another damn second and I rip my own panties off so he'll hurry the hell up.

Works like a charm.

His fingers are sliding over my slick skin and rubbing my clit before my panties hit the floor. Jesus fucking Christ.

I do not want to think about the number of girls he must have been with to find my clit that easily.

I'm going to come so fucking quick, the *weeks* of foreplay priming me to just cream for him. He's still a fucking tease, and when my legs start to tremble and thrash on the bed he moves from my pulsing clit to slip a finger in, hooking it up to rub over my G spot. I nearly jolt off the damn bed.

"Fuck, Mounty. Do you want to come?"

I nod and whimper like a whore. He grins at me, pumping his finger into me before adding a second, groaning at the tight fit. It doesn't hurt, but I'm probably going to knee him in the ribs if he tries for a third.

When I start to tremble, from sheer frustration at the orgasm that's *just* out of reach, he finally moves to rub my clit again, tight, maddening circles and I fucking shatter.

I come so hard I feel it run down his hand and my thighs, my head thrown back, his name ripped out of my chest in a gasp.

When I finally blink the stars out of my eyes I find Blaise grinning at me like the cat that got the cream.

Well, he certainly got mine.

It takes me two tries to find some words. "I don't think I can move."

He laughs at me and if I could move, I'd shove a pillow over his smug face. He moves like he's going to get off the bed and I grab his arm.

"Mounty, I'm just gonna go jerk off in your bathroom. After *that* it's not going to take me long."

I blush like an idiot but I tug him closer. "Do it here. I wanna watch."

He quirks an eyebrow up at me like he wasn't expecting

that at all and, honestly, I wasn't expecting to say it either, but I don't want him to leave.

He kisses me again, so I miss his hand sliding into his boxers, but when he grunts against my lips I break away to rest my forehead on his chest and look down.

Holy fucking shit.

Okay, I'm now a little nervous about having sex with any of them because Blaise is probably the same size as Harley and, sweet fucking lord, how the hell is that going to fit in me? My mind wanders to Ash, because he's the only one I haven't gotten this close to yet, but Annabelle's taunts stick in my head about the extra inches he has. *Fuck.*

Blaise's eyes are glued somewhere between my nipples and the wet mess on my thighs so he misses the little moment of panic I have as he grunts and comes all over his fist.

Fuck.

That's a good look.

Blaise recovers a bit quicker than me, his face flushed and sweaty and fucking *stunning*, and he wipes his hand on his discarded shirt. I wrinkle my nose at him and he laughs at me, rolling off the bed to throw it in our laundry basket and wash his hands.

I still can't move.

It only makes him laugh harder, but I grin back at him, happy to finally see him without the gloom wrapped around him he's been carrying since he showed up in the Bay.

He helps me back into my shirt and then tucks us both into bed, switching the light off. I settle onto his chest, surprised to find myself close to sleep already. My eyes drift shut and he rubs circles on my back.

"Promise me you won't let Avery cut my dick off."

I blink at him, but it's too dark to really see if he's being serious. "What?"

"I sent her a text so she would stay back at our room with Ash and Harley, and we could have the room to ourselves all night. She's just messaged to say she knew I'd be the one to christen her knife. Mounty, I can't live without my dick."

I smother my laugh in his chest and fall asleep.

I WAKE to the smell of coffee, and open my eyes to find Avery wafting a cup under my nose.

I hum happily, grabbing the cup, and when I start to gulp down the sweet, sweet life-giving liquid Avery says, so sweetly, "And anything for your bedfellow this morning?"

Bedfellow?

Oh.

Fuck.

I almost forget the cup of piping hot coffee in my hand as I sit up. Thank fuck we put at least a little clothing back on last night before we fell asleep. My cheeks are burning as I brave a look at Avery. She smirks at me.

"I think he'd rather sleep in." I croak and shift around to try to get out of the bed without her noticing my bare ass.

"Exhausted, is he? Big night?" She coos and I give up, swinging my legs out and preparing to run for the bathroom, bare ass be damned! I need a minute for my brain to unscramble.

"You know he's not a morning person, Aves." I mumble and scurry off to the bathroom. I take my time getting clean, letting the water calm me down. Fuck. What the hell am I going to say to Harley or Ash about this? This is the real fucking test of whether or not they can share.

When I finally emerge Blaise is still snoring. Avery is cooking a mountain of pancakes and Ash is drinking a coffee like his life depends on it. When he hears the door, he turns to offer me a cup, no hesitation or judgment. I let out a breath.

"Harley's coming up when he's finished at the pool and we can study together. Avery is getting twitchy about biology already." He smirks and I join him at the bench. Pancakes aren't my favorite, but I could eat fifty of them I'm that hungry.

Avery snarks over her shoulder at him, "Why do we always have to cut up dead things? It's disgusting."

Ash snorts. "Too bad you're not paired with the Mounty, Harley told me word on the street says her hand is the steadiest."

I elbow him in the ribs while Avery laughs. We get set up on the table, pancakes and assignments spread out around us, and eat while we wait for Harley. I refuse to wake Blaise and I don't mention that it's because I know the real torture will start the moment he does. Avery is distracted, her mind on her phone more than her breakfast. When she looks up I quirk an eyebrow at her.

"Joey has moved to my father's estate in Washington. He has a new dealer and he's already causing problems there."

I pull a face at her. "Problems like a trail of dead bodies?"

Ash snorts. "Senior is not enjoying being on Joey babysitting duty. It was easier for him to leave it to us. He's already stabbed two of my father's men when they tried to stop him from going out."

I nod slowly. I have the opportunity to finally ask why the hell Ash's life depends on Joey breathing but I'm not sure now is the right time, with Blaise snoring and Harley on his way back. Avery sees the indecision on my face and cuts a careful look at Ash.

"Senior has made his *disappointment* very clear that Joey is the only one of his progeny to have inherited his taste for violence."

Right.

Gross.

Harley unlocks the door, for *fuck's sake* they all must have keys, and wanders in. He scoffs at Blaise's snoring form and throws a pillow at him. Blaise doesn't so much as twitch. Harley pulls up a chair next to mine and, though his eyes are intense as he looks me over, he kisses my cheek sweetly and his wet hair tickles the side of my face. I try, and fail, not to start to blush but I'm so fucking relieved.

I clear my throat. "Your dad's pissed because the two of you are ruthless dictators, but also manage to have morals? Jesus fucking wept. I don't want to meet the guy. Knowing and dealing with Liam O'Cronin is enough, thanks."

Ash snorts again and says, "Please tell me you're going to record yourself slitting that cretin's throat so we can all enjoy it."

"It's on my list."

Harley's hand squeezes my thigh, not missing a beat in the conversation he's walked into. "Can we pretend for one second that you're not the most secretive person on the fucking planet and can you tell us what's on the list?"

I blow out a breath and share a look with Avery. "We

should wait until Blaise is up so I don't have to repeat myself."

Avery gives me a sly look and I brace myself for the shit I know she's about to grab a spoon and start stirring. "Ash, go shake the asshole awake. Ask him what he'd like for his last meal on Earth because I'm going to gut him for kicking me out of my own room just so he could get his dick out. Mounty, I hope he was gentle with you."

Kill me.

Just fucking *kill me* now.

I tip my head back and stare at the ceiling for a second, blushing furiously and avoiding any of the eyes that are now glued on me. Blaise decides that *this* is the moment he will return to the land of the living, sitting up sharply, and I'm sure the look he gives Avery will earn him a knife to the kidneys from Ash or Harley.

"Leave her the *fuck* alone."

The look Avery gives him is so fucking cold the temperature in the room changes. "She's my best friend. I can ask her if I need to *kill you* if I want to."

Blaise heaves himself out of bed, looking rumpled and fucking delicious, before stalking over to us. He kisses my head sweetly, cradling my cheek, and snaps back at her, "Don't be a bitch about it. Ask her that shit when we're not around, don't make her feel like shit by putting her on blast. This isn't a fucking game."

I don't know if it's just the ice Avery is throwing, but the whole room freezes. I'm too damn worried to look at Ash or Harley right now so my focus stays glued on Avery. Her eyes narrow at Blaise but he doesn't back down, and I start to sweat at the thought of the brawl that's about to happen. This is exactly what I was afraid would happen, dammit! I open my mouth, ready to try and diffuse the fight, when a slow smile stretches across her face.

"I'm glad you're taking your relationship seriously. Morrison is still second. You two need to step up." She decrees, shooting me a smug look.

Blaise scoffs at her, kisses my head again, and then stomps his way to the bathroom.

Ash gives Avery a hard look. "How? I look in her direction and you have a fucking episode at me."

Avery stands to clear plates away. "I'm not explaining myself to you, Ash. I'm doing whatever I have to do to keep our family safe and happy, even if that means gutting one of you for Lips."

Harley moves to sling his arm over my shoulders and I take my first deep breath since I woke up. His eyes are possessive on me while he says to Avery in a tone haughty, "So we're all being tested by you to make sure our intentions are pure? I'm not fucking worried. I'm sleeping here tonight. I'm fucking sick of spending all of my time with that skank of a teacher."

CHAPTER EIGHT

I'M SITTING in math class, keeping a careful eye on Blaise's blushing desk buddy from across the room, when my phone vibrates silently against my leg. Harley feels it and glances around then frowns at me when it's clear the text has come from outside our little family.

I shrug and wait for the teacher to turn his back before checking the text.

I'm coming to your stuck-up school, little Wolf. Big news, the kind that needs to be delivered personally. The O'Cronin kid can get you into the pool, right? Meet me there at 11pm.

I groan. Just what I need. Harley quirks an eyebrow at me and I flash him the screen to show him Illi's text. His frown deepens and he nods his head a fraction.

I try to get my focus back on the sums in front of me, but the swirling pit of my stomach makes it impossible, so instead I glare at the back of the blushing girl's head.

Harley bumps me gently to get my attention, and asks me what the hell my problem is using just his eyebrows. Yep, I'm fluent now. I know exactly what the golden god who's taken over my bed is saying. Only my bed, he won't take over my body with Avery's watchful eyes around and with all of the extra classes he's barely making it to our room before midnight on the nights he comes to me. I'm sort of hoping Ms. Vivienne will hurry up and make a move on him so the whole thing can be done with, even if it does make me twitchy to think of her touching him.

I'm not sure I can get my eyebrows to say what I need them to in return so I shrug instead.

After class Avery laughs at me as I eyeball the fuck out of the blushing girl. I tuck my arm into hers and stomp to the dining hall for lunch, ignoring the guys as they gloat at each other over last night's fight club.

I already know Ash won.

If the bruised and split skin on his knuckles didn't give it away then the looks of respect and sheer terror he gets from the other students would have clued me in. I hear Blaise joking about sending Harley the video of a particularly brutal fight with one of Joey's ex-flunkies and I make a note to get a copy myself.

For research purposes.

Ahem.

Avery grimaces at her phone before murmuring, "I don't know why you're glaring at that poor little sheep. It's not like he even noticed her, and she was too shy to ever speak to him."

I roll my eyes at her. "Exactly. So if he needs help with his workbook she's not going to be able to do shit if she can't even speak to him. She didn't take a single note the entire class."

Avery chuckles. "Neither did you."

"Difference is, the Mounty has already finished the entire Algebra unit and is now working on the Geometry workbook that the class won't move to for another *eight* weeks. She's so far ahead even Harley's *extra special tutoring* can't get close to her." Ash interrupts, and Avery cuts me a look.

"Are you sleeping at night? How much coffee are you drinking? Do I need to give up ballet and start stalking you to make sure you're taking care of yourself?" She hisses and I laugh at her.

We push into the dining hall and I try to ignore the looks I get. At least I don't have to listen to the whispers while I'm surrounded by the others. The students here seem to think they're the dangerous ones.

Fucking rich idiots.

I grab a tray for myself and Avery, ignoring three sets of glares at my independent move. I make it two steps before Ash wrestles it from me. Chivalrous dickhead. "I'm sleeping just fine. Things are calmer this year, at school at least. I'm not worried about Joey choking you or Harlow fucking poisoning you. I'm not stressing about hot assholes sitting on my couch glaring at me all day." Avery gags at me dramatically and I smirk back. "I'm just getting ahead before everything turns to shit like it always does."

Famous last words.

***

Harley arrives at our door at 10pm.

He lets himself in and I frown, confused about his early appearance. Avery stomps out of the bathroom, wrapped in a fluffy towel, and snarks at him, "The keys are for an emergency! If you don't stop letting yourself in I'm going to start walking around naked!"

Harley snorts at her. "You'll only be risking Morrison's life. I don't wanna see my cousin's tits, but it's not going to scar me for life. Morrison's the one who'll get stabbed for looking at you."

Avery loosens the hold on her towel so it slips a little to call his bluff.

I groan and slap a hand over my face as the two of them glare each other down like some sort of fucked up game of chicken.

I clear my throat to try to interrupt them. "Can we just go, Harley? Please? Or do you want me to put a movie on while we wait?"

He reluctantly looks away and Avery crows in victory. "Grab a bathing suit, we can go for a swim before the Butcher gets here."

I blanch. "I'm shit at swimming."

"Well, I'm not. I'll keep you afloat."

I'm not proud to admit it, but the deciding factor is the very thought of being pressed up against his wet, naked chest.

Yes *fucking* please.

One small problem.

"I don't have a bathing suit."

Harley quirks an eyebrow at me. "You're from the Bay, how do you not have a suit?"

Avery tugs me into her closet and pulls her bathrobe on, rummaging through her drawers until she finds a tiny scrap of fabric and passes it to me.

There is no way it will cover even my small tits.

I cut her a look and she smirks at me. "That asshole should be kissing my feet for giving you that. Try it on."

It's obscene. It's truly fucking obscene.

My entire body flushes as Avery looks me over, clinically approving like I'm her own personal model, and somehow it's so much worse than being naked. It's technically a bandage-style one-piece, but I've seen micro bikinis have more coverage over the important parts. I have under-boob cleavage in this thing, for fucks sake! I turn around in the mirror and, oh look, there's eighty-five percent of my butt-cheeks.

"Let me find you something to cover up with for the walk down there." Avery mutters, as she moves to a different drawer.

Harley lets out an exasperated sigh and calls out, "We're not going to get the chance to swim if you turn this into a fashion parade, Floss. Just grab a sweater to wear once our... *friend* gets here."

Avery ignores him and winds a silky, shimmery wrap dress around me, tying and buttoning and tucking me in until I'm positive Harley is going to have to bundle me back into it when we're finished. When she nudges me out of the closet she snarks at him, "If you run into anyone on the way down and she wasn't covered up, you'd stab them. *You're welcome, cousin dearest.*"

Harley rolls his eyes at her, then kisses her cheek sweetly and tucks me under his arm to walk down to the pool. I wait until we're in the hall before I burrow into the solid warmth of his chest. The rumbling noise of contentment he makes is loud against my ear.

He uses his own set of keys to get us into the building and he disarms the alarm with practiced ease. When he catches my questioning look he shrugs, "Coach knows I come here when I can't sleep. He gets an alert saying someone has disabled the alarm and when he sees it's my code he ignores it."

Huh.

I didn't know that this was soothing for him. They all have little rituals, every one of them. Avery cleans obsessively and puts things in meticulous order, Ash runs until he can't breathe, and Blaise messes around with lyrics and drawings in his notebook. They have all learned how to cope with the dark reality of our world.

I take to my bed and cease existing two days a year.

I'm busy musing over our broken little family when Harley does that move of his and pulls his shirt off one-handed. He grins at me, the absolute asshole because he *knows* he has my attention now, and he pushes his jeans down his legs until he's left in a pair of swim shorts.

Sweet merciful lord.

I would like to climb that boy like a freaking *tree*.

It occurs to me that I can now. *Jesus fucking wept.*

His grin stays in place while he waits for my soul to return to my body and it only falters when I start to fumble with the dress, gritting my teeth at the stupid thing until finally the fabric floats to the ground and I'm left in the sparse black suit.

"Holy fuck." Harley croaks, and I barely manage to blink before he's hauling me up into his arms, my legs wrapping around him instinctively, like they were made to be. Maybe they were; I'm not questioning it. I couldn't right now if I tried.

He holds me up with one arm under my ass, *holy fucking hotness*, and uses the other to gently grip the back of my neck, pulling my lips into his. Just before they touch he whispers, "We are not having sex for the first time in a pool, but fuck me, it's tempting. That suit is the work of the devil, and she's trying to fucking kill me. I need some frigid water to calm my dick down."

I huff out a laugh, but before I can tease him he tugs me into his kiss. I wriggle in his arms a little, just enough that I slide down his body a fraction and feel that, yep, he really does like what he sees. I wriggle a little more, moaning into the kiss and grinding against him, so distracted by his groans that I barely take note that we're moving. It's only when he steps down into the water, slowly descending the concrete steps, that I break away and prepare to be submerged.

"Don't look so scared, babe. I won't drop you." He teases, nipping at my neck.

I don't want to tell him that I'd once been held underwater until my vision blacked out, and doing this with him is using a level of trust I didn't know I was capable of. Not just going for a swim with him, but being this close to him in the water. I clear my throat, and try to chase the ghosts away.

The water is colder than I expect a pool custom built for spoiled brats to be and a little gasp rips out of my mouth before I can bite it back when the water hits my shoulders. Harley smirks at me and pulls me flush against his chest again, grunting when my hard nipples rub against his chest. He walks us deeper and deeper, until he's swimming to keep us both afloat. I try to think weightless thoughts as the tension eases out of his face the further we drift out.

He looks so fucking relaxed.

I don't want Illi to come and ruin this moment.

"I've missed you. I hate being back at school." I say, trying to swallow the lump in my throat at my admission. I try to duck my head away, but Harley cups my cheek and forces me to look at him.

"I miss you too. I fucking hate that dumb slu - *fuck* -

skank for picking me. I was supposed to finally spend the year with you and instead I'm dodging hands."

I pull back from him and fix a stern gaze on him, ready to climb out of the pool and hunt the bitch down, but he shrugs it off. "She keeps stroking my arm and my shoulder. It's not enough to get her under Floss's thumb, but it pisses me the fuck off. Fuck, I don't want to talk about her. Grind on my dick some more, that'll distract me."

He gives me this *wolfish* grin and I cackle at him, so blissfully smug that he wants me just as much as I'm dying for him. I wriggle against his chest again and lean forward to swallow his groan. I'm still not confident in much more than kissing, but his reactions to everything I'm doing spurs me on, like maybe my enthusiasm is enough to get me through this without looking like an inexperienced fool.

Harley swims us over to one side of the pool and perches my ass on a little ledge so he can settle between my legs without me dragging him under the water. He moves to kiss my neck, sucking on the skin below my ear, and I try to grind my hips into his but he holds me still with one hand and a firm grip. Fuck it, I need more.

"No sex or nothing but kissing?" I whisper and he jolts away from my neck. My cheeks are on fire, but the stunned look on his face makes it worth pushing past my nerves.

He stares at me for a second and then says, his voice nothing more than a rasp, "Fuck."

Right.

I was kind of expecting more than that, but before I can *die* of pure mortification, he's kissing me again and grinding his dick into me like he's on a mission. I'm one hundred percent on-fucking-board, and I suck on his tongue until he's panting and groaning, pulling my hips closer until I'm a shaking mess. His fingers dance along the seam of the swimsuit and I nod, trying not to break away from his lips, but good lord, if he doesn't touch me right now I'm going to die.

The bathing suit is so skimpy he can hook it with one finger and tug it aside, he's groaning again as his fingers slide reverently through my slick pussy lips, stroking me like he's savoring the feeling. My breath catches in my throat and the smoldering look he gives me only makes it harder to breathe.

"We can stop." He whispers, stroking the hair away from face with the hand he isn't cupping my pussy with.

I think about inflicting violence on him out of sheer frustration and grit out from my clenched teeth, "If you do, I'm going to stab you."

He smirks at me then grinds the heel of his palm into my clit, pushing a finger into me, and his hips jerk forward when I clench around the digit. He pumps his finger into me, curving it to rake over my G spot, and my head drops back as I moan. He adds another and moves to rub my clit with his other hand, tight, maddening circles until my hips are jerking and twisting wildly. The water seems to heat up around us, like the heat we're throwing off our bodies is changing the temperature of the pool. I can't think straight, and my whole existence is centered around what he's doing to me, and I think I'm going to die if I don't come soon.

"Fuck, you're going to make me come in my shorts like this is the first pussy I've ever touched." His voice is nothing but need and fire, and I shiver, catching his lips with mine to suck on his bottom lip again. I'm so fucking addicted to the taste of him.

It shouldn't be a compliment, but I'm fucking *preening* at his words, even through the haze of my own impending climax. The only problem is, I don't want him to come in his shorts; I want to make him feel as good as his fingers being buried in my pussy make me feel. It can't be that hard, right?

I gulp.

Then I remind myself that I'm not afraid of anything, let alone a *dick*. Even if it is way bigger than I thought I'd be handling and attached to one of the hottest guys to ever walk the Earth. *Deep breath.* I slip my hand down his incredible abs and into the waistband of his shorts. He groans like a dying man as I wrap my fingers around his dick and, sweet merciful lord, I will take that sound to the grave. He wasn't lying, he's throbbing and searingly hot in my hand like he's a few firm pumps away from coming. I'm going to give it a shot.

I manage one stroke before my ringtone cuts through the air and *ruins everything.*

It can only be Illi and we can't ignore him, even for a few minutes because fuck knows what sort of trouble he could get into at Hannaford if left to his own devices. Harley groans into my mouth, and when I break away he curses viciously. "Is the whole fucking universe cock-blocking me?"

I manage something vaguely resembling a laugh but inside, I'm dying over the interruption.

HARLEY CAN'T GET me back into the dress and tugs his shirt over my head instead.

My legs are both restless and wobbling, a dangerous mix, and Harley scoffs at my attempts to walk. "Just sit down and I'll go let him in. Fuck, cross your damn legs! I don't want him seeing that perfect wet pussy."

I blush and do what he says, even though I know Illi has no interest in looking at me. His eyes belong to someone else and I feel a pang in my chest when I think of Odie.

I hope the Jackal hasn't gone after her.

Harley digs around in his swim bag and pulls on his team sweatpants and jacket, zipping it halfway so his tattoo is still clearly visible. I've never seen him in them before and his shoulders look so broad and defined I'm hot for him all over again.

Okay, new rule: no fooling around right before we meet up with Illi to exchange important, possibly life-threatening, information. My hormones are raging and my brain is no longer functioning.

I take a second to try to breathe, before the scuffing sound of Harley walking back pulls my attention back to where it needs to be.

Illi couldn't look more out of place if he tried.

Harley scowls at him, leading him over to the bench I'm perched on. I can smell the acrid scent of tobacco and the twitching of Illi's fingers tell me he wishes he was allowed to light up again. Illi smirks back at Harley, blowing him a kiss and tugging on his leather jacket with a tattooed, scarred hand. I shake my head at him.

"I need you two to get along, Illi, please stop provoking him."

Illi strides over to me, his feet eerily silent in his biker boots, and drapes a casual arm over my shoulders as he sits down. "Anything for you, little Wolf. How's school treating you? The uniform is fucking weird here, you look like a dirty-old-man's wet dream."

Harley was glaring at Illi's arm, but at his little comment

his spine snaps straight and he steps forward to snarl, "*Fuck. Off.*"

Illi holds his hands up in mock surrender. "Look at you, assuming I'm a dirty old man! I've skinned people for less, little mobster."

I roll my eyes at them both and give Illi a not-so-gentle shove away from me. I trust him, with more than just my life, but I don't want him sitting so close to me when I'm barely covered. He cackles and scoots along, giving me more than enough space to breathe. That does more for Harley's temper than words ever could, and he takes up watch on my other side. I slip my hand into his, giving him a little squeeze to try to remind him to stay calm. I doubt it'll work, but I'm freaking trying.

"Right, well, I've had my fun. I was trying to lighten the mood a bit before I break the news to you. We're in a world of shit, kid. I hope you've got something fucking big up your sleeve because we're going to need it."

Fuck.

I'm not sure I have *anything* up my sleeve, let alone something big. I give him a nod and mutter, "What's happened now?"

"I asked around about your little crew to see if there's any word in our corner of the world about any of them, like we discussed. Make sure we're on top of anything that might threaten us. Got a hit back from out of state. Morningstar was approached by Matteo to take out O'Cronin."

"It's Arbour." I croak, as I squeeze my eyes shut and take a second to steady myself.

Illi flicks out a dismissive hand gesture. "Right. So, he was contacted about *Arbour,* but I was expecting that. I wasn't expecting him to also be liaising with the senior Joseph Beaumont about your twins."

My eyes snap to him.

What. The. Fuck.

There's silence for a minute while I try to stop my heart from exploding inside my chest cavity. Illi watches the water and nods to himself slowly, like he's agreeing with some internal monologue he has going on.

"Who the fuck is Morningstar?" Harley snaps when he's finally had enough of waiting for answers.

"The Devil." I whisper, and Illi gives me a chagrined smile.

His eyes flick over to Harley's and for once he doesn't try to provoke him. He just lays out the facts of exactly how bad this is. "He once walked into the biggest MC clubhouse in the country by himself and painted the fucking walls with biker innards. Not a metaphor; the city had to provide crisis counseling to the first responders because it was the stuff out of nightmares. When the cops ran forensics there were fourteen different strains of DNA, but no bodies were ever found and it's still '*unsolved*'. He's a sociopath. He feels nothing. If he goes after you, we're fucked. If he goes after your cousins, *we're fucked*. If he leaves his state, and wanders the hell into Mounts Bay, ***we're fucked***."

Harley groans under his breath and scrubs his face with both his hands. "Why is there *always* someone worse? I thought *you* were the fucking worst there was."

That breaks the somber mood a little and Illi smiles like Harley's just called him pretty. "So sweet of you to say, but there *is* always someone worse. I for one never want to meet whoever the fuck is worse than Morningstar. Any idea on why that fuck Beaumont wants his own kids dead? I thought you said they were good people? I've never known you to put up with dickheads. Well, other than that cock D'Ardo."

I grimace and shrug. "They're the best people. I know some of why their family is messed up, but I'll get the rest of the details and we can work this out. *Fuck*."

Illi cuts me another look. "Kid, there's no dealing with the devil. This isn't a story from old; you can't cut a deal. If he takes the job from Beaumont... they're gone. All of them."

I swallow roughly. There's no way I'm letting that happen. No. Fucking. Way. "Reach out to everyone and tell them the twins are mine. Morrison too."

Illi blows out a breath and rubs his jaw, his skull rings catching the light and grinning at me ominously. "You inducting them?"

Harley watches me closely, but I shake my head. "I haven't asked them, just put it out there that they're under my protection. I don't care how you word it, just make sure it's well known that if anyone touches them they answer to me. If Morningstar takes the job... I'll start calling in favors."

Harley glares at the ground, his fists clenched dangerously. Illi stares at him and then says, softly, like he's testing his grit, "It'll be war, kid."

Harley shrugs. "They're richer than god, if we need to we'll get them out of the country. I hear Antarctica is nice this time of the year. Ash will fucking love that."

CHAPTER NINE

H ARLEY AGREES to keep the bad news to himself until I get the chance to speak to Ash alone about it. I don't want to tell Avery until we have a plan on how to deal with her father and I can't make a plan without knowing what the fuck is wrong with the man.

Getting Ash alone is impossible without an intervention. The five of us are all in the same classes and share our mealtimes, and his extracurriculars are at the same time as Avery's so there's never the chance to be alone together. He's always affectionate towards me, snarking and sarcasm included, but with his sister around I barely get more than a peck on the lips from him.

I feel so fucking guilty.

Blaise pins me to the bed most nights during our study sessions and Harley has been sleeping-over a few nights a week, kissing me senseless before the sun comes up and he has to leave for his swim practice, so it doesn't really seem fair.

I spend two weeks trying to carve out time for a private conversation with him, but nothing works. Avery starts to stare at me with suspicion and on the following Monday, when I ask her what her plans are for the third weekend in a row, she huffs at me in mock upset.

"Which one of them do you have a craving for? I guess I'll go find a park bench to sleep on for the night. Just don't fuck any of them in the kitchen, bathroom, or my bed. Or the couch. You know what, just stick to your bed and change the sheets *immediately* post-coitus."

I roll my eyes at her dramatics and usher her away from the breakfast dishes so I can do them instead. She moves to make us both coffees to-go and I could kiss her damn feet in gratitude.

There's no good way to tell her so I sigh, scrubbing the pans a little harder than necessary. "We promised not to lie to each other so... I'm not going to lie to you. I've found out that we're facing a new threat. It's not something you can help with right now so I don't want to tell you about it yet. You have enough going on with the cougar whore and keeping the sheep in line, and I'm already doing everything possible to neutralize the situation. If the situation changes, I will come to you and we will plan out a new course of action."

Avery hums under her breath softly. "You need some stress relief? Tell me which guy and I'll go sleep in their room. If it's Blaise I need to take my own sheets. I swear he doesn't ever wash his; I've trained the other two better than that."

I scoff at her and wipe my hands. "Actually, I need to talk to Ash. This isn't a... relationship thing. It's to do with the threat. I know you don't want to say anything that might push him when he's not ready to talk about the sheer fucked up levels of *bad* that your father is, but I need to know. The situation has forced my hand."

Avery stares at me for a second, then frowns and pulls out her phone. "I'll cancel tutoring with Blaise, tell him and Harley to stay away for the night, and Ash can skip track." She chews on her lip and then says, quietly, "I should stay too. If it's... if it's a matter of safety I don't want him skipping things or trying to make it sound... less than what it is for your sake. He'll try to shield you from it all like he does with me. I mean, he shields Harley and Blaise from it too."

My heart sinks all the way down to my stomach, but I nod.

AVERY PRE-WARNS Ash of the reason for our dinner so he arrives to our room in a vicious and argumentative mood. Avery puts up with it for about three minutes before she throws a towel at his head and tells him to go cool off in the shower. I make dinner and ignore them both because I'm smart enough to know that you shouldn't involve yourself in a fight between twins.

Avery dishes up our food and pours Ash a bourbon from her secret stash. I raise my brow at the pint sized glass she fills because he'll be slurring his words in no time if he sculls that down. She shrugs and when the bathroom door opens she leans in to whisper, "There's no way he's going to talk about it without a little something to loosen his tongue."

Fuck.

I nod and take a seat. Ash hesitates for a second before taking the seat next to me, kissing the little wedge of skin that's exposed on my shoulder thanks to Blaise's oversized band tee I've, ahem, borrowed.

"Thanks for dinner. I've really missed the slum food since we got back to civilization." He murmurs and I roll my eyes at him while Avery kicks him under the table. I hold up a hand to stop the tirade that's about to spill out of Avery and she smirks at me.

"No amount of shitty attitude is going to stop this conversation. I realize this isn't something you want to do and I'm willing to offer you a trade; I'll tell you my shitty stuff if you tell me yours."

Avery's eyes flare before she can hide it. There's a whole list of things she is desperate to ask me and now I'm offering them to Ash as an incentive to talk. I'd thought a lot about it, but I'll do whatever it takes to keep us all safe.

"Questions, like you did with Harley? Or are you just going to tell me it all?" Ash says, his eyes icy as he glares at his drink. He hasn't picked up the glass yet.

"How about you tell me what you want to know? Because I need to know everything about your father. Why he's trying to kill you, what he's done in the past, why he favors Joey, and anything you know about who he chooses for his cleanup. I wouldn't be asking this of you if it wasn't absolutely necessary."

Ash picks up the glass and drinks half of it in two gulps. When he speaks, it's with clinical detachment and a steady tone. "My father is a sadist. He used my mother as a front for his standing in high society. He'd beat her, slap her around, 'punish' her, but he was never a monster to her. He saved that for the girls he'd buy at auctions. He enjoys hurting people. He prefers to fuck females, but it's the pain that gets him off and really, as long as the person is scream-ing, that's all he needs. The day my mother was killed, she had followed him through the manor to his private cham-bers. They always slept separately and she was never permitted to enter his rooms. He had a twenty-one year-old college student, who had been kidnapped and sold off to him, strapped to a table and he was carving his name into her skin with a scalpel, over and over again, while he jerked himself off over the open wounds."

*Sweet lord **fuck***. Ash takes the glass again, a fine tremble in his fingers, and he finishes the glass. Avery looks like she's going to vomit, like knowing the facts and hearing them laid out right now with our dinner growing cold between us are two very different things.

Ash continues without so much as a grimace. "Joey found us in the kitchen as my mother was getting us out. She had known for years that he was a sociopath too; he'd already broken my arm twice. She had no intention of taking him with us and when he found us he called my father. He caught her by the chauffeured car and dragged her back to the house by her hair. He laid her out on the same table that girl had been strapped to, the blood was still warm, and he got Joey to help him. Then the two of them butchered her. When our nanny brought us down for dinner that night my father had Avery wait outside the formal dining room and he described to me exactly what they had done to her. He called one of his crooked higher-ups in the police department and my mother's death was ruled a suicide."

I swallow the bile in my throat and, very carefully, I reach out and cover his hand with mine. I hold back a sigh when he doesn't shake me off.

"What do you want to know? I'll tell you anything." I say, trying to offer him a break from his demons.

Ash shakes his head sharply and looks at Avery. "He told me that if I didn't 'show some promise soon' he'd be forced to do the same to me. He put Joey in charge of teaching me how to be a *real* man, not a fucking pansy that respects women. He can't stand that I love my sister, that I loved our mother. He just wants a legacy. He wants to die knowing his sons are continuing to torture, beat, rape, and destroy everyone and everything around them. He's insane, but he's also very smart. He looks handsome and put-together in a suit. Not a soul on this earth would believe the things he's done. The only thing reining the two of them in is our standing in high society. He gets away with every-thing because of who he is. If he were to be exposed, he'd be facing the death penalty in at least ten states and three countries."

I squeeze his fingers, but he ignores me. I'm starting to get a little worried that we've broken him. "So they've used Avery as the bargaining tool from the moment they killed our mother. I am to submit to everything Joey chooses to teach me, to do to me, or Avery ends up on that table. I've tested their resolve once, and Harley nearly went to juvie to get Avery to the hospital before she was gone forever too."

Avery shivers and rubs her arms, trying to fight the memories from prickling at her skin.

Ash spins the glass on the table absently, still staring at Avery. "The clean-up is all done by officials. He has so many dirty pigs in his pockets that it would be harder to find someone *clean* then to find someone he owns. That's it, Mounty. That's everything."

I nod and clear my throat. "Do you know why he would contact someone else to kill you? To kill you both? If he's so... proficient and willing, why would he pay an obscene amount of money for someone else to do it?"

Avery frowns at me. "The threat is against us?"

I swallow roughly. "Yes. He's contacted a man about having you both killed. The guy is... actually pretty similar to your father, except everything he does is big and showy. I think he likes the attention of being so good at covering his own tracks that he's untouchable. It just doesn't make sense that your father would contract your murder out when it sounds like he would *enjoy* doing it himself."

Avery stares at me for a second and then her eyes flick to Ash. I wait for the planning to start. I wait for her phone to come out and her sharp, ruthless mind to get to work.

It doesn't happen.

She stands to grab the plate of dinner and shoves it, dish and all, into the garbage. I watch as she grabs everything from the table, all our plates and cutlery, cups and napkins, and shoves the whole lot in the garbage. I hear the glass breaking and ripping the garbage bag, but I let her go.

She has the exorcize the demons out of our space and she won't be able to rest until they're gone.

I sit in silence with Ash while Avery tears the kitchen apart. We're not going to have any utensils left by the time she's settled again, but who the fuck cares when I have a best friend losing her mind and a boyfriend who's just told me he's been the victim of *two* serial killers for the last decade? I certainly don't.

"What do you want to know? I promised you some truths." I whisper, careful not to touch him beyond the hands we have clasped together around his empty glass.

"Not tonight, Mounty. I'll take my payment some other time. Can I drink now? I don't want to become a sulking, morose fuck. We already have one of those in the family, no need for another." He says and I tug him to his feet gently, directing him over to my bed.

He frowns at me and says, "I'm not sleeping. I won't, and Avery is making enough noise that Harley and

Morrison are going to hear it and come looking for our corpses. I need a drink to be able to deal with this."

My lips quirk, but I rest a palm on his chest. "Shh, Beaumont. We're not functioning tonight. You and me will be nothing in here together." His eyes stay fixed to my face and they don't soften at all so I shrug. "If that doesn't work, I'll come down to the track with you and sit on the grass while you run until you pass out, but we'll try this first. I don't want to have to call the calvary to carry you back to the dorms because there's no way I can do it by myself."

I wait him out. Eventually, he slides between my sheets and I climb in next to him, flicking my lamp off so only the kitchen overhead lights are on. It kind of feels like mood lighting and I grimace at thinking such a thing while Ash is lying beside me with all of his internal damage on display. I'm surprised he hasn't hit anything yet. If someone challenges him to a fight tomorrow, I think I'll be calling a cleanup crew.

His story is on repeat in my brain and I start to think maybe alcohol isn't the worst idea. It's all just so fucking sick and twisted, and I'm no closer to figuring out what the fuck I can do to stop the Devil appearing on our doorstep. We're facing the most evil and well connected men in high society and the slums of Mounts Bay.

I really don't do easy, do I?

Ash moves to pull me into his arms, shifting me until my back is pressed to his chest and our legs are tangled together the way he likes, and when his fingers brush my thighs I shiver. His lips press into the soft skin of my shoulder.

"What do I have to do to tempt you into our room, Mounty? I've been very patient while Avery adjusts, but you really need to start sleeping in my bed." He mumbles into my skin and I wheeze a little as my chest tightens. The very thought of spending time in their room, choosing a bed for the night, being in their space - I need to get my head around it first. I need to figure out how to do that without dying of both lust and awkwardness.

There's something else I need to address first.

"You know I've killed people, right?" I whisper, brave now I'm not looking at him. It'll make it easier if he rejects me and walks out.

"So have I. I told you before Mounty, you're not going to scare me off."

I MEET Harley and Blaise for breakfast in the dining hall the next morning. Avery didn't finish her room demolition until dawn, and now there's nothing left in the kitchen or bathroom that wasn't already nailed down. Ash decided he would skip class for the day to stay behind and coax her into sleeping. I brace myself for the questions the other two would inevitably have.

"She didn't take the news well then? She never does when Ash is involved." Harley says, stabbing at his eggs with the type of vehemence that had students giving our seats a wide berth.

"Well, he's always the one being fucking beaten and targeted so I don't blame her. Well, almost always." Blaise mutters, frowning down at his juice like he can magically spike it with a look.

I look between them both and ask, "Harley told you, then? I got the full, unedited family backstory to help us figure out what we can do to stop the hit, and afterwards

Avery needed to scrub some demons out. Be extra nice to her for a while because she'll probably come back swinging."

They both stop and gape at me.

"He told you? He spoke to you about his father and Joey? Ash did? Alexander Asher William Beaumont, my best friend and total asshole extraordinaire, told you about what happens behind closed doors at the Beaumont Manor?" Blaise rambles and I frown at him.

"Yes. It was... really fucking bad, but now I have everything I need to know to navigate this mess we're in." I force confidence into my voice but, fuck, I'm not sure we're going to be navigating shit. It might be closer to blowing everything the fuck up and praying for the best.

They share a look but I ignore it. I push my empty plate away and gulp down the last of my iced coffee before we have to start moving off to our classes.

"Star, he hasn't even told us that stuff. Fuck, he really is serious about you." Blaise mumbles and my frown at him deepens.

"You thought he wasn't? Wow."

He cringes, cheeks flushing slightly, and Harley snorts at him before cutting in to save their asses. "Blaise and I both spend all of our spare time figuring out how to get you alone. Ash doesn't. This dick has been... *concerned* that Ash is having second thoughts because he's never really been the type to embrace celibacy."

Fucking idiot boys! I blush and clear my throat. "He told me last night he's waiting for Avery to stop being defensive. He also told me I should start coming to your room."

I see the predatory gleam in both their eyes and I hold up a hand. "I'm thinking about it. I'm not interested in hearing *more* gossip about how much of a raging whore I am. I'm pretty fucking close to snapping and stabbing some rich dickheads as it is. I don't need to test my patience much more."

Harley glares around the room with that fierce challenge of his and students start averting their eyes, turning their bodies away from his wrath. I'll say it again; I must be so freaking broken because that look is such a turn on. He turns back to me and smirks at my flushed cheeks. He cups my cheek gently, kissing me dirty, deep, and with entirely too much tongue for the audience we have. Blaise cackles at the looks we get from those brave enough to look as we break apart.

"I'll take care of them for you, babe." Harley murmurs and my blush deepens.

"Now who's flirting?"

All eyes follow us out of the room, especially when Blaise slings his arm over my shoulders, I hold my head high. Who the fuck cares what the rich assholes think? Not me.

Okay, I care a little.

Just enough to want them all to fuck off.

CHAPTER TEN

C HOIR IS STILL my least favorite class.
Miss Umber smiles as Blaise and I walk in together and take our seats. She still insists we sit at the front so she can 'monitor us', which is her way of saying 'giggle and blush at Blaise'. I guess this is my life now, such a steep price to pay for the rock god in my bed.

Avery has transferred out of choir to take on extra dance classes and I have no one to share looks with at the lusty eyes Blaise has on him the second he starts singing. I mean, the ones other than mine.

"Okay, class! Time to start thinking about your performance for this year! You will already know from your syllabus that you're going to be working on your own original material to sing this year, an exciting challenge for some of you and a regular occurrence for others." Miss Umber says with a coy and completely inappropriate look at Blaise, who in return looks mildly uncomfortable.

I scoff at him and nudge him in the ribs. He's always been a shameless flirt and I have no desire for him to stop;

he wouldn't be Blaise Morrison without it. He wiggles his eyebrows at me like an idiot.

"You'll be working in pairs, so choose wisely!" She turns to start writing on the board, detailing a list of requirements and resources for songwriting, and Blaise steals my pen from me when I start to take notes.

"I've already written our song." He whispers into my ear, and grins cockily when I shiver.

"I can't take credit for your work." I mumble but he just shrugs.

"Sing it with me, let me record it, and listen to it yourself. That's going to be the hardest work in the assignment and you'll be the only one who can do it."

Fuck.

He's not wrong about it being hard, but I desperately want to be able to do this. For myself and for him. Ash would also probably sell his soul for the song. I've had to ban him from playing the video Avery recorded of me singing around me because he listens to it so often.

"I don't know if I can. Listen to it, that is. I can... if you sing it for me I can copy you with the ear plugs in."

Blaise threads his fingers through mine. "We'll work on it together. We need to get you past this because I'm putting it on my next album. It'll be a single and on the radio and it's going to be huge. I want you to sing it onstage with me someday. We can't do any of that if you can't listen to it."

Holy fuck.

I suddenly feel too warm, too full, too *loved*. I don't know how to deal with it at all so I nod and squeeze his hand.

My good day comes to a screeching halt in our history class.

I look down at the paper in my hands and blink my eyes furiously like that'll somehow change the mark written in bold red ink.

B+

I've never gotten lower than an A+ in my entire freaking life. Never. Even when Harley beats me in our classes it's only by the smallest of margins and yet here I am staring down at a B *fucking plus*.

My head fills with a high pitch buzzing noise and my mind checks out entirely. Gone. Closed for some serious freaking maintenance. My breathing shallows into these weird little pants - I'm probably hyperventilating - and I vaguely feel a hand on my back, rubbing slow circles, while an argument starts around me. I can't seem to focus away from the panic that has broken my brain.

A chair scrapes back sharply, the warm caress of breath down my neck, and then I hear a low rumbling voice as Ash whispers in my ear, "Avery will fix it, Mounty. Just breathe, for fuck's sake! No one is going to *die* over one crappy grade."

That's some perspective, right there. My chest eases enough for a deep, gulping breath. Just one, but it brings the room back into focus and I can hear the war waging around me.

"Mr. Beaumont, get back to your table! And *Miss* Beaumont, I will not be spoken to like that in my own classroom. If your little *friend* is unhappy with her mark, she will just need to work harder." Ms. Vivienne snaps out and, *hoo boy*, big mistake. My eyes finally unglue themselves from the mark and I look up at my best friend as her shoulders roll back and her chin lifts.

The room stops.

Stops talking, stops moving, stops *existing*.

Ms. Vivienne glances around, frowning and unsure of what the hell is going on, like the clueless fool she is.

Avery stands slowly, smoothing her skirt down with a steady hand. She's been teetering on the edge of bloodshed all week and this bitch just stepped into the ring. Ash leans back in his chair to survey the class, but there isn't a single student willing to meet his eye.

Sheep, the lot of them.

"If you think you can come to this school and play games with *my* family, then you're a stupid, desperate, old *cunt* that has a lot to learn. I've been lenient on you; observed the social niceties and played by the agreed set of rules, but now you're going to get the same as every other miserable whore that walks these halls. You have a single chance to give Lips the mark her paper deserves, right now, or you can continue down the path to your own destruction because I assure you, Ms. Turner, that *you* are not in the position of power here. I will wipe all traces of you from the face of the Earth."

Ms Vivienne's cheeks flush and she flicks a look at where Harley's hand is still rubbing circles into my back. Her eyes narrow. The bitch is fucking deranged. If Avery's icy speech didn't make her quake in her stupid whore heels then she's clearly got no survival instincts.

"Go straight to the principal's office, Miss Beaumont. I will meet you there after the bell and we will discuss your actions with Mr. Trevelen. He will find an appropriate punishment for your unacceptable behavior and threats."

Avery tips her head back and laughs, and even I shiver at the sound.

Harley starts packing his bag and when he sees I'm still struck dumb by the red ink he packs mine as well. Ms. Vivienne's eyes flash at him as her focus shifts away from Avery and to the only person she really seems to give a shit about. "Mr. Arbour, I have not dismissed you."

He snorts at her and stands, tugging me to my feet, and Ash and Blaise both get up as well, bags packed and slung over their shoulders. Harley even grabs Avery's bag so she's not weighed down during her rage-filled stomping to wherever-the-hell-it-is we're going.

"What the hell do you think you're doing?! All of you, sit down this instant! I will be calling your parents!" Ms Vivienne screeches, but her eyes are still fixed on Harley. His hands clench into fists and Avery tucks her arm into his to prevent him from smacking the bitch out.

Ash gently pries my numb hands away from my bag and throws it over to Blaise, who swings it over his shoulder easily and walks out of the room with a cocky smirk at our gaping teacher, calling out to her, "Good luck with that!"

Avery stomps after him, tugging Harley with her while he fumes. Ash tucks me under his arm carefully and steers me out of the room, his grip so secure that even my numb legs can't trip us up.

"It's just a mark, Mounty, stop gasping like you're dying. Avery will have it fixed in under an hour." Ash says, and he leads me to the dining hall. None of the teachers we pass spare us a glance and Ash doesn't speak again until he has me settled in our usual seats at the long, empty table with a plate of pasta and an iced coffee in front of me.

He's too damn observant.

I *definitely* need to eat my feelings and the pasta here is unbeatable. I wait for a few minutes so my stomach settles and then I eat like it's my last meal on death row. Ash watches me carefully, like I'm about to break. Great. Now I'm a crazy liability; a shitty mark can set me off into an episode and I have to be coddled out of it. Perfect.

"Stop it." Ash snaps and I shoot him a look.

"What?! I'm eating it, aren't I!" They've all become weird about my food.

"Stop thinking about whatever the hell is making you look so fucking miserable. It's one bullshit mark, given to you by a petty, jealous cunt. What does it matter?"

I put my fork down and glare at him when he scowls at me. I know compared to everything else we have going on it's nothing but, fuck. I wasn't ever expecting my grades to factor into this.

"It matters because my whole life, the only thing that was ever going to get me out of the shit-show I was born into was my grades. I've never had a B+. I've never *failed* because I can't afford to fail. I'm dead if my grades are anything less than perfect. I think I'm allowed to have a minute to freak out over that!"

Ash nods and crosses his arms, leaning back in his seat. I have a little moment of deja vu, having seen him do it a hundred times during our tutoring sessions. "Is Harley not worth the risk?"

I flinch back. "Don't be an asshole, of course he is."

He shrugs. "Then get over it. She did it because you have something she so desperately wants. Avery will fix it. We will fix *anything* that threatens you. This isn't going to work if you don't trust us to back you up. You're not the only one who can defend us."

My stomach turns. I'm panicking for a whole new reason. "I do trust you. I'm still learning how to do this... family thing."

Ash's mask is impenetrable and just this once I wish I could see through it. "I told you, I'll do whatever it takes to keep you. If you need that woman to disappear then she's going to disappear, Mounty, but we'll trust Avery to fix it for now."

I blush and look away. I need to get a hold of myself. Ash scoots across Avery's seat to tuck me into his side again, gently squeezing me until I feel my control slip back into place.

"Like I said last night, Mounty, come sleep in my bed and I'll make sure you're nice and relaxed by morning."

BY THE TIME we're all settled around the table back in our room that night, with takeout and assignments spread out around us, there's a mark change and formal apology in my inbox. It doesn't read as sincere at all, and when I show it to Avery she starts texting furiously.

"Don't worry about it, Aves. The mark is all I give a shit about." I mumble around my dumplings and she hums under her breath at me, distracted by the conversation she's having. I'm a little worried she's ordering a hit.

Her eyes snap up to mine. "How long are we going to be in the Bay? I'm making arrangements to meet up with someone."

Ash sets down his fork with a dark look. "Who?"

Oh dear.

At least we haven't replaced the fine china yet because Avery looks at Ash like she's going to throw a plate at his head. I slip my hand in hers because, well, ride or die. And by the looks Ash and Harley are throwing at us both there might be bloodshed. Harley's leg is tense against mine.

"None of your damn business." She snarls and I know *exactly* what that means.

It's Atticus Crawford.

Ash's eyes narrow and I cut in before our dinner is ruined. "Arrange to meet him for lunch or dinner at the hotel the first night we're there. That way if we have to get out of there after the meeting you won't have to blow him off."

Blaise smirks and I shoot him what I hope is a savage look. He doesn't give a shit. "Maybe *blowing him* is exactly what she wants to do, Star."

My quick thinking saves Blaise's life as I slide my ass into Harley's lap to stop him from getting up and throttling him. He grunts and grabs my hips to hold me still. I don't think about *why* because I don't need to be blushing like a damn fool right now. Ash is surprisingly more forgiving of Blaise's smart mouth and just shoots him a look.

"Right. Now that's sorted, let's discuss the party." I say and when I try to slide back to my seat Harley's hands stop me. Avery does not look happy. In fact, she looks like she's going to scratch his eyes out.

"I'm not allowed to go for dinner with an old friend, but you can grind on Lips at the dinner table? Get fucked, Arbour." Avery hisses, and I start to pray that I can eat my damn dumplings before she flips the fucking table at them. I pry Harley's fingers off of me and settle back into my seat. Everyone is throwing savage looks except me. Yay.

"I think I should go alone. Harley is being targeted by

the Jackal, I don't want to paint targets on Ash and Blaise, and Avery wouldn't be safe there. Illi has offered to pick me up so I'm going to take him up on that."

All of the savage looks swing to focus on me.

For fuck's sake!

"Over my dead fucking body are you going to a party at the docks with *the Butcher* without me." Harley growls.

I grit my teeth. "It's not like I haven't been a million times before and Illi will watch my back. It's not somewhere I want to take you guys."

Blaise scowls, flicking his beer bottle cap at Harley. "Why? I mean, the Jackal could come to Hannaford and kill Harley whenever he wants to, the gossip site has announced our relationships to the world, and we always protect Avery. Why not take us so we can protect you too?"

I scrub a hand over my face. "You want to take Avery somewhere full of drugs, sex, murder, violence, girls being kidnapped, torture, rape, the list goes fucking on? You want that? Because I sure as hell don't."

I expect some sort of reaction from Blaise, but he just stares me down. Ash is the one to snarl, "Well, that settles it. We're all fucking going. End of discussion."

CHAPTER ELEVEN

It takes me weeks to find the things we need to attend the party.

Avery gives me a hard look when I ask her for everyone's measurements and I refuse to tell her why I need them. There is no way I'm telling any of them what the outfits have to be because fuck that. I don't need the headache any sooner than I have to have it.

I have the items ordered at one of the boutique stores in Haven and they arrive on the Thursday before fall break. I email all of my teachers to get out of class the following day and when I ask to borrow Harley's car to go pick them up he stares me down like I'm testing him. When he crawls into my bed after midnight, he informs me that he's escorting me to Haven in the morning.

I wake to Harley's hands cupping my ass and pulling me into his body.

I swear he was put on this Earth to tease me, to break all of my control and turn me into a desperate mess and, sweet fucking lord, he was fucking good at it. I keep my eyes closed as I reach out to find his face, drawing him into my lips for a kiss. I'm too content to deal with today, I don't want to leave the bed and let the outside world fuck with us. I need a break, dammit!

"We could stay here." I mumble and he groans into my mouth.

"Don't fucking tempt me, babe. You said we had to pick up the shit you ordered and it's already late. Ash and Blaise took Avery down to class hours ago."

I frown at him like a pissy toddler. "That's not helping. I don't want to leave this *warm bed* in my *empty room*."

Harley groans and pushes away from me, stumbling out of the bed and rearranging his dick in his shorts like that'll somehow help the raging hard-on he has. "If we don't leave now we can't stop for French toast at the coffee shop and we both know you'll lose your shit if you're hungry. If we leave now, we can get everything finished in time and I'll convince Avery to have a sleepover with Ash."

I shiver because, *fuck yes*. "Get dressed, Arbour. I need food."

We have to stop off at the guys room to grab Harley's spare set of keys after he turns the living room back at my room apart looking for his original set. I make a mental note to myself because I've been burned by missing keys before.

We take Harley's 'Stang to Haven and I get to admire the way he drives it like it's an extension of himself, effortless and smooth. I love watching his hands, big and rough and scarred, and then my lungs forget how to work as I remember what they feel like on my body. Fuck, I need to inhale my food and get this shopping over with.

Harley smirks at my flushed cheeks like a smug dick.

We park behind the cafe because it closes the earliest, and then I bite my lip as Harley refuses to let me pay for our food. I make a note to *never* tell him I've been the one giving him money since I inducted him. He might have a stroke.

We sit, side-by-side, in one of the corner booths at the back. The waitress keeps looking at Harley like she'd bend over any available surface for him and the haughty, disinterested look he gives her in return makes me concerned about eating the food she serves us, but it's worth it.

"How is Avery handling the news about Senior's plans to have them both killed?" Harley mumbles around his mouthful of eggs. It should be gross but the guy is so fucking hot he could get away with anything.

I shrug at him. "Our room has never been cleaner. Avery is pissed there's nothing she can do to help and now Ash is fucking livid that it'll all rest on my shoulders to get them out of this."

Harley scowls. "Well, of course he is. We all are. It's hard enough keeping you safe and alive as it is, we don't need some psycho coming to the Bay to join the mix."

I snort at him, ever the lady, and poke a fork in his direction. "I survived without you guys having my back for seventeen years. I'll be fine, it's all of you lot with your shitty families that are the concern."

Fuck. That reminds me... I clear my throat. "Look, the meeting isn't just about the Vulture's death. We're also going to go through the usual bullshit and I've put something big in motion. I've... fuck, okay... I've called in some favors to get you free and clear from your grandfather once and for all. You need to be prepared for that meeting. You need to stick to all of the rules I've told you and be on your best behavior because once we're through it, we'll have one less threat stalking us."

Harley chews slowly, frowning down at his plate. I wait

him out, the last thing he needs is to be pushed about his issues.

Finally, he flicks his eyes up to mine. "Are you at risk? Is this putting you in more fucking danger?"

I shake my head and he sighs, scrubbing a hand over his face. "Okay. Okay, I'll play along. I don't want my grandfather coming after me and finding you, so if this gets him off my ass then I'll do it."

I lean over and try to kiss him sweetly, something I'm still unsure of because I don't know how the fuck to be *sweet*. He cups my cheek to hold me there so I think I succeed.

"Come on, let's get your shopping and go back so I can do more than just kiss you."

HARLEY CARRIES all of the bags in one hand and threads his fingers through mine with the other. He swings our arms playfully as we head back to the alleyway we'd left the car in, so relaxed and unlike himself that I laugh like a besotted idiot at him in return. I guess that's exactly what I am.

The streets have cleared now that the sun is going down. Only the bar is still open, and it's on the other side of the sleepy town, so we're alone and happy to walk in silence, soaking up each other without the distraction of words.

We turn into the alleyway, and Harley gives my hand a little squeeze before letting go to fish his keys out of his jeans. My senses pick up the slight rasp of feet attempting to be silent behind us half a second before Harley realizes what's happening. My hand is already slipping into my pocket to grab my knife when the body slams into Harley from behind.

The bags all go flying into the air as Harley throws his arms out to break his fall.

I freeze for a second, assuming it's a rich asshole from Hannaford trying to eke out a revenge beating for a failed fight in the boys dorms, and then I see the flash of light hitting the steel blade in the attacker's hand.

It's a hit.

Lips retreats back into the farthest reaches of my mind, where she's safe and protected, and leaves me with the Wolf.

Harley manages to dislodge the guy enough to roll over and I see first hand that he's a fucking good brawler; strong, fast, and willing to fight dirty. The problem is that Harley's only going to knock him the fuck out, and if we let him live it's a sign of weakness. Something that will eat away at the carefully constructed image I've built as the Wolf, and our lives all depend on that image. If we let him go alive, the Jackal will just keep sending guys until eventually one of them kills Harley.

I cannot let that happen.

Harley knocks the knife away and grabs him with one hand by the throat. I take my chance and use every ounce of strength I have to ram the blade of my knife through the base of his skull, the quickest and most effect way to kill someone. Harley's strong grip gives me just the right resistance to help push the blade through the spinal cord and it's lights out for the attacker.

He's dead instantly.

When the guy's arms drop and he slumps down,

Harley's eyes flare and fix themselves onto my knife. I shove the limp body off of him before I yank the knife out because the last thing I need is for him to be covered in blood and have some sort of flashback to his dad's murder. Harley jumps up and stares down at the guy, then at me.

My hands are steady.

I stare at him blankly, waiting for him to start screaming, or hurling accusations, or for something else to happen, and when he takes a step towards me I move back instinctively.

He looks fucking devastated as he holds out a hand to coax me over to him. "Shh, babe. I just need to know you're okay."

I blink.

I blink again.

Nope, still no idea how the fuck he can be worried about me when I'm the one who's just killed a man. Shouldn't he be afraid of me? Shouldn't he be calling Avery and getting the family far, far away from me?

"Babe, please. Don't freak out." He pleads and I think the word 'please' eases the trance I'm in and I step into his arms. He holds me to his chest with the sort of ferocity that you can only feel when there's a leaking corpse at your feet.

He buries his face into my hair and says, "Tell me what you need me to do."

I think he means emotionally, but I lost the ability to feel anything about this sort of death years ago. I pull away and shove the guy onto his back with the toe of my boot to get a proper look at him. Great, I know him. He goes by Whip on the streets in Mounts Bay, fuck knows what his real name is. He's a scumbag, constantly hanging around the docks trying to get close to the Jackal's men. He thought being a gangster sounded cool.

It hasn't worked out for him.

I look back at Harley and he's watching me carefully, his eyes cataloging every breath I'm taking. It's oddly reassuring.

"Call Avery. Tell her it's a 911 and ask her if there are any cameras in this alleyway, she needs to get them wiped immediately."

Harley nods and I stare down at Whip's vacant eyes. It's weird how quickly the life leaches out of them and leaves behind nothing, even though the eyes themselves haven't changed.

I shake myself to regain some focus.

Harley murmurs quietly enough that I can make my own call without moving away. I don't want to leave him here alone with the body. He has a rap sheet, a tattoo on his face, and a bad attitude towards authority and, well, anyone outside our family. If by some cruel twist of fate the cops showed up, he'd get himself shot in a heartbeat without supervision.

"Wolf." The Bear doesn't bother with pleasantries, thank fuck. I don't have it in me to fake it.

"I need a priority cleanup crew." I rattle off the address and I hear him directing people in the background. Harley hangs up and makes a series of complicated hand gestures that I assume mean there's no cameras around. I make a note to start teaching him and the others military hand signals in our oh-so-plentiful spare time.

"Two minutes away." The Bear says and I shift my focus back to him.

"Perfect. Payment?" I say, tone cool and calm. Harley scowls down at the body like he wants to revive the fuck and kill him himself. He's weirdly protective of my diamonds.

The Bear grunts, "It's nothing, kid. I have a job for you,

a quick in-and-out you can do in an hour. So if you get it done while you're here for the meeting I'll take care of this and owe you another."

I tilt my head in consideration. I guess that's more than fair. I don't want to give up a diamond even though I have more from him than any other member. "It's a pleasure to work with you, Bear." I say, my tone still flat and he grunts out a laugh at me.

"See you in the Bay, kid."

Harley tells the others the finer details of what happened while I shower.

I'm still struggling with the detached feeling, and no matter how hard I try to slip back into Lips, when I dress and leave the bathroom I am still the Wolf.

They all look at me like I'm a ticking bomb.

I stare back blankly.

Avery is the one to try to approach me, to take my hand, and when Harley hisses out a warning she falters for a second. I don't move back because I trust her and the adrenaline isn't riding me hard anymore like it was when Harley first tried to touch me.

Avery sighs and goes to grab a tub of my cherry ice cream out of the freezer, jamming a spoon into it and then she holds it out to me like a peace offering. I look at it for a second, puzzled, and then take it. The tension in the room eases a little.

She gently guides me over to the couch and tucks a blanket around me. I'm not cold. I don't know why she does it, but it's easier to keep my mouth shut and let her go. She grabs her own tub of ice cream and settles at my side with her phone out, tucking her arm in mine. I eat in silence while the guys all move aimlessly around the room.

"I'm fine. It's not like I haven't done it countless times before." I murmur, and Avery nods without looking up from her phone. It's easier to talk without her eyes on me.

"I know, you're one of the strongest people I know. This is for me. I need to know that you're okay and being here with you is comforting to me. It's a part of being a family, Lips." She explains gently, with none of her usual fire.

I nod and relax back into the chair. I can do this for her. I'm not sure there's anything I couldn't do for her.

By the fourth spoonful my body relaxes. By the tenth I'm Lips again.

Hours of tense silence later, Ash and Blaise climb into my bed with me. Neither of them give me any space, Blaise's chest pressing my back into Ash, whose face is buried into the nape of my neck. They both touch me like they need reassurance that I'm still here, whole and unflinching.

Harley takes the couch because he knows he's not going to sleep.

He watches the door until dawn.

CHAPTER TWELVE

ASH INSISTS on chaperoning Avery's dinner date with Atticus when we arrive at the hotel and I think she only agrees because she's terrified it's not a real date.

It gives me some time to shower and shave, well, *everything* in preparation for the party. I still haven't told everyone that the dress code is strictly lingerie and briefs.

The Jackal is the host and he's trying to provoke Harley into taking a swing at him. My stomach feels like it's full of lead because he just might succeed.

I leave the bags of the guy's clothes in their rooms and lock myself in the bathroom at ten pm to start getting ready. Blaise offers to wash my hair for me, saying he'll even let Harley help him soap me up, and Harley cusses him out when I blanch like a virginal idiot. I'm so fucking tempted. Wet, naked, and pressed in between them.

Sweet merciful lord.

I'm standing in front of the mirror wrapped in a towel and putting on my makeup when Avery knocks at the door and joins me.

I raise an eyebrow at her and she blushes.

"I think he wanted it to be a real date. He stared at Ash like he wanted to break his arm when he walked down with me. I've just sat through their sniping for the last two hours."

"Why didn't you just tell Ash to leave? He would've." Maybe. Okay, doubtful.

Avery pulls off her stunning and elegant red silk dress that I'm sure Atticus took one look at and wished he'd be the one removing it. "Maybe I want to be chased. Maybe I think I deserve to have him work for me. I've been on a platter for him for years and he's turned me down."

No maybes about it; the guy can *grovel* for her. But if I've learned anything about girl talk, it's that you ask questions and offer to gut anyone who slights your bestie. "Did he ever say why he wasn't interested before? The age gap might have freaked him out. I mean, maybe he's been waiting for you to get a bit closer to eighteen so he didn't feel like a creep."

Avery hums and slips into the shower, scrubbing at her skin like she always does. I wince at how rough she is. "I tried to speak to him about that during freshman year. I told him I would wait if he was interested in something in the future. He told me he refused to tie me down. It was like a knife in my heart. That's when I started seeing Rory."

I pretend too gag. "Don't say his name! I was close to forgetting he exists. I wonder how he's doing these days?"

Avery smirks at me as she cuts the shower off. "Ash keeps an eye on him to make sure he's miserable and very far away from me. Apparently the spinal injury has affected more than just his ability to walk."

Ahh, perfect. Nothing the rapist deserves more.

I sigh happily and then again with less joy when I open

the bags holding the lingerie I've bought for Avery and I to wear. She wraps herself in a towel and peers into the bag.

"You're joking, right?" She says and when I shake my head she cackles. "Ash is going to be *pissed*." She gasps out as she laughs even harder.

I begin to wriggle my way into the stupid teddy-thing, but it's a struggle to get it on my body. It's made of lace and pure white, but with too many straps and a white choker. It looks like something an angel would wear if it gave bondage a whirl.

"I got us both the most coverage possible while sticking to the rules." I grumble, as I accidentally snap one of the many straps against my skin and curse viciously under my breath. It doesn't hurt, but I'm so fucking frustrated at this stupid thing. Avery giggles at me and takes pity, deftly fixing the mess I've made with it. She slips hers on with far more ease and I glare at her for being so graceful. And *bendy*.

"Do we have to wear the shoes? I'm not really a 'combat boot' sort of girl."

I roll my eyes at her. "Like I haven't noticed you'd rather break a fucking ankle than wear flats. The party is at the docks, in a warehouse, with probably a couple of thousand people attending. You'd die in heels and you'll be wearing *that* so you can't make Ash carry you. Imagine the therapy he'd need."

Avery snorts and frowns at me like the spoiled brat she really, really is. I grin at her with a little sarcastic edge. "You should be grateful, do you know how long it took me to find boots that were *completely* white? A long fucking time."

Avery sighs again, like I'm mortally wounding her, and there's a pissy thump at the bathroom door before Ash is growling, "This is a fucking joke, right? I'm not going to a party in fucking tightie-whities."

Avery's eyes turn into saucers. We both shove bathrobes on and then I fling open the door.

Ash is scowling at us both and he's dressed in the 'clothes' I left for him. They're definitely *not* tightie-whities, but they are underwear. He's standing there in a simple pair of white boxer briefs that I cannot help but look down at because *holy shit, there's his fabled giant dick.* Even without an erection it's huge. Fuck. Fuuuuuuuuuuuck.

I gulp.

"Are you *fucking kidding me*, Mounty?" Avery hisses, and then I remember that I'm literally just standing here staring at my hot ass boyfriend's dick while his sister watches my brain melt out of my ears.

I clear my throat and try to ignore my blush. "I told you I could go by myself. You all insisted on coming. This is what it takes to get in."

Ash snorts under his breath, and tugs me until I'm tucked under one of his arms. I start to sweat because I'm too close to his giant dick. He doesn't notice. "Like we'd let you traipse around in your fucking panties by yourself. How much therapy am I going to need when I see what you've put my sister in?"

Avery grabs her phone and then frowns when she realizes she doesn't have anywhere under the bathrobe to stash it. "I'm not sure we can afford the extent you'll require. We certainly can't afford the amount I now need."

I groan at them both when Blaise comes stumbling into the room in his own pair of white boxer briefs, laughing at Harley who is frowning and tugging at the waistband of his.

Avery mumbles under her breath and stomps over to her overnight bag, digging out one of her beautifully tailored coats. When she slips out of the bathrobe to pull it on Harley's frown turns into a snarl. *"What. The. Fuck. Mounty."*

I sigh and hold a hand out, the other one keeping my own robe firmly closed. "Look. That is the most modest lingerie I could find her and she's covered more than when she's in a bikini! It has to be completely white. I did my fucking best and, *once again,* I said I'd go alone. At least it has a covered crotch."

Harley's eyes snap over to mine and away from the white, vinyl, halter-neck teddy that is showing a whole lot of Avery's cleavage and molds to her body like a second skin. There's a little chain holding the two strips of vinyl in place over her tits and it's looking a little strained. Every single male Mounty at the party may die tonight if that chain breaks.

"And what the fuck are you wearing to this shit-show?" Harley snaps, and I glare at him as I wrap the robe around myself even tighter.

"I'm not showing you until we get there. I'd rather drive there in peace and quiet."

Harley rolls his eyes at me and bends at the waist to shove his phone in his boot. Fuck me, that ass of his is *bitable.*

As a grumbling Ash helps Avery into her coat, his eyes fixed sullenly on the floor, Blaise pointedly keeps his own eyes on me and firmly away from her. He smirks and crowds me into the wall until his chest is pinning me and I can't breathe with him surrounding me. "Give me a peek, little Star. I won't tell the grumpy dicks."

Oh, the cheeky asshole is aiming for a punch to the kidneys. I scowl at him even as I hold the robe out for him to peer down.

The look in his eyes turns me into a fucking puddle.

He bites his lip and leans down to kiss me fucking senseless.

"Get the fuck off of her in my presence, Morrison! I know what she's just shown you and if you're now sporting a boner, I'll cut it the *fuck* off!"

We break away and Blaise smirks at me as I blush. He helps me into one of Avery's coats while shielding my outfit from the others, and then walks me down to his car. I sit in the back between Ash and Harley and I keep my eyes on the windshield so I don't ruin my lingerie. Well, anymore then Blaise's kiss has already.

I have to direct Blaise to the docks and the giant boat-shed where the Twelve park their cars. The security guard at the fence looks in and dips his head in respect when he sees me. Avery giggles about it, and Harley mutters, "I told you guys, it's fucking weird."

We park between a Rolls Royce I'd guess is the Lynx's and a Bentley that has to belong to the Crow. The guys eye them appreciatively as they all get out of the car. I give myself a minute to slow my heart rate and shake my nerves.

Harley leans against the open car door to wait for me, debating with the others about which car is nicer. I take advantage of their distraction and slide carefully out. With a deep breath, I take the coat off and drop it on the backseat. I push Harley gently out of way with a palm on his back to shut the car door and he turns to me to get an eyeful of the lingerie. His jaw drops, stunned, and then he's cursing viciously.

"Not a fan?" I gripe as he turns away from me.

"I'm walking around the fucking docks in the slums of the Bay, in nothing but boxers, and now I can't even enjoy seeing you in whatever the hell you call *that* because Avery will actually fucking castrate me if she sees how much of a *fan* I am."

Oh.

Right.

"Fuck." Croaks Ash from behind us and I startle out of the daze Harley's words have put me in. Avery is smirking evilly with her hands on her hips, coat off and her phone in her hand. Ash's face settles into his cold mask as he takes a step backwards. "No. No, Avery, go on ahead." He snaps and Avery groans like she's being murdered.

Blaise roars with laughter, completely at ease with the whole situation. "Good, isn't it? Aves I don't mind you seeing what the Mounty does to my dick, we can walk together."

"Fuck. Off." She hisses at him, and grabs my arm. "You three can walk behind us until you learn to curb your fucking hormones. It's nothing you haven't seen before."

I smirk at them and turn to walk with Avery, flashing them the back of the teddy. I hear groans and give my ass a little wiggle for good measure.

"This way Aves, remember to let me do the talking."

THE CHUMP at the door stares at us all.

I don't know him, he's obviously new, and I do *not* like the way he's staring at Avery. I knew this would happen! I fucking warned them all and if he doesn't stop looking at her Ash is going to beat him then Harley will seal the deal and slit the fucker's throat all while Blaise watches them with glee.

"If you're trying to sneak into this party, you chose the wrong color. The Wolf doesn't bring friends. Ever."

Avery giggles mockingly, the sound like glass shards and open arteries. I smirk and take a step forward. "You should let us pass. You're going to regret it if you don't."

He looks over my shoulder at the guys and snorts. "I'm with the fucking Jackal. You think three pretty boys are going to scare me? You all reek of money, but cash ain't gonna get you in here."

He pauses again and gives Avery a slow sweep over with his eyes. He's so busy making an assessment of her that he doesn't notice the wall of muscle that appears behind him. Avery's body goes rigid as she takes the newcomer in, her only sign of fear, and the chump mistakes the reaction as a response to his assessment of her.

"Maybe I'll let you lot in, gimme that little rich cunt to break for the night and the rest of you can go through."

I lock eyes with Illi and say, "No one calls Avery a cunt, Illium. *No one.*"

The chump pisses himself when he turns to see the Butcher grinning at him, clad only in a pair of white boxer briefs and white combat boots. Well, he also has several knives, a gun, and his signature meat cleaver strapped to his body but personally, I know it's the grin that means danger.

He leans forward and reaches into the chump's pocket. Avery raises an eyebrow at me and my smile in return is smug as fuck.

"Y'know why your boss handed you this little torch?" Illi croons as he pulls said torch out and waves it in the guy's face. I laugh quietly under my breath.

Avery is going to lose her mind.

"It-it's to identify-" The guy fumbles his words so hard Illi pats him on the shoulder and interrupts him.

"Yeah. It's to find marks that don't show up otherwise. You used it tonight? You waved it at anyone or are you more of a big-man type? Ah, no, you like raping little girls. You like using your cheap little Jackal tramp-stamp to get you some unwilling pussy. I know *all* about your type."

Illi switches the torch on and aims it over his cheek.

The Wolf insignia glows.

I startle when I see it because I didn't mention it to him when I took him on. I didn't feel comfortable asking him to do it and now Harley's going to pitch a fit at me. *Fuck.*

The chump fumbles over his words again, pathetically, "I know y-you belong to th-the Wolf. Everyone does. B-b-but-"

Illi flicks the torch light over to me and Avery gasps as my skin begins to glow.

"Fuck!" The guy screeches and as he tries to scramble away Illi stabs him, right in the gut, and gives the knife a little turn for good measure. I didn't even see his hand move towards the knife; he's just that good.

I lift a brow at him as the guy squeals like the stuck pig he is.

"What? He'll live! You said no one insults your little bestie so I'm making sure it never happens again. You're *welcome*! I'd hug you but, honestly, seeing you in that thing is like seeing my sister naked. It's fucking disturbing and let's never do this again."

I laugh and grab Avery's hand, tugging her forward and glancing over my shoulder at the guys. They're all staring at Illi with a deep distrust, hatred, and just a little bit wary. I won't fault them; he did just stab a guy.

"So, this is Illi. He's a treasure."

Illi cackles and wiggles his fingers at the guys like he's an eighty year-old woman trying to coax them into trying his cookies. Harley scowls at him, no longer looking nauseous around him which I'm taking as a win. Blaise shrugs and smiles at me, trusting me implicitly. Oh, my sweet naive rock god.

Then there's Ash.

He surveys Illi with a detached look and then looks at me. "This is the Butcher?"

I nod and wait him out.

"Anyone touches the Wolf or my sister while they're under your protection and I don't care what the fuck they call you, I'll be the one doing the butchering."

Harley looks at his cousin like he's lost his damn mind, but also like he's fucking *impressed*. I'm swooning a little because only Ash would threaten a man whose latest victim is still bleeding at our feet.

Illi smirks at him, his eyes twinkling like a proud fucking father. "I'd expect no different from the son of Joseph Beaumont."

* * *

THE WAREHOUSE IS WRITHING with people, the music is so loud it takes a second to learn how to breathe again, and Avery clutches at my hand as the bodies close in on us.

Illi leads the way and it's not until we hit the platform with the staircase that the black lights hit me, my tattoos instantly glowing, and the crowd parts like the Red Sea. Avery lifts our linked hands then stares down at my arm, turning it and marveling at the tattoos. It's too dark to read her face properly, but I know she's going to snark me out for this.

The second story is invite-only and safer than the bottom level. When I had told Illi that everyone was coming he'd arranged to have some guys keep an eye on Blaise, Ash, and Avery while we're in the meeting. I'm wary about it right up until we meet them at the bar and they dip their heads at me with that fear-drenched respect that can't be faked. Their eyes don't touch Avery at all and when Illi signs to them to guard her with their lives they agree willingly.

I make a note to ask Illi what they owe him for.

I kiss Avery's cheek and give her hand a reassuring squeeze which she returns easily. Ash and Blaise both do eyebrow acrobatics at Harley and then give me a quick peck on the lips as we move off. Harley wraps his arm around my waist and pulls me into his body. I let him, offering him that little reassurance I can before we hit the elevator.

There's only one way in and out of the room we're heading to, and that's the service elevator. The thug guarding it flinches when he sees Illi and fumbles over himself to get us in it. Illi grins and waves at him as the cage-like door shuts and we start to move, excruciatingly slowly.

I pull away from Harley's body but keep a hold of his hand, taking one last deep breath.

"Illi, we need a minute." I murmur, and the tattooed mass of muscle moves soundlessly to the corner, staring down at his shoes. I hate that Harley doesn't like him because he's actually the best guy, just a little fucked up and dangerous. Like me. He's going to be able to hear every damn word we say, but he's trying to give us some sort of space which is fucking decent of him.

Harley's hand tightens in mine. "I know the rules, I'm not going to lose my shit."

"He's going to try to provoke you. Look at what he has

us wearing. Just ignore him and remember that I'm going home with you and sleeping in your bed tonight. I've made my choice, and he's not it."

Harley nods and presses his palm over my heart. "You got your knife on you? Or is Illi the only one who's going to be stabbing people tonight?"

He called him Illi, not the Butcher. I'm taking that as a good sign. Illi chuckles quietly and I scoff at them both. "I have one in my boot, but I trust Illi. I've seen him throw a cleaver before, he's got this under control."

Harley scowls and drops his hands from me. He looks over his shoulder at the Butcher and says, "Who the fuck did you throw a cleaver at in front of her? For fuck's sake."

Illi grins and steps back up, taking his place behind me right as the elevator grinds to a halt. "I threw it at the guy who held a knife to little Wolf's throat when we broke into the Vulture's den of evil to spring my wife. Caught him in the throat and the cunt squirted blood all the fuck over us like in the movies. Was so fucking cool, and little Wolfie made me promise her I'd show her how to do it. I did by the way, so don't piss her off in the kitchen."

The doors scrape open right as Harley nods at Illi and mutters, "Okay. You're a decent enough sort of guy."

Illi roars with laughter and we step into the meeting room together.

Holy fuck.

I hope I know what the hell I'm doing.

CHAPTER THIRTEEN

THE TABLE for the Twelve is round and I quickly choose my seat to be in-between the Coyote and the Bear. Before I sit down Illi snags a jacket from Luca, who is more than willing to help me cover myself thank fuck, and Harley helps me slide into it. He even zips it all the way to the top for me while his eyes twitch like he's trying not to glare at every guy in the room. I'm oddly proud of him for controlling his protective urges. Then my guys take up watch by the wall with the rest of the henchmen, flunkies, guards, and overprotective husbands.

Well, there's just the one over-protective husband and he's glaring at Harley like he thinks my boyfriend is going to try to jump the Lynx's bones. I frown, and then I see the woman herself is staring at Harley like she'd happily drop to her knees at his feet to worship his dick.

Fuck.

Just what I need.

I glance around and see we're still waiting on the Boar. The Jackal takes a seat directly across from me and I refuse to look in his direction at all. He's dressed impeccably in a three piece suit. Only the Fox and the Coyote are in the required underwear, everyone else has approached the Jackal for a pass to get themselves in without stripping.

I refused to speak to him after his spat in the car so lingerie it is. I quirk an eyebrow at the Coyote, the youngest member after me at twenty, and he smirks at me.

"Why the fuck not? I'm going pussy hunting after this, it's been a while since I left my dungeon."

I chuckle under my breath at him. He's the hacker of the group, there's no digital information in the world that's safe from this guy, and he's a certified genius with tech. Someday when I get a permanent residence I'm getting the fucker to set up my security system.

"Who's the hot piece you came in with? She a part of your crew?" The Coyote continues, and I give him a look.

"She's mine." I say with a flat tone and I meet the Crow's gaze across the table. My breath catches as the steel gray of his eyes cut me. He's as dangerous as the Jackal and I don't need any extra bullshit going on in our lives right now.

After a minute he dips his head to me and says, "Has my protection been sufficient?"

"Exemplary, as expected." I say and he nods, almost amicably.

The Boar finally arrives, clothed and with three giant bikers with big bushy beards and cuts with patches all over them. His crew is not one I'd be getting into a bar fight with willingly and I'm not exactly pleased when they stand next to Illi and Harley. Fuck.

The Jackal calls the meeting to a start and I'm forced to look at him. His gaze stays fixed on mine and he's not attempting to hide the possessive obsession from the others anymore. Just what I need. I stare him down because sending a guy to my school to kill Harley was the last fucking straw. I'm done trying to find a casualty-free way of fixing this.

I'm going to war.

The Jackal runs through some squabbles the bigger players are having with turf wars and cops getting involved and I keep my mouth firmly shut. No one cares about my opinion on these things and I don't care enough about it to offer them any advice. I just want to be left the fuck alone. It gets heated pretty fucking quickly and I sit back to enjoy watching the Crow shut the Jackal down at every pass. With their empires rivaling each other in size, the Crow is often the one to shut the Jackal down.

If only he weren't a terrifying, coldly-calculating man, I'd actually like the Crow.

Finally the Ox speaks and shuts the rest of them up, "Are we not going to talk about the fact that the Vulture is dead and his killer is standing here with us, protected by one of us?"

I don't freeze or flinch. I just stare them all down.

"Are you going to explain yourself, Wolf?" The Jackal taunts and I finally look up at him. He's smug and so fucking arrogant as he calls me out but fuck him.

"No. I'm not. Unless you have proof the Butcher did it, move on."

The Viper sneers at me, "He killed a member. If you're willing to look over that then you're spitting in the face of the institution of the Twelve. Maybe we need to dispose of you too."

I hold my hand up because I know Illi is just about to start throwing knives and shooting people in my protection and I don't even want to know what's going through Harley's head. Fuck.

"I have known Illi a long time and we've been negotiating his induction for years. I believe him when he says he had nothing to do with the Vulture's death. If any of you have proof that he is guilty I will happily hand him over." Blatant fucking lie, I'd never sell him out and he knows it, but he's also sworn there's no evidence of his crime so it's a lie I'm willing to take the risk in telling.

"He's been telling people for years he'd kill the Vulture for what he did to that pathetic French slut, of course he fucking did it!" The Viper snaps and again I hold my hand up though I know it must be killing Illi to stay silent on this one.

"Exactly. If he's been saying it for years, why now? Why wait until the Vulture's business was bigger, his protection stronger, and thousands more girls have been sold? He wanted to kill him, but he didn't want to mess with the Twelve. Now the Vulture's death tipped in my favor and he's finally agreed to *my* terms to become one of mine. So, I'm not saying I'm happy the Vulture is dead but I'm very pleased with my outcome."

The Bear nods at me like my reasoning is sound and for a second I think I've won.

Nope.

Of course not, the Jackal would never let it go now I've openly defied him.

He smirks at me like this is his favorite game, cornering me and bending me hoping I'll break. I know for a fact it is. "I don't find that plausible at all. Majority rules, Wolf, and unless you're going to call in your favors you're not going to get the majority here."

My favors. He wants to force me into using them. Even he doesn't know how many I really have and, though I don't want to use any more than I have to tonight, I will. I only need six votes.

"Fuck the favors, the Wolf has my vote." The Boar grunts and the Jackal's head snaps over to him. I admit, I'm kind of shocked too. He's probably one of the last members I'd expect to back me.

He shrugs. "She's been nothing but true to the Twelve, and she's taken every job I've ever asked from her. If she wants him in her crew then so be it; it's her own back that will be knifed if he's not loyal."

The Jackal grits his teeth and says, "Any other votes in favor."

I hold my breath.

After a beat, the Bear, Fox, Coyote, and Lynx all make some noise or motion of voting yes. I only need one more and just as I open my mouth to call in a favor with the Ox, who owes me quite a few, the Crow says, "Aye. Majority wins, the Butcher is spared."

I glance over to him, but his eyes are on the Jackal. Their little rivalry has worked in my favor, *thank fuck.*

"Any other issues before we move onto the settling of the Vulture's business?" The Jackal snaps and I smile at him, giving him my best fuck-you impression of Avery. The girl is an ice queen after all. I've been planning this for months, knowing the Jackal expects the quiet, reserved Wolf he knows to be in this room and not the fierce, protective Wolf that's formed now I have a family behind me to guard. I throw myself in.

"Two things. Firstly; I would like to address some threats that have been made against my people. I would like to formally remind the Jackal that Harley Arbour is mine, and if he sends any more street rats to knife him in dark alleyways I will see it as an open act of betrayal against not only me, but the Twelve as a whole."

Silence.

I think I can hear the blood pumping furiously in the Jackal's veins from across the table and the slight flare of his eyes is the only sign I've just shocked him.

"Why would I have him killed?" He says, carefully now the Crow and the Boar are watching him closely.

"Because you're pissed I turned you down. I may choose not to grow an empire but at this table, I am an equal to you. Send someone after my people again, and I won't have to call in favors to have you taken care of. The Twelve will have no choice, but to do it."

The Jackal doesn't try to argue or deny what he's done, he just stares at me like he wants to punish me the same way he's punished me for years, labeling it as training. Well, fuck him. I've learned a fuck-tonne in the two years I've been away from him and it's only made me more dangerous. Now I have people to protect.

"Jesus Christ, is your pussy gold plated or some shit?" The Coyote murmurs in my ear and I have to resist the urge to shove him the hell away from me.

"Either the institution stands, or it doesn't." I say and tension snaps through the table. I can hear the group behind us shifting on their feet, preparing to dive into the fight that we're edging our way closer to.

"The second thing, Wolf?" The Boar asks, clearly wanting to steer the conversation away from bloodshed and war within our own ranks.

I bend and retrieve the velvet bags I have stuffed in the tongue of one of my combat boots. I stand to place the pile in the center of the table. Eleven bags, eleven diamonds.

"You all know what I'm asking for."

The table all stare at the diamonds with ravenous hunger and I nod.

"Good. Now we can move on."

I'M FORCED to sit through an hour's worth of arguing about the skin trade and no resolution is found, just as I suspected. The Crow refuses to back down and at one point I think the Jackal starts to plan exactly how he's going to dismember him when the chance arises. Again, it works in my favor because the rest of the table sees it too.

The Jackal is unstable.

His time of being harmonious among us is counting down.

When the Jackal finally calls the meeting over no one stands to leave. He flicks his wrist at one of his men and the elevator starts up. The Twelve all slowly collect their diamonds and stash them away as we wait.

I take a deep breath.

This part is going to be immensely satisfying, but it's also the part I'm most worried about Harley seeing. I have thirty seconds of regret for not warning him, for not wanting him to argue with me about the price of his safety, before Liam and Domnall O'Cronin walk into the meeting room.

Neither of them notice Harley amongst the group of men, they both only have eyes for me as I stand. I'm so glad Illi got me the jacket as I place my palms on the table in front of me and lean forward to address the fucking scumbag mobsters.

"Thank you for joining us, Liam." I say in a dark tone, hatred and disgust clearly present. Domnall twitches at my complete dismissal of him and I mentally high-five myself for it.

Liam's lip curls. "Not like we had much fuckin' choice,

ey? What's all this about? You've already stolen my heir, what more could you want from me?"

I ignore the disrespect he's showing me and smirk at him. "Oh, I didn't steal him. He sought me out. He decided that he wanted real loyalty, not the bullshit your family dishes out. But that's all beside the point. I've brought you here to inform you that your family is done. The Twelve are finished with the lot of you. You'll need to pack up and find a new state to live in. I hear Alabama is nice this time of year, try running your '*empire*' there."

Liam's face grows slack as he stares at me and then his eyes frantically dart around the table at the others. When no one speaks up to correct me his face slowly turns purple.

"Our family has lived and worked here for generations, you can't just fuckin' freeze us out!"

Again no one moves or speaks, exactly as I've instructed. I'm the one with power over the O'Cronin family now. My smirk only gets wider.

"I could be persuaded to let you stay. Maybe even keep your businesses running with us."

Domnall finally spots Harley and he freezes, his body locking up completely at the sight of his hulking, enraged, practically-naked nephew standing beside the Butcher, who I'm sure looks positively psychotic with the tats, and the grin, and arsenal of weapons strapped to him. Both of them clad in my color; both of them belonging to me.

Liam rolls his shoulders back, contempt deepening the curl in his lip. "What do I have to do to *persuade* you? If you want the boy that much then fuckin' keep him. If he's sold himself to you then he's as weak as his fuckin' Da."

Fuck.

I hear Harley's first step and my breath catches in my throat.

Then silence, thank fuck. I lean forward again and stare Liam straight in the eye, unblinking.

"I want my money. I want the inheritance your grandson is due that you're hiding from him. I want every cent of it, transferred to my accounts, with interest. I'm guessing it's been making you a nice return? Well, that money is *mine*."

Domnall has lost the ability to school his features and he's openly glaring at me now. I arch an eyebrow at him and Illi takes a step forward. "Watch yourself, mobster. Only a stupid man would provoke the Wolf and I'm fucking *itching* to split you open for her."

I sit back down, smoothing my hands down the jacket as if it's a silk gown and I'm Avery Beaumont, all classy and shit. "I thought about buying a judge to retrieve the money. Easy, quick, simple. But I wanted the satisfaction of watching you realize that your little power moves didn't work. That money is mine and you're going to hand it over to me. If you don't, I will consider your refusal a declaration of *war*. I'll destroy every last O'Cronin in the state."

Liam does one last sweep of the table and then gives me a look that would boil the blood of a lesser man. Good thing I'm neither a man, or less than the deadly, calm Wolf. I nod at him like he's agreed with me. "If it's not in my account by Friday I'll be finding you, Liam. I'll be coming for you all. Maybe I'll start with your new heir, what's his name again? Oh, Aodhan? Maybe I'll come see if he wants to join me as well. I'll bring Illi to help sway him."

Domnall blanches at his son's name and I smirk. Hook, line, and sinker; they know they're fucked.

Liam spits out from his clenched teeth, "Deal."

THE MEETING ROOM empties soon after the mobsters storm out. Illi and Harley step up immediately to join me and I avoid looking Harley in the eye. I don't want to see his reaction to my confrontation with his family while the Jackal is staring holes into us from the other side of the table.

The Crow takes his time getting up, and I know he's pushing every damn button on the Jackal he can when he gestures to the elevator and says, "Ladies first. I look forward to seeing you at the next meeting, Wolf."

I incline my head at him respectfully, and when I turn around to face Harley, he makes eye contact with the Jackal over my shoulder. I grab his hand gently, both to warn him and to tell him I'm fine, and he squeezes mine back. Illi snorts and crosses his arms next to him, obviously pissed off at the Jackal's actions and ready to throw down with him for Harley in a second. I'm so relieved they've found some sort of truce that I don't notice what the fuck Harley is doing as he maintains eye contact and -

And, fuck me with a cactus, he unzips the jacket, pushing it off my shoulders while running his hands all over me with such fucking possession my knees threaten to give out. I look up to find him *smirking* at the Jackal and then he kisses me like he's trying to fuck my mouth, my face cradled in his big hands.

Fuuuuuuuck.

Illi cackles and nudges Harley with an elbow. "Grab your girl. I need a drink and a fucking smoke after that. Let's go find the rest of our little motley crew."

Harley breaks away from my lips with another smirk, this one at me, then he just grabs my ass and hauls me into his arms, walking us over to the elevator.

"Did you just spend eleven fucking diamonds on me?" He mutters against my neck, and of course that's his priority, even with the psycho behind us making eye contact with me. There's nothing but bloodshed and slaughter in the Jackal's eyes but I hold them, steady and calm. Harley steps into the cage and the door shuts.

"Did you just taunt the Jackal about being mine?" I retort, still a little gobsmacked.

"Fuck yes, I did. Fuck him, babe, you've just told them all about what he's doing. Besides, if he doesn't let you go we'll just get the Butcher to throw a meat cleaver at him."

Illi cackles and runs a finger down said cleaver lovingly. I laugh and wriggle out of Harley's arms to stand between them. I feel lighter, like I've taken the last step away from the Jackal and now I'm standing on my own two feet. It's fucking terrifying to feel so alone without his protection, and for a second it knocks the breath out of my lungs, but then I hear Illi cracking jokes and Harley grunting out a chuckle at them and I remember the family I'm carefully building is worth the risk.

Illi leads the way back over to the bar area where we find a fucking wasted Blaise, Avery holding a drink and staring down at her phone, and a very antsy looking Ash. When I point to Blaise with an eyebrow lift Ash rolls his eyes and points towards the other end of the bar, where there's a growing crowd of salivating Mounty girls, watching him like they want to eat him alive. Illi laughs when he sees them and wiggles his fingers at them, easily dispersing the crowd with one action.

I feel too hyped up to drink, but I need *something* to

take the edge of my adrenaline off.

Ash watches me closely, then tugs on my hand and tilts his head towards the dance floor. Harley nods at him for me and I turn to gesture to Illi to get him to watch Blaise and Avery. Avery smirks at me with a little evil grin and lifts her cocktail at me in a salute. Okay, so tipsy Avery is much more agreeable to the guys turning me into the meat in a hot guy sandwich. Good to know.

As we move through the crowd, Harley presses me into Ash's back. The second story is safer, but still teeming with sweaty, intoxicated, writhing Mounty's and without the black lights touching my skin none of them know who it is walking amongst them.

Ash leads us far enough away that Avery won't be able to see us clearly and that's my first clue that he's up to no good.

The second is the fucking panty melting grin he gives me when he turns around to dance with me. I can feel Harley's chest rumble with laughter on my back as Ash stoops down to kiss me, clutching my hips to move us both in a grinding sway with the music. He's not a natural at this style of dancing like Harley is but, fuck, the grind of his hips and the sweep of his tongue on mine render me incapable of doing much more than swaying. The other people dancing disappear completely as my world narrows down to the three of us and the touch of their skin on mine. Harley's mouth traces the tendons of my neck, nipping and sucking, and I know for sure that I'm not going to leave this party with my dignity.

It's fucking worth it.

Harley's hands slide up from where he was gripping my waist to slip underneath the lace of the teddy and roll my nipples until I'm grinding back on his dick and panting into

Ash's mouth. Ash cups my soaking pussy through the lingerie and pauses for a second until I nod, breaking away from his lips to drop my head onto Harley's shoulder and moan like an utter slut. I fucking love it.

Harley bites down on my shoulder as his eyes glue themselves down my body to where Ash is tugging and shifting the teddy until he has room to touch me properly. The teddy has snaps along the crotch and I'm so fucking desperate I think about ripping it open, but I don't think either of them would be happy with me being bared to the whole dance floor like that. I don't think anyone has noticed us, there's a couple fucking on the bar so no one gives a fuck, but I know my guys.

It's like my nod to Ash unleashes the restraint he's been showing for weeks and he's merciless now he has his hands on me. He slips a finger inside me and after a few quick pumps he adds another, raking them over my G spot sporadically like a fucking tease until I'm a babbling mess. I give him a stern look, but he's smirking at me like a smug dick and when his thumb brushes over my clit, in the lightest freaking touch, I want to cry.

The more he teases, the more I grind back on Harley's dick and his chest is heaving against my back. I can feel how much Ash is getting off at drawing this out, at driving me out of my mind, and when I'm about to shove him away and demand Harley finish the damn job he grinds his thumb into my clit and I break into a thousand jagged pieces. Only Harley's arms around me keep me upright as Ash strokes the orgasm out of me with nothing, but his demanding fingers.

When my brain comes back online, Ash slips his fingers out and stares at me, unblinking, as he pushes them into my mouth. Okay. Never tasted myself before but sweet lord *fuck*, that's hot. It only gets hotter when he leans forward to chase the taste with his own tongue and Harley's fingers slip down into the mess they've both made.

I gasp into Ash's mouth and when he breaks away I grab his biceps to steady my jelly-legs now Harley's steel grip has eased off. There's an odd pause where they both tense for a moment, and then Harley's fingers start to move against me.

He's obviously not trying to get me off, his fingers just playing in the come that's dripping its way down my thighs, and he presses his mouth to my ear to shout over the music.

"I'm cleaning this up, babe, I don't want you wasting it down your legs."

My brain short circuits a little because he's right, I don't want to go back to Avery with a soaked crotch, but there's no bathrooms here. I should have thought about that before I let them both distract me with their hotness and their hands.

I don't make any attempts to resist as they move me over to a small alcove-like area near one of the enormous speakers. I wait for Harley to give me some sort of idea of how he's going to make me presentable before we see Avery, but instead he swaps positions with Ash until he's standing before me and the look they share spells trouble. Deadly, sexy trouble.

I narrow my eyes at Harley but he ignores me, swooping down to kiss me, pressing me into Ash's chest as his arms band around my hips like steel. I have just enough room to wriggle between them, grinding against their dicks, torn between pushing forward or back. For the first time I think about having sex with more than one of them and I'm not scared. Jesus, what are they doing to me? I shiver and moan all over again, breaking the kiss with Harley.

Then he smirks at me and drops to his knees.

Oh.

Oh fuck.

My heart starts pounding in my chest. His hands skim up my thighs until he finds the opening at the crotch of the teddy and rips the snaps open, baring my pussy to him. Thank god I really did shave everything because I can feel his breath dancing over my skin as he leans in, and my eyes roll back in my head.

I'm trembling as I wait for his mouth to touch me. Then Ash's arms drop from my hips and he pushes me forward slightly as he leans down to hook his arms around my knees. He lifts me up and *open*, spreading me wide so my pussy is on full display for Harley. My cheeks burn, but before I can protest this *mortifying* position Harley sinks his teeth into my thigh sharply until I look down at him, and once he has my eyes glued to his he finally drops his mouth down to lick and suck at my pussy like he's been starving for this.

I can't keep my eyes open, not as his tongue swirls around my clit and toys with it until my thighs are trembling in Ash's hands, so I squeeze my eyes shut and drop my head back against Ash's shoulder. I want to wrap my legs around Harley's neck and grind on his face, but those hands are immovable even as I try to squirm. Instead, I wrap one hand around Ash's wrist to keep me stable and the other I twist into Harley's hair, pulling him closer and I feel his groan against my sensitive skin.

Holy fuck, if this is how I die then I accept.

I know if I look down at Harley I'm going to come straight away and I don't want him to stop the amazing torture. I can't think past what his mouth is doing to me and when he drops down to push his tongue inside me I cry out into the deafening noise of the party, no one any wiser of the dirty dreams Harley is fulfilling for me.

When I can't stand it any longer and his tongue is working my clit like he's trying to melt my brain, I open my eyes and the roaming lights of the warehouse hit Harley's face as he stares straight into my eyes. I come so fucking hard, my back arching to grind my pussy into his mouth even harder and Ash slackens his hold just enough to let my writhe my release out on his cousin's face.

When my head drops back onto Ash's shoulder again my eyes land on the balcony above us, to find the Jackal is watching us, flanked by his men. He's gripping the railing and his back is so deadly straight I'm surprised he hasn't pulled his gun yet.

I stare up at him, defiance in every inch of my body, as I realize Harley and Ash have known he was there watching all along. This was as much a claiming of me for them as a fun public fuck.

I can't see the Jackal's face clearly, but the lights keeping hitting us at random intervals and he's been able to see exactly what we've been doing.

Ash gently lowers my legs to the ground, kissing my neck possessively, and when he looks up at the Jackal I see the arrogant taunt; the challenge he's giving the sociopathic Jackal to come down and fight him for me. I suppose being raised by Senior has made Ash a little reckless.

Harley tugs the crotch of my teddy back together, closing the snaps carefully to cover my pussy from view, before standing and turning away from me. I glance away from the Jackal to see the deadly glare he's throwing at the leader of a fucking huge criminal organization like the haughty golden god he is, and on impulse I lean forward to kiss the solid muscle of his back.

I will not submit to the Jackal's demands any longer.

Even if it costs me my life.

CHAPTER FOURTEEN

$\mathbf{A}$ VERY IS tipsy enough that she doesn't notice the state of my teddy or the wet spots on the guy's boxers, and I've never been so fucking grateful for margaritas in my life. Blaise has to be carried out and I tuck my arm into Avery's to keep her walking straight.

"Fuck guys, Lips. Just fuck them." She giggles and I notice tears in her eyes even as her giggles turn into a full belly laugh.

I *am* hoping to fuck three of them in particular, but I keep that little nugget of wisdom to myself. "What's happened? Atticus being a dick again?"

She tucks her face into my neck and I try not to breathe on her. The last thing in my mouth was Ash's fingers coated in my come so I really don't want her smelling it on my breath. I don't want to think about her reaction to that!

"I told him I was out on the town and he said I'm not the type of girl that should be out at parties. I didn't even tell him where I was! He thinks I'm some perfect china fucking doll, maybe that's why he won't fuck me."

My brain goes blank, and when Ash's head snaps

around to look back at us he's all fury and rage. I shake my head at him with a *look*. Glass houses and all that.

"I'm confiscating your phone. We're making him come to you remember? If he wants to try to tell you what sort of girl you are instead of seeing it for himself then he's a dick. You'll feel better in the morning, and if he tries to make you feel bad about it, I'll stab him. Or we can ask Illi too, he loves that shit."

Avery laughs again and whispers, far too loudly so everyone hears her, "You didn't tell me Illi was so fucking hot! Do you think his dick is tattooed too?"

I see the tension form in Harley and Ash's shoulders as I giggle. I deliberate for a half a second but think, fuck it.

"Odie, his wife, told me he has her name tattooed down his dick because any girl that dares to go near it should be warned it belongs to her. I'm not sure if she was being serious, but I do know he has a piercing there. I haven't seen it! A few Mounty girls told me about fucking him. Before Odie, I mean."

Avery stumbles and my leg protests so fucking painfully as I hold her upright.

"A piercing?! Do you think he'd show it to me?"

"*Avery, shut the fuck up!*" Ash snaps and I snort with laughter at them both as we get to the car. Avery frowns at him, but at least the tears are gone from her eyes.

Harley drives us back. I sit in the back, with Blaise draped over my lap and Ash seethes about Avery's drunken ramblings next to us. I feel like warning him that she's just doing it to piss him off, but Avery needs to get her kicks somewhere, I guess.

When we get back to the hotel room, the guys drop Blaise on the couch and then Ash stomps after Avery to start an argument with her.

I wriggle my feet out of the boots, grabbing my knife to take with me to bed, and then move to follow the twins into our room. Harley catches me around the waist and drags me into his body.

"Did you forget something, babe? You're in my bed tonight. It's my reward for not mouthing off to that sick fuck."

Oh, right.

I turn in his arms, rubbing my face on his bare chest as I yawn, dead on my feet.

"I'm not sure you deserve it after your little private show for him."

Harley hoists my into his arms and carries me to his bed. "That's *exactly* why I deserve it, babe."

I'M WOKEN by a text from Doc checking in to see if I still need to see him.

I flick him a quick text saying I'll be an hour and then I crawl out from underneath Harley and jump in the shower. I order an Uber as I throw some shorts and one of Harley's tees on, then shove my cherry Docs on at the door and swipe a room key from the side-table at the door.

"Where are you sneaking off to this early in the morning?" Ash whispers, and I jump about a mile in the air. Creepy fucker. He's standing there, already dressed and with a cup of delicious smelling coffee in his hands. I think about wrestling it off of him.

"I'm going to see Doc. I have an appointment." I

whisper back, and try to ignore the blush that immediately starts.

Ash eyes my cheeks and quirks an eyebrow. "I'll drive you in. We can pick up breakfast on the way back."

Okay, that sounds amazing, but the chances of him waiting in the car while I'm in with Doc aren't great. He hands me his coffee while he grabs his shoes and I drink the rest of it in a giant gulp. "I need to speak to him about birth control and my period. I didn't think you'd want to sign up for a front row seat for that."

Ash smirks and grabs his keys. "I'm glad you're thinking about birth control, Mounty, and I'm not squeamish. Who the hell do you think helped Avery when she first got hers? I don't give a shit. Now, do you want to take the Maserati or the Mustang?"

Fuck.

I guess he's coming.

We take the Maserati because he has the keys for that already and I don't want this to end up a field trip to my uterus by asking Harley for the 'Stang keys.

It's strange to me that Ash has access to the largest amount of money and yet we're borrowing cars from the other two. When I mention it, he smirks at me. "I have a collection of cars and if I brought any of them to the slums of Mounts Bay, I would have to stab someone for breathing too closely to them. I leave them safely in the garage at Avery's horse ranch."

Huh.

Avery has a horse ranch?

Ash laughs at my expression. "She bought it freshman year and she's been renovating it since. She's been careful about keeping it a secret from Joey and Senior. She hates horses because she's a germaphobe, but the land is in a prime and secluded location. She built a garage for me and she's been renovating rooms for us all too. She'll start bugging you about moving into it during summer break soon."

Huh.

Maybe I do have a house I need to have secured by the Coyote? I make a note to ask Avery about it.

Ash is shockingly good with directions and remembers how to get to Doc's house without much prompting. The drive is clear of cars and he parks out front, unbuckling his seatbelt and pausing when I don't make a move. I don't like admitting when things hurt or are concerning me, I'd rather make a sarcastic joke, so I give myself a second to get my shit together.

Ash watches me fidget for a second, and then gives me a look. He says, with a surprisingly neutral but stern tone, "I'm coming in. I don't like him and if he has someone else in there I don't want you walking in alone."

I nod, but I don't move to get out.

"Is there something else?" He says, and it's in that soft damn tone he uses at Avery. I cave.

"I get severe cramps. I've been getting the birth control injection from him for years to help lessen the pain but it's not working out, and being at Hannaford makes it hard to get them on time anyway. I'm asking for something else."

Ash frowns at me and shrugs as he opens the car door. "Stop worrying then. Let's get this over with so we can go get breakfast. I need another coffee."

Doc opens the door before we make it up the steps. "Hello, my girl! Brought a friend again, I see. I'm glad you're being a bit more social."

I can barely hear him over the noise of the kids running around the house and Ash is scowling around the room at them all. I wait until we're locked safely in the exam room before I quietly murmur to Doc, "This is Ash. He is the one who tried to help Maria."

Ash's eyes snap to mine. "What do you mean tried to? She got out, didn't she?"

Fuck. I grimace and Doc smiles wryly at Ash, clapping him on the shoulder. He doesn't act like a man deeply mourning, but I can see the strain in his face, the signs of his devastation there if you know him like I do.

Doc answers Ash for me while I'm still fumbling for the right words. "You did get her out and I cannot thank you enough. But she was a silly, love-sick girl and went back to Matteo. She's gone now. Those noisy little beasts out there are all I have left now."

The mask snaps back over Ash's features and I curse myself for not telling him earlier. Doc gives him another little pat then directs us to sit down.

"Here for a shot? You're late, my girl. I hope you're not here about babies."

I flush and grit my teeth at him. "No, Doc, I'm not here about babies. The shot isn't helping anymore and I want the rod. That's the next thing to try, right?"

He hums and starts rummaging around in his drawers. "Do you want babies? We could just cut it all out. That can be effective in stopping the pain. Not always, but it's an option."

Sweet mother of god.

Why did I bring Ash here again?

Fuck.

While I'm too busy freaking the fuck out about this, Ash snaps at Doc, "You're not cutting *anything* out."

Doc gives him a stern look. "Not your choice, boy."

Ash surveys the room with contempt. "If she wants

anything cut out, I'll take her to a real hospital, with real doctors, so she doesn't bleed out at the hands of a second-rate hack in the slums."

I groan and bury my face in my hands. Is anyone safe from Ash's sharp tongue?

Doc looks at him for a moment and then laughs, thank fuck, pulling out the equipment to insert the rod in my arm. It takes under a minute and once he's finished sticking the band-aid over the wound he gives me a stern look. "Any changes from our last visit? Do you need me to test you? Boys lie about being safe and clean, you know, even rich ones."

I shake my head, still flushed, and Ash glares him down like he's going to stab him.

"7 days until it's effective to stop babies."

I wish he would stop saying babies to me, fucking *lord*.

Ash slips his hand onto my thigh and sneers at Doc, "Are we done?"

WE STOP for waffles on the way back at Avery's request because she has a savage hangover and bad temper with it. Harley texts to say she's already kicked Blaise out of the room and bitched him out for his antics last night. All I can think is thank fuck she didn't know what I'd done with the other two.

Ash orders my coffee without asking what I like and when I raise a brow at him he smirks. One sip of the sweet nectar of the gods tells me the smug asshole has been watching me closer than I think.

He holds my hand the whole way back to the hotel, up the elevator, and down the hall to our rooms. I'm so happy I even hum a little under my breath, and he pulls me in closer to his body so he can hear it. I should know better than to let myself be happy.

There's a box waiting outside the door to our room.

There, in bold black letters, is my full name across the top. Middle name and all. My stomach drops instantly and Ash's hand tightens around mine. I wait for a second and then step up to open it.

"Mounty, you can't just fucking open it!" Ash hisses, and I ignore him.

I use my knife to slice it open. Ash snaps at me again and I cut him off, "Avery, Harley, and Blaise are in that room and there's no other way out. I have to see what it is."

I flick the box open and the smell hits me.

Fuck.

Fuuuuuuuuuck.

It's a head.

There's a head in the box.

I flick it shut again and stand up abruptly. Ash steps forward, my body shielding the contents so he still has no idea of what's just been delivered to us. I know my face must look all sorts of fucked up as I try to figure out what the fuck is going on because his hand slips into mine again. I mean, it's not the first time I've seen a dismembered head, but I'd let my guard down again this morning. I'd let myself slip back into Lips and away from the Wolf.

"Is it dangerous?" Ash mutters. I shake my head, but when he moves to have a look for himself I tug him back.

"I need your phone. I left mine behind." I say calmly, and he hands his over without question.

"What's up, kid?" Illi answers, and I don't bother asking him how he knew it was me.

"Priority call, Illi. I need you to come to the hotel. We've had company this morning and they've left us a gift."

Illi snorts. "How kind. Gimme ten."

I gesture for Ash to get the door and then, grimacing, I pick up the box and carry it into the room.

CHAPTER FIFTEEN

T HE HEAD in the box belongs to Lance, my stalker
from last year.

Harley and Ash both refuse to wait for Illi and have a
look, jaws clenched. Blaise gags at the smell but has a look
too, and he's the first to figure out who it is. Avery doesn't
look up for her phone and she demands that Ash puts her
waffles in the fridge for later, when there's not stray body
parts appearing out of nowhere.

Illi arrives and snaps on a pair of latex gloves before
lifting it out. Avery gets one look at it and barely makes it to
the bathroom sink before she vomits, then she refuses to
leave until the head is back in the box. I don't blame her;
she's hungover and it's not exactly *fresh*. She's going to clean
every square inch of our room for hours when we get back
to Hannaford. She'll probably have the guys room gutted
before the panic subsides.

Illi moves to empty out the rest of the contents of the
box and finds nothing but the head and the plastic sheet
lining the cardboard.

Nothing.

Fuck.

Illi stares at the box with a frown over his face. I don't like the look of that frown one bit because the same one is on my face. Fuck, he sees it too. He meets my eye and nods.

"I'll ask around a bit more. You might want to call the Crow, or even the Coyote, see if they know what the fuck this means."

I scowl and nod; we're going to need the extra help. Ash frowns at me and says, "This isn't the Jackal? It looks like a sick token of affection to me. Like he's proving his devotion to you. I'd assume after last night he was making a stand."

Blaise rolls bloodshot eyes around at us all. "What happened last night? Did Arbour piss him off in the meeting?"

I flush scarlet and desperately wish Illi wasn't so fucking perceptive as he grins at Blaise. Fuck, does he know what we'd done? I need some fucking whiskey.

Illi opens his mouth and I cut him off. "He saw Harley, Ash, and I dancing after the meeting. He was watching the three of us and I have no doubt he was planning out my punishment."

At that, the smirk melts off of Illi's face and he snaps his gloves off. "This isn't retaliation. This was done at least three days ago, and D'Ardo would leave a calling card. This isn't his style. Fuck knows *whose* style this is, but it's not his."

Harley groans and curses at the ceiling. "Mounty, is there any fucking chance you could stop attracting psychos and serial killers for five fucking minutes while we dig our way out of the mountain of shit we're already in?"

I shift my scowl over to him, sitting on the couch to rest my leg. "If I knew how I was doing it, clearly I would stop."

Illi snickers at us both and tucks the box under his arm

without a care in the world of it's contents. "I'll deal with this. If the rest of it shows up we might have more of an idea of who's behind it. Stay safe, kids!"

He takes two steps towards the door and then swings back to smirk at me, his eyes fucking dancing around like he's never been happier. Fuck.

"If you decide to indulge in anymore *public frolicking*, please warn me. I've had a few threats neutralized already this morning, little Wolf."

I don't think it's possible to blush any freaking harder than I am as he laughs at me and walks out.

As the door clicks shut behind him, Avery comes out of the bathroom, her face still a little green, and slumps down next to me, eyeing the color on my cheeks critically. I tuck my arm into hers to distract her and she croaks out, "Fuck margaritas."

Blaise is still staring between us all like he's missing something big. I really hope that when he figures it out Avery and I aren't around.

"I don't like him." Ash snaps, and I glance up to find him staring at the door Illi just exited.

Harley shrugs nonchalantly. "He grows on you. Give him time to get under your skin."

Blaise laughs at them both quietly, like his head is still pounding and his usual raucous laughter wouldn't be worth the pain. "Well, I don't have a single fucking issue with the psycho. He doesn't look at Star's ass even in those booty shorts, he stabs people without her even having to ask him, and he gets rid of decomposing body parts with a smile. Don't be a jealous dick and just leave him alone."

Ash's eyes flare and he fixes them on me. Fuck, what next? "Oh, Mounty, how could I forget? Your name was on that box."

I tense up and throw him a stern look. His answering smile is a taunt. Fuck, I should've gone with a pleading look, but it's just not my style.

"Yes, Ash, we've just spent the last hour discussing her crazed stalker. Have you suffered some sort of brain damage I'm unaware of?" Avery hisses and he smirks at her.

"I was referring to Lips' middle name."

Fuck. I glare at him and Blaise bursts out laughing. Harley looks between them and then frowns at me like this is my fucking fault. Nope, I will not feel bad that he's practically pouting at me. No. Stay strong, Lips. *Fuck.*

"Ash, I would appreciate your discretion." I grit out, overly polite because I don't want to rage blackout and stab him for digging this hole for me. For the record, it would be justified.

"How does Blaise know it?" Avery says sweetly, and it's a total ruse. She might slit my throat while I'm sleeping for not telling her.

"She loves me the most!" Blaise sings and shakes his ass as he heads towards the balcony for a smoke. I stare at his ass for a second too long but, *damn*, he can move those hips of his.

When I look back at the others Harley is staring at Blaise like he's planning exactly where he's going to stab the fucker. I hold out my hands as Avery scowls at me. "He found out while I was off my head on those pain pills you gave me. I made him swear not to tell anyone because it's fucking embarrassing and I'd rather die than ever hear it said out loud."

Avery rolls her eyes at my dramatics, but Ash stares at me for a second longer. Something in my eyes makes him shrug. "Fine, I'll keep it to myself."

Avery just shrugs and smiles at Harley. "Mounty will tell me when we get home. She loves *me* the most."

I squeeze my eyes shut so I don't have to see his reaction to potentially being the only one not knowing the damn name and snap, "It's Starbright, okay? My name is Eclipse *Starbright* Anderson. My mom was high and thought the moon was fucking cool and just ran with it. She didn't give a fuck about how it would affect me for the rest of my life. Fuck, she couldn't even stay sober long enough to get through her pregnancy or my birth, for fuck's sake. Okay? Cool. Glad everyone is on the same fucking page. Where's the fucking whiskey, I'm going to drink myself to death, or until I forget about it. Whichever happens first."

THE BEAR CALLS me with his job midway through the break and I instantly know it's going to be fucking messy.

He wasn't lying, it will be quick, but the chances of me getting it done without one of the guys or Avery finding out and throwing a fit is pretty slim.

The outfit requirement alone is going to piss them the fuck off. They're pretty twitchy about my ass in booty shorts, especially since all of the supervised eating has put a little meat on my bones. Harley in particular can't seem to keep his hands away from the curve and I find myself fantasizing about what it'll feel like to have his big hands spread me open.

I take a lot of cold showers.

After I get my brief from the Bear, I drag Avery into our

shared bedroom at the hotel and give her a very basic and vague rundown of what I'm going to do. Naturally, the evil genius figures it out before I've even finished with the watered down sentence.

"So what you're trying *not* to say is you're going to assassinate the leader of a prominent illegal organization because he pissed the Bear off?"

Right. Well. I can't really argue with that assessment. "Yeah. I am. Is this going to be a problem?"

Avery switches her phone on silent, I trip over my own feet in shock, and then she props her chin up on her hands and watches while I throw together a good Mounty outfit. I need to blend in.

"No problem. How many times do I have to tell you, I'm on your side. I trust that you wouldn't be going and killing a decent person. Honestly, I don't think I would care even if he were decent. If he's in your way, take him out. Our family first; fuck everyone else." She says, her eyes taking in the tiny shorts and skintight razor tee.

Fuck, I really would kill and die for this girl.

I do a full face of make up, and then cover all my visible skin in the tinted moisturizer I use to cover the tattoos to get through clubs without notice. Avery helps out with the backs of my legs and when I grab my shoes she gets up and starts digging around in my bag. When she pulls out another pair of shorts and a Vanth tee Blaise gave me I raise my eyebrows at her.

"Don't be dense, Mounty. I'm coming with you and we'll tell the boys we're having some girl time. That way they won't try to jump in, as if you're some kind of damsel that needs saving, to mess this up for you, and I'll get to watch you work. There is nothing quite as satisfying as watching you destroy the male population one by one." She says and when she pulls my clothes on I nearly choke at her transformation into a Mounty girl. Sweet lord fuck, it's only a matter of time before some guy hits on her and I'll have to fucking kill him too.

Yep, just a regular girls night out in the Bay.

As predicted the guys all pitch a fit when they get an eyeful of Avery and figure out what we're doing, and she shoots them all down *beautifully*. She has an answer for everything and when Blaise tries to hand the keys for the Maserati over she smiles sweetly at him, waving her phone in his face.

"Mounties use Uber. I'm going to live like the locals for a night. I feel desperate already."

Ash snorts at her, pissed at the both of us, and I step away from them before I get caught in the crossfire.

Harley hooks an arm around my waist and pulls me into his body. When he whispers in my ear, I shiver. "Promise me you're not going somewhere dangerous, babe. Promise me it's just a girl's night."

Fuck. Avery shoots me a look and I fumble to talk my way around it without lying. "I'm taking Avery on a job with me. I wouldn't take her if I thought there was a chance it could get dangerous. Her safety is always a priority for me."

He nods and ducks down to kiss me, his hand trailing down my back to squeeze my ass in my shorts and I shiver. "Do you have any shorts that cover more of your ass?"

I pull away, scoffing at him even as I blush. "I have to blend in. Avery's wearing the longest ones I own, anyway, and on her long ass legs they still look indecent."

At this, Ash levels me with a look. I freeze for a second

before snapping, "What the fuck have I done? I was going to go alone!"

He turns on his heel, stalking over to the bar to find the bourbon, and we take the opportunity to leave before he changes his mind and follows us both out.

Avery sits in the Uber like she's afraid she'll catch a venereal disease from the seats. I send a photo of her to the guys and she snarks at me like I'm a traitor to all womankind.

It only makes me laugh harder.

The bar we're heading to is seedy and dark, perfect to murder some asshole in.

I know the guy at the door, and a curt nod is all it takes before we're both in. I slip a little clip of cash into his pocket as we pass and then Avery's hand is tucked carefully into mine as we navigate our way through the room, blending seamlessly into the crowd of drunken locals.

Well, I blend in. Avery is shuddering a little too much to look local to the discerning eye, but no one here is sober enough to give her revulsion a second glance.

"That guy back there had cum stains on his shorts, Mounty." Avery hisses and I laugh at her, pulling her along until finally we reach the bar at the back.

Stephen is one of the bartenders on tonight.

Excellent.

I catch his eye and he smiles cheerfully at me, finishing up with his customer and making his way over to me before the busty blonde helping him can piss me off. The look she's giving Avery pisses me the fuck off before I realize she's glaring at the Vanth shirt. Right. A priceless collector's item.

"There's my favorite little ass shaker! Here to dance the night away or should I be worried? Picking things up or making a mess?" Stephen says and pours me a whiskey without asking. He tilts the bottle in Avery's direction and she nods, her eyes glued to the glaring blonde the same way you'd stare at a box of snakes.

"Making a mess, sorry. You'll have to call your boss." I murmur and he only smiles wider.

"Oh, he called and told me to expect you."

He hesitates for a second, wiping a glass with a rag I hope Avery isn't looking at, before gesturing at her. "A friend of yours?"

I nod and down my shot. "She's with me. I'm looking out for her."

"You know your friends are my friends, kid. I'll keep the hoards of ravenous cock in the bar away from her while you shake that ass of yours. Have fun!" He says with a wink and I laugh at him. He pours me another shot and walks back over to the crowd of people waiting to be served.

I survey the room and find the guy I'm looking for sitting in one of the booths with two other guys. They're talking, or more likely arguing as he shakes his head and sneers at them. I jerk my head at Stephen and he nods, grabbing a bottle of vodka and walking it over to the booth. I need the guy to pee.

"This is not what I expected. It's a lot more... open than I thought it would be." Avery murmurs and I shrug.

I smile at Stephen as he comes back over to the bar, the dirty rag slung over his shoulder like it's an everyday occurrence that he helps out with a hit. Belonging to the Bear, it may well be.

"Stephen belongs to the Bear. He owns this place and is kept safe by that loyalty so he's safe to talk to. He got the heads up and we drink for free. You'll always drink for free here now, by the way, not that you need the hand out."

Avery nods and downs the shot, pushing the glass away

from herself to signal she's done for the night to the bartenders. Stephen grins and slides a bottle of water down the bar to her like the sweetheart he is.

While I wait for my mark to break the seal, we get approached by no less than five guys, each wanting to fuck us both. I shut the first guy down hard and Avery sends a blow-by-blow to the group message because she secretly hates me, I'm sure. I wait for her to jump in and destroy the Mounties but she just watches and assesses my words.

When my mark finally stands as the fifth guy approaches, Avery cuts him off before he can even open his mouth. I'm relieved until I see the evil little twinkle in her eye.

"She has three cocks waiting at home; she doesn't have anymore *vacancies* to fill."

Good lord.

The guy smirks at us both and reaches for my hand, "If you like groups, baby girl, my friends and I can show you a good time-"

I break his hand, then stomp on his foot with my good leg. The thick soles of my Docs make it hard to tell if I've broken his foot, but the squeal that comes out of him is disgraceful.

I lean forward to speak directly in his ear, "Leave while you still have hands for me to break because one more word and I'll cut them off, dickhead."

He scurries away and Avery gives me her best broken glass and bleeding hearts giggle. I make a note to never give her whiskey again. Apparently even in small amounts it turns her into a smug, shit-stirring siren.

I should get that on a shirt for her.

I wait until my mark moves towards the restroom by himself and I give Avery a stern look, motioning for her to stay put. I catch Stephen's eye, and then quickly duck behind the bar and into the store room. I've been here many times before and when I crouch down by the shelves, holding dusty boxes of red wine no one in the Bay will ever drink, I find my supply bag where I left it back in the summer break. There's nothing in the bag that could lead anyone back to me, but I've never worried about it. Stephen would never risk answering to the Twelve by moving it; he's just not that stupid. I make quick work of slipping my Docs off, wriggling my toes and centering myself. I don't have much time to waste, so one last deep breath in and I let the calm Wolf settle over me.

Time to work.

I grab the latex gloves and snap them into place. There's a plastic jumpsuit in there too, but it'll make too much noise.

If I need to go home bloody, I will.

I push the false back out of the shelf and squeeze through the small opening, checking to make sure no one is in the toilet cubicle on the other side before pulling myself the rest of the way into the restroom. Another sweep under the stall to make sure there are no witnesses, but the cash I parted with on the way in will keep the room clear.

The men's always stinks. It's fucking foul.

My mark is on the phone at the urinal, loud and brash down the line like he's invincible. I wait until he hangs up and his dick is safely tucked back into his pants before I step up behind him.

His eyes meet mine in the mirror and I see the exact moment he realizes he's dead.

The hot spray of his blood over the tiles just confirms it.

I CAN'T GET into an Uber stinking of blood.

The giant hoodie I had in my supply bag covers most of the damage and I'd scrubbed my legs clean before I'd left the restroom, but the tang of copper is overpowering where it's stuck to me.

I should have worn the plastic jumpsuit.

Avery is calm as we sit on a busy road in the slums, waiting for the guys to come pick us up. I let my mind wander as my eyes track the cars passing us, on guard as always in the Bay.

She breaks the silence first. "That was surprisingly easy."

It wasn't easy; it just ran smoothly. It's something I've done so many times, something I've studied and practiced and executed hundreds of times, so now it seems simple.

I'm too tired to explain it to her so I shrug, letting the silence fall over us again. Avery fidgets with her phone, distractedly. I watch her from the corner of my eye for a while before she scoffs at me, hesitating a little then slipping her hand in mine.

"I wore gloves, you're safe." I murmur, misreading her hesitance.

She shakes her head at me like I'm simple. "Harley told us about what happened after you... eliminated the threat in Haven. About how you didn't want to be touched. I don't want to push you if you're not ready."

I swallow, nodding my head. "It's getting easier. The lines between who I was and who I am now, they're blurring so much I think I'm just going to be the Wolf again."

Avery smiles at me and, *holy shit*, rests her head on my shoulder. I can't believe she's willing to get that close to all of the blood.

"You'll always be the Wolf. And we'll always be yours."

I rest my cheek on her hair and we fall quiet again, waiting to hear the roar of the 'Stang.

At peace with the family we've fought, bled, and killed for.

CHAPTER SIXTEEN

W E DON'T TALK about the smell of blood in the car, and the guys all pretend they didn't notice the piles of ruined clothes in the bathroom the next morning.

Blaise decides he'll singlehandedly clear the somber mood from the air and spends the rest of the fall break teasing Harley about being the last one to know my full name. I stay the *fuck* out of it because I don't need any extra drama in my life. It's only when Avery comes tearing into the bathroom the morning we're due back at school, screeching like a banshee about public sex acts, that I realize Harley finally snapped back.

Oh *joy*.

Which is how I find myself sitting in the Maserati with a whiny Blaise and a gloating Ash, while Harley is driving Avery back and listening to her tirade about *discretion* and *subtlety* and *keeping the details of our relationship the hell out of general conversation.*

I do not envy him.

"I can't believe you let Harley eat you out in *public* and

I was too fucking wasted to watch. That's against the rules!" Blaise groans at me for the billionth time.

"What fucking rules, you insufferable dick?" Ash snarks from the backseat and I ignore them both, trying to focus on my reading for our literature class. I'm on the last book for the year and I'm determined to have it done before we arrive back at Hannaford.

Blaise fucking *pouts* like a brat at me, but I continue to ignore him. "I think there should be some rules and *that* is number one."

Ash scoffs and crosses his arms. "I should have ridden with the other two. I thought the Mounty would need help dealing with your attitude, but she can't even be bothered listening to you."

I turn the page, casually. "Oh, I'm listening. I'm just choosing to ignore you both because this topic is stupid."

Blaise snickers at me, aiming a sly look in my direction. "Wasn't he any good at it? Do you need me to come stay with you tonight and do it properly? Aves will be pissed but, now I know you *love* an audience, we can just ignore her yelling. Do you think Ash will hold you up for me too?"

I blush and then I decide that the cheeky fucker won't stop until I shut him down. I'm so fucking proud when my voice comes out strong and even. "I came so hard I creamed down his chin so no, it was better than good. Can you please shut up about it now?"

Blaise groans at me and his eyes dart lustfully between the road and me. "Star, that was the hottest fucking thing I've ever heard come out of your mouth. Say something else! Wait, no, wait until we get back. Come whisper dirty things to me tonight. I promise I won't be a dick about it and I'll even make sure everyone is present. I'm a team player unlike the other two scheming assholes."

I try not to squirm in my seat and Ash smirks at us both, his eyes catching mine in the mirror. "Are you going to start sleeping in our room now, Mounty? Or are you still too scared?"

I give him a glare over my shoulder. "I'm not fucking scared, asshole. I just don't want to hear more gossip about myself."

Ash leans forward in his seat to kiss me, his hand gripping the back of my neck firmly, and I try to hold back a moan when he bites my lip.

He breaks away and speaks lowly, his voice annoyingly unaffected by the searing heat of the kiss, "I'll deal with the sheep. Prove to me that you're not being a scared little girl and come sleep in my bed."

He's baiting me, it's so fucking obvious he's using Beaumont Bullshit to get his way, but fuck it if it's not effective.

I lean in until my lips brush against his as I speak, "If I have to stab someone because of this, you're paying the cleanup fee."

Ash smirks and gives me one last peck, more teeth than sweet. "I think I can handle it."

AVERY TUCKS her arm in mine as we make our way back up to the girls' dorms.

The guys head off to their room, still bickering and shoving each other like children, and I groan to Avery about Ash's demands to sleep in their room, wanting nothing more than a little vent. She, *of course*, wants to talk about it.

"Well, just go sleep there. *Are* you scared? Should I find

you a therapist of some kind? I'm pretty sure sex therapists are just sex workers who charge more."

I blush and try to avoid her eye. "I'm not scared! I just... all three of them will be there. I've only been in their room once and... it's just a lot, okay?"

Avery snorts at me and unlocks our front door. "Is it more than having Harley perform oral sex in the middle of a crowded dance floor while my brother twiddled his thumbs and waited his turn?"

I flush scarlet and mumble, "It wasn't the *middle* of the dance floor, and *technically* Ash went first."

Avery shudders dramatically and pulls away from me, cackling when she sees the color of my cheeks. "Go there during the day while they're gone. Eat their food, smoke Blaise's stash, get comfortable in one of their beds. By the time they get home you'll be calm and less twitchy about it. I'll get you a key. It's only fair you have one since they all have copies of ours. If it turns into an orgy please put sheets down, because I do spend time over there. I don't need to find myself sitting in Morrison's DNA."

I elbow her gently while she laughs, and hum under my breath for a second while I think but it's a really great idea. She's a fucking genius, I almost feel bad for the sheep of the world. I'm also so glad we can ignore the weirdness of me being in a relationship with, you know, all three of her people.

When she's locked the door behind us, and I'm busy toeing off my shoes, Avery frowns and stoops down to pick up an envelope that's on our floor. It's been shoved under the door while we've been away. I never get mail so it barely registers with me.

I move away from her, already thinking about assignments and quiz notes, when I hear Avery's teeth grind together. Seriously, I'm kind of afraid they're going to crack under the pressure from her jaw.

"What now?" I sigh, rubbing a hand over my face. Avery watches me carefully, assessing me and cataloging every little sign my body is showing her. I know I'll look tired, grumpy, and a little hungry because when am I not up for food?

"Don't worry about it. I will deal with this." She finally says, eyes icy but firmly fixed on my face. I swallow because whatever the fuck it is must be bad for her to be looking at me like that.

I nod and let her. I have enough on my damn plate and she can hold her own.

I grab a tub of ice cream and spend the rest of the afternoon working on my studies while Avery deals with whatever was in the letter. By the time the sun is setting and I'm feeling a hell of a lot better about my studies, Avery is cooking enough food to feed an army and the sound of keys at the door tells me they've arrived.

I offer Avery help but she shoos me into the shower to clean up before dinner, snapping at Blaise when he once again offers his assistance. One day soon I think I'm going to take him up on his offer.

When I get out, rubbing my hair with a towel and my belly rumbling at the incredible smell of the food, Harley kisses me softly and directs me to sit next to him at the table. I usually sit between him and Avery so it's not an unusual thing to do but the way he's handling me sets off warning bells.

"What the fuck was in that letter?" I grumble, and Ash gives me a look, like he's already plotting the deaths of whoever sent it.

Avery rolls her shoulders back and starts to fix me a

plate, her mothering only making me more concerned. "It's a notice. A warning that you'll be put on probation if you continue to behave in a manner unbecoming of a student at Hannaford."

I blanch and Harley grabs my hand under the table, threading him fingers through mine. He speaks softly, not to keep the others out of the conversation but to soften the blow of his words, "Someone got to the security video of us meeting Illi at the pool before Avery wiped it. He's not in the footage but we are. It hasn't been leaked but the principal and school board know it exists."

Unbecoming behavior. *Sweet lord fuck*, there's a video of Harley fingering me in the pool out there in the world. I think I want to die. I sure as fuck want *someone* to die.

"Mounty, Avery will deal with it. Don't panic." Ash says, and I snap back like a bitch for him assuming I'm breaking over this.

"I'm not fucking panicking. I'm *jumpy,* remember? Consider this me *jumping*! Avery, who the fuck am I stabbing? I'm stabbing someone!"

"Harley, for insisting on constantly putting his hands on you in public?" She snarks, but she tucks her arm into mine as she says it. "I've sorted it out with the school board and Trevelen. You'll have another formal apology by the morning because they can't punish you over a rumor of a video. I've put an official complaint in about Ms. *Vivienne* because this reeks of her."

I see red and clamp my eyes shut, counting backwards in French until I'm not likely to stomp my ass downstairs to hunt the cougar skank down.

I hear them all start to eat around me, ignoring my bloodthirsty rage in favor of the hot meal in front of them, and that cools the fire more than they could ever know.

By the time I start in on my food, Avery has finished hers and is teasing her brother about her admiration of Illi.

"He's the perfect man for me, Ash. I'm a little disappointed he's already married. All those muscles and the way he just stabbed that disgusting guy without Lips even telling him too. He even wore gloves to handle the box!"

I cut in. "Do you have any idea how long it takes to get the smell of rotting human flesh off of your skin if you touch it bare-handed? No thanks! Odie would have shanked him if he went home stinking of corpses."

Avery gags and I rub her shoulder a little because I've got this best friend business down like a pro. Blaise swallows and turns a little green. When he notices the other two nod along he turns on Ash.

"What, you've handled *rotting human flesh* before?"

Ash stares at him for a second and Avery's shoulder tenses beneath my hand. Fuck. Finally he shrugs and nods. Blaise gapes and then mumbles under his breath, "What the fuck have I gotten myself into?"

"Second thoughts, Morrison?" Harley sneers, still pissy at him over the conversation in the car. Ash had, *so kindly*, told him the details.

Blaise glares at him. "No. It's just that every time I think I know just how fucked up we all are the bottom falls out and I find a whole new level of depravity. Ash; when, where, and why?"

Avery pulls a face and wriggles in her seat, looking down at her phone and effectively putting a barrier between herself and the conversation. I'm sure now that the death isn't what's bothering her; it's the *rotting* that turns her gut.

Ash stares at his glass and says, monotone and dry, "I had to help Joey dig up one of my father's toys. I think we washed more of her down the drain when we washed our hands afterwards than what was left of her on the bones when Senior finally fired up the incinerator."

Blaise swallows.

Harley nods, then grunts and pipes in, "One of my grandfather's lackeys was sunk in the bay, out past the docks. He'd been skimming, caught red-handed, and they chained him up and dropped him off a boat. He floated up a week later. I'll never forget the smell, Domnall made me help him scoop the gross fuck into a net and he paid some biker guy to dissolve what was left of him in acid."

I nod at him. "The Boar. You would have seen one of his guys. Pricey, but you're never going to get caught if he's the one getting rid of your problems."

Harley's eyes flash and he leans over to drape his arm around my shoulders. "He was the one that vouched for you and Illi, right?"

Avery's head jerks up. "That reminds me. We need to make a list of the members of the Twelve we like."

I groan and rub a hand over my face. "I'm not sure we *like* any of them. It's more like the ones who want us dead and the ones who could be persuaded to spare us."

Harley snorts. "There's also the ones who want to fuck you, babe."

Ash cuts me a glare. "Is that list longer than the Jackal?"

Harley's eyes only get more intense now he has backup in this brewing argument. "One of them asked if her pussy was gold plated."

Fucking rich, entitled, bratty boys.

Blaise snorts, enjoying this conversation a little too much at my expense, and I smile at Harley like I'm baring my teeth at the asshole. "Aves, we also need to add the Lynx to the list of cougars chasing Harley's dick."

Blaise's raucous laughter almost drowns out the frustrated groan Harley lets out.

I WATCH the cougar skank with rage in my blood and fire in my eyes. I watch her every move in my presence, cataloging her quirks and ticks, all the little mannerisms until I have a full picture of who Ms. *Vivienne* is.

She's a slut.

I know, I know, I've banned the word, but fuck if it isn't the right one for her. She doesn't just fawn over Harley. She touches every guy in our class and when I see her out in the dining hall she touches every being with a dick that crosses her path. I'm sure she must be hosting orgies in her room every night with the amount of winks and knowing looks she's getting.

Okay, glass houses and all that shit.

I'm not technically having any orgies, despite Avery's snarky comments. Also, how many people does there need to be involved before it's classed as an orgy? Fuck it, off topic.

I manage to keep my cool until classes finish for the day and then I drag Avery down to the gym for a training session, intent on sweating my rage out.

She's gotten pretty good at kicking my ass. I'm still going easy on her because I know she's a little hesitant about the knife, but I've found the best way to get her over that is to talk about what I've done in the past. She loves it when I walk her through scenarios, like she's learning a skill and piecing together more of my past. I think she wants to know everything that has ever happened to me, but there will always be things I'd rather never speak of again.

When my body hits the mat for the fifth time my fury has burned out enough to talk it out.

"Why Harley? Like, of all the dicks on this school she could climb, why him?" I'm totally fucking pouting. Thank fuck he isn't around to see it. His head would probably get so big it would explode.

Avery helps me off the floor and then hands me a bottle of water. "I've looked everywhere for a link to the Jackal and I can't find one. They've never crossed paths as far as I can see. I think she's just a desperate whore. A dirty, desperate whore who enjoys a challenge."

I nod and wipe my face with my shirt, ignoring the face Avery pulls over it. "He is fucking gorgeous, the bastard."

Avery shrugs. "There's plenty of gorgeous guys at Hannaford that she can have, you just don't notice them because you're too busy drooling over the three you're obsessed with."

"Rude." I grumble and Avery cocks an eyebrow at me, smirking at my attitude.

"It's an observation, not a judgment."

"Fine but you don't need to be so smug about it." God, I sound whiny. I need to harden the fuck up.

She scoffs at me and gets back into position. She changes the subject because she's a *saint*. "I spoke to Atticus again. He's pretty adamant I go to the Charity Gala this year, and he said he's going to dance with me there."

Fuck. I need to look this guy up, make sure he's not some rapist asshole. I make a note to talk to Ash and see why he hates him so much. I wonder if Harley likes him?

"Ash and I both have invitations with plus ones. I'll take Blaise and Ash will take you. Harley has a swim meet and now that he's taking his swimming more seriously he's going to go. He'll be pissy, but there's nothing I can do about it. Well, I could have the Gala date moved I guess. How badly do you want to see Harley in a three-piece suit?"

I try not to drool at the thought. She doesn't need any encouragement in her assessment of me. "It's fine. I'm sure being around you lot there will be other *Galas* to attend."

Avery laughs at my fake-ass airy tone and waves a hand at me. "Okay, no more distractions. Walk me through another. I think I'm almost ready to start stabbing my enemies myself."

I raise an eyebrow at her. "Any requests, Miss Blood-thirsty?"

She nods and hesitates for a second. I roll my eyes at her. "Just ask. I'm not going to lose my mind over it and if I don't want to do it I'll say no."

The door to the gym opens and I don't have to turn to see it's the guys. They're bickering and talking shit loud enough for Illi to hear it down in the Bay.

Avery lowers her voice. "I want to know how you won the Game. How you beat the last two men."

I stare at her for a second and then shrug. It's an old memory, not something I think too much about. Why not use it?

Blaise slips his arms around me and tugs me until I'm leaning back against his chest. I smirk at Avery and say, "Sure. We even have volunteers to be our victims."

Blaise cackles, squeezing me a little, and Harley swoops down to kiss my cheek, murmuring quietly, "I'll be your victim any day, babe."

I smirk at them all and pull away from Blaise, directing them all until they're where I need them to be. Ash stands with Avery, intent on learning everything I'm teaching her as well. It's a well calculated move from him; they all need to know how to read a situation and no one is better at it than Avery or me. If they're going up against the Jackal with me, they need to learn when to fight and when to manipulate.

I point at Blaise. "Do you want to be a loud idiotic beef-cake or a silent, calculating sociopath?"

Harley cuts in before I finish the sentence. "He's the idiot. Where are we standing?"

Blaise scoff but nods along, "If anyone is the beefcake it's you, dickhead, you're going to fucking sink next time you get in the pool. Lay off the weights when you're frustrated at being stuck with the cougar, man, maybe have a wank instead."

He continues, but I zone out their bickering easier than I breathe air so I just direct them into their places and then I stand between the twins. Avery cools the arguing off with a single look and I'm a little jealous at her superpowers.

"Right, Blaise is Geordie. He's made it to the last three by sheer size so far. He's easily four times bigger than me, he sees me as a nothing job. He doesn't pay any attention to me at all."

Avery nods and tilts her head. "He's focused on the other male contender."

"Exactly. Harley is playing the part of Xavier. The best way to describe him is to say he was a sober Joey. All of the psychosis, none of the manic."

Avery shudders and I squeeze her hand. "Just watch and listen this time. Right, Geordie lunges at Xavier. What's the plan, Aves? Ash?"

Ash waves a hand. "Let them fight. Then you only have one to take out, and hopefully whoever is left is injured."

I nod, oddly impressed that he's thinking it through. I shouldn't be; he's always been the level headed one. Except for the entire year he insisted I was evil; that one time he was an emotional asshole.

Avery frowns. "You can't just watch them though, if Geordie lands even a single hit on Lips she could be out. You'd have to be watching for an opening to take him out."

Harley crosses his arms, watching me just a little too closely. "Xavier is the real danger. Joey sees fucking everything, even as high as he is. He picks up all the little shit that you guys do. If you're standing there watching, he'd be trying to find a way to throw Geordie at you."

Avery shrugs. "What did you do, Lips?"

I step up and slip the fake knife we practice with out of my pocket. Harley gets Blaise in a headlock at my directions and I stand behind him.

"I danced around them, never letting them get too close to me intentionally. I knew I had to wait for Xavier to be dealing the killing blow to Geordie. This was before my leg was destroyed and I was faster than any of them. Eventually, Xavier got impatient and stabbed Geordie, waiting long enough for blood loss to weaken him and then went about strangling him."

I press the knife into Harley's Achilles tendons and push him to kneel, dragging Blaise down with him, grunting in protest, but being a good sport overall. Fuck. I didn't think this one through at all.

I shoot Avery a look and she raises an eyebrow at me. "Remember you asked me to show you. This was your doing."

She frowns at me and Ash crosses his arms. "Well, hurry up then."

Ugh. I lean forward and whisper in Harley's ear, "Please don't be a dick about it, Avery will murder us both."

And that is the only warning I give him before putting him into a chokehold and using my free arms to grab a fist full of Blaise's hair to hold him still while I 'stab' him through the eye and 'kill' him. How did I have free arms to do this while strangling Harley, you may ask?

My thighs.

My *thighs* were wrapped around Harley's neck, ankles locked and squeezing just enough that he knows how fucked he really would be if I wanted to take him out.

"*Holy fucking shit, Star!*" Blaise sputters as he watches Harley very slowly, and I hope peacefully, grow weak from lack of oxygen. I let him go before he actually passes out and Ash gapes at me.

"Then once he's out I find a boulder and smash his skull in. There was a crowd watching and I didn't want anyone watching thinking I was afraid to get my hands dirty. Half of the power of the Twelve is the rumors that precede us and as a starving teenage girl, I couldn't risk looking weak."

There's a sort of reverent, stunned silence for a second.

"Okay, teach me how to do that. Now, Mounty, I need to be able to do that. You looked like an assassin seductress, I'm *in*." Avery gushes, her eyes lit up like I've just handed her a box of blood diamonds.

"Fucking Christ, we're going to have two of them blood thirsty and trained." Harley croaks and I lean down to kiss him sweetly in apology. He smirks into the kiss, fisting my hair in one hand and cupping my jaw in the other.

"I can think of worse ways of dying, babe. Your legs

wrapped around my neck might just be my preferred way to go."

Avery snaps at us both and I pull away, ready to torture my boyfriends for a few hours while I arm Avery with enough knowledge to be a danger to society.

Well, *more* of a danger then she already is.

CHAPTER SEVENTEEN

W E FALL BACK into a steady routine, the events of the party and our time away during fall break fading into the background with so much classwork to get done.

Harley is still barely around and I miss him so goddamn much it's like a hole in my chest. Ash is quieter and more reserved the longer we're back, but I decide to wait him out. There's no point pushing him, he'll only snark and hiss like the lovable asshole he is.

Blaise becomes so focused on his studies that I'm fucking impressed as shit at him. He refuses to fool around until his studies are done and we've worked on my vocal training. I'm usually so shaky after we're done that he won't do much more than kiss me, but fuck it feels good to finally hear myself sing without vomiting.

I think Blaise likes being able to help me, to teach me, and not always be the student. Plus I think he finds my voice a turn-on, more often than not he has to use his bag to cover himself when Avery gets back from ballet. There's nothing that girl likes more than threatening some dicks.

I start to relax a little., Just enough that I'm once again caught unaware by the next move on the board.

I'm sitting in Choir with Blaise, trying to ignore the sick feeling of dread in my stomach as we warm up, when my phone starts vibrating insistently in my pocket. My rock god boyfriend raises his eyebrows at me and I shrug, knowing there's only one person outside of Hannaford who would be calling.

Well, two but I doubt I'm on the Jackal's speed dial these days.

When class finally comes to an end I check my phone and see Illi has called eight times and left three messages. I duck into a little alcove in the hallway to call him back, anxiety creeping up my spine. Blaise crowds into the little nook, his broad shoulders covering me from prying eyes and I lean my forehead onto his chest while I wait for Illi to answer.

"Is Odie okay?" I whisper the second I hear the phone pick up. Blaise wraps me into his arms at my quiet tone.

There's a beat of silence and then Illi sighs heavily down the phone. "You're too good for this fucked up world we're in. My girl is safe, kid. I'm calling to let you know I've just had to have a stern chat with three more guys sent by our friend." Translation: he's just killed three of the Jackal's men. He doesn't wait for me to comment, "They were sent up the coast, kid. They were sent after Iris, to finish what that dickhead Liam started."

I suck in a breath. Fuck. How the hell had I forgotten about Harley's mom? Of course the Jackal would go after her, she's a sitting fucking duck! Blaise runs a hand up and down my spine gently, resting his cheek on the top of my head.

"I'm only saying this in a phone call because I don't

want to leave her. You might want to suggest to your little mobster that he send her somewhere a little more secure now he has the funds."

I finally find my voice again. "I'll sort it. Thank you, Illi. I don't know what we'd do without you."

He chuckles down the phone and says, "You have my back, kid, and you have from the first day we met. I'll have yours until I stop fucking breathing. Tell Arbour not to worry, I'll keep her safe until you can move her."

I end the call and let Blaise hold me until I can figure out my plan of action.

Avery is already handling Harley's fortune. The moment the money hit my accounts I had her move the money into investment accounts she had set up for him. It's a fuck-tonne of money, and he could easily pay for his mom to move to any facility in the world. Avery will know what to do.

The problem is I have to tell him first.

"Is his wife alive?" Blaise mumbles, and I shake myself out of my thoughts and pull away from him.

"She's fine. We need to go. We need to find the others, fuck." I mumble, and he tucks me under his arm.

"Avery's already text to ask why we're late to lunch. Let's go eat and you can tell us what the hell is happening now."

I nod distractedly and let him guide me to the dining hall. The others have already gotten our lunches and are sitting in our usual seats. I'm relieved there's a little buffer of empty chairs around them and one look at the thunder on Ash's face tells me he's the reason.

"You okay?" Harley calls out as soon as Blaise has me in earshot and Blaise shrugs at him.

I step up to my usual seat next to Avery but I take a

second to think before I sit down. Apparently that's the wrong thing to do because the tension at the table suddenly heightens until I'm choking on it.

"What the fuck has happened now?" Ash hisses, and I quickly drop to my seat.

"I'm trying to decide if I should say it here or drag Harley away so he doesn't rage out and flip the whole fucking table." I mumble and Ash's eyes narrow.

I sigh and turn to Harley before blurting it out. "The Jackal sent men after your mom."

His face shuts down, his body turning to stone and his cutlery drops to crash down on his plate. I reach over and grab his hand, squeezing until I know he's listening.

"Illi dealt with them. He called to let me know he's staying with her for now, but we need to move her somewhere more secure, somewhere far enough away that the Jackal forgets about her until we can... deal with him."

Avery immediately takes over. She's out of her seat and snapping orders down the phone as she moves to the door for privacy. We're too close to where the teachers are sitting for comfort. The Jackal has eyes in the school and we still don't know who they are.

"I'm sorry." I croak, and Harley's eyes flash up to meet mine.

"Don't apologize for that sick fuck; this is payback for us provoking him. Well, fuck him. I'm not giving you up." He says, his free hand closing over the little gold locket at his neck.

I feel like a monster.

All my bullshit is at our door.

Ash watches us both and then says, "Liam's been trying to kill her for years, Mounty. Adding the Jackal to the mix barely changes things. We all have demons stalking us, don't take it out on yourself."

My eyes flick over to him. "What's eating you today?"

His mask settles into place and he turns back to his food. "Joey."

I groan. Haven't we gotten away from that psycho? "What's the little fucker done now?"

Ash gives me a curt shake of his head that I interpret as *not here* but could be *fuck off* for all I know. Blaise snorts and starts on his lunch.

Harley turns his hand to lace his fingers through mine. "I guess I'm going to have to thank Illi now, aren't I?" He says, a little wryly.

I fight the smile threatening to break out over my face and say, "He loves a good muffin basket. Even better if there's blueberry."

By the end of the day Avery has Harley's mom transferred to a safe facility in Switzerland with a permanent armored guard. Illi stays with her until she's on the plane and, though he won't admit it, Harley is fucking relieved to have him there.

I still feel guilty.

I go through the motions for the rest of the day; dinner with Avery, studying with Blaise, then we work on my singing until Avery comes home. Blaise notices how crappy I'm feeling and slips me his iPod before he leaves, kissing me sweetly until Avery bitches him out on her way to the shower.

I climb straight into bed, messing around with the iPod to find a song that will help slow my brain down, when I hear the sound of keys in the door. I frown at the sound. It's barely ten pm, Harley never gets here before midnight.

Ash locks the door behind himself and stomps over to my bed, pulling the sweatshirt he's wearing off and climbing in wearing only his boxer shorts. He sighs and flings an arm over his eyes, channeling the drama of his morbid best friend, but the move only makes his chest look broader.

Oh fuck.

I try to focus on the blank mask over his features, because something has pushed him to come here, but he is something else to look at. A half naked Ash Beaumont has angels freaking weeping at his feet.

I clear my throat twice while I attempt to focus on something other than his nipples but it's hard work. He snorts at me, rolling over to tug me into his arms, and the icy depths of his eyes cool me off a little.

"Has something happened?" I murmur, holding my breath as I wait for his answer because I have so many things on the planner I can't think about another one. I had pushed Joey out of my mind for now, Senior being the bigger threat.

"Are you planning on killing Joey?" Ash mumbles, his eyes screwing shut, and I grimace.

"I think I'm going to have to. He's going to force my hand and he's not someone we can neutralize long term. I have to figure Senior out first, because he's already made it clear that he'll kill you and Avery if anything happens to Joey but... yes. I'll take him out."

Any hesitance I had in telling Ash I'm planning on murdering his brother is obviously pointless because he just nods thoughtfully.

He strokes his long fingers over my face, brushing my hair back absently as he thinks. "The gossip site posted about our relationship and Joey messaged me to threaten you. He told Senior about you too. Mounty, I'm not going to let them get to you."

I swallow roughly at the emotion in his voice, something I'm not sure I ever thought would be aimed at me. "Don't think about it. The Crow will keep Senior away until we can deal with him properly. The only reason I haven't gone in to deal with him myself is because you and Avery are underage. Too many variables. Avery seems to think Atticus would step in for you both but-"

"Fuck Atticus. I'd rather live in the slums with you than owe that dickhead anything." Ash hisses. It's fucking hard work, but I contain my eye roll. How does he go from sweet to asshole in a flash?

I ignore his tantrum and say, "Like I said, too many variables. If we can keep him away from you, and somehow keep fucking *Morningstar* away, then we'll be able to wait until you're eighteen. Then I'll sneak into his bedroom and slit his throat while he sleeps. Or Illi can take a meat cleaver to his throat and then dismember him."

Ash mutters unhappily under his breath at the mention of Illi and I nudge him playfully. Avery exits the bathroom, quirking a brow at Ash's appearance but doesn't make a comment as she climbs into her own bed and cuts the lights. I hear her iPod start up and smile at her attempts to give us a little privacy.

I let my eyes drift shut, ready to sleep and forget about the sociopaths looming over us, watching our every freaking move. Ash presses his lips to mine and kisses me so sweetly I can't believe it's him. He usually kisses me with fire, with dominance, with that arrogance that only a Beaumont can have.

I tremble like a freaking wilting virgin in his arms.

When he breaks away to press his forehead against mine, he whispers, "If I lose you, then everything we've done has been for nothing. If he takes you away from me... I can't let that happen. Every time I close my eyes I see you strapped to that fucking table, bleeding out while they watch, and I won't live through that again. If there's a chance of that, then we need to kill them both. I almost wish you weren't so strong, that you'd dropped out freshman year, because even though I wouldn't have you, at least you'd be safe and far away from Senior."

I will not cry, I won't let myself, but fuck it's hard not to.

When I'm sure my voice won't betray me, I say, "If I had dropped out, I'd be the Jackal's personal whore by now. He would have chained me to his bed and fucked me until I was nothing but an empty, manipulatable shell. Then he would control two seats in the Twelve and be unstoppable. We'll get through this together, like we'll get through everything else life throws at us. As a family."

He nods against my neck, biting the skin softly until a shiver runs down my spine.

I don't know how long it takes me to fall asleep but I'm woken by the dip in the bed and smell of chlorine hits me before his voice does.

"What the fuck has happened now?" Harley whispers, pulling me back into his arms and Ash grunts unhappily in his sleep.

"Nothing. He just needed... me."

Harley nods and kisses my neck, right over the bruise Ash left behind. "We all need you, babe."

CHAPTER EIGHTEEN

THE ONLY WAY TO spend any time with Harley is to study down at the pool while he's at practice. It's stuffy from the water heaters and my notes somehow end up watermarked every time, but it's worth the trouble when Harley walks out in his swimsuit.

As my eyes trace the ridges and plains of his muscles, the Adonis belt I swear had to to be seen to be believed, I absently wonder if I'll ever be able to look at him without feeling lightheaded. It's not like he's some idealized dream; I've seen so many of his highs and lows already, I know he's human. I know he's not some perfect man. But, sweet lord, to look at him is like looking at the fucking sun; searingly hot and dangerous to your health.

I'm distracted from my lusty daydreaming by Ms. *fucking* Vivienne sitting her whorish ass next to me with a smirk.

"Stunning, isn't he?" She says, coquettish in her breathy tones.

I could rip her fucking head right off of her body.

"I would think a teacher in her, what, thirties would

know better than commenting on the physical appearance of students." I snark, channeling Avery Beaumont at her scathing, polished best.

Ms. Vivienne just smiles at me. "Becoming a teacher didn't make me immune to the charms of the younger males. He's only a few months away from turning eighteen and then we'll be free to... explore the attraction we share."

I snort at her, shaking my head at the crazy that's spewing out of her mouth. Harley glances up at me and frowns when he sees the cougar bitch. I give him a sarcastic little wave and palm my knife. He notices and smirks at me, blowing me a kiss.

"Boys that look like him, they turn into men that won't settle for little girls like you. He needs someone with more experience, someone who is more worldly. He's not going to share you with his friends forever."

Huh.

She's just voiced my biggest fear about my guys, and yet the moment the words leave her mouth I know exactly how wrong she is. We're damaged, we're broken, we're desperate, but we're together and we're a family.

There was no jealousy or hesitation in Harley when he found Ash in my bed, only concern for what drove him there. Blaise only gets pissy about being left out of the group... activities, never about sharing. And Ash... Ash wants me safe and happy.

This bitch wouldn't know a fucking thing about what Harley needs, but I do.

"Keep pushing him, Ms. Turner. You'll learn that he's nothing like the pretty little boys you're used to playing with and I am *nothing* like the girls you've threatened away before."

Ms. Vivienne's spine snaps ramrod straight and the

smile on her face now has a viciously sharp edge. "I was told you're a brilliant student, that your IQ is at genius levels, and yet you can't identify when you're outplayed."

"If I'm such a genius why am I not a part of your study group? Why isn't Ash? He's just as smart as Harley. You're a sexual predator and you belong behind bars. If you had any sort of intellect you'd leave Harley alone, because the path you're on leads to a six-foot deep hole."

She blinks at me, then turns on me with vicious intent only to falter as Blaise's says, "There you are, Star. I've been summoned to rescue you from the cougar. Harley's afraid you'll catch the clap from sitting too close to her."

His shadow hits me as I look up at his smirking face, every inch the spoiled rock god of my dreams in his leather jacket and ripped jeans. He winks at me playfully when he catches me giving him a lusty once-over. I might be horny, sue me.

The look on Ms. Vivienne's face... fucking priceless.

"How *dare you* speak to me like that!"

I scoff at her. If I were a nice person I'd warn her of Morrison's poison tongue but, y'know, fuck her.

"You're a desperate, panting whore who can't accept that you're over the hill so you fuck teenage boys to get validation."

She turns beet-red with outrage and I chuckle under my breath, stashing my books away. I don't need rescuing, but it's nice to sit back and watch Blaise destroy someone who's not me for once.

"Yes, I know, you're going to call my parents and go to the principal. Problem is, my parents don't give a fuck and Trevelen is under Beaumont's thumb so... maybe you should chase after someone else's cock and leave Arbour's alone. Also, if I ever see you so much as side-eye Star again

I'll personally destroy you. Are you aware that my aunt is on the school board? Shriveled old hag, but she has a soft spot for me. How badly do you need this job? I think I'll start by taking it from you and working my way up from there."

Blaise's face only gets more vicious as the stunned silence drags out from the cougar and he holds a hand out to help me up. "Avery's waiting to have dinner with us in the dining hall before her ballet class. We shouldn't keep her waiting."

I tuck myself under his arm and don't spare the whore a backwards glance.

———

My PHONE WAKES me the next morning and I don't recognize the number. Avery frowns over at me, unhappy at the early wake up call, and I force my tone to be even and cold.

When I hear the Coyote's voice I straighten.

"I'm not a fan of early mornings either, Wolf, but this is an emergency. I have some information for you and a job. I'm willing to hand over a favor if you're reluctant."

I bite my lip. "What is the information first?"

He huffs down the phone but I wouldn't say it's a particularly joyful sound. "You've royally pissed off the Jackal and now he's gone fucking insane. He's hitting back at the members who took your side in the vote. He's just popped by for a visit here but he seems to have forgotten that I live in a bunker and it could survive an atomic bomb blast."

I groan and rub my eyes. "I apologize that my... issues are now affecting you."

The Coyote laughs at me, still no joy to be found. "I don't regret voting for you. He'll have to try a bit fucking harder than this to push me into taking his side on anything. I'm just calling to let you know he's on the fucking rampage and no one is safe."

Avery gets up to make us both coffees and I switch the phone onto speaker so she can hear the conversation. "Right. Well, I appreciate the courtesy call. What's the job?"

There's a pause and then he murmurs, "You're in love with the mobster's kid, right? He's worth all of this?"

Avery hands me a cup of coffee and climbs into my bed, the side Harley crawled out of hours ago to head into swim practice. "I am. If I have to go to war for him then I will."

"The Jackal threatened my girl. I need you to get her to me and away from him before he gets his hands on her."

I shrug. "Easy. Name and location."

He hesitates and I cuss him out under my breath. "She knows she's your girl, right? I'm not kidnapping some girl you're cyberstalking, am I?"

"We've met."

Fuuuuuuck. Seriously?!

I sigh loudly at him, something I wouldn't do to any other member of the Twelve. "You want me to kidnap a girl you've met but aren't in a relationship with because the Jackal somehow knows you're into her and is threatening her. Does that about cover it?"

The Coyote laughs and says, "Yep. You in or not, kid?"

Avery cuts me a look, cold and calculating, with her phone in her palm ready to start work if I deem this a job we're taking. There's no way around it though, we need as many members of the Twelve on our side as we can manage.

"Sure, I'll do it for a favor. Send her details through to me and I'll have her to you by midnight tonight."

The Coyote chuckles at me. "Oh, I think you can have her here a little faster than that, kid. She sleeps down the hall from you."

Avery's eyebrows nearly hit her hairline and I'm sure mine are close too. The Coyote is stalking a Hannaford girl? For fuck's sake. "Who the fuck is she?"

The chuckles turn into a full fucking belly laugh. "Well, her dad's a senator and her mom's a news anchor so it may make some waves when she disappears."

Avery drops her phone. I have no idea of who this girl is but by the look on Avery's face I've just made a critical error. "Viola Ayres? You're cyberstalking Senator Peter Ayres' daughter?"

"Is that the hot girl you brought to the Lingerie Party? I never caught your name, hottie."

Avery sneers at the phone and I cut in, "Just answer the question, is Viola the girl you're stalking?"

"Yes and I'm not stalking her, I'm just *casually* keeping an eye on her from afar. I mean, I could hack her webcams and watch her sleep at night, but I *don't* because I'm not a pervert. Honestly, Wolf, it's like you don't trust me or something."

I don't trust him, or any other hacker on the planet. Which reminds me; my eyes narrow down at the phone as if he can see me. "I thought you wiped my middle name from existence? I keep getting packages with the name listed."

He scoffs. "I did. There's no way anyone has looked you up and found out your dirty little secret. Must be someone you know."

Fuck.

I can't think of anyone other than the Jackal who knows it.

Fuck.

I share a look with Avery. "I'll have her to you by midnight. Even if I have to gag 'er and drag 'er, she'll be in the bunker by midnight."

To say that I don't have time for Mr. Trevelen's bullshit is putting it fucking mildly.

Avery gave me the rundown on Viola Ayres while I forced myself to eat breakfast, my stomach roiling with nerves over the potential issues, and I try to scrape together a plan for how the hell I'm going to make this work. I sent word to Illi to do the drop off for me, he was far too cheery about it for my liking, and then all I have left to do is... kidnap the girl.

Fuck.

I'm busy trying to look calm around the guys so they don't get involved and complicate things when Trevelen pulls me out of math class. It's our first class for the day, and the second he calls out my name my stomach drops and I share a look with Avery.

Nothing good ever comes from being pulled out of classes.

I pack my bag, my face the picture of calm and stable, while Harley glares at Trevelen like he's seconds away from shanking him. I squeeze his arm gently, discreetly, then follow the principal down to his office.

A shiver runs down my spine as he directs me to sit. The last time I was in this room I was facing suspension and the Jackal got me out of it. I watch Trevelen attempt to pull himself into a power pose but he lacks the spine required to pull it off. I raise an eyebrow at him like a spoiled rich kid and he clears his throat.

"Miss Anderson, I'm going to get straight to the point. There have been... further accusations of unbecoming behavior against you put forward by an anonymous party. This time video evidence has been provided and the school board has made the decision to-"

The door slams open and an enraged Avery Beaumont stalks through, graceful even at her most furious. Not that you'd be able to tell from looking at her that she's pissed, it's more the air around her that gives it away; even the dust particles are running away from her.

My hands have a fine tremble in them, but I clench my fists and my jaw to ward them away.

"Mr. Trevelen-"

"Miss Beaumont," He interrupts and I tense. "There is no reason for you to be here. This issue is about Miss Anderson and her status as a scholarship student. It is none of your concern, no matter how much you wish it were so."

Fuck. Avery is going to destroy him.

Her eyes narrow and she leans forward in her chair, menacing and calm. I speak for her, just to make sure she has all the facts she needs to dig me out of this.

"Who was the anonymous source? I think I have the right to know who is trying to have me kicked out and defend myself."

Trevelen's eyes flash to mine and the regret that flashes there has nothing to do with me and everything to do with his own ass that is now firmly on the line.

He clears his throat again before saying, "She- the source has been granted anonymity by the school board to ensure there are no unjust repercussions. Your roommate has a... reputation for such things."

Avery smirks at him and I settle back in the chair, content to watch her work. I bleed people out for her and she does this stupid political crap for me.

It works.

"I have far more important and pressing issues to deal with than some desperate slut because we both know this reeks of jealous little whores. I'll have your job for this, Richard, we both know I own you. If you're lucky, we won't take your head with it."

"You can't just go around threatening people's lives, Miss Beaumont." He says but his forehead is covered with a thin sheen of sweat that belies the truth in his words.

Avery laughs at him, and I shiver at the sound.

Fuck, I love her.

"Oh, you're mistaking me! It's not a threat, it's a fact. If you fuck with my family, you bleed. Have you not met my father, Richard? The apple doesn't fall far from that tree, I assure you."

Trevelen is now moping his sweat up with a handker-chief, his fingers shaking. "Miss Beaumont, there is nothing I can do about it! The video has now been watched by the entire school board and the ethics committee will have my ass if I don't act upon in. Maybe Miss Anderson should have acted with-"

"Was Miss Anderson the only student in the video? Was she acting indecently by herself? No. This is all an attempt by Ms. Turner to separate Harley and Lips because she's a sexual predator. Are you aware she's fucking a fifteen year old student, Richard? How does your ethics board feel about that? Oh, I'm sure they're fine with it because she's fucking them too. I don't care what it takes, you will make this disappear. If you don't, I'll send my own anonymous letter out to the police and tell them exactly where you buried your first wife. Does Lucinda know the back porch she so dearly loves to sit on and enjoy is built on the unmarked grave you dug?"

Holy.

Fuck.

I did not see that coming.

CHAPTER NINETEEN

V iola Ayres is *nothing* like I was expecting the
daughter of a Senator to be.

She's a senior and has a private room so when we knock
at her door, she frowns and ushers us in. She's taller than
me, but that's not hard. Her hair is streaked with purple
highlights and there's a stud in her nose so tiny you can
barely see it flashing in the light. The teachers here would
struggle to spot the dress code violation and I instantly like
her more than any other girl I've come across. Well, other
than Avery obviously.

The room only confirms she's a different breed. Everything is painted black, and there's whiteboards everywhere
with physics equations and coding on them. She's a genius.

She's also fucking perfect for the Coyote.

"What exactly have I done to deserve a visit from the
reigning Queen Bees of Hannaford?" She drawls, flicking a
wrist between us.

I scoff at her. "I'm not a queen bee, that's more Avery's
kind of thing."

Avery giggles at me, stroking my arm lovingly. "Lips

doesn't like admitting she's alluring and powerful. She would rather enjoy lurking in the shadows and silently slitting throats."

Viola squints a little, glancing between us to try and spot the lie. "Right. Sure. What have I done?"

I rub the back of my neck a little sheepishly, not having thought this out much. I wasn't planning on liking the girl. I thought she'd be some rich bitch I'd just threaten and kidnap, but Viola is... kind of cool.

"Look, there's no easy way to say this so I'm just going to lay it out there." I start and Avery gives me a look.

"Let me, you're not very... diplomatic. Viola, are you currently dating? Or hoping to date someone?"

She scoffs at Avery and makes her way over to the kitchen. "I'm not chasing after your boys if that's what this is about. I don't need to be getting involved with taken guys."

That's it. I love her, too. Fuck the Coyote for making me kidnap her.

Avery smirks at the look I'm giving her. "No, someone else. Someone older, perhaps?"

Viola frowns as she pulls cups out of drawers and starts to make us all coffee. Another mark in her favor. Fuck, I should induct her and keep her safe myself.

"Maybe you should just let the Mounty be blunt about it, I'm not following you at all."

I take the coffee from her and sip. Not bad. "Do you know a guy, around twenty, who's tall as fuck, blond hair, brown eyes, good with a computer? Like, able to hack into the US Defense Force levels of good?"

Viola's eyebrows twitch, an easy tell to spot. "Jackson? Why do you need to know about him?"

Jackson.

I guess he kind of looks like a Jackson. I mean, it must be him. I can't imagine there would be that many guys who look like him and can do what he does in the state. Fuck, at least I hope not.

"Are you interested in him? Crush or something?"

Viola sets her cup down on her table, wrapping her arms around herself defensively. "Why are you asking this? If you're going to try and use me against him, you're out of luck. He's already told me he's not interested."

I groan without meaning too. I hate relationship drama and this reeks of it. "Look, I need to take you to go see him tonight. Something has come up, something life threatening, and you need to go see him. He's... a friend of mine."

Her eyes narrow at me when I pause. She hisses at me, voice scathing, "Are you fucking him too? Are the *three guys* crawling into your bed at all hours of the damn night not enough?"

Oh look, I found a nerve.

I raise a single hand up to stop Avery from pouncing on her, because I don't even have to look at her to know she's about to tear strips off of the girl. "I'm guessing you really like him and I assure you, whatever he said to you about not wanting you, he was fucking lying. I'll let him talk his way off of your shit list. For now, can you just come with me? I just want to get you to him safely so I can crawl into my bed with whichever guy deems it's his turn."

I even wink at her to try to soften her up a little. Avery looks pissed but stays quiet, letting my words sink into the girl's brain.

"Fine. He fucking owes me an explanation for this shit."

Yes, he does.

I CONVINCE Viola to pack a bag, then we walk her down to the staff parking lot where Illi is waiting for us standing beside the most beautiful muscle car I've ever seen. I sneakily take a photo for Harley to drool over later.

Viola takes one look at the Butcher of the Bay and freezes, planting her feet into the gravel. "I'm not getting in that car. He looks like a thug! Are you trying to extort my father for cash or something? I could have saved you the effort, you've picked the wrong kid. He prefers my younger sister."

I share a look with Avery, the quirk of her lip telling me she's just made note of that little gem. I'm not sure what we'll be extorting Senator Ayers for in the future but we have him if we need.

"His name is Illi and he's just driving you over there so stop looking worried. He's my... foster brother." I say, winking at Illi.

Technically, I did meet him in foster care, back when his name was still Johnny, his best friend was Matteo, and together they taught me the meaning of ride or die. Until one day they weren't. My heart feels sore in my chest just thinking about it.

"Come on, little girl, I'm glad to be of service." Illi does a ridiculous little bow and I snort with laughter watching it. He's too fucking huge to look anything but hulking and intimidating.

"I'm not stupid, there's no way I'm getting in that car." Viola snaps, and I decide I love her a little less.

I hold my hand up to stop her from running off, then pull out my phone. I hit dial on the Coyote's number.

"Trouble, Wolf?" He says, smug and playful as always.

I smirk and I'm sure he can hear it in my voice. "Hello, *Jackson*. It's your dear friend Lips here. Viola is all packed up and ready to have a sleepover at your place though she's unhappy that our mutual friend Illi will be driving her over."

The Coyote groans. "Seriously? You're trying to get *him* to drive her?"

"You do understand I'm at school and have no car, right?" I snark and he laughs at me.

"C'mon *Lips*, we both know your little harem has plenty of vehicles for you to borrow. Alexander has eight Ferrari's, for fuck's sake."

Eight?! Jesus.

"That's beside the point. Tell her to get in." I hiss, and hand Viola the phone.

She looks at it like I'm handing her a snake or some shit and I try to make my smile sweet. Avery cackles at me so I clearly fucking failed.

While she's busy arguing with her maybe boyfriend, I sidle up to Illi and bump my shoulder against him like we're close or some shit. "How's things?"

He smirks. "Great. I've killed eleven guys this week for our little crew. I took on a job up the coast while I was there with Iris too, so send me your bank details so I can tithe to you."

Tithe, the cheeky shithead. I snort at him. "Fuck off, I'm not taking your money. Consider it payment for running around after me."

He laughs. "Kid, I live for this shit. I even got to torture the last guy. I *julienned* him as if I were a sous chef and he was nothing but a fucking carrot. I'll send you the tape, looks fucking *sick*."

Avery gags dramatically from where she's eavesdropping and Illi roars with laughter at her. Their easy acceptance of each other is such a fucking gift to me, I wish the guys would take a leaf out of Aves' book and just welcome him into the fold. It's not like he wants to move in, he's got an amazing apartment overlooking the docks in a shady looking warehouse so he can... work from home if required. He does that a little less now Odie lives there too.

"I've moved Odie to a safe house, kid. Since the video of you getting freaky with the mob boy started circulating the lowlifes have been coming at us in droves."

I freeze. Video circulating? Illi notices and swears under his breath. "I thought you knew about it? Sorry. You got more enemies than the Jackal, I'm guessing?"

Avery snorts. "Lips collects them, like trinkets and pets. Nothing she loves more than pissing people off by living her very *best* life."

I groan at her. "I'm just trying to survive! Fuck. Okay, What do you need from me, Illi? Name it, it's yours."

He scoffs at me and bumps shoulders. "Whatever. I'm your *brother* remember? I'll drop the prissy girl off at the Coyote's bunker and then I'll go hunting. Maybe it's time to take the fight to D'Ardo. Stop defending and start attacking. Speaking of that, any of your boys good with a gun?"

I swallow. "Harley and Ash are. I'm not sure about Blaise. I'll check."

I WAIT until family dinner on Friday to bring up the gun question.

Avery cooks a stir fry and for once I take Ash up on his offer of whiskey to go with our meal. I feel like a nice buzz will help me with the headache this is going to cause me. I wait until the table is quiet, the guys all shoveling the food into their mouths like they're starved Mounty street girls, and then I ask Blaise.

The guys all pause their eating. Avery continues, unruffled and smug because she knew it was coming. There's nothing that girl loves more than to be in on the joke.

He blinks at me owlishly, and Harley swears viciously. "What the fuck has happened now? We aren't going to make it to fucking senior year at this rate."

Avery laughs, flicking her wrist at him the way a cat plays with it's prey. "We're doing a fine job. And you can't talk, it's your fan club that is causing all the issues. The video being leaked reeks of Annabelle. Or possibly Ms. Turner. They both stink of desperation so it can be hard to differentiate sometimes."

Blaise snickers at the dark look Harley gives her but she's right. I stay out of it, as always, and nudge Blaise with my foot under the table.

He gives me a little mocking smirk. "Footsies during dinner with Avery? Star, I would have never pegged you as the type to flirt with danger."

Ash chuckles at my withering look and Harley mutters, "She does more than fucking flirt with it."

I roll my eyes at them all. "Just answer the question, Morrison. Do you know how to use a gun? Properly, not just point and pull the trigger. I mean like, assemble, reload, clean, the whole fucking shebang."

He looks uneasy at me again. "I do. I'd rather not though. I'm more a beat-the-life-out-of-them kind of guy."

Ash flicks a sliver of carrot at him. "That isn't any better so don't think you have the moral high ground. You're saying you want to feel the life leave your victim rather than have the clinical, impersonal kill."

Blaise glares at him. "Oh, are we trading psychotic tendencies now? What's your preferred method of killing a man?"

Ash smirks and says, "Whatever is required to make sure they stay dead."

I should find this conversation unsettling.

Whelp, but I don't. I'm suddenly squirming in my chair at the dark parts of them all.

I clear my throat twice, a sure giveaway of what is on my mind from the looks they all give me, and say, "I'm going to get everyone ghost guns. Completely untraceable. Just for emergencies now that the Jackal is being careless and sending guys out to catch us unaware."

The guys all share a look and something tightens in my chest. Avery slips her hand in mine, ready to take my side with whatever they're planning, and I'm so fucking glad she's with me.

Finally, Ash takes a sip of his bourbon and pegs me with a look. "We need to stop with this 'waiting around' bullshit and start being offensive. He's not going to stop until we take him out."

I try not to groan at him but it escapes me anyway. "Do you understand the risks of that? Really? Do you get how much blood will be on your hands, and the cleanup involved? I know we have the finances to back us but fuck, it's a lot. I've lived it. I woke up every day knowing I'm going to kill countless people and pray I'm not going to go down for it. Are you all prepared for that too? Because I've been working my ass off to keep you all out of it and... clean."

Harley cuts me a look, arrogant and haughty. "We're not clean though, are we? None of us are. Even Morrison has blood on him. We're going to figure this out and we're going to fucking kill the Jackal and every last one of his loyal followers. No more peaceful attempts at resolution."

I give Blaise a curious look, interested to know what blood he has on him. I know he's not afraid of a fight, and will jump in to defend his friends without a second thought, but I'd never guessed he'd done anything more than that.

They're all watching me, watching for an answer and I'm not sure I really have one but I squeeze Avery's hand anyway and say, "Okay. Offensive it is. We'll hunt the Jackal."

CHAPTER TWENTY

F RIDAY MORNING I find Blaise missing from our
history class, and I can't concentrate on a thing the
cougar whore says because I don't know where the fuck he
is. When Harley notices me twitching and tells me he's
gone to an appointment in Haven and I send the *utter* dickhead a pissy text about *security* and *threats* and *murderous
sociopaths stalking us all.*

He ignores me.

Ash walks up to my room with me and collapses on the
couch with a sigh, throwing his bag down and ripping his
shoes off. Avery's mother hen act drops in an instant and
she's snarling at him for messing shit up. I head to the coffee
machine. Caffeine is necessary for my survival.

Blaise arrives to family dinner half an hour later covered
in bandages and for a second my heart stops, then I see the
easy grin on his face and I know he's fine. He winks at me
and I blush when Avery cackles at the stupefied look I
give him.

"I told you, I'm filling in the rest of my canvas, Star." He murmurs as he bundles me into his arms, kissing me chastely under Avery's watchful glare.

"Are you going to tell me what you got?" I grumble and he laughs at me.

"You'll have to wait and see. Or bribe me, I'm easily bought. Flash me some pink, Wolf."

I jab him in the stomach but his solid muscles only hurts my hand. Ash smirks at me and tugs me over to sit on his lap in front of the TV while we wait for dinner. Avery is on an Italian kick and refuses to let me help out now she's making pasta by hand.

She's the weirdest rich kid in the fucking building but god do I love her.

"Stop giving my sister lustful looks, Mounty." Ash snarks, and I elbow him.

"She's my favorite, I hope you know that." I snark back and he slips his hand down my waist until he gets to the hem of my shorts. My eyes flare and then narrow at him.

"I'm your favorite." He mumbles into the skin on my neck.

I shake my head, mostly to clear it. "Nope. Definitely Avery. You're my second favorite Beaumont though, so don't feel too bad about it."

His eyes fucking sparkle at me with evil intent and I gulp. I try to move out of his lap and his arms only tighten, trapping me.

"Don't run off. I'm fucking hungry, Mounty."

I blush. My heart stutters in my chest at the warm honey tone in his voice, something I've never heard from him before. Even when we had laid together in bed all those months ago in the Bay, his dirty talk had been whispered and decisive. Not this coaxing.

I can't fucking handle Ash Beaumont seduction if it's like this.

"Dinner's ready!" Avery calls out, and Ash huffs.

"I don't think I'm ever going to get my hands on you at this rate." He grouses, and I kiss him sweetly because I'm just as fucking frustrated.

We all take our usual seats at the table and Harley has already changed into his swim uniform to leave as soon as he's eaten something. The second I see it I remember the last time I saw him wearing it and heat floods my body until I'm blushing like an idiot.

I stare at my plate like it's the answer to all my damn problems because there's no way Avery won't notice the puddle I've turned into. Dammit, I'm drooling again.

Blaise unwraps one of his hands so he can handle his fork but I'm too busy trying not to ogle Harley to see the new ink.

"Did you get stars tattooed on you? You know that tattoos are the curse of relationships, the kiss of death." Avery says in a haughty tone, spinning her long strands of fettuccine perfectly between her fork and spoon.

Blaise gives me a look and I smile at him. I don't think tattoos are the kiss of death for fucking anything. I'm just not that superstitious.

His foot runs along mine under the table and my smile turns into a grin. His eyes fucking sparkle at me and I flush, looking back down at my food and refusing to look at him. Great. So only Ash is safe for now, because he's snarling at his sister.

"Why the fuck didn't you tell me Joey was coming to the Hannaford Family Dinner?"

Ugh. The stupid dinner all juniors and seniors have to attend, even if they're emancipated orphans, to sit and discuss their bright futures with their teachers and families. Fucking yay.

I glance up and see him glaring at Avery, all fire and rage that I don't usually see him aiming at his sister.

Oh fuck.

"You know as well as I do that Lips had Senior removed from the picture until graduation, so he's sending Joey in his stead. There's nothing I could do to stop it, but why would I tell you about it any sooner than I have to? Harley is already an insomniac, we don't need two sleep-deprived, grumpy assholes in the family."

Ash scoffs and downs the rest of his bourbon in one gulp.

What a lovely dinner we're having.

Blaise shoos Avery out of the door for her ballet class and flicks the lock with a little flourish.

"Oh, look. I find myself alone with my Star. Whatever shall I do?"

I smirk and point at our textbooks. "Studying is what you *shall do*."

He laughs at me and pulls his tie off, popping the first few buttons open on his shirt. Fuck. He's worked out that little trick too, the one where my brain melts the second any of my guys start showing extra skin.

I'm fucking doomed.

"You have three assignments due next week." I croak, so fucking ready to cave and he smirks at me.

"I'm just getting comfortable. Didn't you want to see my new tattoos?"

Right. Tattoos. Yes.

I nod and he peels the bandages, tape, and plastic away from the puffy, raw skin of his hands and neck. Avery was right, he's now covered in stars. There's even a little one inked behind his ear, right where he usually kisses me.

"You'll have to tape me up again. My hands are killing me." He grumbles, and I go to rummage around in the bathroom for the first aid kit. I'm especially good at taping hands back together with all of the practice I now get with Blaise and Harley's boxing, and Ash's fight club matches.

Once he's looking more bandaged than a mummy I try to get him to study but he's too damn jittery.

"I'd concentrate better if you were naked." He drawls, running a thumb over the swell of my chest. I bat his hand away.

"No you fucking wouldn't. If you fail this test I will be so pissed."

He shrugs. "I won't. I've been studying at night before bed too. I'm going to pass these classes and next year we'll take all the same classes again so I can keep an eye on you, and then we'll go on tour together before you run off to college to become a doctor or an astrophysicist or... whatever the fuck geniuses become."

I smile at him and close the textbook. "Why would I go on tour with you? Do you need a groupie on hand at all times or something?"

He leans back on the cushions, smug and relaxed. I bite my lip at the sight of him, all bandaged up, secretly marked with *me*. Maybe I hate my name a little less.

"I like the idea of you being there for my every need, but no. I meant because you're going to be singing with me. I'm going to release your song on the album... if I ever fucking release it." He sighs, and rubs his eyes.

"Why haven't you? I mean, the songs have been done for months."

Fuck it, I climb into his lap. He groans in frustration when he can barely hold me, but I do my best to avoid pressing on any raw patches.

"I'm thinking about leaving my label. Don't tell anyone that, not even Ash. He'll have a fucking aneurysm at me over it. But they keep interfering with the song writing and I'm just... I write and play to get shit out of my head. Because I love that I can turn the weird thoughts and pain into something I can hand to someone else. The band's agent wants me to clean up the lyrics and go more mainstream. He didn't like the new songs, he said they're too raw. Fuck him."

I frown at him and say, "They're amazing. They're the best songs you've written so far. I should know, I've heard them all."

He quirks an eyebrow at me, playful again. "You haven't though, have you? You never did open my present."

Fuck. I hadn't.

I shake my head and he smiles at me. He cups my face gently, pushing my hair away from my face and kissing me sweetly.

"I was so pissed that day. I'd put my fucking heart in that box and you wouldn't open it. I can't blame you, I'd been such a fucking dick to you, but I had put myself out there and hoped you'd see it... see me. It doesn't matter, Star, I have you now. My little muse. My sweet Nightingale, pretty and sings so sweet."

He starts to ramble, my crush only getting worse as he begins to describe all of his favorite parts of me, most of them naked body parts, but some of them immensely more intimate, like the scar the bullet from Diarmuid's gun left on my skin and the soft patch of skin on my shoulder they all seem to be obsessed with.

I WAIT until Avery heads to ballet the next afternoon and I dig out the package Blaise had sent me, untouched and hidden in my duffle bag under my bed. I'd been so tempted, so many times, over the summer break but it was like Schrodinger's box. What if I opened it and it was just candy, something small and meaningless? Or, more terrifyingly, what if it wasn't?

Now I know it's his heart, I have to see what it is.

I use my knife to slice the tape open and my hands shake as I lift the lid. I find a notebook and an iPod older than the one we now share.

I grab the notebook first and find poems, lyrics, stories, etchings in the margins and gold ink accents everywhere. The lyrics are all of his new songs, things he's written in the last two years, but they're all just a little different from the polished versions he's given me to listen to. I read the entire notebook, cover to cover, in disbelief.

It's about me.

The whole thing is a love story about me.

The drawings are of my hands, the scars on my leg, the dark shadows of my eyelashes on my cheeks.

The plump curve of my lips.

The songs have my name in them, over and over again, the longing and worship on Harley's face is reflected in the melodies of Blaise's songs. I can't breathe to read them, my lungs squeezing tight until I feel dizzy.

Thank fuck I didn't open it last year.

I would have had a stroke and died.

When I finally move away from the notebook, every word and image seared into my brain for all of time, I turn the iPod on to find it full of every single Vanth Falling song, even the covers Blaise recorded and released before he was famous. There are songs I hadn't ever heard him sing so I know they've never been made public because I followed his every move online back when I lived in the Bay.

Fuck.

It's every little piece of him I've always wanted, and I've been hiding it under my bed for months.

CHAPTER TWENTY-ONE

A VERY IS FUSSING with her already perfect hair and I'm busy trying to figure out why the fuck we're being forced to a 'Formal Family Dinner' at Hannaford if none of us have family attending when a booming knock sounds at the door, like a giant's fist is trying to punch it's way through.

I frown, motioning for Avery to stay in the bathroom, and move to open it.

Illi and Odie grin down at me.

Holy sweet lord, this cannot end well.

"La Louve, I am so happy to see you! When Johnny told me he was coming up to see you, I insisted on coming too! He said you're the top of all your classes, that's incredible! Oh, I've missed you." Odie *gushes in French, wiping at her eyes delicately.*

She smiles sheepishly at me and I sigh, holding my arms out so she can hug me. She doesn't realize I've had my family slowly teaching me to be normal, to tolerate all of the touches that happen between friends.

Avery eyes Odie critically for a second and then holds out her hand. "*Avery Beaumont, it's lovely to meet you.*"

Odie grins at her, her eyes flaring in delighted surprise, and takes her hand to pull her gently in to kiss both her cheeks in a very European flourish. "Odette Illium, but I prefer Odie. Your French is perfect! It is such a relief to meet more of la Louve's friends and be able to talk to you is wonderful. My English is still very poor."

I shake my head at her. "It's very good, you're just a perfectionist. What are you two doing here? I'm glad to see you but it's risky."

Illi tucks Odie into his side and says, in English because his French is less than perfect, "The Crow has managed to keep Joseph Beaumont Sr. from coming to the family dinner, but I heard he's sent the little freak to take his place. Joey's been asking around about you and I think it's time to deal with him. I can make that as permanent as you want, kid."

I nod and cut Avery a look. She knows better than any of us what the repercussions of Joey's death will be.

"Senior will strike at us if anything happens to Joey. If Morningstar refuses to take the job then Senior will come and do it himself."

I cock my head at Illi. "What's your assessment of Senior?"

He eyes Avery for a second like he's worried about her reaction to his words, a very rare consideration from him, and says, "I think he's a fucking psycho and with the amount of money he's sitting on like a gargoyle we need to be very careful about how we get rid of him. We'll be better off taking him out and then the little freak."

I can't help smirking at his nickname for Joey. "Not a fan of Junior?"

Illi grins and kisses the top of Odie's head. "I'll skin the fucker alive for you, kid. I'll do it with pep in my fucking step. If he looks sideways at you or your girl tonight I'll gouge his eyes out."

I nod and turn to Avery. "You might want to warn him. Illi would do all of that for us and infinitely more for Odie."

And there's no man on the planet that wouldn't look lustfully at Odette Illium. She's everything the cougar whore is trying be; a sensual, blonde bombshell who oozes sex appeal. She looks delicate against the wall of muscle and violence that is Illi, but she's tall and curvy in all the right places.

The price she sold for at the skin markets was fucking *terrifying*.

Avery nods and pulls out her phone while I grab both of our blazers, a full uniform being a requirement to attend the dinner. Illi cracks another joke about the skirts and socks, and I shoot him a vicious look while Odie giggles at us both.

I open the door to leave and find the guys waiting for us. Harley smiles and kisses me, then does that weird, bro head dip at Illi who claps him on the back like they're best friends. Ash grimaces at them both, sidling past to get to Avery. Joey's attendance tonight is wound tight around his neck like a noose.

Blaise looks like he's going to vomit.

"What's wrong?" I murmur, and I step out of our room towards him.

Holy.

Fuck.

"Lips, these are my parents. Blaine and Casey Morrison. They've decided to attend tonight's dinner even after they disowned me and told me they no longer see me as their son." He says, his voice steady, but the look on his face makes me want to reach for my knife and start stabbing. His mother just stares at her feet like she'd rather be anywhere else but her son's school.

The look his father gives me would make me cringe with shame if I weren't the Wolf.

"I thought you said she was your girlfriend? Why is she kissing your friends?" He says, leering at the scant inches of my bared skin. I want to throat punch him so freaking bad.

Blaise ignores him and slings an arm around my waist, whispering so low I struggle to hear him, "Sorry, Star. They just showed up, I had no idea they were coming."

I nod and move away from the doorway so the others can get through. I glance up and see Illi's mischievous grin. Oh, fuck yes.

"Blaise, you remember my foster brother Illi? He's brought his wife to see me and they're both joining us for dinner. They're very excited to be here." I say, and Odie grins at Blaise with a sweet little, "*Bonjour.*"

Illi grins at Blaise, then turns that baring of teeth towards his parents. I swear I see Blaine Morrison shit his pants.

Perfect.

Blaise squeezes my side and Illi winks at us both.

One big, happy family.

THE DINING HALL has been transformed into a luxurious looking restaurant, complete with Christmas decorations and waiters in three piece suits. Illi snorts at the entire thing and Odie giggles at him like she's the school girl here. I smile at the sound until my eyes hit Joey Beaumont and it slides right off my face again. Fuck, I hate that psycho.

"The seating is assigned. I made sure we'll be seated together." Avery whispers, her arm tucked in mine tense as she eyes both of her brothers.

Illi stares between them with the bloodthirsty glee that I usually see from Blaise, but he's still too worried about his own family's appearance to enjoy the bloodshed that's potentially about to happen.

Ash pulls out my chair for me while death glaring at his brother, ever the reckless asshole, and I sit between Illi and Avery. Joey takes Harley's seat across from me and I shake my head at him.

"Are you trying to provoke us? Because we're just here for the food." I say, more to remind Ash than Joey.

"My little Mounty. I really didn't think you'd make it at this school for so long! And without fucking anyone! I heard the bet was still ongoing. I'm starting to wonder if you're hiding a cock under that skirt and that's why you won't fuck anyone."

Odie makes a sound of disgust and turns to Ash, "How is this disgusting man related to you and Avery? He shows none of your high breeding or decorum when he speaks."

Joey smirks.

I learn that all three Beaumonts speak perfect French when he replies for Ash. "I'm the better sibling. If you want to stop fucking gang bangers, I'll happily choke you with my cock."

I count Illi's breaths as he slows them down, deep inhales and long exhales. I stare at Joey while I wait, crunching the numbers on how much a full cleanup will cost us if Illi slams his meat cleaver through Joey's throat and bleeds the fucker out.

Fuck I'd love to see that. I think I'd sleep better at night afterwards.

"I call dibs. I'll let Ash help but I'm skinning the fuck." He finally murmurs to me and I nod.

Odie looks down her nose at him, and then says in perfect English, loud enough for the Morrison's to hear, "*Mon monstre*, cut his heart out for me when you're done. I would like to eat it."

The people within earshot all freeze and turn to look at the stunning blonde, but she stares Joey down like there's nothing even slightly worrying about the psycho.

I guess if you share a bed with the Butcher you're immune to these things.

Illi raises her knuckles to his lips and kisses them like she's the very center of his world. My heart aches a little and I remind myself that if they can find each other and survive what they have together, then I can survive the threats we're facing, with my family intact.

After another minute of silence, I hear Blaise's dad start questioning him about his classes but he's too far away from me for me to chime in. I huff in annoyance but then I hear Harley snap, "He's in the top of his class in every subject and he's got a 3.5 GPA. *Fuck off*."

The food had better be fucking amazing.

Ash stares Joey down, watching his every move while he grins at me. I ignore his eyes, focusing on his hands to gauge how doped up he really is. The tremble is there, enough to know he's recently gotten his high and he's still riding the effects. When the crash starts there's going to be bloodshed.

I can fucking taste it in the air.

The waiters all start to serve dinner and I stare down at the plate in front of me with disgust.

"What the *fuck* is this?" Illi says, and both Odie and

Avery laugh at him, sharing a look that sets off warning bells in my head. Avery is the ice queen and, fuck, Odie is sultry fire. If they hit it off the whole country will fucking crumble. Sign me up for front row tickets. I meet Illi's eyes.

My sadistic glee at their camaraderie is written all over him as well.

The waiter fumbles over his words, intimidated by the fierce look on Illi's face and the manic bouncing of Joey's eyes. I wave him away before he pisses himself and Illi mutters at me, "What the *fuck* is a study of peas? They're vegetables, they can't go to fucking college!"

I nod, agreeing completely and craving some burgers. Avery and Odie both eat the blobs of colors delicately and I just swirl my spoon in it to make it look like I've eaten some of it.

There had better be a steak coming up next or Illi's going to riot.

"I heard you're fucking half my family now. What's my brother's dick got that mine hasn't? Other than the clap now he's wetting his dick in slum pussy." Joey says, ignoring his plate entirely. I watch from the corner of my eye as Ash carefully sets down his fork.

The hand around his knife only tightens.

I sigh, and make a big show of looking around at each member of my family, all of them glaring at Joey. I decide that if we're hunting the Jackal, then we're done dancing around Joey too. I can put him in his place without killing him... maybe.

I set my cutlery down and cross my arms, staring at the drugged fuck with unflinching rage. "You've made your decision to come here and start this fight with me. I've warned you, over and over again, that you have no idea who you're dealing with."

Joey laughs at me, too loud and with that crazed edge it always has. The Morrisons both angle away from us even though I know they'll hear every damn word. Good. I want them to know who they're pissing off every time they belittle and scorn their own damn son.

"I'm not afraid of some little slum whore who fucks thugs for protection."

I smirk at him. "Your siblings are under my protection and you can tell your father that. If either of you attempt to harm them in any way you answer to the Wolf of Mounts Bay."

Joey's eyes narrow, the knife in his hands still pointing in my direction. "Are you fucking him too?"

Illi snorts, "How the fuck are you still alive? Go back to the children's table, dickhead. The crack has set you back a few years if you can't figure it out."

Ash smirks at Illi. "He's alive because he hides behind his father. He's too fucking stupid to be a real danger. If we wipe him from the board we'll face Senior but we can take him on. I vote we kill him."

Avery sighs quietly, low enough that Joey won't hear it but I have. I slip my hand into hers under the table.

"Yes, well little brother, you should know by now that Father will kill the little slum cunt. And the pathetic bitch you shared a womb with. I'd personally like him to take the blonde slut too. She'd look perfect strapped on his table. All that blonde hair... just like Mom."

Harley manages to get an arm across Ash's chest before he flips the table but it's Avery I'm watching. I need to know if we're changing the plan because there are too many witnesses here.

Joey laughs, throwing his head back and sounding like a

fucking loon. "You'll always be fucking weak if you're taking orders from pussy."

Ash smirks and points the knife at Joey. "That's your problem, Joey. You're too fucking stupid to notice when you're outmatched, and, brother, you're so far out of your league now you can't even see it."

THE COURSES STEADILY GET WORSE.

By the time dessert comes out, I won't even say what it is but I don't think Illi will ever hear the word 'foam' without feeling queasy and enraged again, Joey's hands have progressed from the fine tremble to full-blown shakes. Avery watches them as closely as I do, her appetite disappearing as it becomes clear he's going to rage out.

Joey takes a phone call and leaves the dining hall, blowing Odie a kiss because he must be the dumbest motherfucker on the planet, and some of the tension leaks out of Avery.

The waiters clear our plates and everyone stands to leave. Well, we stand to leave. The other students, parents, and teachers all start to mingle and network like this has been a lovely, productive dinner and I'd rather gouge my own eyeballs out than stay here.

"I'll hunt the little fuck down for you and finish him off." Illi murmurs, and I shake my head.

"Despite what Ash said, the plan is still to leave him for now."

Ash snorts and tucks me under his arm protectively. "I

think we should contact Morningstar and give him a counter-offer. Whatever the fee is I'll pay it."

I groan at him but it's not the worst idea.

As we walk back towards the dorms, Blaise's dad starts to grill him about me.

Namely, why Ash is draped all over me if I'm Blaise's girlfriend. I pretend that I'm ignoring the dick but I hold my breath while I wait for the answer.

"We're in a poly relationship. It works." Blaise says, and Avery's eyes are *impressed* as they catch mine.

His father makes a noise of disgust and I tug out of Ash's arm, just enough to turn around and give the vile man my best impression of Avery's ball-shriveling glare.

"You seem to be having trouble getting it; no one here gives a fuck about you or your shitty opinions. If you want to keep breathing, you'll keep them to yourself." I say, low and even toned. The color seeps out of his cheeks and he glances at his miserable son.

"What the fuck have you gotten yourself into now?" He mumbles, snapping his fingers at Blaise's mom and tearing off down the hall without even saying goodbye.

I take a deep breath to stop myself from chasing him and stabbing him through the eye, and Ash tugs me back into his side.

"Sorry, Star." Blaise murmurs and I shake my head at him.

It's been a clusterfuck sort of night.

Avery slips her arm through mine and frowns down at her phone as I help direct her. Illi grouches about the shitty dinner and Odie laughs at Harley's snarky comments. I enjoy it for about thirty seconds, then we round the corner and find Joey and two of Senior's bodyguards waiting for us at the bottom of the staircase. Great. Perfect.

I move to tuck Avery behind Blaise and he nods at me, understanding my silent instruction to protect her if this goes to shit. One of Joey's babysitters takes a step forward and then falters when he sees Harley, second only to Illi in sheer width of muscle. Harley is itching to make them all bleed. Now he knows the extent of what Senior and Joey have been doing to his cousins, he wants to bleed them all the fuck out. He was civil enough during dinner because of the witnesses but now we're alone, Joey is on thin ice.

I step forward, drawing his attention away from Ash. "You really are too stupid to survive, Joey."

He grins at me, the whites showing all the way around his eyes so he looks fucking deranged. "Father has told me to bring you home, Mounty. He's eager to meet the fabled Wolf of Mounts Bay."

Then he reaches out to grab my wrist, his fingers nearly brushing my skin, and Ash moves faster than I've ever seen a fucking human move. I swear right this second he's found his superpowers.

Joey is against the wall, pinned by his throat, before his bodyguards realize what's going on.

"Lay a hand on her again and I'll fucking bleed you out. I'm done with your games and your little lessons. I'm done toeing the line. Come after Lips or Avery and I'll destroy you both."

Joey's eyes dance around Ash's face, searching for some hesitance or faked bravado, but there's only the cold killer his father wishes he would embrace there.

Illi gently moves Odie so she's standing with Avery behind Blaise, then he flanks Harley with that little fucking grin of his slashed across his lips. His movement catches Joey's attention, but he only addresses the bodyguards, dismissing the psycho entirely.

"Do you two really want to die for this dickhead? Because this isn't going to be a beating; I don't do beatings. It's going to be your blood on my hands and your body melting away to nothing in a vat of acid. Is that how you were planning on spending your night?"

Joey's eyes flash back to Ash's face. "Do you really think some little gangster queen can keep you safe?"

Avery snorts at him, her tone as cold as ice as she says, "We've found bigger monsters than you to call our own. Run along to Senior and tell him that, too."

Ash chuckles and shakes his head. "He's not going to run anywhere. I've waited a long fucking time for this."

Harley doesn't peel him off of Joey until the little fuck is unconscious and unrecognizable.

CHAPTER TWENTY-TWO

For possibly the first time in my life I am excited for Christmas.

Well, not Christmas Day, I'm still trying to weasel my way out of that but the rest of winter break is going to be perfect. No plans or expectations, I'm going to eat my body weight in ice cream and figure out how the fuck we're going to hunt the Jackal without getting ourselves killed or found out by the Twelve.

Illi sends me a giant box of information he's been compiling, file after file of shady shit the Jackal is pulling on the other members of the Twelve, including putting a mole in the Boar's MC clubhouse. I know for a fact the giant biker will personally wage war with the Jackal if he finds out.

He's fucking touchy about his clubs.

The file about me curls my gut, but at least we now have a full list of the teachers on the Jackal's payroll. Ash is going to have to quit the track team until we can oust Mr. Ember from the coach's position and Mr. Trevelen is on borrowed time.

The guys move into our room and rotate between my bed and the pullout. Avery takes it all very well, happy we're all safe and in one spot, and the guys are all on their best behavior. Mostly.

Blaise makes it his mission to piss Harley off, over some spat I have no interest in taking sides over, and he starts to play his guitar and make up stupid songs at all hours of the day and night. Ash and I secretly love it. Avery puts in her headphones and ignores us all in favor of flirting with Atticus over text messages. It's messy and loud and fucking perfect.

I wake on Christmas morning to Avery's face hovering over mine. I startle, making Harley grunt and mumble in his sleep, and she motions for me to stay quiet and follow her to the kitchen. It feels like a trick, like she's using her Beaumont Bullshit to force me into accepting the day, but I smell the coffee she's brewing and decide to play along.

For now.

I sit at the table and Avery fusses over me until there's a perfectly made hot coffee and a plate of French toast in front of me and I'm a happy girl. Avery waits until I've eaten the whole plate before she speaks.

"Tell me why you hate Christmas." She says and I groan at her.

I take a deep, *deep* gulp of my coffee. "Did you know that even foster kids and kids in group homes get presents from Santa? Every kid on my street used to ask what I'd done wrong every year when I had nothing. Once, when I was eight, I decided it had to be because we never had a tree. So I made one from shit in the backyard and decorated it with all the crap I'd made at school and put it all up in my room. I wrote a letter, asking for food because I didn't want a bike or a fucking doll or some other shit. I was hungry. I woke up to nothing, like always and sat there and wondered what the fuck I'd done to piss the fat man in the suit off. The next Christmas I was in the group home, and I puked when I saw my name on a present. I gave it to one of the other girls. I hate it. Last year, your present was the first one I've accepted. I fucking hate this day and I hate how fucking weak it makes me feel. Can I go back to bed now?"

Avery stares at me and I'm so freaking glad there's no pity on her face. I know she's feeling it, but she must know how badly I don't want to see it. All I can see in her eyes is the bloodthirsty Beaumont rage.

"Thank you for telling me. We should start working on our plans to hunt the Jackal soon. I'm not going to involve the guys in it. We'll make better plans without them getting all alpha-male over this."

I nod and sip my coffee. If there was any day I needed the caffeine to kick in and give me super powers, this would be it. Avery doesn't push me or ask any questions, so we sit in silence while we try to think of a way through this mess but no matter what angle I take, it all boils down to one thing.

"The problem is Luca." I say, frowning down at my now empty coffee cup.

"The hot guy that always kisses you in front of Harley? I thought you said he was nice."

I blow out a breath. "Yeah, he's nice but he's also loyal. I think he's so nice to me because he thinks I'm someday going to submit to the Jackal and become his boss too. He's always around and I haven't seen anyone get past him."

Avery taps her chin delicately. "You don't think you could get past him?"

"If they haven't switched up his security I could be in

and out in under a minute and none of them would know the Jackal was dead until morning."

Avery nods. "But they would have changed everything since the meeting."

I hum under my breath and think it through. Should I go to him or draw him out? "I can't just send Illi in; I would never risk him like that and stealth will be our biggest asset. Plus, the other members can't find out what we're planning."

I need to take the guys to the gun range and see if any of them have some skills I'm unaware of. I know Harley has been trained by the O'Cronins and Diarmuid is the best sharpshooter I've ever seen. If Harley inherited those same family traits then maybe I can set him up on a roof to take the Jackal out that way.

"I need to meet with the Crow and discuss how we're going to handle the Jackal. He seems to be waiting for him to spiral and from what the Coyote said that's already happening."

Avery sighs and gets up, grabbing my plate for a second helping of breakfast. As she's piling on the toppings Harley groans and rolls out of my bed, rubbing his eyes like he needs another ten solid hours of sleep. I know the feeling well.

He kisses my cheek and then joins Avery in the kitchen to make himself a coffee.

"You forgot the sprinkles." Harley mumbles and starts rummaging through the kitchen cupboards until he finds them.

Avery arches an eyebrow at him and he scoffs at her. "It's Christmas morning, Lips deserves some fucking sprinkles on her breakfast."

I blush, swooning a little that he even remembers that,

and Avery sighs at us both. "If the two of you can't contain your sickening love-struck selves I'm moving out."

I laugh at her, pissing her off until she drops a small perfectly wrapped box in front of me.

"You promised me no presents." I glare and Avery shrugs, smug-as-fuck.

"I already know you got us all gifts. You think I didn't search the entire room while you were in the shower last night? Please, I know you're not that dense. The boys even helped me."

I glare at Harley and he just shrugs sheepishly. Sighing, I shake my head. "There's no way you found the presents. I hid them too damn good from you."

Avery leans back against the table and smiles at me. "Sure I didn't."

Ugh. Fuck.

She has to be bluffing because there's *no way* she figured it out.

Avery laughs at the look on my face and flounced off to wake the other two guys up so we can start this awful day. Harley puts the plate of extra breakfast, complete with sprinkles, in front of me and kisses my cheek again.

"Thanks for joining us." He mumbles and moves to the couch.

Okay, maybe it's not completely awful.

I finish my toast and have a quick shower. Ash doesn't move until Avery wafts a coffee under his nose and Blaise bitches us all out for waking him. I end up on the floor in Blaise's lap by the time Avery wrangles everyone into exchanging gifts. She doesn't mention my sad little story this morning and I could fucking kiss her for it.

"I remembered that you didn't want things bought for you." Blaise mumbles into my shoulder, slipping our shared iPod into my hand. I smile, because a new playlist sounds *perfect*, and all that I really want. He smiles back at me like I'm the freaking sun, and my heart does this silly little back-flip in my chest, then he turns the iPod on to show me the name of the song.

It's our song.

The one he wrote for us to sing together for choir. He's recorded it for me, somehow in secret because I know Ash still hasn't heard it yet. I furiously blink back tears. I will not cry in front of everyone, dammit!

Harley makes a pissy noise and I glance up to find him shaking his head at Blaise. "Of course you gave her a fucking song."

Blaise snickers under his breath and I elbow him. "What's wrong with a song? I love it."

"It's cheating because you're the hardest fucking person to buy for and Morrison has a secret fucking weapon." Harley mutters under his breath, but he hands me a small box with a card taped on top. I find a hot wiring kit and a promise to teach me to boost cars over the summer break. It's actually fucking perfect because when I am not wanting to learn more skills to keep me alive in the Bay?

I kiss him, with a little too much tongue for Avery's liking, and then Ash tugs me away from him and hands me a large black box, tied with luxurious black ribbons, and I start to panic a little that he's forgotten how weird I am about money and bought me something expensive.

"If that is sex toys or lingerie then please tell Lips now, I don't need to know the specifics of your relationship." Avery snipes, and Ash gives her a cool look as he hands her a much smaller box with a kiss to her cheek.

"I saved that one for later." He whispers into my ear and I shiver. I don't know if I want him to be joking or not.

I take a deep breath and open the box to find a bullet-proof vest, brass knuckles, a tactical pen, and a new belly holster for my new ghost gun.

"Ah, nothing says Christmas like weapons." Avery snarks, but I smile at Ash and give him a quick peck now Avery's pissy.

"Good call; I don't even care how much it all cost you. I love it, thanks."

Then I stand up and move the cabinet under the TV to the side until I can access the loose floorboard there that houses my safe this year. Avery groans and jabs Harley in the ribs. "I told you she'd hide the presents in there!"

I laugh at her and open the safe, slipping the little velvet bags out for each of them and handing them over.

They all look at the bags with varying degrees of curiosity and apprehension. And lust but, unsurprisingly, that comes from Avery.

"You're giving us favors for Christmas?" Ash says.

I shake my head. "Just look in them, for fuck's sake."

Avery squeals when the deep blue diamond rolls out, caged in a delicate platinum sphere and hanging from a chain. Each of the guys have them as well, though the spheres look less *pretty*.

"Whose color is blue?" Blaise says with a frown, and I smile at him.

"Mine. I don't give out favors, but if any of you need to I want you to have the diamonds ready. If something happens and I'm not there you can use that as currency."

Avery clears her throat and puts the necklace on, clutching at the diamond like it's the most precious thing she's ever held. "And how exactly did you pay for these? There's at least three million dollars worth of diamonds here."

I smirk at her. "I didn't pay for them. The Vulture did. The favors he owed died with him and I had eleven diamonds from him. More than enough to cover these."

Blaise grins at me and blows me a kiss, breaking the awed tension in the room. "Aw, you want to start your own gang. Do I have to start calling you boss?"

THE NEXT DAY, I wake up early feeling better now that Christmas is over with.

Avery refuses to take the day off from her rigorous training sessions for ballet, and I walk her down to the gym even though we're basically alone. She reads out her conversation with Atticus to me and I do my best to be supportive. It's fucking hard because I'm still firmly on Team Atticus-can-fucking-grovel but what Avery wants, Avery gets.

And Avery wants Atticus in the worst way.

When I've dropped her off at the gym and I'm sure there's no random spies hanging around, I head back to our room to wake the guys up and have breakfast. I want French toast again, because when don't I? Ooh and ice cream, and a giant mug of coffee. If Harley makes me breakfast I might kick the other two out to show him my, ahem, gratitude.

I'm still chuckling at my own hilarity when I unlock my door and step in, freezing as the door swings shut behind me.

Three sets of eyes take me in.

Harley is shirtless, holy hot *damn*, sitting on the couch holding a bottle of whiskey. Ash looks deliciously sleep rumpled and he has shot glasses lined up on the coffee table in front of them both. Blaise looks tired and grumpy from where he's sprawled out on the floor.

"Wanna play a game, babe?" Harley says, waving the bottle at me as if that will entice me into playing along. I blush as I come out of my trace and I kick my shoes off, stalking over to slump down on the couch between the cousins.

"Can we just drink? I was also kinda hoping for breakfast." I grouse, but the second Harley slings an arm around my shoulders I'm in. Why does he smell so good?!

"I've got my truths up my sleeve. You owe me." Ash says, his tone like warm honey and it's almost enough to distract me from the words themselves.

Fuck.

I'd forgotten about that.

"Well, what do you want to know then?" I feign indifference but his smirk tells me I fail miserably.

Harley frowns at him and cracks the bottle of whiskey open, taking a swing and then handing it over to me. He hates not knowing shit about me, and Ash having the upperhand will be grating on his nerves.

Ash keeps his eyes locked on mine as he swipes the bottle from me, laying out the shot glasses and filling them to the brim. "I'll be gentle, Mounty. We'll play by your rules and if you don't want to answer something just take the shot, and I'll wait until it's just the two of us to get the real answers."

I groan at him because nothing in this world will piss Harley off more. "I'll answer your questions. You guys can take shots if you don't want to. You go first, Ash, since I owe you."

He stares at me for a second and I almost think I see

some regret on his face, but he asks the question anyway. "Why do you hate your birthday?"

I take the shot.

Harley curses under his breath, I think he's ready to argue with Ash for me, but I wave him off. "I can tell I need to be drunk for the rest of this conversation. I hate my birthday because my mom died on my birthday. Next question."

Blaise glares at Ash and tugs me until I end up in his lap. They've all taken to just picking me up and moving me where they want me and I'm still deciding if I like it or not.

I grab the bottle and start in on it. "C'mon, ask your questions. I'm giving you ten minutes and then I'll be fucking wasted and useless."

Ash opens his mouth but Harley cuts him off. "I thought you hated your mom. Why miss out on your birthday every year to mourn someone you hate?"

Another gulp, I'm not going to make it to ten minutes. "I'm not mourning her. I'm commemorating the day I got sent to a group home and met a boy there with big brown eyes and sweet words who told me he'd protect me and keep me safe. I'm commemorating the last time I blindly trusted someone and he turned out to be the biggest fucking monster under the bed. I'm mourning naive Lips Anderson who had no idea that boy had been watching her for months and sold her mom the dirty batch of heroin. I might have met him there but he'd been watching me for a while and my life ended the same day she died. Lips died too, the Wolf is all that's left. Next question?"

Harley takes a shot and then punches Ash in the arm so hard he winces. "Ask one of us one, babe. It's not just you playing."

Oh. That could be fun. I hand Harley to bottle and tap

my chin with a finger dramatically. Blaise snorts with laughter at me, his back pushing into me as he leans forward to grab a shot and down it.

Fuck it, I'll go for the throat. "Why don't you two get pissy that Harley always sleeps in my bed? Why is some shit harder to compromise on than others?"

Ash scowls at me, sighing and rolling his eyes. "You won't know this because Harley always sleeps well around you but outside of your bed he's an insomniac. Last year we had to drug him to get him to close his eyes for longer than twenty minutes at a time. I'm not going to get *pissy* over him finally having some sort of regular sleeping pattern. Would you say no to me sleeping in your bed while he's in there?"

I shake my head. It's a stupid question, I've had all three of them in there before.

"Well, there's your answer. Yes, I'd like you on my own occasionally but I knew what sharing you entailed when I agreed."

I look at Blaise and find him nodding. "I'm less... grumpy about it, I guess. I don't give a fuck who's in your bed or who you're fucking, Star. As long as I'm one of them."

I blush because that's sweet but also I feel a little like a skank for wanting them all. For enjoying the hell out of them sharing me. Ugh. I'm a total whore.

Harley brushes his knuckles over my cheek. "Stop over thinking things again, babe."

Blaise takes another shot and then moves me around in his arms like I weigh *nothing* which isn't fucking possible with the amount of ice cream I now get to eat every week.

He pouts at me and my eyes glue themselves to the inviting sight of his lip. "Why is this only truths? I want there to be dares as well. Kiss me, Star. I dare you to."

I laugh at him and squeeze his arms, the whiskey lighting my blood up until I'm all soft and pliable. "You don't have to dare me to kiss me."

He bites down on my shoulder and I have to consciously tell my hips not to rock forward into him. I glance back to find Harley and Ash are both watching us, not a shred of jealously in either of them, but I can taste the *want* in the air.

Fuck.

This is heady and overwhelming and fucking perfect.

Then keys slide into the lock and Blaise is cursing low and vicious under his breath and I'm the one pouting.

Firm hands band around my hips and Ash pulls me out of Blaise's lap. "Time's up, Mounty."

ON THE SUNDAY before classes go back Harley sends everyone else back to the boy's room while I'm in the shower getting ready for bed. When I step out and find him alone, perched on my bed in nothing but his boxers I gulp. Not in fear but in pure fucking lust.

"Uhm-"

He cuts me off. "I need another truth from you, babe."

I frown and step up until I'm standing between his legs, his big hands spanning my hips and drawing me in until he's taking up all of my senses. He raises his eyebrows at me and I nod.

"Avery went through my budgets with me when my inheritance came through and I told her to take out the exact amount I owed her. She was short and when I confronted her about it she told me you've been paying for my shit. Is that true?"

Fuck.

Avery hadn't warned me about this, dammit!

Harley nods like it's written all over my face even though I'm sure it's not. "So while I was being an asshole to you, you were paying for my tuition, my hotels, my fucking food. Everything."

I clear my throat. "Look, I had to. The Jackal was looking for any little opening to take you out and having you on the Beaumont payroll would have been the easiest opening for him. I was keeping you safe."

He shakes his head and lets his hands slide down until he's palming my ass, squeezing and kneading. "I'm not angry, babe. I'm hungry. I'm fucking starving and you're the only thing on the menu I want. One taste of what you've got and now I'm fucking addicted. Spread those legs for me."

Oh *god*. How the fuck did I end up with three Alpha males? And how the good *goddamn* did I find the only Alphas in the history of the Earth that are happy to share with each other? Sweet lord, I'm going to have a fucking heart attack.

Harley gets tired of waiting for me to come to my senses and do what he's asking, so he grabs the backs of my thighs to lift me and spread me out on the bed how he wants me. I'm only wearing my shirt and panties, and the tiny triangle of lace covering my pussy is torn from my body like it's a fucking insult to his very nature, and he groans like he really is a starved man.

"Take a deep breath and settle in, babe, because I'm not stopping until you've come on my tongue at least eleven times. One for every fucking diamond you lost that night for me."

I squirm and try to sit up, his hang ups on the favors and the money grating on me, but he flattens a big palm against my chest and pins me to the mattress. I want to say the dominant action pisses me off but the trickle of my wetness that lands on my sheets prove that's a lie.

"There is no way I can come eleven times." I croak and he scoffs at me.

"Start counting, baby."

By the fifth orgasm I'm nearly crying from the overstimulation but he's ruthless, driving me out of my mind with sensation until I'm a sobbing mess over the bed. Number eleven leaves me with numb fingers and toes, I'm fucking destroyed and he's the most smug asshole you've ever seen as he curls me onto his chest. I can feel his dick digging into my belly and I quickly decide that even Avery walking in here right now couldn't stop me from making him come too. I give myself thirty seconds to figure out how to work my limbs again and then I flip up to straddle his legs.

Harley's eyes flare but he gets on board with my plan pretty freaking quick, sitting up and pulling me until I'm right where he wants me.

"Get this fucking shirt off." He mumbles, and I laugh as he rips it off of me. My hips roll down on his, grinding away mindlessly and leaving a wet patch on his boxers. He groans like he's being murdered and I swear it's the hottest noise *ever*.

"Fuck babe, these tits." He bites his lip so hard I expect to see blood, and his eyes worship all of the newly exposed skin. His calloused hands are rough against my soft skin as he cups them, rolling my nipples like he had back at the docks.

"Do they feel fine?" I snark at him even though my breath hitches in my throat and I sound like a tramp. I'm still just a little pissed about his comment last year and fuck it if I'm not going to give him shit for saying it. He doesn't take any notice of me; all of his focus is centered on my boobs.

His hands squeeze and stroke, he mumbles, "Perfect," and then he ducks down to suck my nipple into his mouth. *Holy sweet lord fuck.* I'm dripping. When he moves over to the other nipple he catches my eye and, with a wink, he growls, "Taste perfect too, babe."

I moan and try to remember what the hell I'm doing. Right. I'm going to suck Harley's dick and I'm going to do it right. I pull his face back up so I can kiss him, pulling his hair to angle him just right. Fuck, he's like a drug.

"Why aren't you naked yet?" I mumble, biting at his lip.

He chuckles at me and then tugs at his boxers, lifting his hips and grinding into me as he gets them off, and then he's naked as well. Oh, Lordy.

He kisses me, deep and long and entirely too fucking hot, while he strokes himself. I whine into his lips and wrap my hand around his dick as well, craving the heat and the weight of it and needing a few seconds to figure this out. He grunts into my lips, moving my hand until I'm stroking him exactly how he likes it, firm and curling around the head.

Fuck him and his rational thought.

I wriggle down his body until I come face-to- well... dick. Harley's legs tense up. I glance back up at him and he's gritting his teeth like the sight of me face-down in his lap is all his dreams come true. Huh. Maybe it is. He moves his hand away from his dick as I lick my lips.

Good, I don't want him playing with what's mine right now.

I wonder if the guys would tattoo my name down their dicks, too?

I wrap my hand around the base and give it another tug, enjoying the heat and weight of him in my hand. Harley runs a gentle hand through my hair, his eyes soft on mine, but I don't want soft. I want him shaking with need like I am whenever he touches me.

"You've been tested lately, right? I refuse to swallow if you haven't." I say, arching an eyebrow at him even as my face flames.

He freezes for a second and then all of the gentle in him burns out, replaced by heady lust. "We all got tested when we agreed to share you. We're clean. Now make me come, babe. I want to taste myself on your lips."

I groan, my pussy waking up for round *twelve*, but there's no time for that now. I run my tongue up the length of him, swirling around the head like he's a spoonful of ice cream and I'm craving that sweet cherry on my tongue. Harley grunts when I do it again, slow and teasing, I want to push him like he pushes me.

When I see his jaw clench I finally close my lips around him, taking as much of him in as I can, forgetting I need to breathe now I have him in my mouth. I pause for a second, just long enough to get my bearings and then I suck, pumping at the base with my hand because there's no way I can fit his whole dick in my mouth or my damn throat.

Fuck, I can't wait to feel him buried deep inside my pussy. I groan around him and the noise he makes has me humming to keep him on edge.

He starts to ramble on, mindless streams like he can't control his mouth. "Fuck. *Fuck*, baby. Oh... that's my girl. How the fuck is this the first time you've done this, fuck me. You were made to take my cock, babe."

I know when he gets close because his hand threads into my hair and fists tight like he's going to pull me away but

I've made up my mind. I'm going to swallow, at least this once. If it's gross I'll never do it again. He tugs a little and I only suck harder until he's coming down my throat.

It's not French toast and ice cream, but it's not terrible either.

Harley pulls me up and into his arms, moving me around until he can kiss me, slow and sweet. He's fucking perfect.

I could sleep for a week.

When I tell him that he tucks us both up in my bed, flicking the light off, and pulls his phone out. I assume it's to ask Avery to sleep in the guy's room but when he chuckles I suspect he's fucking bragging.

"What do you think you're doing?" I murmur and Harley pulls me onto his chest, cradling me gently against him.

"Just making sure Blaise knows I don't need any lessons on how to make you come, baby. The little fuck could learn from me."

I roll my eyes. "Of course you've made it a competition. Of course."

Harley drops a kiss on my head and murmurs, "It's not a competition. We both just want you. But if it were a competition, we both know I'd be winning it."

I bite him in retaliation and I fall asleep to the rumble in his chest under my ear.

CHAPTER TWENTY-THREE

S OMEONE IS BREAKING IN.
   I hear the window open and a body climb lithely in. It's too skilled to be a student, this is the efficient work of someone who breaks into places a lot and they're moving quietly enough that even Harley doesn't wake. I reach over and grip my knife as I hear the clinking noise of chains rattling on a pair of boots. *Great.* I know who those belong to; I've heard that noise too many times in the past before.

I slide a hand over Harley's mouth carefully and he wakes up instantly.

"You might want to get some bars on those windows, girlie."

Harley curses loud and vicious as he gets out of the bed. He pulls on boxers before he hits the lights. He grabs one of Blaise's shirts that's hanging on my bedpost to pull over my head, using his body as a shield so his uncle doesn't get an eyeful. Diarmuid watches us both with a cackling laugh.

"I thought you didn't mind sharing her, *buachaill beag*?"

One minute Harley is helping me lift the blankets and get

out of the bed discreetly and the next he's landing a severe right hook into Diarmuid's cheek, knocking him to the ground. I scramble forward to grab Harley but he doesn't lay into him. He just stands over him with fire in his eyes and says, "If you imply she's a slut up for grabs again I'll fucking kill you."

Diarmuid rubs his jaw and stands, frowning. "Makes no fuckin' sense to me. I hear a rumor the girl you're in love with is out with both your best friends and I expect you to be dealing with it like a man would. Instead you're fuckin' sharing her?"

Harley shrugs. "I don't care if you get it. Is that all? See yourself out."

Then he turns his back and leans down to kiss my forehead gently, cupping my cheek sweetly until I'm a puddle on the floor.

"Right. Wolfie's off limits. I'm not here to talk about your love life anyway, I'm here because I'd like to join your merry little band."

I freeze and cut a look at him.

I do *not* trust Diarmuid. I don't trust him one fucking bit. Harley glares at him and then flicks his eyes over to me, his eyebrows doing a complicated dance I don't quite understand.

Fuck it. "Why?"

Diarmuid pulls out one of the chairs at the bench and slouches down into it, too casual for my liking. This is still my fucking room and I'm the Wolf of Mounts Bay, for fuck's sake.

"The Jackal wasn't very happy with me choosing your side in the car. He's making my life pretty fucking difficult so I need to swear allegiance somewhere. The Crow is a cock, no chance of me signing up under some suit pretending to be rough. I'm not a fucking biker, so the Boar's out."

I roll my eyes at him and cut him off. "Well, I don't take people in out of fucking pity so no. Try the Viper or the Fox."

Diarmuid grins at me and shrugs. "They've both sided with the Jackal. Besides, you took the Butcher in. He'd be dead without you. If my little nephew isn't sharing you with the sick fuck then what's he giving you? I'll pay double."

I use Harley's body as a shield to pull yoga pants on without flashing my ass at his uncle and then I stalk forward to stand in front of the Irish bastard.

"He gave me his loyalty, without question, like he always fucking has. You don't have a loyal bone in your body, O'Cronin. Fuck knows how Éibhear had it because the rest of you lot certainly don't." I snap, and hope that isn't crossing some line with Harley.

Diarmuid's eyes flick between us and the way his face sets I know Harley's backing me perfectly. Thank fuck.

"Right. You want loyalty, little girl? Name your price and I'll pay it. What's it going to take to prove my loyalty?"

Harley scoffs at him. "Maybe start with showing her some fucking respect."

Diarmuid's jaw clenches. "My apologies. Wolf, what can I do?"

I roll my shoulders back and stare at him while I think. I don't want to induct him, I don't want a fucking empire, but we could use another set of skilled hands while we're being hunted. Fuck it.

"The Jackal has put out a hit. I need every single man, woman, and child in the Bay to know that touching anyone under my protection is signing their own death warrant. The Butcher is aiming for subtlety at the moment so we don't rock the boat with the other members."

Diarmuid snorts. "The Jackal has flipped the fuckin' boat. The boat has sunk, litt- Wolf." He catches himself and shoots a look at Harley.

"Right. So I need you to be obvious about it. If you want to prove you're going to be loyal and one of mine I want the entire fucking state to know that they could catch a bullet between the eyes at any second from the best sniper in the country if they cross me."

Diarmuid's eyes narrow at me and I stare him down. Harley steps up until he's at my side and close enough that if his uncle tries something stupid, like pulling one of his guns on me, he can take him out before he can pull the trigger. I'm not worried. Diarmuid will never be a trusted member of our family, even if he does prove his 'loyalty'. He's only ever looked out for himself. He might be pissed about his father killing his brother but he didn't come looking for that revenge until Harley was old enough, and big enough, to do the dangerous work himself.

I don't trust this man.

"Fine. I'll start shooting every Tom, Dick, and fuckin' Harry that so much as whispers your name wrong. At what point does this get me in?" He says, standing and straightening his jacket and running his fingers through his mussed, shoulder length hair.

I shrug at him, nonchalant. "Impress me."

He snorts, then gives me a ridiculous and very obviously mocking bow, then leaves through the door. Harley watches his every step and doesn't relax until the door clicks shut behind him.

"He's not being inducted." He says, and I shake my head.

"No. He's not. But he can lighten Illi's workload for a while until we know if there's another reason he's coming to us."

I WAIT until family dinner before telling the rest of the guys about our midnight visitor.

Avery immediately gets on her phone and orders bars for the windows in both our rooms and I kick myself for not thinking about it sooner. Blaise gets on Harley's case about his fucked up family and Ash ends up snapping at them both to cut their shit out.

"The real problem here is what the hell is going on in the Bay." He says, and I nod.

"It's war. The Coyote warned us, and now more of the Twelve are choosing sides. We have the Crow, because he will never side with the Jackal so as long as we toe the line we have him. The Coyote and the Boar have both refused the Jackal. I need to find out where the others fall."

Ash snorts. "We're not toeing the line though, are we? Sending the O'Cronin dickhead after the Jackal's minions is a move against another member."

I smirk and shrug. "What the Crow doesn't know won't hurt him. Or us."

Avery sighs and stabs at her curry with extra force. "If we're turning this into a business meeting then I think you should all know that Annabelle is amping up her slander campaign and I'm having to clean up after the disgusting gold-digging whore. She's gone to every member of the school board about your relationship and said that she doesn't want Lips slandering the good name of Hannaford by... participating in orgies."

Blaise chuckles under his breath. "Are you three having orgies without me? I thought we discussed this, all for one and one for all."

I slap a hand over my face to try and hide my blush while Avery screeches like she's been stabbed.

"It's not fucking funny." Harley snaps, and Blaise flicks a pea from his curry at him.

"It's called lightening the mood, asshole. What can we do about Annabelle that Avery isn't already doing?"

Avery cuts through them both before they can start fighting again. "Kill her. I vote we just get rid of her."

I blanch and gape at her. I mean, I knew she was a bloodthirsty dictator but I kind of thought I'd have to convince her to let me kill Annabelle. Well, I assume I'm the one killing her. I doubt anyone else will put their hands up for the task.

"We talked about this. She's a dumb slut. We can't just run around killing dumb sluts." Harley says and takes a swig of his beer. I narrow my eyes at him and he grins sheepishly.

Ash looks between us both but I can tell he's uncomfortable. "I'm with Harley. If we kill her we're as bad as Joey and Senior."

I shrug and look at Avery, but she too busy rolling her eyes. "And of course Blaise will side with you and majority rules. I'll just keep running around after her when we have a permanent solution at hand that we ignore."

I bump her shoulder with mine. "I'll gut her for you the second she looks sideways at you. Or tries to touch one of the guys."

Avery huffs. "And what about you? I want her in the ground so she stops spreading bullshit about you."

I grin at her. "Aw. That's why you're my favorite."

WHEN CLASSES START after winter break, I bury myself in homework again. I finish all of the readings for our literature class, the workbooks for math, and I blitz past Harley in our history class. I even offer to do his half of the assignments so he has less on his plate and can spend more time with me.

The look he gives me would kill a lesser person.

I shrug at his pissy attitude and focus on Blaise's tutoring instead. I don't want to sound like a smug-ass-bitch but my smolderingly hot rock god is in the top half of all of our classes thanks to our study sessions. I stand firm on my rules, no fooling around until everything is done, and that motivates him like nothing else.

The nights we run out of time before Avery arrives home I go to bed cranky and frustrated. The only thing that helps is knowing Harley will climb in later with his wandering hands.

I wake on Friday to find him still fast asleep next to me. He always wakes before me, he has swim practice and never shirks any of his responsibilities. I frown and deliberate over waking him but the dark circles under his eyes worry me enough to leave him.

Avery makes us both coffees, moving as quietly as she can, and I shoot her an appreciative look. She shrugs and joins me in the bathroom as we get ready for classes.

"He needs to drop the study sessions. The cougar skank

is working him too hard." She murmurs, and I try not to let the fury in my blood take over.

Working him hard.

I'll fucking stab the bitch.

Avery cackles at me, running her fingers through her hair even though it's already perfect. I scowl at her but with the toothbrush in my mouth I just look stupid.

The bathroom door opens and Harley blinks at us both, his eyes bloodshot and bleary.

"You could fucking *knock*, you Neanderthal." Avery snaps, but he just shrugs.

He kisses her cheek as he passes by her, then cups my cheeks as he kisses me. When he moves to the toilet I shove Avery out of the bathroom so he can get ready in peace. He's so fucking tired I might stab someone on his behalf today.

I hope Annabelle pisses me off and it's her blood on my knife.

Avery heads out for our classes but I wait for Harley to finish up. He takes twice as long in the shower and I make the decision that he's taking the day off. He can sleep in my bed all day.

He stumbles out of the bathroom in his uniform and I point at the bed with a stern look.

"In. Now. Don't argue with me, Arbour."

He smirks lecherously but the yawn that takes over his face destroys any chances of flirting his way out of this. He pulls his tie off, smirking again, then I watch and drool while he strips down to his boxers.

Fuck, temptation has a name and it's Harley fucking Arbour.

"I need to get to class but you're sleeping today. I'm not asking." I say, but the raspiness of my voice ruins the stern words. He walks over to me, his eyes burning my skin with the intensity of his gaze, and I gulp.

"I'm fine, babe. I wouldn't mind spending the day in bed with you though."

I gulp again and shove him into the bed, my hands lingering a little on him by accident. Totally an accident.

I tuck him in, ignoring the looks he gives me even as my cheeks flame, and I kiss him softly. "We need to sort Miss Vivienne out next. I'm finishing the bitch and getting you back."

He smirks. "Whatever you do, make sure I'm there to see it."

CHAPTER TWENTY-FOUR

THE WHISPERS that follow me only get worse now Annabelle is campaigning.

If I spot her in the hallways she scurries off like a fucking cockroach because she knows I'll break her in half if she so much as opens her mouth in front of me.

Avery watches her every move, waiting for an opening to destroy her. I try my best to forget about her. As long as she's not trying to touch one of the guys she's not my problem.

Weeks later, I wake to Blaise stroking my hair away from my face, whispering sweet words into my ear until I'm shivering and reaching for him.

"My brother was born this morning and my mom called me. She wants me to go see her, I think she's fighting with Dad over it. I'll be back in a few days, Star."

I blink up at him and then press my lips to his gently, a sweet kiss to say all the things I can't speak out loud to him; I'm sorry, I'm worried, I hope you're okay... I love you.

"It'll be fine, Star. I just didn't want to leave without saying goodbye. I'll text you when I land." He murmurs against my lips, his fingers still stroking away like he knows the anxiety that's curling in my gut.

I need to get past my worries about being away from them, but with the threats we have nipping at our heels I just want us all together and watching each other's backs.

"Come home the second it gets bad, Blaise." I whisper back, and he shrugs, nodding a fraction but in that distracted way that tells me he's already preparing to be in his father's presence again.

When Avery and I meet Ash and Harley for breakfast in the dining hall Ash is in a foul mood.

I quirk an eyebrow at Harley and he scoffs at me. "Isn't it obvious? His boyfriend is gone so he's pouting."

The look Ash gives him is so fucking cutting, I'm surprised Harley doesn't actually bleed from it.

"He's just gone home to meet his replacement sibling at his mother's demands but the woman is so fucking spineless that the second his father starts his bullshit she'll cave and send him away. Sorry for being concerned he's going to come home in a pine fucking box."

I swallow roughly and Avery sighs. "Can you not freak Lips out? She gets twitchy the second one of you are in trouble and I don't feel like making a cross-country trip on the fly. I never pack what I need under those sorts of pressures."

I try to focus in my classes but my mind keeps wandering away. I'm so far ahead it doesn't matter but I know it freaks Harley out when I space out. He keeps touching me, just little brushes of his fingers on mine, to try to pull me back into the real world but nothing works. Those three words keep circulating in my head: pine fucking box.

I decide it's an ice cream for dinner sort of day and

Avery brews me a perfect cup of coffee, perching on the couch with me while she texts Atticus. Their flirting has been taken to the next level, constant and consuming. The little smiles and giggles she gives her phone make me so freaking happy but just as terrified.

What if he's a dick? Or a rapist too? What if he hates me and I have to pretend to like him? Ugh. When I say this to Avery she laughs at me.

"Don't be stupid, Lips. He has no choice but to love you. You're nonnegotiable."

I sip my coffee with a little smile as Ash stomps through the door and gives me a look that spells fucking trouble.

"What now?" I groan, and he grabs the remote and flicks through the channels until he lands on a news station.

There's Blaise standing outside a hospital in New York with his dad at a press conference. He looks fucking miserable and the smug satisfaction on his dad's face makes my jaw hurt from clenching so fucking hard.

"My son was born in the early hours of this morning. He's healthy and my wife is now resting in the capable hands of the hospital staff."

Even his voice pisses me off. I cut a look to Ash and he murmurs, "Wait, he's about to sign his own fucking death warrant."

My eyes snap back to the screen.

"Yes, we've made the decision to remove Blaise from the family business and trust. He is old enough now that he can make his own decisions on these matters. He has a... flourishing career ahead of him in the music industry and the Kora board has moved to sever all ties to him."

Sever all ties to him?

This dickhead has just publicly announced he's disowning his fucking kid?

"I'm going to gut that motherfucker." I snap and Ash nods at me.

"Only if you get to him first."

BLAISE TEXTS TO say he has business meetings all week with his agent about the new album he's been putting off releasing. I tell him he has seven days to get his ass home before Ash and I charter a flight to come drag him ourselves. He sends me a bunch of hearts and laughing emojis.

I'm not joking. Ash texts him the same thing and I think he finally gets that we're dead fucking serious. Five days later, while I'm alone in my room after classes, a little lost without our tutoring sessions my door opens and Blaise stumbles in, drunk off of his ass. I groan under my breath as I move straight to him.

"I think I need a lie down, Star. Just give me a minute. I need - I need a minute." He slurs and I get him over to my bed.

A man walks in behind him, but I ignore him as I help Blaise strip down to his boxers then tuck him into my bed. I rummage around in the kitchen until I can find a bucket to leave on the floor for him. I pray he doesn't need it.

The man is so quiet I almost forget he's there until he says in a lecherous tone, "So you're the pussy he's tied himself to then? I was hoping it would be the little dark-haired one, the icy bitch. She would be fun to have on tour."

My spine snaps straight and I look over at the fucking perverted dickhead. "Excuse me?"

He smirks at me, stepping towards me with a swagger

like he thinks I'm into forty year old guys with thinning hair and dopey, drugged up eyes.

"I heard you like to be passed around. I would've preferred the other pussy but I'll take yours."

I look down at Blaise but he's passed out. I'm guessing this is his agent, David Fyre. I don't want to fuck up his career by killing the dickhead but I'm also never going to accept being spoken to like this. I also know for a fact Blaise would lose his fucking mind if he was sober enough to hear it.

I palm my knife. "I'm assuming you're the agent. You have ten seconds to get out of this room before I remove you myself. I'm only asking once."

The smirk on his disgusting face only gets bigger as he takes another step forward and the gods smile on me because the sound of the door unlocking stops him in his tracks.

Ash storms in and stops when he gets a look at the expression on my face and my hand in my pocket. His eyes cut to the agent and his lip curls.

"Fyre. You should leave." He says, cold and no-nonsense.

The fucker tips his head at him like they're such good friends and leaves with a little sleazy wave in my direction. Ash opens his mouth and I cut him *the fuck* off.

"I will never stand in the same room as that man again without stabbing him. I'm not going on tour with him. Firm pass. Avery is *never* allowed in his presence again. Nonnegotiable."

Blaise mumbles in his sleep and rolls, groaning. Ash throws a pillow at his head as he steps up to me. "What did he say to you? I'll go and deal with him now."

I shake my head. "Blaise can decide what to do with the sleazy pervert. Just leave it. Why are you in a shit mood?"

He grabs my wrist and tugs me until I'm in his arms, pressed against the hard lines of him. I tell my treacherous knees that they shouldn't be quivering now I've spent this much time around the asshole but he's too fucking hot to be real sometimes and the possessive way he just moves me where he wants me does something to my insides.

Also my panties fucking disintegrate but I swear I'm running out of them being around these guys.

"You're sleeping in my bed. Not tonight now that idiot is home and wasted, but tomorrow. I'm done waiting and if any little fuck starts talking about you being in there I'll gut them."

I WAKE the next morning to three large boxes at our door labeled, 'not heads' in Illi's scrawling handwriting.

I snort and text him to tell him he's an idiot.

I don't bother opening them, I already know exactly what they are. Blaise groans like he's being murdered and Avery snarks at him, though she's a little more gentle about it than she normally is. I make him coffee and nudge him towards the bathroom to get him moving. He's already missed a week of classes and I don't need him falling behind just because his father is a fucking asshole.

After classes I drag everyone back to the room. I hand the boxes for the guys over and they open them to find Illi has decked them out for murder. Ghost guns, knives, holsters, and a promise to teach them all how to use them effectively over the summer break.

Blaise's eyes are still bloodshot and bleary as he mumbles, "Fuck. We are a gang now right? This definitely means we're a gang."

I consider stabbing him just a little. He cackles at me like he knows exactly what I'm thinking, the asshole.

Harley pulls a holster out of his box and adjusts it until it sits over his shoulders nicely, then he rolls his shoulders back like he's testing the feel of it. "These are good. Comfortable and lightweight. We should be able to wear them under a jacket without the sheep noticing."

I smile at him and knock his shoulder with mine, teasing him, "Are you good enough with a gun to be carrying all the time? Maybe you should wait for your lessons."

"Get me a rifle and a scope and I can hit a beer bottle lid a half mile away with wind resistance." Harley shrugs, and I gape at him.

That's pretty *fucking* good.

"Maybe we should be getting you to take the Jackal out from a distance. I feel like now we're building a fucking tactical team when I was supposed to be coming to school to get away from that life." I mumble, and Avery tilts her head at me.

"We don't live in a safe world, Lips. We don't live in the normal, blue collar world on the television. We'll always be chased by demons because we have power."

I nod and huff out a breath while I reevaluate my entire exit plan.

Finally, after stewing on it for five minutes, I get up to make another cup of coffee. "Do we have any ice cream left? I need the calories to plan this shit out."

CHAPTER TWENTY-FIVE

W ITH ASH's demand for me to go stay with him still
ringing in my head I decide to just get the fuck
over the whispers and the risks of the school board finding
out and to stay there for a night.

I wait until Saturday when they're all busy; Ash is out
for a run and the other two are at the gym for their usual
afternoon of boxing. Blaise has a lot of rage to burn through
these days thanks to his dickhead father and Harley is
bearing the brunt of it in the ring. Good thing he's stacked
and can take it.

I tell Avery my plans and she smirks at me as she hands
over the key. When I blush she snarks at me, "I'll text them
to be gentle with your sweet virgin body."

I think about killing her.

Okay, lie but I do think about messing with her scarves
until she has to press and refold the whole damn box tower
but the psycho would probably enjoy it.

I don't bother packing a bag because Avery has a drawer
full of clothes over there and I'll steal a toothbrush from one

of them if I have to. It's just me, my knife, and my newly cut key.

The boy's dorm is thankfully quiet.

I hold my breath until I'm safely inside with the door locked behind me. The room is different from last year and I toe my shoes off to walk around. Blaise's bed has been shoved in the corner to make room for a mountain of music equipment, speakers, and guitars in black cases. His bed is covered in lyric books and guitar picks, his acoustic guitar slung over his pillows like he set it aside seconds before leaving. His last album hasn't even been released yet so it makes no sense to me that he'd be working on new songs. Maybe it's all just stress relief.

Harley's bed is bare, his books still in boxes and the patchwork blanket missing. He's barely sleeping here anymore and with the extra study sessions with the cougar whore he hasn't even had a day off to unpack even though we've been back at school for months. I make a note to force him to have another day off.

Ash's space looks the most lived in and I instantly feel guilty as fuck over it. I know he's trying to be respectful, I know he's trying to make sure nothing gets broken by pissing Avery off, but fuck. I need him. I need his snarking and his asshole nature. I need his fierce loyalty and the ruthless way he defends what he loves.

I know that now includes me.

I text him to tell him I'm waiting in his bed, and seconds later he texts the group message to tell everyone to fuck off for the night. I blush and giggle like a freaking schoolgirl then I climb into his bed and bury my face into his pillow while I wait. My eyes drift shut and I fall asleep even as the excitement builds in my belly.

The dip in the bed doesn't worry me at first because I'm

so used to waking up to one of the guys climbing in to join me. It's only when I hear the high-pitch and, definitely, female giggle that I bolt upright in the bed and snap the light on.

Annabelle *freaking* Summers has crawled into the fucking bed.

She stares at me in shock and then sneers, "You!"

I shove her off the bed with my foot, ignoring the shooting pain it causes me, and then I seriously fucking consider stomping on her face until she stops breathing.

"What the fuck are you doing in here?!" she screams and I gape at the bitch.

"Are you fucking kidding me, it's my boyfriend's bed! What the fuck are *you* doing in here? How the hell did you get in?" Fuck am I glad I fell asleep before I stripped off. I scramble out of the bed and grab my phone. I spot Harley's missing keys dangling from her fingers and see red.

Annabelle stands and looks down her perfect nose at me. "I'm not stupid, I know the boys will get sick of slumming it with your cheap, Mounty pussy. It's only a matter of time before they come back to me."

Yep. She's clearly fucking crazy and that's all I can take.

I take the keys from her and if I snap one of her fingers while I do it then the bitch deserves it. I ignore her screaming and cussing me out while I shove her out the door.

It's completely irrational but I get fucking livid and throw a little tantrum. If the psycho bitch goes to the school board again, I'll be expelled. I let Ash talk me into sleeping here and now I'm dealing with his *shared* psycho stalker ex. I call him ready to leave a scathing voice mail but he picks up.

"That impatient for me, Mounty? I'm already coming up the stairs."

I snort at him and snap, "Annabelle fucking Summers just climbed into your bed and woke me up from my nap. I've kicked her the fuck out and I'm going back to my own bed while I wait to see if this gets me expelled. Just a courtesy call." And then I hang the fuck up to the sounds of him cursing the whole damn universe out.

I LOCK the door and turn off my phone while I try to calm down.

It's only when I hear the door unlocking that I realize they all have *fucking* keys and can get the *fuck* in and I need some *fucking* space! I stomp to the bathroom and lock that door instead. They'd have to break the damn thing down to get to me and if they do that, well, I'll stab them.

I turn the shower on and then sit on the floor, doing some deep breathing to calm the fuck down. Like Mariana's fucking Trench levels of deep.

The soft knock startles me and I frown. I can't imagine Ash knocking like that.

"It's me, Mounty. Ash called me to deal with Annabelle and I told him to deal with his own sloppy leftovers." Avery says, and I unlock the door for her, cutting the shower off now I know I don't have to pretend. I can't look her in the eye, I feel all raw and exposed at my little tantrum. Fuck, I'm being pathetic.

I say that to Avery and she breathes ice at me. "No judgment. *Fuck* them."

"I just- I knew it was a bad idea to go there. I knew it! I let him talk me into it and now I've been spotted in his bed by that bitch and for all I know she's managed to get a photo of me there. You're going to have to save me from being expelled again and the fucking whispers are only going to get worse!"

Avery nods and fluffs with her hair in that way she does when she's plotting and texting. I wait her out, pulling my socks off and starting to strip to have a shower. Avery does always tell me hot water heals all.

When I step under the hot spray, Avery hums quietly under her breath and lifts her phone to her ear. I can't hear whoever is on the other end of the line but I watch instantly as a slow smirk slides across Avery's mouth.

"Oh, I'm sure it *is* a pleasure to hear from me, Summers. I have some news for you... I did warn you. If you piss me off again, I'll have your scholarship revoked... well, crawling into my brother's bed pisses me off... I can and I will... how about instead of slutting your way around my family you find another cock to worship... I hear Remy is desperate and he's due to come into a reasonable sum...you're not in a position to be picky Summers. Oh, and if you go to the school board about Lips again I won't put out a social hit. I'll end you."

She hangs up and smiles at me, genuinely sweet, as she leaves me to my shower. "I'll go make us a coffee. We can pull the drawers in front of the door so the idiots can't get in and then watch Dirty Dancing with ice cream."

I laugh at her enthusiasm for fucking with the guys and nod, lathering up and cleansing the shitty mood right out of my skin.

When I'm finished and wrapping myself in a big fluffy

towel the front door bangs open and I stop breathing so I can hear who the fuck it is.

I hear Avery snap, "If you walk into that bathroom, she will tear your testicles clean off of your body, and I'll stand by and let her."

The bathroom door slams open and Ash storms in, kicking it shut behind him. I clutch my towel like he hasn't watched Harley eat me out in public and blush like an idiot.

"I have had the patience of a fucking saint." He says, and I gape at him.

"Do you want a fucking medal?" I sputter and he steps forward until he's crowding me back into the bathroom sink.

"No, I want you to trust me and trust that there's nothing that trashy whore could do that I couldn't fix for you. They want to kick you out? I'll fix it. They want to bad mouth you? I'll fix it. They want to hurt you in any way? *I'll fucking fix it.*"

His eyes are like the center of a flame, searingly hot blue that burns me until I'm panting up at him. I can't function or form a reply when he's looking at me like that.

I pull away and root around until I find a clean set of bra and panties, matching and chosen by Ash last year. I try not to blush and fumble as I slip them both on while his eyes roam over my skin possessively. When I reach for my shirt he grabs my hand and tugs me into his chest. Snapping the bathroom door open, he barks out, "Go away, Avery."

Avery startles from where she's sitting at the kitchen bench with her coffee texting, her eyes wide as she takes us both in.

I gape at Ash, and from the indignant noise his sister makes I know she's just as pissed about it. "This is my fucking room, asshole!"

He smirks at her and my heart stops. Oh fuck. "Well,

I'm about to lay the Mounty out on the closest flat surface and spread-"

"DO NOT FINISH THAT *FUCKING SENTENCE!*" Avery screeches, scrambling out of the chair and grabbing her ballet bag. Cursing him out, so fucking colorfully I can't believe it's her doing it, she storms out, slamming the door behind her.

I could die.

Ash only looks more determined once we have the room to ourselves.

"I'm still pissed off." I say, because a sweet little declaration hasn't changed my mood. Okay, it has changed it a little but I'm still practically vibrating with anger.

"Good. It'll only make you come harder."

Sweet merciful lord.

"Wait, you can't just-" he cuts me off with a blistering kiss and then I forget why the fuck I was arguing with him.

One of his hands wrap around my throat so his thumb fits under my chin, tipping my head back to where he wants it. It should *not* be a turn on, especially with his family's history, but I fucking *gush* at his firm grip.

He walks me backwards until I'm pinned against the table by his body, his dick pressing against my stomach and holy shit I forgot how big he is. I forget I'm kissing him, dazed and a little terrified, and he scoffs at me, tapping my hip until I hop up onto the table. When I move to wrap my legs around his hips he holds my legs down, spreading them wide. I frown at him, because I might be nervous but I don't want to stop, and the smirk on his face only gets wider.

"Lie back. I want to enjoy the lingerie I picked for you. I've spent a long fucking time thinking about how it would look on you."

I blush but do it, gasping as my back hits the cold table.

The possessive look is back as he runs his hands down my chest, squeezing and teasing my tits, then sliding down until he can stroke back over the scrap of black lace between my thighs. I shiver, choking on the moan that claws it's way out of my throat when he rips the lace clear off of my body. The rumble deep in his chest lets me know what he thinks of the sight of my wet pussy spread wide for him.

"Avery will have an aneurysm if she finds out we did this on the table. She's been clear about her stance on the furniture." I choke out, and he drops to his knees.

"Don't tell her then, Mounty." He says, and any reply I could have come up with disappears the second his mouth touches me.

Holy. Fuck.

Holy Jesus *fuck*.

Okay, getting head is the best fucking thing and why did I wait so damn long to start dating? Stupid question, I was waiting until I found the three *hottest guys* who ever walked the Earth and then somehow managed to convince them all to share me. *Fuuuuuuuck*. As he teases at my clit my brain switches off and I start to grind against his mouth, chasing the sensation until I'm splintering apart at the fucking seams but he doesn't stop. He's fucking merciless as he pushes and pushes until I come again, gasping and crying out into the silence of the room.

Lord, he is good with his tongue.

When my thighs finally stop shaking, I sit up and tug at his shoulders until he stands, kissing me until we're just panting into each other's mouths, sharing the taste of my slick pussy between us.

I want him.

I don't think beyond that, sliding off of the table and onto my knees as I reach for his belt with steady fingers. He smirks at me and helps to undress. I swallow roughly at the sight of his chest, all the lean solid muscle of a runner. Only when he's kicked his pants and boxers off do I glance down but my eyes land on a smudge of ink right above his dick.

I can't even focus on anything but the tattoo.

"Are you serious right now?" I croak.

"Yes, I'm serious, that is my dick. I appreciate the awed tones though, Mounty." He drawls out, all fucking smug and I can't. I just fucking can't.

"No, I mean, do you seriously have the words 'you're welcome' tattooed above your dick? I changed my mind, I'm not doing this."

Ash chuckles at me as I move to stand up then he holds me down with a firm hand on my shoulder. Oh look, there's my damage again but sweet merciful lord if that doesn't make me gush all over again.

"It's Morrison's fault, get pissy at him, not me."

I scoff at him and then try to focus on his dick instead of the arrogant, smug, *totally-fucking-Beaumont* tattoo he has.

Sweet lord in heaven.

I forgot he was fucking huge. I gulp. There is no way that will fit in me. Not right now, and possibly not ever. I might dislocate my jaw doing this.

"You'll be fine, Mounty."

I punch him in the leg because I'm *excellent* at foreplay. He grunts at me, probably because the hit was a little too close to his monster cock for comfort, but when I wrap my hand around the base of his dick and pump he shuts up real fast.

He's right, I don't dislocate my jaw but fuck it if it isn't a stretch. He's less worried about hurting me than Harley is, his hands in my hair tugging and pulling while his hips jerk forward, but that only makes me moan louder. He doesn't warn me that he's going to come either, just grunts and shoots down the back of my throat. It's the soft touches afterwards that tell me how much I mean to him, and I love every fucking second of it. I could do that every day of my life and die a happy lady.

When he helps me up from the floor and kisses me, I can't stop myself from snarking at him. "You're going to have to make do with blowjobs for a while. That is not going to fit in me. I'm half the fucking size of you as is."

He laughs at me, completely unconcerned by my stern warnings, and walks over to climb into my bed. Fuck, his ass is all toned muscle. Perfect to sink your teeth into.

"Get in here. I need a nap."

Ugh, bossy asshole.

But I do exactly what he says.

THE NOTIFICATION of my in-school suspension comes through as an email the next morning and I read it out to Ash while he sips at a coffee in bed, sleep mussed and fucking delicious looking after spending the whole night with me.

"I told you, Mounty. Trust me."

CHAPTER TWENTY-SIX

I REFUSE to let the house arrest stop me from doing whatever the hell I want, trusting in Ash and what he said to me.

Avery starts working her way through the teachers and students that have helped Ms. Vivienne and by the end of the week two teachers quit and eight students transfer out of Hannaford. There's nothing quite like Avery freaking Beaumont when she's on the social warpath.

On Sunday, after a long day of studying and trying to catch up on sleep, Ash texts me a demand to meet him in the boy's room and when I try to get him to come to my room instead he calls me a coward.

The manipulative asshole, except it's effective and I stomp over to rant at him in person.

When I unlock the door and fling it open the words die in my throat at the arrogant fucking smirk on his face and the fact that he's lounging on his bed in his fucking boxer's. Dammit. His nipples are like my kryptonite and I think somehow he's figured it out!

"Do you want to argue, Mounty? I'd rather we go for round two but I'll fight if you need the foreplay."

I cut him a look but I lose the higher ground by drooling all over myself as I climb up onto his bed to get to him. "Shut up and kiss me, asshole."

Ash chuckles and nips at my lip, "Why, Mounty, I didn't think you'd be up for ass play just yet but if you ask nicely I could be persuaded."

Aaaaaaand now I kinda wanna die.

He doesn't let me pull away, his hand firm on the back of my neck as he strokes his tongue over mine until I forget why it was I was so embarrassed in the first place. I feel like a fumbling idiot as I clutch at his shoulders because his hands are steady and sure as he strips my shirt from me and with a quick flick of his fingers my bra is off and across the room.

I'm panting the second his hands cup my tits, kneading and toying with my nipples, and for a second I'm so distracted I don't feel the buzzing of my phone. It's only when Ash curses into the skin of my neck that I realize what's pissed him off.

911. Our room. Now.

I glance at the text from over Ash's shoulder as he works his way down my chest. I'm only checking it because I know it's Avery and my stomach fucking drops. I shove at his chest to move him and dial her number frantically.

"Atticus asked me on a date! A real one. He's going to come pick me up after my recital tomorrow night. We need to plan out everything, Lips. My outfit, my hair, my opening line, how I'm going to turn him down if he tries to kiss me because I want to string him along a bit. Stop sucking face with your man-meat and get over here."

I groan at her. "911 means life threatening, Aves, not

help-I'm-freaking-out-over-a-guy! Fuck, I nearly shanked Ash to get to the phone."

Ash grunts, flopping over onto his back dramatically while I drool at the sight of him, and snaps, "I'm not giving Lips up just for your pathetic boy troubles. Which idiot did you snare this time? If you say Sebastien I will walk to his room right now and rip his fucking throat out."

I cringe and he eyes me for a second before it clicks.

He snatches the phone away from me and hisses, "You are not going on a date with that spineless fuck Atticus! Over my dead *fucking* body, Avery."

She screeches at him so ear-piercingly that I hear every word. "Well I guess you're dead then, asshole!"

I refuse to get involved in their little spats but I do leave Ash to go help Avery. He's fucking livid about it but I know it's about Atticus and not me leaving him. He even tries to talk me into helping him turn Avery against Atticus but I stand firm.

Avery deserves to be fucking happy and if Atticus is it, then he's it. I'm not questioning it.

Avery is standing in the living room in her skimpiest lingerie when I arrive and I decide that Atticus is a fucking lucky guy. She's a hot piece of ass and any guy would be fucking begging to have her.

"Would you go with the red or the black? Atticus always likes me in black." She says without looking back at me.

I kick my shoes off and join her. The dresses are both stunning and sexy without showing much skin. There's nothing Ash could possibly complain about when he sees her in them.

"Black with red lipstick. The dress and your hair will

make it pop and he'll be falling over himself to kiss you. It'll make it that much better when you decline his advances."

Aves smirks and cuts me a little smug look. "This is why we're friends. How would you say no to kissing him?"

I snort out a laugh at her. "Well, I'm not a refined and graceful lady like you. I usually say no by breaking people's bones."

Avery hums and runs a hand down the black dress. "How did you say no to the guys while you were oblivious to them last year?"

I groan at her. "I didn't. I kissed them and then remembered I couldn't and told them that. Well, except that one time with Harley where he was the one who stopped us because I couldn't help myself."

Avery pretends to gag but she laughs while she does. "Was that before or after he got you drunk and found out you were a virgin?"

I head for the freezer. If I'm going under the Spanish freaking Inquisition them I need some cherry fucking ice cream. "I *am* a virgin, and it was before."

Avery hums and throws a robe on, grabbing a spoon to dig around in my tub of cherry goodness. "I would never have believed those three horn-bags would take this so slow. My screeching is working wonders."

I cackle at her. "And how much of your screeching is real discomfort?"

She shrugs. "I'm pretty sure you could fuck Morrison on the couch in my general vicinity and the only real concern I'd have would be the clean up required. Oh, and the fact I'd have to see his dick, ugh. But they don't need to know that."

I WAIT until Ash takes Avery down to the gym for her last ballet practice before her recital and I call Illi. There's no way I'm going to let Avery get involved with Atticus before I've done a full background check on the asshole. Rory had looked like the perfect gentleman on paper, great breeding and the poster boy for an all-American footballer, and he'd tried to fucking rape her in a bathroom for dumping his cheating ass.

Blaise arrives as Illi picks up and I motion for him to stay quiet.

"What's up, kid? Who's dead now?" He laughs and I snort at him.

"You shouldn't joke like that when we're being fucking hunted like game. I need a full-scope background check. I'm going to call the Coyote also but I need your sources as well."

Illi grunts and I hear him moving around. The blaring horns and shouting tell me he's out on the Bay, probably chasing up the Jackal's hired muscle. "Who's it for?"

"Avery's new man. Don't ask, it's a potential shit-show waiting to happen. Ash is going to gut the fucker if he so much as side eyes her."

Illi chuckles. "Good fucking luck to him. She might be prissy but the girl has claws and the grit to back it up."

That warms something in my belly. I love that he can see her worth just as much as I can. "She's fucking besotted so we need a full check. The last guy she got into... we had to deal with. Piece of shit. So, we're doing this right, Illi."

"Of course, kid. Gimme the dickhead's details and I'll

rummage through his fucking sock drawer until we know he's clean."

"Thanks. I owe you."

"Shut it. Hey, what happened to the other guy? He still breathing?"

I grunt. "Unfortunately. Harley had him permanently taken out, and now he's in his own version of hell. A wheelchair and a non-functioning dick."

Illi roars with laughter. "That's fucking good. Send me his name too. Tell the Ice Queen it's an early birthday present from Odie and me."

I cackle and hang up, texting him through Atticus and Rory's details. I should just leave the rapist asshole to his own hell but fuck it. The world will be a better place without him around wasting oxygen.

Blaise sidles up behind me, resting his hands over my hips and kissing my neck. "Why are you telling Illi about Rory? I thought we were done with that dickhead."

I shiver and try not to melt into a puddle of goo at his feet. "I need to get Atticus checked out. What do you think of him? Besides hating him on principle for Ash's sake?"

Blaise huffs and his breath tickles at my neck. I have to take a step away from him so I don't embarrass myself. Well, more than usual.

"I think he's an arrogant dickhead but I also think he's kind of perfect for Avery. Don't tell Ash I said that, he'll fucking slit my throat in my sleep. He hates him. Actually he fucking despises him."

I frown and move to make us both coffee. Blaise doesn't drink coffee much but I refuse to let him drink beer while he studies so I'm slowly converting him.

"Why? Did something happen or does he hate him on principal?"

Blaise slumps down onto the floor in front of the TV in his usual spot. "Aves was fucking devastated when Atticus stopped talking to her. She holed herself up in her room and watched those stupid romance movies for weeks. It was pathetic. Nothing like she normally is. Harley ended up moving in here to make sure she didn't do something stupid and Ash went on the warpath. He nearly got kicked out for how often he was in the fight club fights. Avery eventually came around and dealt with the fall-out but Ash hates the idea of Atticus in her life again because he already knows the power he has over Avery."

I grimace and join him on the floor, smiling as he sips the coffee without pulling a face. I must be getting better at making his super sweet. I may like my sweets but my coffee needs to be as black as the stain on my heart to keep me going.

"I don't think it's worth getting into a relationship with someone if you feel anything less than that."

Blaise leans back and watches me carefully. "Less than what?"

I shrug. "Less than all in. That's how I feel about you. And Ash and Harley. It's how I know you guys are worth all of the danger and risks to keep alive. Why start something with anyone who doesn't hold that power?"

Blaise grins and when he glances down at his textbook there's color on his cheeks that squeezes my heart a little.

"Why the fuck are you blushing over that?" I laugh. Boys are fucking confusing.

He shrugs at me and flicks a pen in my direction. "I know you feel like that because you risk your neck for us all the time but you don't really say it. It's just fucking weird to hear you say it."

I huff at him. "I don't mess around, Blaise."

He shrugs again and I let it go, focusing on his assignments until I'm happy he's going to nail every last one of them.

When Avery gets back from dance, Blaise leaves with a lingering but sweet kiss and I ignore Avery's questioning look. I wait until she's showered and in bed before I tell her about my conversation with Illi.

"I don't need him to kill Rory. I'm comfortable with where he is."

I nod and switch the light off. "It's the principle of it. Illi doesn't ever let rapists live. What happened with Odie taught him that lesson the hardest way possible."

***

Ash and Avery leave for the recital early the next morning. I text Illi and he promises to follow them there, though he doesn't seem very happy about tagging along to high society functions. I think dinner at Hannaford has ruined the illusion that the higher societies have better things for us.

They certainly don't have better food.

I go to classes with Harley and Blaise, and we eat lunch in the dining hall. The whispers that follow me are even fucking worse now that I'm on my stupid school arrest but I grit my teeth and just fucking deal with it. Harley offers to start practicing with his new knives I got him for Christmas loud enough that the little freshmen assholes near us hear and scurry away.

I smile and say, "I can show you the best places to stab

without making too much of a mess. DNA can be hard to completely clean off."

Harley smirks and shrugs at me. "Do tell, babe. I love hearing about your life skills. The Bay does teach girls valuable lessons."

I quirk an eyebrow at him and Blaise cackles at us both. "You two flirt like fucking serial killers, it's fucking hilarious. C'mon then, Star. Tell us where you'd stab.... that guy. The one who will die if he keeps staring at your tits like that."

The guy, who's sitting three chairs down, shits himself and darts off, leaving behind his bag, lunch, and dignity.

"I wouldn't stab him. I'd castrate him. Have you ever skinned someone before? If you do it right, it takes some time to work your way down to the layers of fat and muscle. You can technically peel a dick like a banana until there's nothing fucking left."

Blaise turns green and gags but Harley smirks, his eyes twinkling.

"Who taught you that, babe?"

I shrug. "Doc. I was thirteen and he taught me the birds and the bees. Then he rolled a corpse in and showed me all the best ways to hurt any guy who tried to touch me without consent."

Blaise nods but still looks green. He really does love his dick that much.

I finish my lunch in peace now we've subdued the sheep and Harley tucks me under his arm to walk us back to our classes. There's something about being pressed against his body, safely tucked into him, that slows my brain down and brings me some peace.

I only wish I could have it all the time.

CHAPTER TWENTY-SEVEN

"WHAT'S THIS?" I wave at the board even though I can see exactly what it is. I'm more worried about why she has it.

Avery stops in front of it and props a hand on her hip, blowing on her coffee absently. "I feel like the best way to keep everyone on the same page about what we're dealing with is the board. I'll let the boys all know they can add to it if a new threat appears. We can't keep overlooking things because one person knows something the others don't. One board, total honesty, and fuck everyone who gets in our way."

I snort at her and take a gulp. "If a new threat appears we might need to move the boys, Diarmuid, Illi and Odie into our room. Stash them under the beds or something."

Avery grimaces. "I can't think of anything worse. Odie's fine and Illi's hot enough but Diarmuid sounds like a dick."

I smirk. "We could take bets on which guy snaps and kills him first?"

"I'd be the first. I'd pay Illi to do it for me." Avery snarks and sips at her drink.

I nod along. "I know how worried you've been about Harley. Inducting him is fucking risky and I'm still not sure how I can get out of it without making him our next threat. Snipers and sharpshooters are not people you want hunting you."

Avery squints at me, then sighs. "I want to take him out for what he said about you. What, you're the only one allowed to be protective? You're my Mounty, I'd stab anyone who implied you're a whore for loving those idiot boys. I'm still trying to figure out if I'm locking the doors and setting this place on fire after graduation or poisoning the water to take out all of the little jealous bitches here."

I blush and take another sip of my coffee. Changing the subject seems like the best idea. "What are we going to do about the Morrisons?"

She frowns. "I'm going to very slowly, and very carefully, destroy that man's business, family, and will to live. The Morrisons are clean but everyone has a price. I have some... feelers out."

Right. Feelers. Why does that make me feel fucking nervous? "Don't do anything to put yourself in danger, Aves. I can just climb through his window and slit his throat in his sleep."

Avery laughs at me, like it's all just a big joke. "I will say, getting Ash pissed off about everything that's going on was the best present you have ever given me. He's been very... motivated to help me."

Fuck, that makes me even more nervous. "What have you guys done?"

She lifts her coffee cup up for a sip. "You'll see, Mounty. You worry about your issues on the board, and I'll take care of mine."

EVERY TIME I take a breath at Hannaford and think my life is settling into a pattern something else happens to remind me that isn't my life.

We're in my least favorite class of the day when Miss Vivienne decides to make the next move on the board in her attempts to pry Harley away from me.

She looks over the class with this smug little smirk that sets my teeth on edge and is my first warning that she's about to start her personal brand of bullshit.

"I've made some changes to the syllabus to reflect on the changes that have happened in our classroom."

What the actual fuck is she talking about?

I tense and Harley cuts me a look. He knows I've finished all of the damned assignments already and this just means more fucking work for me. This bitch. Ugh.

"We're going to discuss personal history, because that's what all of this is really about. Sometimes I think, as scholars, we can forget that in every battle and in every significant moment in history, it's all centered on people. Living breathing human beings. So, shall we discuss some of our own history?"

Fuck that with a cactus. I'm not discussing shit with her or any other rich kid in this class. A few hands raise and some girl starts spouting on about how her family got richer than god, a great opportunity for the narcissists to talk about how great they are.

I relax a little in my chair and let my mind mull over all of the plans I have going on.

"Miss Anderson, would you like to share with the class?"

I meet her eyes and the smug smile is fucking infuriating. "No, thank you."

The other students all giggle and whisper to eat other, like I'm some poor little Mounty girl to pity and poke fun at, but I ignore them all. The whispers will never end at Hannaford, no matter who my real family now is.

"I'm sorry, I worded that incorrectly. Miss Anderson, please share something about your own personal history."

I glare at her, flirting with danger because fuck it, and say, "My personal history is I grew up in Mounts Bay, worked my ass off to get a scholarship to come here, and now I'm at the top of every class because, again, I work my ass off."

She steps around her desk and stares at me, shaking her head. "That language shows your poor breeding. However I think it's commendable; most babies born addicted to heroin don't fare so well in the IQ lottery."

The breath leaks out of my lungs as the giggling starts up again.

This cunt - yeah I said it - this *fucking* cunt has looked up my medical history.

I'm proud of my steady tone when I reply, "What can I say, I'm a fucking lucky girl."

She smirks again. "You weren't so lucky when you broke your leg. How did that happen?"

I lean back in my seat and cross my arms. Harley finally snaps and says, "None of your fucking business."

Ms. Vivienne glances over at him, all doe-eyed again, and says, "Now, now, Mr Arbour. Don't let the crass language of the Mounts Bay local rub off on you."

He smirks at her. "Maybe while you were digging your

fat nose into your student's private files you should've looked at mine as well. I grew up in the Bay with Lips. So *fuck off.*"

Avery giggles and the sound slices through the whispers happening around us. Ms. Vivienne looks ready to argue with us when Ash joins in the fray.

"If you don't stop, I'm going to bleed you out. Slowly."

Blaise snorts with laughter and calls out, "Shit, Beaumont never threatens pussy. You're really something *special*, Ms. Whore."

He looks back and winks at me. I'm still too stunned at Ash's words to react. Miss Vivienne is about the same.

I watch as Ash pulls his phone out and hits play on a video he has recorded. The obscene sounds of moaning and grunting start playing.

"Oh, Ms. Vivienne, I don't see any of your high society breeding here while you're being fucked over a table by Mr. Trevelen. What does his wife think of this? The alive one I mean, not the one who's mysteriously 'disappeared'."

The whispers turn into giggling and catcalls. Ms. Vivienne's teeth clench and she takes a single step towards Ash before he stops her with a look.

He taps on the screen again and the moaning changes. "Does Trevelen know you're fucking Sebastien Steele? Does Sebastien know you're fucking his dad? And his uncle, both of whom are on the school board. Isn't that against the corruption clause? Something about keeping your dick out of school business? Hmm. Well. Maybe I should start sending these out."

"No-"

Every phone in the classroom buzzes. "Too fucking late."

Ms. Vivienne's eyes narrow at him but she keeps her

head held high which is stupid. She's lost what little credibility she had in the classroom and now every student is sitting there whispering and giggling at her. Ash leans back in his chair, arms crossed and I know he's got his signature smug smirk across his mouth. Avery glances back at me and smiles, winking.

"Mr Beaumont, that is a gross invasion-"

"So is looking up Lips' medical history and telling the whole class. So is stealing the recordings of two of your students going for a midnight swim. Fuck, I'd say nothing is as *invasive* as showing up to your study sessions with no panties and cum leaking down your legs but you didn't mind then."

My eyes flick back to Harley and he's watching Ms. Vivienne with that satisfaction that can only come from being pushed too fucking far. No panties. I could rip her fucking face off.

She dares to call my *breeding* poor?!

Her life is saved by a knock at the door and a red-faced Mr. Trevelen escorting a substitute teacher for the class.

My in-school suspension is lifted and we don't see Ms. Vivienne in our history class again.

AFTER FAMILY DINNER THAT FRIDAY, I sit with Blaise while he strums our song out on his guitar. I hum softly under my breath, just enough that he can hear to tune and the smile on his face is only a little sad. I hate the miserable cloud that's hanging over him again but no playlist, make out session, or gallons of ice cream have managed to fix it yet.

"Ash told me my agent said something to you." He mumbles, and I shrug. I've been waiting for this conversation. I knew it would happen at some point.

"He's a pervert. I can't promise you I won't skin him if I see him again."

Blaise just nods and finishes off the song with a little flourish. "I'm going solo. It's just me and Finn who do everything anyway, and he's sick of Fyre trying to clean up our songs."

Finn Benson, the drummer. I try to keep my face blank like I haven't stalked the utter crap out of Blaise's career and know everything about the only other person in Blaise's life he trusts, but he smirks at me and it's clear I fail.

"You're not going to fangirl all over Finn, are you? I'll be hurt you've replaced me."

Avery scoffs at him. "No, you'll be jealous as hell because you enjoy being her idol. Besides, you can't go solo. Do you have any idea how much it would cost you to break your contract? Without your inheritance, you'll be bankrupt and begging on the streets. I think you're forgetting that you're a millionaire now, not a *billionaire*."

"I'll be fine." He says, nonchalantly shrugging and Avery's eyes narrow as she looks at her over her phone. She's been texting Atticus at all hours of the day and night, and I'm waiting for the engagement announcement. I'm sure it'll come any day and Ash will start flipping tables and stabbing people. I make a mental note to hide his weapons.

"You can't even wash dishes without guidance, Morrison, how the hell are you going to survive poverty?"

The bathroom door swings open and Ash strolls out, tucked neatly into his pajamas and I look the fuck away before I get caught drooling over him. I try to fix my eyes on my literature assignment, still spread out in front of me from where I was studying before Blaise distracted me, but Catcher in the Rye just can't compete with Ash Beaumont's nipples.

Blaise smirks at Avery and calls out to her twin, "I'm breaking my record contract and paying the company out. I'll be destitute."

Ash doesn't break his stride as he walks over to his drinks tray and pours himself a bourbon. "I'll sort out an allowance for you until you're back on your feet. It's for the Mounty, right? Harley will match it, for sure. What do your monthly expenses look like these days?"

Harley is down at the pool, putting in extra training sessions for his upcoming competition. Without Ms. Vivienne's bullshit study group he's thrown himself back into a rigorous training schedule, but he's so much fucking happier now.

Avery's scowl darkens, and when I open my mouth she shoots me a look. "You bled for your money, Lips, let the fucker *starve*. And, for that fact, Harley isn't paying *shit* after everything the Mounty did to get it back for him."

I join her on the couch and tuck my arm into hers. "His agent told me he'd enjoy his turn with me on tour. He was only disappointed it wasn't you getting passed around."

Blaise stiffens and looks up. Apparently knowing it happened and hearing the specifics are two very different things.

Avery gags dramatically. "Fine. Ash and I will pay an allowance but you better make your solo record the best damn thing anyone has ever heard."

Blaise is still looking pissed, and he only looks away

from me when Ash hands him a beer. "It is. Star is going to sing on it too."

Ash sits next to me and slips a hand onto my thigh to trace little patterns while he drinks his bourbon. "And when do we get to hear this song?"

I clear my throat. "When I can sing it without puking."

CHAPTER TWENTY-EIGHT

WE FALL into a new routine now that Harley's days aren't full of cougar flirting and bullshit study groups. Sunday's become my favorite day of the week, waking up tangled up in boys and nothing on my schedule now that I've finished all of my assignments.

Now that we know Mr. Ember is on the Jackal payroll and Ash quit the track team, he's joined Harley and Blaise for their boxing sessions. He still runs but he does it in his own time.

When I try to apologize for my baggage ruining the sport for him he gives me a shitty look and snaps, "I don't give a fuck about team sports, Mounty. I was just doing it for the gym credit."

After a late breakfast, I walk Avery to her dance class and then head to the gym to meet the guys. I thank god, the universe, fate, and a million other things I don't believe in when I arrive to find all three of them stripped down to work out. *Hoo boy*, I have to talk my vagina down because I might just pass the fuck out at the sight of them.

They all snigger at me like smug fucking dicks, and I

huff at them, stomping over to set up camp on the mats in front of the ring. I should have brought a coffee and ice cream because this is better than any TV show *ever*.

Harley swoops down to kiss me, dirty and raw like the urge to fight is thumping in his chest alongside his heart already, and I bite his lip in protest because I don't know what I want more; to watch him fight or to wrestle with him myself.

Oh, god.

Yes, please.

Ash smirks at my stupefied look and kisses me too, then joins Harley in the ring. He's wearing the tiny shorts again because apparently, he wants my brains to melt and leak out of my ears. They don't wait for a bell or one of us to call out or anything, they just throw themselves at each other, fists flying and grunting when they hit their mark. Watching them spar and grapple is just... porn. It's porn.

Blaise sprawls out next to me and roars with laughter when I get my phone out to record them. I ignore him because, well, a girl's gotta do.

The second Ash gets Harley on the mat I'm sweating and panting harder than they are. Harley rolls him off easily but his size isn't as much of an advantage as you'd think. Ash is fucking *quick* and brutal, completely unconcerned with the getting hurt. I guess that's the real lessons Joey and Senior taught him. I shiver and try not to follow that thought. It'll just ruin the high of watching them.

Blaise grabs me around the waist and pulls me into his lap, one hand creeping under my oversized tee and grunting when he finds my hard nipples pushing against the thin lace of my bras.

"Are they turning you on, Star? We could fuck on the mats right here if you want to. I could eat that sweet pussy right here while you watch them." He whispers, then bites down on my shoulder as I groan.

"I've just had my suspension lifted, I can't get caught doing shit again," I mumble, and he hums against my skin as he marks me up until I squirm in his arms.

"Get off of her, dickhead. There are cameras in here." Harley calls out and Blaise curses, pulling away and glaring viciously at him. I slide out of his lap and away from his temptation. Harley shoves Ash out of the ring and glares at Blaise until he sighs, kissing me again before taking his turn.

Ash slumps down next to me; sweaty, bleeding a little, and looking fucking delicious. I hand him a bottle of water.

"We need to talk about Atticus." He says, and I groan at him.

"Why? His background check came back clean so he's Avery's business, not ours. Why are you so fucking against him? I know he's hurt Avery before but... I understand the why of it. He's clearly not a creepy pervert trying to touch fourteen year old girls. That's a mark in his favor and you know it."

Ash's jaw clenches. "His father buys girls like Senior does. They have similar tastes but Crawford doesn't murder his girls. Just breaks them and put them back in the auctions. I don't want someone like that around Avery."

I nod and watch Blaise and Harley jab at each other for a second. Sweet lord, it's a fucking sight to see.

I clear my throat. "I think we both know that having a piece of shit for a father doesn't automatically make you the same."

Ash shakes his head. "I don't like him. I don't trust him. You can decide for yourself at the Gala next week."

Fuck. I groan. "I forgot about that. For fuck's sake, what

the hell do you think Avery is going to make me wear to a *Gala?*"

A slow smirk spreads across his face. "Oh, I'm sure I'll enjoy it."

The Gala is the same night as Harley's swimming competition and he's *pissed* he won't be coming back to the Bay with us. When he tries to convince Avery not to go she threatens him with her knife. I go take a shower to get the hell away from their spat.

I'd put money on Avery in that fight.

Once I'm dressed again, I lean on the I text Illi for back up because the thought of leaving Harley without someone to watch his back gives me hives. I might not throw a tantrum like Harley is but I'm just as pissed off.

I'll watch the little mobster. Have fun in your pouffy dresses and flower crowns. You know that's what they wear to those fancy parties, right?

I stare down at my phone in horror. Now, he could be fucking with me, but he's also lived in the Bay his whole life and there's every chance he's been to a Gala before. He'd have been there to kill someone but he could've seen the dress code.

I feel sick.

I must look fucking bad when I step out of the bathroom because Avery stops mid-rant and says, "What's happened?"

I look up at her and croak, "What's the fucking dress code tomorrow night? I refuse to wear anything flowery or that a wouldn't look out of place on a Disney princess. Avery, I have a reputation to uphold."

She blinks at me like I've lost my mind. "I would never make you wear a flowery dress. I'll have to tell Morrison to stop planning your wedding though. I'm sure he's planning to get you into a full skirt."

She cackles like an evil witch at the face I pull but I let out the breath I was holding and send Illi a savage text back.

What a *dick*.

The next day, Harley kisses me at the Maserati, pressing me against the closed door like he wants to imprint himself on my skin and keep my safe.

"Promise me you won't go anywhere without Ash or Blaise. Promise me, babe." He murmurs against my lips, ignoring Avery cussing him out from the front seat.

"I will. I promise. You need to be careful as well, Annabelle has signed up to help with the time trials so she'll be stalking your ass the entire time you're away."

He smirks and sucks on my bottom lip, rolling it with his teeth gently like he's trying to stop himself from eating me. "You own my ass, babe, she can't have it. Send me photos of the dress and tell Morrison if he tries to fuck you at the buffet to outdo me, I'll skin him."

I blush and nudge him away, glaring at him while he opens the car door and tucks me in like he's a chivalrous gentleman. Dread pools in my gut but I don't know what it is that's freaking me out so much, we've been separated before and there haven't been any new threats.

I wave at him as we take off, Blaise blasting some techno crap just to get a rise out of Avery, but I can't look away from Harley's slowly shrinking form.

"What's wrong?" Ash whispers, but I shake my head.

I'm being stupid. But I also trust my gut.

I flick a text to Illi to tell him we've left and then I try to focus on the conversation happening around me.

I hope I'm wrong, but that feeling tells me something fucking bad is going to happen.

That feeling says I won't see Harley again.

CHAPTER TWENTY-NINE

THE DRESS AVERY puts me in is fucking ridiculous.

There's so much delicate lace covering my arms and my shoulders that I feel like a fraud. I'm not a lace person, I wear booty shorts and band tees for fuck's sake! Avery clucks at me like I'm an unruly child and I sulk a little because why the fuck not. The slit up the skirt is a plus though, all the way up one thigh, making it impossible to wear underwear without revealing it. I quirk an eyebrow at Avery and she shrugs, smug as fuck.

One look at Ash's eyes when I walk out and I remember why Avery is *the* evil dictator in power.

Blaise smirks at him, muttering about drooling, before kissing my cheek sweetly and holding an arm out for Avery to take. He looks sharp in the suit, the new ink on his hands and neck a statement to the crowd of higher society we're about the walk into.

I'm so fucking proud of him.

Ash waits until Blaise and Avery move to the door before stalking over to me, his icy blue eyes stripping me, layer by layer, until I feel like he's exposed my soul.

"Fuck the Gala. We're staying here." He snaps, and Avery snarls from the door at him.

"Keep it in your *fucking* pants! I'm here for Atticus and you *promised* me you'd be on your best behavior."

His eyes squeeze shut like Avery is sucking the life out of him and I scoff at him. "We can go down for an hour and then come back up. Blaise will probably drink like a fish and watch out for her."

He glares at me for taking Avery's side but tucks me under his arm anyway. Blaise shoots me these lusty looks over his shoulder and I know he's doing it to piss Ash off, the little fucker. When we get to the elevator and step in he says, "I'm not drinking tonight, Star. Atticus is a dickhead but he's also a fucking pussy for Avery so we can leave her with him. I'm pulling that dress off of you."

I glare at him but Avery takes his comments a little harder than I do and stops on his foot with her stiletto heel. He grunts and cuts her a look that has me cringing. She's going to stab him. Or choke him out now I've taught her the best ways to do it.

"I'm taking you down, I'm bringing you back, you're sleeping in my bed," Ash says, breaking their intense face-off, his voice steely, and Blaise breaks eye contact to glare at him too. Ash nods like he's won and the elevator door slides open, his hand curved possessively over my hip.

I feel a little like I'm walking on stilts and, although I'm not totally happy with the caveman glares Ash is throwing at Blaise right now, I'm grateful he's holding me because I'm sure I'd be on my ass by now without him.

Avery smirks at the sheep as we pass. It doesn't matter that they're all twenty-plus years older than us, they all stare at her like she has an executioner's order with their name on it.

I fucking love it.

It's nice to see those looks directed at someone else and to know that I'm not alone in my infamy. Avery Beaumont has already carved a place for herself in high society as a force to be feared *and* reckoned with.

"I'm going to find Atticus. Blaise, you may as well stay here and dance with your girlfriend because I won't tolerate your moping." Avery says, smiling sweetly at me and then sashays towards the bar. They serve her, knowing full well she's only seventeen, and Blaise trails after her.

"Do you want a drink, Mounty?" Ash murmurs in my ear, and I shiver at the warmth of his breath dancing down my neck.

I clear my throat. "Why not, I'll have a whiskey."

Ash jerks his head at Blaise and then he walks me over to one of the sitting areas. The plush lounge feels expensive and I'm instantly uncomfortable perched on it. What if I spill something on it and it's worth thousands? Rich people are stupid.

"Stop frowning at everything." Ash says, as his fingers dance along the slit in my dress. He murmurs happily when he finds my skin and then groans when he realizes I'm *only* wearing the dress.

"Are you trying to fucking kill me? The crowd here is a little less oblivious to public sex acts but I'm sure we could find a bathroom somewhere. I'll even let the brat join in this time." He snaps right as Blaise walks up with our drinks.

"How fucking *kind* of you. Here's your bourbon, asshole, next time get your own." He snarls and then drops down on my other side until I'm wedged between them both. I sip the whiskey quietly, trying not to get involved in their drama.

Everyone around us is wearing hundreds of thousands of clothing and I don't want to think about where the decimal point would land on the jewelry. The women all float around like this is the highlight of their year and the men all eye them predatorily. This party is the same as the ones in the Bay, just better dressed and less open. I'm positive there are drugs being used, crime being organized, and if there isn't some dirty fucking going on secretly somewhere then I'll be damned.

I let my eyes continue their path around the room when I spot Avery and the man with his arms around her waist, holding her against his chest.

My heart stops in my chest.

I scramble to grab Ash's arm, tugging to get his attention, and he frowns when he sees my face.

"Who is that with Avery?" I croak and he jerks to look in the same direction I am.

"That's Atticus. Fuck, Mounty, you scared me. I thought she was being fucking attacked by the look on your face." He snaps, and I glance away from the horror in front of me.

"Blaise, go get her. Now. Go get her and meet us back at the room. Don't be obvious about it, say I'm sick or something. Just get her." I ramble, and Blaise nods, moving quickly away.

Ash's face turns thunderous and I tug him off of our seat. I get us both moving out of the room as quickly as I can in these stupid fucking heels.

"What the fuck is going on, Mounty?" He growls and I shake my head, moving as quickly as I can. We get to the elevator at the same time Blaise pulls an enraged Avery along behind him. When she looks up and sees me she freezes.

"You don't look sick but you don't look okay, what's happened?" Avery says softly, tucking her arm into mine.

The elevator door opens and I pull her in, jabbing at our floor number violently as if that will make the thing move faster. As the doors slowly shut behind us I glance up and make eye contact with Atticus Crawford.

The Crow of Mounts Bay.

"I AM NOT LEAVING this elevator until you tell me what the fuck is going on, Lips." Avery says, and although her words are sure, her voice shakes.

She's guessed what the problem is.

"I know Atticus. I know how he makes his money, I know why he wouldn't let you intern with him, I know *everything* about the world he lives in, Avery, and I need to get you out of here."

Avery's eyes well up but she doesn't let the tears fall as she gives me a curt nod, stalking down the hall the second the elevator doors open. Ash grabs my elbow and pulls me into his body sharply.

"Who *the fuck* is he, Lips? Tell me right now."

"I'm not telling you before I tell her, now let me go. We need to get her out of here." I snap back and jerk my arm away from him. He shouldn't be arguing with me, he *knows* I always put her safety first.

Once we're back in the hotel room, I snatch my shoes off of my feet and try to herd Avery towards our room. "You need to pack. We have to leave now, he saw me. He knows that I know."

Avery nods but she stays put, her face calm and blank now she's had a second to compose herself. "Who is he? I have to know."

I glance back to find Blaise and Ash standing in front of the door like they're waiting for someone to break it down. With the empire, Atticus controls he fucking could.

"He's the Crow. He's a member of the Twelve. He's more powerful than any person in our world, except for the Jackal, but even they are equal. He's the one I called the favor in with to keep Senior away from you because I knew he had ties in the upper class."

Avery's lip quivers just a little but her eyes stay dry and unwavering on my face. "What does he do? Why are you so afraid of him? You said the Crow deals in information, why does that mean we have to leave?"

I open my mouth to answer her when my phone begins to buzz on the coffee table. Dread trickles down my spine and I move to answer it.

I know it's him before I pick it up.

"Which room are you in? We need to talk."

I squeeze my eyes shut but my voice is steady. "We're leaving. We're going back to Hannaford. Avery is under my protection and if you want to discuss the parameters of that protection with me, we can do it at the next meeting."

I hear him sigh down the phone. "Open the door, Wolf."

THE SMILING man that was holding Avery gently

against his chest is not the man we open the hotel door to. This man is purely the Crow.

Avery is sitting, rigid and scowling, on the plush living room chair and I position myself a few feet in front of her, the guys flanking me. Ash is trembling with rage and blood lust, ready to just kill the Crow and be done with it. He never trusted him in the first place. Blaise takes one look at Ash and rocks back on his heels, ready to throw down the second this all turns to shit.

The Crow steps forward and inclines his head to me respectfully but the cold, cutting edge of his gray eyes rake over me like he's planning on bleeding me out for this. Fuck. Has Avery just been some pawn in his game for power? A Beaumont on his arm and in his bed?

Joke's on him. He picked the wrong girl, in the wrong family.

"I already told you we're leaving." I say, my voice pitched low and even.

His eyes stay fixed on mine, kicking the door shut, and even though he's moving smoothly I can see the tension in him. My mind runs through every little scrap of information Avery has ever told me about her crush, the man who has become her obsession.

I wonder what his father would think if he knew the power his son had amassed. The conversation I'd had with Ash earlier flashes back to me. He's probably just like his disgusting father.

"I'm not leaving here without her. Name your price." The Crow says, and fuck if that isn't the worst thing to say.

"*She's not for fucking sale.*" Ash hisses and there it is; the ruthless, killer Beaumont blood. Threaten Avery and you'll push Ash right into the dark place that exists in his soul. The darkness that lives in him and burns in his eyes when his mask slips. The same fire his father and brother both use to destroy women, Ash uses to protect Avery.

I know I'm pushing my luck when I hold up my hand to stop him. His eyes break away from the Crow for a second to aim that fire at me. Blaise stiffens next to me and I can feel the heat of his glare swing around to narrow in on Ash, not liking the shitty attitude one bit.

This is big. This moment could change everything between us all. Ash is holding a grenade and toying with the pin if he doesn't trust me now then this relationship, and I suspect our family, are going to be blown to pieces. I hold his gaze and I *pray*.

His eyes don't lower. He doesn't back down at all.

I feel a tiny crack start on my heart and then he crosses his arms and swings back to face the Crow. I don't know if he's chosen to trust me or not but I have to follow through. I have to make sure we're all safe. I glance back at Avery and I see it in her eyes that she knows. She trusts me to get us all out of this safely.

"How much? How much is she worth to you?" I say coolly.

The Crow's eye never leave mine. He doesn't so much as glance at her. Another black mark against him. "Three favors."

Fuck.

Fuck.

This man never gives out favors. I've had three favors from him already but those were torn from him in moments of true desperation, for things only I could do for him. For him to offer me three for Avery alone... *fuck.*

I shake my head at him and he grits his teeth.

"Six but I'll have your word that you will never tell the Jackal about her."

I freeze.

The Crow *never* breaks the rules of the Twelve and that's pretty fucking close to crossing a line. That's not what I'm expecting at all. Granted we all keep our cards pretty close to our chests but it's the unwritten law that we never conspire and scheme against each other. I know he's been biding his time, waiting to take the Jackal out, but he's *always* played by the rules. Even now the Jackal's gone fucking rogue. What the hell is he playing at?

I look at him then, a proper once over without the rage clouding my eyes.

His face is blank and unreadable but his body speaks loud enough. His fists are clenched, his shoulders stiff, and his elbows are bent slightly like he's poised ready to attack. He's not the Crow, here to buy some skin for the night like his father would or a pawn in the game we're all playing. He's Atticus and he's waging a war for Avery. The feelings he's had for her are real, real enough that he's here for her, risking the wrath of the Twelve and losing the empire he's built.

I take a step forward and when his chin lifts I narrow my eyes at him, the tension in the room crackling like electricity.

"You're in love with her, aren't you, Atticus?" His eyes narrow to slits at the sound of his real name. I've broken protocol but I don't give a fuck. He's going to have to come clean if he wants to leave this room with any sort of a relationship with Avery.

Or his life, because Ash is fucking teetering.

"I told you, I'll-" he starts but I cut him off.

"She's not for sale. Not to you, not to Matteo, not to anyone. Either admit you're here because you have real, genuine feelings for her or leave. And to be perfectly clear, there is *nothing* I wouldn't do to keep her safe. I'll risk the Twelve if I have to."

His eyes finally leave mine and swing down to land on Avery. I see it then, the feeling in my gut is right, he looks at her like she's the center of his world. He looks at her with longing and sweetness and worship. He's here to *save her from me.*

His eyes only get more vicious when they cut back in my direction but he softens at the sound of Avery's voice, "The Wolf is my family, Atticus. I'm not leaving with you."

Some of the tension in Ash eases a little like he was afraid Avery would skip off into the sunset with this guy and he'd lose her forever. I make a note to talk to him *again* about letting her make her own fucking choices.

The Crow slips away, something I've never seen another member of the Twelve do, and it's Atticus standing there with us again.

"You can't let Matteo know about her, or what she means to me. He'll fucking destroy her. It's bad enough she's with you." He sinks down in the armchair and rubs his hands over his face. The room seems to take a deep breath.

"You don't need to explain to me what that man does to innocent girls when he has an agenda." I whisper, and I see the regret flash on his face so quickly I think I might have imagined it.

He chuckles darkly, "I guess I should remember that better than anyone. I was there when he snapped your leg with his bare hands. What were you, twelve years old?"

Blaise's hand runs down the inside of my arm until he threads his fingers through mine, tugging me back until I'm back at his side. I don't want to look at any of them while we talk about the damage done to me. "Thirteen. I was thirteen and I had just won the Game. He told me he wanted to teach me how to deal with pain but really he was trying to break me in. Nothing he hates more than a female he can't break."

"Well, he didn't break you, did he? Here you stand with two Beaumonts and the richest kid in the country. You've inducted the heir to the O'Cronin family into your fold and let's not forget the Butcher. I'd wager *this* wasn't Matteo's plan."

I chuckle, a little shocked that I have it in me to do so, and then I sit on the couch, tugging Blaise down with me. Avery moves to sit with us, perching on the arm of the couch stiffly, and then, slowly, Ash joins us. When he slips his hand to rest on my thigh my shoulders finally relax. Atticus watches us all carefully.

"I was under the impression you were with the O'Cronin kid? That's what Matteo thinks anyway. I heard a rumor of... more but I thought that was just his delusions."

I feel a blush start and Avery scoffs at me. "Seriously? We're in a life-threatening situation and you're getting all shy about your harem of obsessed boys?"

Blaise nudges Avery's leg with his shoulder and cackles at her. "Leave her alone, she's used to being a badass under pressure."

Atticus watches her the exact way that Harley watched me during our sophomore year, back when I was oblivious to want it meant. God, I was so fucking blind. "This isn't a life-threatening situation, Avery. As long as you are safe, I'm not going to do anything. The last time I saw the Wolf I knew things had changed between her and the Jackal but I couldn't risk being wrong. I couldn't leave your fate up to chance because the Jackal would do things to you that I've spent *years* making sure your father didn't fucking do."

Atticus's voice is kind and gentle. It's fucking weird. I've only been around him a handful of times and he's always a cold, ruthless dick. Probably because I was always with Matteo.

Avery stares over at him like he's a stranger to her and if I didn't hate his guts for lying to her, I'd feel sorry for him.

Avery is ride or die, and I think Atticus is now firmly on her shit list.

"It's Lips, and I'm not Matteo's protege or girlfriend or whatever it is that the Twelve think. He sponsored me for the Game and he's helped me out but he's also done things to me that I can't ever forgive or forget. I went to Hannaford to figure a way out. That's what we're doing, we're finding a way out of all of this."

Atticus nods and rubs his chin. He looks older than twenty-two but then he's the leader of one of the largest criminal organizations in the state, possibly the country. Rivaled only by the Jackal's numbers. I had never thought to approach him for help in getting away from Matteo, his cold manner making me wary. I'm starting to see that was a mistake.

Avery hesitates for a moment and then asks with a surprisingly strong voice, "You were at the meeting with Lips and Harley, do you think the Jackal is going to continue to send people to kill him?"

Classic Avery; she's just found out the guy she's been in love with for half her life has been lying to her and she's instantly thinking about what information she can mine for the protection of her family. I both love her and want to shake her. She should be chewing this fucker out.

"He's in less danger now he's under her protection. He was on very limited time with his grandfather before then, despite my efforts. Matteo can't just kill him, he has to find some sort of betrayal or dishonesty to be able to take him out. He doesn't just answer to the Wolf if he does, he answers to the Twelve. He's a big player but he's not the biggest and definitely not bigger than us all."

"And what if he continues to try to kill him stealthily? I'm sure you're aware he's spiraling and recruiting."

Atticus grins and cocks an eyebrow at me. Again, I blush which is fucking ridiculous.

"Oh, after the Wolf's declaration at the meeting the Jackal has been served a severe warning about touching her toys. The rest of the Twelve are much more aware of his... instability now. Those who have chosen his side are in as much danger as he is."

I ignore the look Atticus is giving me, and lean forward in my chair. "If I induct these three as well, would you be willing to back me up in the meetings if Matteo starts with his shit?"

Ash's leg tenses against mine. I haven't spoken to him about this but I know how badly Avery wants it. It's a move on the board against their father. He could no longer threaten them without risking the wrath of the lower criminal organizations. Lower in social standing but certainly dangerous to him and his business.

Atticus stands and runs a hand down the front of his suit jacket. A slow smile forms on his lips and he suddenly looks closer to his age. "If you cut yourself off from the Jackal and start calling *me* when you need help instead of him, then I will take him on with you. Induct them, keep Avery safe from the Jackal and her father, and I will offer my help with *anything* from this moment onwards. Whatever the cost."

That's *exactly* what we need.

I glance up at Avery. This is her choice, if she doesn't want to trust this guy ever again then we'll figure something else out. If I decide for her then I'm just as terrible as everyone else in her life.

She's staring at Atticus, her eyes guarded and her mouth turned down a little. I'm not sure he'll ever be able to repair the damage this has done in her trust of him. She sighs and gives me a little nod. I look at Blaise and he leans in to kiss me under the ear, sweet and sure. Then I take a deep breath and turn to Ash. He's looking at my thigh, where his fingers are drawing lazy circles on the skin exposed by the deep slit in the dress. I wait him out, this isn't something I'd ever rush. This is lifelong. As long as I breathe, I am the Wolf. If he chooses this then he will be tied to me forever. His fingers still and then he gives me the smallest squeeze.

"Done." I say to Atticus, and he shoots a resigned smile at Avery, who stares back at him like she's plotting his death, before turning to the door.

He hesitates for a second and then turns back to me. "Don't ever let her wear red again. She wears your color or mine."

And then he's gone.

Blaise gets up and locks the door behind him and Avery slides down to take his seat, her hand finding mine.

"His color is black. Mine is white." I murmur and she nods.

"I'm guessing the Jackal's is red from that little display. I'll burn it all. What does induction look like? If you tell me I have to be naked or bleed I'm pulling out. My brother too, I'm not having him frolicking around the city in the nude."

"Should have told him that earlier." Blaise murmurs and then laughs at the glare he gets from Ash.

"It's done. I told the Crow, he passes it on. It's weird but, yeah, it's that simple."

CHAPTER THIRTY

MY PHONE WAKES me at three am.

I have to struggle my way out from under Ash to reach it, and when I see it's Harley I answer immediately.

"What's happened?" I whisper, not wanting to wake Ash if it's nothing serious.

The line stays quiet, I can hear a rhythmic rustling, a sort of swishing noise, but nothing to tell me what the hell is going on. I sit and just listen for a second, and realize his phone is in his pocket and the noise is the sound of his pants as he walks.

I'm on edge immediately.

Why is he walking around at this time? Why has he called me only to put his phone in his pocket? Butt dialing isn't really a thing anymore, is it? Is he in danger?

What the fuck has happened in the last three hours?

I keep the phone to my ear and climb over Ash, who's the deepest sleeper out of all of us and barely mumbles as my weight hits his chest. I grab his phone and then use his finger to unlock it, like some creepy stalker girlfriend but fuck it, this feels like an emergency.

I fucking hope it's not an emergency.

I dial Illi's number with my heart in my throat.

"What's happened?" He answers, an echo of my own worry.

"Do you still have eyes on Arbour? Something is wrong."

Illi grunts and starts to move. The swishing noise in the other phone stops, and I heard a door open and shut.

He swears low and colorful under his breath. "He's just taken a girl into his room, kid. Fuck. He's clearly fucking wasted, she's practically holding him up, but cheating's fucking cheating. I didn't fucking see him doing this, he's so fucking taken with you. Fuck. You need me to kill him? I can do it with a bullet, nice and quick if you feel squeamish about it." Illi says, gentle in a way I didn't know he had in him.

But fuck that.

I know Harley and I fucking trust him.

"No killing, no matter what. Go and get a look at what the fuck is happening in that room."

Ash grunts and his eyes open, an arm winding around my waist before his eyes even open. He blinks up at me and frowns when he sees his phone at my ear. I cut him a look and, thankfully, he keeps his mouth shut.

"Right. I'm outside the room and - *FUCK!*"

The booming sound of a door being kicked in startles Ash and he sits up, his arm keeping me stable on top of him.

"What the fuck?" He mouths at me and I swallow roughly.

"Harley." I croak, my eyes welling up, and Ash can't contain the vicious curses that spill out of his mouth.

He sets me down on the bed and starts pulling his clothes on, yelling for Blaise and Avery. I can't move. I can't do anything until I know Harley is alive and safe. Whatever the fuck has happened I'm frozen until I know he's okay.

But the second I know he is, someone is going to fucking *bleed* tonight.

Through Harley's phone, I can hear screaming and sobbing. I recognize it immediately and look up to find the others, dressed and ready, waiting for me to tell them what the fuck is going on.

"Annabelle *fucking* Summers. I don't know what's happened but Illi's there and she's sobbing." I croak and Avery collapses on the bed next to me. Her eyes are wide and when she tucks her arm into mine I can feel the tremble running through her.

"Call 911, you dumb fucking slut!" Illi roars, and Harley's phone makes a scratching noise before the line goes dead.

Holy fucking shit.

Avery's shoulders shake and Ash yanks her up off the bed as Blaise pulls me to stand. I protest, I don't want to hang up, but he maneuvers me into a pair of yoga pants. Then he hoists me into his arms and carries me like I weigh nothing.

"We're going to him. Tell me once you know where the ambulance is taking him."

I nod and he sets me back onto my feet in the elevator. Avery is taking deep, shuddering breaths, and Ash is scowling, his hands clenching.

IT TAKES us over an hour to get to the hospital, even

though Blaise drives like a fucking maniac the entire way. I can't think, or breathe, or function. My mind just keeps playing Illi's voice over and over again, the urgency when he screamed for Annabelle to call 911. The dread in my gut has grown, spread down through my limb until I walk into the hospital lobby on numb legs. Only Blaise's strong arm banded around my waist keeps me upright.

Avery snarls at the reception staff until they tell us Harley is in surgery. My brain sort of shut off after that, like a rage blackout except I can see Avery nodding and taking in all the information for me while I freak the fuck out. Then we're directed to the waiting room.

Illi is already there, vomit and blood covering his clothes.

I could fucking pass out.

He looks at me with such fucking sorrow for a second I want to punch him. He nods at me. "This way kid. I've got what you need in here."

I stupidly think he's taking me to see Harley but no. He directs me over to a supply cupboard and jiggles the door until the lock pops. Inside, Annabelle goddamn Summer's is hogtied. All trussed up like a turkey at Thanksgiving, and what good luck because I'm going to fucking carve her up.

Illi motions me in and then I block everything out, every sound, sight, and smell while I stare down the pathetic *whore* who's tried to take Harley from me. If he dies... no. I can't even think about it. He's going to live. He has to.

I step forward and yank the gag out of her mouth, watching with grim satisfaction as she tries to swallow and winces.

"What the fuck did you do to him?" There's nothing human left in my voice.

She whimpers pathetically.

"Tell me." I say, and she sneers at me, all the fake simpering vanishing like the manipulative skank she is.

Eclipse Starbright Anderson ceases to exist. I don't know who takes her place because the Wolf has *nothing* on the deadly rage that takes over me. I stay completely aware as I pin Annabelle to the wall by her throat. I watch with a detached sort of fascination when her eyes light up with terror and, as my hands tighten around her neck, her face darkens until she looks almost purple.

I only squeeze harder.

I don't notice the argument happening behind me until a large, colorful hand wraps around my wrist and a broken voice croons softly in my ear, "Let go, Star."

I shake my head. I'll never fucking let her go again.

She dies *today*.

"She can't speak if she's dead." He says calmly, and my grip loosens a fraction. I must have spoken that thought out loud.

Her eyes are still bulging as she sucks in air, and she fixes her gaze over my shoulder like she always fucking does. No one else matters to this fucking despicable, money-hungry whore but the guys she's fixated on. My *fucking* guys.

"Blaise, please -" She gurgles and he cuts her off.

"Just get the facts out of her so we can get back to Arbour. That's where we need to be, babe."

Babe. Only Harley ever calls me that. My lip threatens to wobble but it's like my emotions are just out of reach. Annabelle's eyes stay glued to Blaise like I'm not even there, pinning her to the wall by her throat. I can't get what I need like this. She won't look at me with Blaise in the room.

"I'll get the truth. You should go."

Blaise moves his hand from my wrist to my hip, covering

my body with his own until I'm surrounded by him. "I'm not leaving you with this cunt. I don't care what you do to her; I'm with you."

Annabelle starts fucking crying and I can't contain my snarl at her. "She won't focus with you in the room. She'll just spout her usual fucking lies."

Blaise grunts and shifts on his feet like he's going to put up a fight. Illi speaks up from the doorway. "Go on, kid. I'll watch your girl and you can go help the other one watch over the Crow's little ice queen. Nothing will touch her with me around, I'll see to it."

When the door clicks shut Illi speaks, "The doctors said he was dosed with ketamine. A dirty batch."

This fucking *cunt*.

I stare her down but there's no remorse in her. "So you were going to rape him?"

She scoffs at me. "Girls can't rape guys! I just needed him to forget about *you* and your fucking *magical slum pussy* for an hour and then we could be together again. Everything was finally working out; he has his money and we could be together without the other two. How the fuck was I supposed to know the pills would do this?"

She's dead.

The second I have the story out of her, I'm gutting her. Nice and slow. Clean up will be a bitch but, fuck it, I'll call in a favor and the Bear can pin it on some underling of his. While I'm plotting her disembowelment she continues on her little rant until something she says pings in my memory.

"What dealer?"

She sputters to a stop. "What? Some guy. What does it matter? He was from the slums like you and gave me the pill in a little bag."

Slums.

The Bay.

My voice shakes. "Show me."

"What?"

"*Show me the fucking bag.*" I hiss at her.

She fumbles around in her pocket before dropping the little clear bag on my palm. I know it's the Jackal's before I turn it over and see his insignia. Even with Illi taking out the stream of underlings the Jackal hired he's still found a crack in our defense.

I stare at her, long enough that it finally dawns on her that she's utterly defenseless, hogtied in a closet with a murderous girl and her thug-looking mountain of a friend.

She's fucked.

"Look, I didn't fucking know it would do this to him! I just wanted him back!" She sobs, and I feel fucking nothing but icy bloodlust pumping through my veins. I drop my hands away from her and start to look for my knife. Blaise had grabbed it and stashed it in his pocket for me while I'd been frozen in fear, waiting with my phone pressed against my ear. Illi steps up and takes my arm, pulling me out of the room and into the hallway, pushing me until I find myself wrapped in Blaise's arms.

"I'll sort this for you, kid. It's my job and my fucking pleasure to take care of this for you."

I stare at him, cold and detached. He nods at me like he knows how blank I am inside.

"She fucked with the wrong family. I'll treat her with the same *patience* and *understanding* as you did with the guy who bid on Odie. Stay with your mobster kid. I'll check on you guys when it's done."

He ushers us back out to the waiting room and at the last moment, he grabs Ash's arm. Ash stares at him with the rage that's filling every fiber of his being. If anyone else did that Illi would thumb their eyes out, but he just nods at him with respect. "Welcome to the family. We're going to burn this place to the fucking ground."

And then he leaves with a deftness no man his size should have.

Ten minutes later, we're all still sitting in the waiting room when Diarmuid shows up. He takes one look at me and collapses on a chair across from us.

"Liam?" He snarls.

I shake my head. "Matteo."

He nods and unsheathes his favorite knife. Blaise tenses for a second but the Irish bastard pulls out a whetstone and begins to sharpen the blade. It's an old habit, something he does when he's plotting. I don't know how we're going to do it, but the Jackal just signed his own death warrant.

FIVE HOURS later they finally let us in to see him.

The overpowering smell of the disinfectant burns my nostrils and my chest tightens instantly. The beeping of the machines monitoring him just makes me want to scream and fucking chase Annabelle down, slamming a knife through her gut before Illi gets the chance. He would have already taken care of it but fuck, I wish I would have fought a little harder to make the kill myself.

Blaise helps me climb onto the bed next to Harley as Ash lifts wires and tubes out of my way without unplugging anything. It's a tight fit with how big he is but I make it work. Avery sits in the chair by the window and watches me with vacant eyes.

It's not until I cry that her soul seems to come back to her body. The tears start as silent streams of salty liquid, leaving tracks down my face. Then comes the sniffling until finally, my whole body is trembling at the force of the sobs I'm desperately keeping in.

I'm taking today.

I'm giving myself today to lay here with him and touch him and know that he's alive. Tomorrow I'm going to start a war, I'll call in every last favor until the blood pours like fucking rivers through the streets of Mounts Bay and every damn man, woman, and child knows to stay the fuck away from my family. But today is for Harley.

Hours pass like that, me crying into his chest, while the others all try to find some comfort on the cheap, spindly plastic chairs. Blaise eventually passes out on the floor, his jacket balled up under his head, and Ash sprawls out over four chairs with his head in Avery's lap.

I am nothing but blind rage and gut-wrenching fear.

"I've never seen you cry before." Avery looks absently out the window and strokes at Ash's hair. I don't speak, I can't open my mouth without the sobs coming out messily, so she continues. "I've always known you liked them. I mean, you protect them all so fucking fiercely, it's obvious it's not just for my sake. I just... I didn't realize you loved him like this."

I take a minute to wipe my eyes and collect myself. It takes every last ounce of my strength I have left.

"I've never given anyone the power to break me. Harley is... on paper, he's the worst choice for me. He's a mobster's son. He's from the Bay. He's lived in the world that has tried to kill me every fucking day of my life. He's a killer, he has that darkness in him that every single man in my life so far has used to hurt me. Trying to get away from that life means he's the *worst* option. But he's... a part of me. It goes so far beyond having my heart. Hearts can be broken, torn out, fucking burned. Harley owns a part of my soul and, if he wanted to, he could destroy me in ways Matteo never fucking could. They all do, Aves. It's why I couldn't fucking choose in that bathroom back when you asked me because how do I choose between the parts of my soul?"

I lift my eyes to her and I feel the calm settle back over me. "Avery, I'm not going to take careful steps anymore. I'm going to wipe the fucking board clean until there isn't a threat left. I'm going to take out the Jackal, the O'Cronin's, Senior, fucking *Morningstar himself* if I have to. Every single one of them will die before I let this happen again."

Avery's eyes stay fixed on mine, unblinking and unflinching in her resolve. "I would watch the whole world burn to keep our family safe, Lips. I'm calling Atticus. I don't forgive him and I don't want him anymore, but I'll use him until every last threat is gone. We're done playing it safe and keeping the body count low. Whatever it takes, to the end."

CHAPTER THIRTY-ONE

Harley doesn't wake up for two awful, gut-wrenching, devastating days.

I don't leave his side, only getting out of the bed when the nurses need me to, and Avery works her magic to have supplies brought to us.

Ash takes up watch by the door like he thinks the Jackal is going to come down here personally to finish Harley off. I think he's actually hoping the fucking sociopath will. We all want him dead in the worst way for this.

Blaise only lasts a few hours before he rigs up a stereo and starts singing the most ridiculous songs. When Avery snaps at him he shrugs and says, "Quickest way to wake him up is to piss him off, and nothing pisses him off like my taste in music."

I could cry all over again but my tears have all dried up.

Now there's nothing but rage left in me. Rage at the Jackal, rage at Annabelle, rage I didn't kill her myself. Rage that he won't wake up. I need him, dammit. I fucking need him.

When he finally opens his eyes Avery is busy fussing

with his blankets while I'm cuddled up on his chest, making sure his damn heart is still beating.

"Fuck, Harley! Lips, he's awake!" Avery shrieks, and my neck damn near breaks as I snap upright to get a look at his bleary eyes, doped up and fussy.

He's never looked fucking better in his whole life.

Avery jabs at the call button for the nurse as I lay there just staring at him like an idiot because I can't fucking move or think now he's awake.

"What's wrong, babe?" He mumbles, slurring a little, and I kiss him gently.

"Nothing. Everything is going to be fine. Just rest." I mumble against his cheek, and he nods.

The nurse bustles in and Avery starts to snap out orders at her, ever the dictator. The nurses all tiptoe around her, having learned on day one of our stay not to piss her off. Ash helps me off of the bed so the nurse can check Harley's vital signs and reflexes now he's awake.

I stand by the bed, ready to stab the bitch if she so much as flinches in his direction because now I'm convinced everyone is a fucking Jackal spy. Avery does the same, even though she liased with Atticus to have the hospital swept clean before the surgery was even over.

When the nurse mumbles she's happy with his reactions, she starts to mess around with his IVs and Diarmuid walks in, Illi on his heels looking pissed the fuck off.

Diarmuid gives a wry smile when he sees Harley's eyes open and reaches out to sling an arm around me. I flinch away from him, I don't want to be touched by anyone but my family and I don't trust this asshole. Not one bit.

"*Don't fucking touch her.*" Ash hisses and Diarmuid snaps away from me.

"Right. I'm just here to check if my nephew is okay.

Now I can see he's awake I'll leave you all to it. Call me if you need help making this right, Wolfie."

I shake my head at him and he leaves, Illi glaring at his retreating back. Once he's out of sight I share a look with Illi. He doesn't trust him either.

"How your boy, kid?" He murmurs, and I nod.

"He's awake and he's going to be fine. I need you to clear your calendar for the summer. We're going hunting."

***

A week later, we travel back to Hannaford in the Maserati and I clutch Harley's hand in my own like he'll somehow slip away without my touch. Ash notices my anxiety and slips his hand around my thigh, what little weight I was managing to keep now gone so there's not much for him to get a hold of.

Blaise drives much steadier and slower than normal, and Avery stays glued to her phone the entire time. When I'd told Harley the truth of who the Crow really is he'd snarled at Avery to ditch him. It's a testament to how worried we've all been about him that she let him go with nothing but a kiss on the cheek for his troubles.

It's mid-afternoon on a Tuesday, so when we pull up there isn't a person in sight.

Harley is grouchy as fuck, irritated to be fussed over and when Blaise offers to carry him back up to our rooms he snarls and takes a swing at him.

Blaise just laughs because everyone is fucking relieved to be out of that fucking hospital room.

Avery and I are a little more discreet in our fussing, but

we're still fucking fussing. Avery's fingers fly over the screen on her phone as she covers for our absences and plots out our next move. I watch Harley's every step as if he's going to drop dead any second and when we get to the stairs right as classes let out for the day, I death glare every single student who dares come near us.

I can't trust that the Jackal hasn't sent someone else to finish the job.

The whispers follow us; about Annabelle's absence, the takedown of Ms. Vivienne, why we've been gone. I try my best not to roll my eyes at them but Ash is openly smirking like a smug dick about it all. When I jab him in the ribs he shrugs, "I'm just enjoying the theories of the sheep. Imagine their faces if they knew the truth."

He's not wrong.

Blaise and Ash go back to their room and I coax Harley back to our room with the promise of ice cream and coffee. He doesn't give a shit about either of them, I start to suspect he's just humoring me. It's only after dinner I find out his real plan.

"Over my dead fucking body are you going to swim training. I will knock your ass out."

He frowns at me, cutting a look at Avery like she'll help him but she's firmly Team Sit-The-Fuck-Down. "I'm going fucking insane, babe. You gotta ease up."

There's no way I can let him out of my sight without the panic clawing at me.

Instead of admitting any of that I glare at him and point to the couch. "Sit your ass down and don't move. Your doctor said no swimming for another week, *so no fucking swimming for another week.*"

He growls at the two of us, like that will scare us into submission, and Avery laughs in his face. He cusses the two of us out to hell and back, and I ignore him on my way to the shower. When I'm done and brushing my teeth, Harley calls out to grab my attention.

My heart skips a beat, as I scramble but I find him on the couch where I left him only now Avery's joined him and Harlow Roqueford's face is on national TV, with an Amber Alert out on her. Her father stands at a press conference, blotting at his eyes, and listing all of her saint like qualities.

"What school did she end up at?" I ask, and Avery answers without looking up.

"Huxerly Prep in Boston. Her father has business associates there to keep an eye on her. She did her stint in rehab, too. She's probably just fallen off of the wagon. I'll make some calls and make sure she hasn't run back to find Joey."

I nod, but there's something not right about this.

The sound of the door unlocking breaks through our thoughtful silence but we don't look up, confident only Blaise and Ash can get in here, and it's Blaise's voice that calls out.

"Star. You have another package."

THE DIFFERENCE between finding Lance's head and finding Harlow's is fucking huge.

Avery starts to collect every frame of footage taken at Hannaford for the entire day while I call Illi, staring into the box at Harlow's vacant eyes. He picks up immediately.

"Don't fucking tell me. You have another package."

I curse under my breath. "How did you guess? What the fuck is going on?"

He groans at me. "Because a headless corpse just got found at the docks, strung up like a fucking crucifix. It's a girl, fake tits on her and nails like a fucking housewife. Who is it?"

I rub a hand over my face. "Oh, you know, only the oil magnate's beloved daughter who's got every fucking cop in the country on the lookout for her."

"Okay, kid. We need to have a chat about who the fuck is stalking you."

I snort at him. "No shit. Can you make it up here to get the package? I can call the Bear if it's too much."

"We can't be trusting any member of the Twelve right now. Leave it with me, I'll be there as soon as I can sort... the rest of it out."

He hangs up and I tell Avery what he said. She stares at me for a long time, silent and calculating.

She shakes her head. "It doesn't make sense. It can't be the Jackal. Senior doesn't play these sorts of games. Who else would be this invested?"

I shrug at her. "Whoever it is, they're not killing people I like. They're killing people who've threatened me... or our family."

We've managed to attract some sort of sick, twisted guardian angel.

Fuck. Me.

CHAPTER THIRTY-TWO

Harley goes back to school on Monday and I continue to watch his every move, waiting for something to happen and for him to drop dead. I've never been this fucking paranoid before but his hospital stay has fucking broken something in me.

He deals with my over protectiveness for exactly three classes and then finally he snaps and tells me to get the fuck over it.

I just nod along; it's easier to agree with him and then do whatever the fuck I like.

We eat dinner in the dining hall because Avery has an extra dance practice and none of us feel like cooking. Ash leaves for a run straight after, kissing me far too possessively for public consumption, but after Annabelle's disappearance the other students are now silent in our presence. No whispers follow me and even the clueless freshmen give me a wide berth.

The rumor is I ran her off.

The truth is worse.

Harley tells Blaise to go ahead and start studying back

in my room, and I give him a curious look. He shrugs, "I want you to myself for an hour after your freak out all *fucking* day."

"I can't help it. You *died*."

He nods and tucks me under his arm, walking me back up to his room. None of the guys in the hall dare to look at me and I can't say I'm unhappy about it.

Harley kicks his shoes off at the door and waits for me to do the same, then he grabs my ass and lifts me into his arms, burying his face into my neck. I wind my arms around his neck and thread my fingers through his hair, sighing.

What the fuck would I have done if he'd died?

"Stop fucking thinking about it." He mumbles into my skin, and I shiver uncontrollably.

I shake my head at him. "I can't help it. I haven't ever had someone to lose before and now I have four people I can't live without. Six if you count Illi and Odie, and I do. Fuck. I don't think I'm cut out for... loving people. I can't fucking breathe when I think-"

"Well, stop fucking thinking then." He growls and kisses me, effectively turning my brain off the way only he can.

I groan and kiss him back, pushing and desperate because how fucking dare he nearly die on me? After everything I've done to keep him breathing, dammit!

He grunts and walks us over to his bed, falling until he's on top of me, catching himself with one hand so he doesn't crush me. He feels fucking perfect on top of me. I wriggle until the heavy weight of his hard dick rubs against my clit through our uniforms.

I definitely want to suck him off. I want to taste him and remind myself he's okay, he's here, he's mine.

When I tell him that, he grunts and kisses his way down

my neck. His hand slides underneath the tiny triangle of lace between my thighs and two of his fingers ease into me, my pussy already wet and aching for him. "You first, baby. I need you first."

I think about arguing with him but I swear his mouth is magic and the second his lips and tongue touch me all rational thought just leaks out of my brain until I'm writhing underneath him. When his mouth closes around my clit and he groans, the vibrations tip me over the edge until I'm screaming and thrashing, clenching down on his fingers, held down by his firm grip on my hips.

He chuckles under his breath at me, all satisfied alpha male at making me lose my damn mind, and I yank at his hair until he crawls but up my body.

When he kisses me, I groan at the taste of myself on his lips and decide that this isn't enough. I can't wait any longer, we've been slow enough. I need every fucking inch of him.

"I need you. I'm on birth control, and I know we're both clean so I need you inside me right now." I whisper against his lips. He groans and pulls away, his hips jerking to rub his dick against the soft skin of my belly. He opens his mouth and I cut him off.

"I know what I'm doing. Okay, I don't know exactly what I'm doing but I know that I want you so don't argue with me."

He scoffs and laughs at me then slides his hand back down my stomach until two fingers slip back inside me. I frown at him, ready to chew him out for trying to distract me, when he adds a third and my heart stutters in my chest at the stretch.

Oh.

Right.

I scramble until I get my shirt and bra off, my skirt and panties are a little more tricky because Harley refuses to stop kissing and touching me, even for a second, but I manage it somehow. I feel a little frantic as I yank his shirt off, my legs starting to shake as he crooks his fingers inside me and rubs my G spot mercilessly. I gasp out his name as I come again, and my hands become useless. I swear I must black out a little because then next thing I know he's gone, standing to take the rest of his clothes off, thank *fuck*.

He's fucking perfection, and I can't breathe when I look at him. How is that still possible, after months of kisses and touches, orgasms and blowjobs, how can I still feel light-headed just looking at him?

He smiles at me, slow and so fucking adoringly I want to *die*, and then he settles back on top of me again, kissing me until I'm panting.

"You sure?" Harley mumbles against my lips, and I bite his lip until he grunts back at me and shifts his hips, lining himself up and pushing in.

The stretch is uncomfortable, just this side of pain, but I'm no stranger to things that hurt and he kisses me to distract me. I'm so fucking full of him, I can't breathe but I don't even want the air in my lungs anymore if it means we have to stop.

"Babe, fuck, babe..." he mumbles into my skin and I nod, tugging and pulling until finally he moves, rolling his hips and *holy fuck* this is it. This is how I want to die. Impaled by Harley's fucking dick, stretching and filling me until I'm his.

He catches my lips with his in another blistering kiss and rocks slowly inside of me until I can't take the easy pace anymore, desperate for *more*, and I bite his lip again.

His control snaps and the next stroke is harder, building

and building until he's slamming into me, and fuck if that isn't exactly what I need. I hold onto his shoulders, his neck, fucking *anything* I can and he doesn't stop.

It's fucking perfect.

He shifts to hold himself on one arm and slips his hand between our bodies and the second his fingers touch my clit, I'm gone. All I see is white light and pure fucking bliss. I hear him grunt my name and his hips stutter to a stop, grinding rather than pounding.

When I blink up at him, trying to get my eyes working again, he grins down at me like I'm the most perfect thing he's ever seen. Like I'm his soul, his reason for being.

I have to duck my head and blink rapidly because I will not be that pathetic girl who cries after her first time, and he scoffs at me, pulling out to go clean up and I kind of think he's giving me a second to pull myself together. It's sweet.

Harley cleans me up too because apparently he's a gentleman, then he climbs back into bed and bundles me into his arms. I rest my head on his chest, secure in his arms, listening to his heartbeat like I had for days in the hospital. His mom's heart locket catches in the light as he catches his breath.

"How did Joey get a hold of the locket? You said you'd been trying to get it back for years."

He grunts and shifts so he can thread his fingers through my hair, stroking my back until I'm a boneless mess.

"The first time I went to juvie was the first time Avery and Ash even knew I existed. Senior wouldn't let Alice and my mom see each other. Used to fucking kill Ma, they were as close as Ash and Avery were as kids. So they didn't know about me until Social Services knocked on the big, ugly fucking door at Beaumont Manor and Senior had his staff turn them away. But the kids all heard my name, heard how

I was related and Avery started to pull strings until I got out. She got me into boarding school with them, got me away from my grandfather. I was too fucking scared to wear the locket in middle school. Scared I'd lose it, scared I'd break it. It was like a fucking night light, I'd go to sleep with it in my hand. Joey found out and broke into my room and stole it. I raged out destroyed the whole room, went after Joey, the only reason I didn't kill him was because Ash and Blaise stopped me. I fucking hated Ash for stopping me. I didn't know... I didn't know what was going on. I thought he was picking that psycho over me. Avery had to do a fuck load of mediation to get us through that. Now I feel like a dick. He was being fucking tortured and protecting us all and there I was being pissy at him for it."

I blink away tears and clear my throat. "He doesn't blame you. He only blames Senior and Joey. He's just as fierce as Aves with his love. He's just a dick about it."

Harley chuckles, the rumble loud and warm against my ear. "I don't regret anything, babe. It got us here. I'd do it all again, and Ash and Morrison would too."

CHAPTER THIRTY-THREE

H ARLEY TELLS me not to make plans for my Saturday.

When I ask him why, he gives me a smug, haughty smile. I'd be pissed about it but all three of my guys keep sharing these little secretive looks and eventually I give up and just go with it. I'm stupid enough to ask Avery if she knows what going on and she gives me her own smug fucking smile.

"Why don't you ask your *lover?*"

I could die.

She screeches with laughter at my blush. "I'm so glad to know that having sex hasn't stopped you from blushing like an eighteenth-century contessa on her wedding night."

So that's the end of my inquiries.

I wake to pancakes and coffee for breakfast and then Harley drives us all into Haven in the Maserati. Apparently he won a bet about Avery but I'm too afraid to ask what the hell it was. Blaise sulks in the back with me, dicking around to piss Harley off but my golden god is above the petty bullshit today. I finally break and ask him why he's so happy and he gives me a smug look in the mirror.

"We're getting tattoos. Do you have any idea how long I've waited to get your insignia on me? I fucking hate that Illi's had it all this time and I haven't."

I blanch, fucking shocked that *that's* what's going on. "You don't have to. None of you do."

He gives me a look in the mirror. "I only waited because the others hadn't been inducted. I'm not waiting anymore."

Avery rolls her eyes at him, then smiles at me. "We are all doing this. As a family, even if there are *needles* and *bodily fluids* involved."

Blaise roars with laughter at her. "How's Atticus faring with your hatred of bodily fluids? Does he know he's going to have to wear a hazmat suit to fuck you?"

I groan as Ash turns to stone next to me but Avery snarks back before he can come to her defense.

"I don't want *his* fluids or any other fucking piece of shit man that walks this Earth. I'm taking a vow of celibacy because you're *all* fucked." She says through clenched teeth and my stomach drops. Fucking Atticus.

I sigh, and wonder how the fuck I'm going to help her with this now we've agreed to work with him. That's a fucking headache to think about later. I lace my fingers into Ash's.

"Do you know where you're getting yours?" I murmur, trying to distract him from the conversation happening around us. If I didn't already know, his clenched jaw would tell me everything I need to know about his feelings towards Atticus.

He stares out the window, a frown over his brow and replies, "We discussed it after the Lingerie Party, we're all getting the same thing. Well, not Avery. I'm sure you'll find it suitable, Mounty."

I nod and rub my thumb along the back of his hand.

Harley parks behind the tattoo parlor and as we all pile out of the car I rub my arms, the chill in the air biting at me. Ash tucks me under his arm and leads me in.

The guy sitting behind the reception desk nods at Blaise and they start talking shit about how his last tattoos turned out. One of the tattoo artists looks Avery up and down dismissively, obviously used to Hannaford girls and their rich bitch attitudes, and she stares him down like he's a steaming pile of shit.

Then his eyes flick over to me and he frowns. Ash cuts in front of me and snarls at him, "What the fuck is your problem?"

The guy raises his hands in submission, "Nothing man. She just looks familiar, that's all. I thought I recognized her."

Blaise starts to snicker under his breath and I sigh.

"Any chance you're from Mounts Bay?" Avery says, sickly sweet, like poison.

He nods and pulls his chair up, ready to draw up the design they want. A group of high school girls come in for piercings and I start getting twitchy at the looks my guys get. Avery rolls her eyes at me but joins me in glaring at them.

When Harley tells the guy they all want the same thing he cracks a lame joke about boy bands and Ash looks ready to gut him.

Then Harley gets a UV torch out of his pocket and shines it on my face.

The tattoo artist shits his fucking pants.

Oh, *goodie*.

"You get that it takes a week to heal, right? You can't go to classes with that on your face!" Avery hisses, but they all ignore her completely.

I sit in the corner in a state of shock.

The tattoo artist from the Bay took a good ten minutes to calm down enough to trace the image out nicely, but the tremor in his fingers is finally gone. I try to look friendly and approachable but I think that only freaks him out more. Something about me being an assassin and renowned killer has him freaked out. Who knew?

Then he hands it off to the second guy and we're in business.

Harley and Blaise go first, unflinching and completely at ease as the needle drags through their cheeks. The jaw bones and sharp teeth only make them look hotter, the assholes, and the giggling girls in the corner refuse to leave after their belly button piercings are finished. Finally, after one of them tries to talk to Harley, the receptionist kicks them out. The blonde gets snooty and tries to play the rich daddy card but Avery only laughs at her, the cruel edge cutting.

"These are gang tattoos, you dense bitch. Do you want to risk a bullet by fucking the boss's boy?"

They scurry out quickly after that. I glare at Avery and she shrugs, smug as always.

It takes an hour and Ash smirks at Harley when he gets taped up, puffy and grumpy at the inconvenience. Avery cringes the second the gel hits her skin to transfer her little wolf onto her wrist but she doesn't flinch at the needle piercing her skin. Hers only takes ten minutes, being so small, and I make my decision to cement myself in the family with them.

I catch the tattoo guy's eye and ask him to tattoo me as well. He blanches for a second and them recovers nicely, nodding and clearing his throat.

When I point out Harley's tattoo he agrees quickly but when I move to take my pants off all hell breaks loose.

"What the fuck are you doing?!" Harley hisses, and Avery giggles at him.

I glare back at him, and then over his shoulder at Blaise. "I'm getting a tattoo as well. Go wait with Avery, it'll only take a few minutes."

Harley plants his ass in the seat next to the tattooing table and refuses to move like the stubborn asshole he is and Blaise takes up watch by the door. I roll my eyes and try to ignore them as best I can. By chance I'm wearing my most modest panties but, given that Ash picks them out for me, they're still fairly sheer. Harley glares at the tattoo artist like it's his damn fault.

"I want it on my panty line, where my hip meets my thigh, because it's fucking personal and the only people I want seeing it are you three dickheads so lay off." I snap, and he calms down a little.

Then I zone the fuck out while the family creed is inked into my skin, a permanent reminder that I belong to them just as much as they belong to me.

I couldn't be fucking happier with it.

We take the next week off while the tattoos heal and spend it in the boy's room watching trashy thriller movies Blaise loves and drinking too much whiskey. Avery continues to go to classes and tells the teachers we've caught mono, something they all accept without question because who in their right mind argues with a Beaumont?

Blaise and I practice our song together, him playing the guitar and me sweating without my earplugs in but fuck, we sound perfect together. Ash bans us from singing it around Avery because the second we start he ends up hard as stone and drooling for me. It's a nice fucking compliment, better than any stupid roses he could ever give me.

Harley cooks me French toast and insists I eat it in bed, sulking when I refuse to do it naked. I'm positive it would quickly turn into an orgy if I did and I'm not quite sure I'm ready for that. There's an unspoken agreement amongst the boys not to talk about my new non-virginal status, thank *fuck*.

On the Sunday before classes go back I step into the shower, getting ready for bed and pouting that my week off has come to an end, when Harley ducks in behind me. I give him stern look that quickly melts away because sweet lord *fuck*, he is glorious to look at.

His personality ain't bad either.

"You're going to flit back to your room tomorrow and I'll have to make do with the smell of you on my sheets. You've turned me into some pathetic sap, it's fucking sad."

I snort at him, blushing wildly, and then I grab the soap to wash him, any excuse to run my hands over the solid plains of muscle on his chest.

"You'll just come sleep in my bed anyways. I'll try to sleep here a bit more. We can work something out. What are we going to do after summer break when we're all used to being in the same bed all of the time?"

Harley groans and rubs his dick against my belly. "You're going to move in here next year. Fuck it, Avery can get the room next door and we can live together. We all know she could make it happen."

My teasing dries up in my throat because, fuck, that sounds perfect.

CHAPTER THIRTY-FOUR

THE SCHOOL STAFF decide that the students need motivation going into the last few weeks of classes before exams so the class rankings are posted on every door. Our first class for the day is History, and I do a double take when I see that the second spot, under me, is Ash. Not Harley.

Oh fuck.

"Are you *fucking* kidding me?" Harley snarls, and the look Ash gives him is total arrogant asshole.

Do I stand between them or just let them fight it out? Stupid question, I get the fuck out of there and zone them the fuck out. When Harley finally takes his seat, I smile at him only to have him glare back at me.

Fuck.

"Maybe if you hadn't spent half the year with the cougar and a little more time studying with the Mounty you'd be getting those marks too." Ash says from his seat in front of us, and the smug tone only makes Harley's rage spread.

I decide to walk away and let them battle it out amongst themselves.

Harley spends the rest of the day furiously writing notes and snarling questions at our teacher like that alone will raise his mark the fraction it needs to reclaim the second spot. We make it through history in one piece only to find that Ash has beaten Harley by the tiniest of margins in every. Damn. Class.

Harley wouldn't take the news well at the best of times but Ash makes it his personal mission to mock his cousin mercilessly until I'm sure I'm going to be helping Avery clean intestines off of the walls by dinnertime.

Blaise enjoys the show just a little *too* much. He's practically bouncing with glee when we get back to our room and when I drop onto the couch next to him he pulls me into his lap.

"Wanna fuck on the couch and see if that distracts them?" He murmurs, but it's loud enough that Avery hears him and throws a dirty look at him.

"No fucking on the furniture, Morrison, or I'll burn all of your guitars."

He pouts at her and she snarls at him as she shoves Harley towards the bathroom to cool off. I abandon Blaise and his wandering fingers, too much of a temptation, and I convince Ash to walk me through my share portfolio. I hope it'll distract him enough to leave Harley alone.

He relents, but only if I'll sit in his lap. Avery side-eyes the fuck out of him but I don't care. It's easy enough to learn and seeing my profits makes me wriggle in his lap with excitement.

"Now, now, Mounty. Avery's already on the warpath. I don't need to die just because you got over excited over your money and want to fuck me at the table." He says and I blush furiously.

"Who said I want to fuck you?" I whisper, eyeing Avery's back as she stirs the curry she's cooking. Her new obsession is cooking her way through cookbooks and I for one am not complaining.

"Other than your hard nipples, and your thighs? If I touched you right now I think I'd find you dripping."

Oh, Lord have mercy on my poor soul.

Yes, yes he would find me dripping. Even more so now he's whispering dirty things to me again. I try to move away from his lap but he slaps my thigh and tells me to focus on the laptop screen or he'll have to spank me, loud enough that the entire damn room hears him.

Avery's death glare at him only makes my blush worse.

I would have never thought I'd be up for being spanked but holy god damn. I think I could be convinced.

We're all seated in chemistry together when there's a bang outside and the building rumbles.

A few girls squeal and dive under their desks, but the teacher stands and locks the classroom door, calling for us all to stay calm.

My phone buzzes in my pocket at the same time Harley's does. He gives me a look and Avery turns in her chair with an eyebrow raised. Great. Another mass text, what the fuck now?

Every damn student forgets about the lockdown and

checks their phones to see what the hell has just been sent out.

It's a video from Joey.

My heart stutters in my chest for a second when I see the entrance of Hannaford on Harley's phone screen but then it video pans down to the staff parking lot and the cars there.

Harley's Mustang and Blaise's Maserati.

I start to pray he trashes the fucking Maserati and leaves the 'stang the fuck alone. Blaise could not give less of a fuck about his car but I can't bear for Harley seeing another version of his dad's car destroyed.

Joey doesn't just trash the 'stang.

He fucking *blows it up*.

I should've known by all the noise but I'm still shocked to see the video. Ash groans and Blaise starts cursing Joey out in new and thought-provoking ways. Harley doesn't say a word, he just stops the video and slides his phone back into his pocket, before getting back to his chemistry notes. I chew my lip for a second and then grab his hand under the desk, rubbing his knuckles with my thumb like he does for me when my world starts to fucking break. He nods at me without looking up and something in me breaks a little.

I meet Ash's eyes over his shoulder and nod. Joey is escalating and I vote we kill the psycho fucker now too.

When the school admin finally let us out and cancels classes for the rest of the day while the police and fire department clean up the mess, we all go back to our room so Avery can rage clean and drown herself in coffee.

I keep a hold of Harley's hand the whole way up there, trying to ignore the fearful stares from the other students. Everyone knows who's car just got bombed.

"He's fucking pathetic. He knows he can't take any of

us in a fair fight so he's going after shit he thinks will hurt. Well, fuck him. The car is important to me, but it's just a fucking car. Ash and Avery mean more to me. He's just proving how fucking weak he is." he murmurs, and I wonder if he's explaining it to me or trying to convince himself.

I squeeze his hand and smile up at him, trying to lighten the mood. "Remember you're fucking loaded now and you can get it fixed. Or buy a new one."

He scoffs at me. "I don't want a new one. Morrison bought me this one, and it doesn't matter that I've paid him back; he did it because he's family and we do that shit for each other. Fuck Joey and his pissy attitude."

Be still my fucking heart.

Blaise turns and bats his eyelashes at us both to be a dick and Harley snarks back at him. I can take a deep breath again but my chest still fucking hurts.

Joey knows that the only way to truly hurt his siblings is to hurt our family and that makes him a fucking danger.

When he gets back into our room my phone buzzes again and I find a text from Diarmuid.

I can hunt the Beaumont down for you. Will that prove my loyalty? He'll be dead by sunrise.

I show Avery and she stares at me for a second, running the risk analysis in her head for the hundredth time. Finally, she sighs and shakes her head.

Joey lives to die by my hand another day.

CHAPTER THIRTY-FIVE

MUCH LIKE LAST YEAR, I feel fucking sick to my stomach the morning of our choir performance.

Harley wakes me with kisses and soft touches, stroking my face and neck possessively, and I enjoy it for about three seconds before I remember what I have to do in a few hours and then I'm shaking again.

Avery cooks me French toast and I choke down a single piece, my stomach revolting the entire time.

She hides the coffee from me.

I've never been so fucking angry at her, not even when she was trying to destroy me in freshman year. When I snap that at her she just nods and smiles in this infuriatingly kind way that sets my teeth on edge.

When I snarl at Harley to piss off and let me shower by myself she laughs at his kicked puppy expression. "She's not going to be our Lips today until she gets this over with, Arbour. Just leave her to wallow Morrison style."

When I get out of the shower, stomping and throwing myself around, I find the whole family out in our room waiting for me, staring with various levels of sympathy and glee.

Ash can't contain his *fucking* glee.

"I've been waiting all year to hear this, Mounty, Morrison's being fucking shifty about it. He never records songs without letting me listen to them, I've been feeling put out." He says as he tucks me under his arm. I can't do much more than nod and grimace.

We walk down to the Chapel and I sulk the whole way. They all ignore me, which is usually what I want but just this once I'd like Avery to save me from this fucking assignment. I don't feel ready to sing yet. I don't feel ready to listen to myself do it but I've promised Blaise and... fuck. I love him.

I fucking love that asshole.

I sigh and pull myself together. We leave the others on their claimed bench in the front row. Avery squeezes my hand as we walk past and I attempt some sort of smile at her. I can't look at the other two, afraid they'll try to kiss me and I'll puke on them.

Blaise sweet talks Miss Umber and gets us the first slot so I only have to wait five minutes while they set the piano up. Then we're being introduced and the squealing of the freshman girls at the front has a little of my usual fire returning.

Blaise roars with laughter.

"There you are, Star. I was afraid I'd lost you." He teases and laces his fingers through mine.

"I fucking hate this, you're lucky I love you." I mumble and his hand jerks in mine. I frown and glance up at his shocked face. He swallows roughly but I'm too busy freaking out to realize it's the first time I've told the idiot I love him.

We walk out on the stage and Blaise grins easily, waving and bowing like the natural performer he is. I stomp out like I want to commit mass murder on every fucker in the damn room. Well, everyone but my family.

I sit on the piano bench, away from the crowd so I can hide behind Blaise's broad form. He smiles and bumps my shoulder as he rolls his own back, loosening up before his fingers rest on the keys.

"Ready." He murmurs and I give him the slightest nod. I swear I'm going to puke.

His fingers start to dance over the keys in a somber, lilting dance and my heart finally slows down until it's following the beats of the song.

My mind turns off, my eyes drifting closed, and I let myself fall into the song.

I hit every note and my voice doesn't falter.

I'm so glad Blaise's chest is shielding my face from the audience because the second his voice joins mine in the first chorus tears prick at the back of my eyes. We sound fucking perfect together.

I sneak a peek at him and find him staring down at me, ignoring his music sheets and playing the song by heart. He's practiced for this moment for hundreds of hours all year.

We've fucking smashed it.

I feel more powerful than I've ever felt before. Better than standing across from the Jackal drawing lines in the sand.

I've reclaimed my voice for myself and I'll never let anyone take it again.

We're going to war and for the first time, I feel confident that we're going to fucking win.

As Blaise finishes the notes there's a stunned silence like

the whole room is holding it's breath and then the applause is deafening. I can hear Avery screaming again, exactly like she did last year, but I can't look over. I'm still trying to pull myself together.

Blaise grins out at the Chapel and gives a little wave, before turning back to me and wiping my cheeks with one of his big, colorful hands even though they're dry.

The microphone is still on so he can't speak without the whole room hearing, so he quirks his eyebrows at me until I nod, I'm okay. I'm not broken. I'm just so fucking relieved to be healing finally.

He stands, making sure he's still blocking me from the crowd, and then tucks me into his side to walk us both off of the stage. Miss Umber catches his arm at the bottom of the stairs to gush but I don't want to look at her while I'm still so raw.

Ash pries me out of Blaise's arms and wedges me between him and Avery. I take a shuddering breath and Avery slips her hand into mine.

"That was fucking incredible, Mounty. I have goose-bumps." She whispers, and I nod. I swallow and smile at her, my eyes still a little watery.

I hear snickering behind us and the look Harley serves the freshmen there would shrivel the balls of any gangster in the Bay.

I try to find my voice so they don't think I'm going fucking crazy. "I'm fine. It's just-"

"I know." Avery cuts me off, running a soothing hand down my arm. "You're slowly being put back together."

This girl. Where the fuck would I be now without her?

Blaise takes his seat next to Ash and we sit through the rest of the performances, none as breathtaking as ours had been. My hands stop shaking, and by the last song, I can hum along under my breath.

The grin Ash gives me when he hears me is worth all the fucking tears I've ever spilled.

THE CHAPEL EMPTIES out and we wait until the crowd disperses. I look like I've spent a week in bed moping like some pathetic heartbroken teen and I don't want photos of that shit on the gossip site for the Jackal to see.

He'd probably enjoy them too much.

"Right. Dinner? I think we should order in, I feel like sushi." Avery says, and everyone agrees though I just want coffee and ice cream after my stressful day.

We stand and start towards the door only to be stopped by an unfamiliar voice.

"Blaise." A woman's voice calls out and I frown when he freezes, then jerks his head around to follow the sound.

It's his mother.

Harley curses viciously under his breath and moves in front of me while Avery and Ash both stare over at her like they're hoping she'll drop dead.

I try to stay calm.

"What are you doing here?" Blaise croaks, and my heart breaks a little more at the haunted tone in his voice.

Casey Morrison steps forward and wrings her hands nervously, clutching at the - *holy fuck* - baby strapped to her chest. "I wanted to see you. Your agent called me about your contract, I know how hard you worked for it and I can't believe you'd throw that away for... for a girl."

Oh.

Hell.

No.

I step around Harley and cross my arms, pegging this weak and fucking gutless excuse for a mother with a look that rivals the Beaumont's in ice. She winces and gives me a watery smile.

"I didn't mean it like... no, I did but that was before I heard the song. It was beautiful. You both sound so lovely together."

I try to ease my glare up a little but it's impossible to shift. Blaise shakes his head at her but his eyes are glued to his little brother.

"So you've seen I'm fine and now you're going to, what, leave? Scurry back to Dad? Fuck, I can't call him that anymore, can I? Go back to your husband, Mrs. Morrison. I'm fine, my girlfriend is none of your concern, and my choices are no longer yours to help shape."

Casey takes another step forward and looks around at the other parents here, at the teachers all watching their little reunion with badly veiled interest. Being the wife of a billionaire in this level of society must be like living under a microscope.

"I am still your mom and now I've left your father. He... he's left me with nothing and our pre-nup has protected his right to do that but I can't live without you in my life. I thought... I thought I could but I was wrong."

Ash snorts and steps up to Blaise, angling his chest until he's covering his best friend from the prying eyes, the same way Blaise had just done for me.

He looks at her like she's *nothing*, and says in a low voice, "If you had ever given a fuck about your son you would've stood up for him against that miserable, egotistical excuse of a man years ago. Choke on your apology. Come on, Morrison. We have a *family* dinner to get to."

Then he stalks off. Avery shares a look with me and then follows. Harley tugs at my hand and I nod, shooing him away after his cousins until I'm left standing there with broken mother and faltering son.

Blaise sighs. "Give me your number. I'll call you later and we can... figure something out."

Casey smiles and I try not to stare at how much she looks like Blaise when she does. It must be all the fucking sadness in her eyes but I'm not letting her off the hook. Not at all.

Blaise takes the baby from her while she fumbles around for her phone. He smiles down at his little brother and my heart clenches in my chest at the look of wonder.

Lord help me.

"Isn't he cute?" He mumbles at me while he pulls faces and I clear my throat.

"He looks like you, so yeah he's cute."

Blaise grins and tries to hand me the baby.

No.

No, thank you. I do not hold small humans. Not ever.

Blaise cackles at the terrified expression on my face, snapping a photo on his phone because apparently, he can just ninja the baby around in his arms like a freaking wizard without dropping it. I feel a little lightheaded and kinda wish I'd left with everyone else.

"Calm down, I'm good with kids. I'm surprised you're not." He says and I roll my eyes at him.

"I have enough on my plate keeping you lot alive, I don't have time to... hold those things."

Avery will not stop laughing over the photo.

"I'm framing it and hanging it above your bed, so you remember even during coitus that you shouldn't ever get pregnant."

I side-eye her but nod, because I should never, ever have a baby.

Ash scoffs at her. "I was told very sternly by her doctor that those decisions are hers alone, Avery."

Avery hands him a glass of bourbon and says, sickly sweet, "I have far more say in it than you ever will. Besides, how would that even work? Would you guys draw names out of a hat to see who gets to pass their DNA on?"

Fuck this.

I join Harley on the couch to hide from their snarking and he folds me into his chest easily. Blaise is distracted, tapping away on his phone to his mom and I chew my lip as I watch him.

"We'll be on suicide watch by the end of the week," Harley whispers.

I wince but I think he's right. "He can sleep here tonight. I'll see if I can talk him into keeping his expectations low."

"Good fucking luck."

After dinner has finished, and Harley and Ash have gone back to their room, I cuddle into Blaise's chest and sigh. He rubs his cheek against my hair and whispers, "I promise I'll be okay, Star. I'm not going to let her drag me under again."

I wish I could believe him.

CHAPTER THIRTY-SIX

M Y PHONE PINGS after midnight and I have to wriggle out from under Blaise to reach it, my rock god boyfriend wrapped around me like a second skin. He doesn't falter in his faint snores and Avery's headphones are in her ears blaring still so neither of them have woken at the sound.

The dining hall. Now. Don't bring your little friends unless you want me to slit their throats while you watch.

I stare down at the Jackal's text and a cold wave of dread takes over me for a second. Then I get angry.

Really fucking angry.

I slip out of the bed and into one of Harley's hoodies and some yoga pants because I'll be damned if I let that psychopath see me in booty shorts ever a-fucking-gain. My knife gets slipped into my pocket and, after a moment of hesitation, I slip my gun into the waistband of my yoga pants.

Then I stand over Avery for three minutes, my heart in my throat, debating telling her but, fuck, she might follow me down there or call for back up and that's a bad situation looking to turn nuclear.

When I'm out of the room, door locked firmly behind me, I text Illi.

The Jackal is here. I'm going to meet him. If you don't hear from me in thirty minutes call Diarmuid for backup. Tell the boys I love them and Avery she's the best fucking thing that ever happened to me.

It's sappy as fuck, and Illi will give me so much shit for it, but I need them to know how much they mean to me if I'm... dead. Fuck, I hope I'll be dead and not taken.

But I'm done bowing down to this man's whims.

I walk slowly, calmly, down the silent halls of Hannaford as if I'm not heading into the very hell I enrolled here to escape. Luca is waiting outside the dining hall doors with three other flunkies. I dip my head and for once Luca doesn't grin and flirt.

"He's not very happy with you, princess."

No shit. "He doesn't have to be happy with me. He's forgotten he's an equal to me in our world." I'm proud of how strong my voice sounds.

Luca just looks at me for a second longer, his eyes searching mine, and then nods.

I give him a nod back like I'm not concerned in the least, and he opens the door for me. I keep my eye on Luca and not the man dressed in a sharp suit, sinfully handsome and utterly soulless. He ushers me in with a firm hand at the small of my back I try not to flinch away from and helps me to my seat across from the outwardly calm Jackal.

He's sitting in Harley's seat.

He knows everything that happens in this school.

I meet his eyes and, fuck it if he doesn't look menacing in his suit. I suppress the shiver that tries to take over my body. He looks calm, with his hands on his knees below the tables, but that only intensifies the dread clawing at me.

"Good evening, little Starbright. I hope I didn't wake you?"

I raise my brows at him. "Don't you know? I assumed you'd have found a way to get a camera in my room by now."

He smirks at me and tips his head. "But of course. I have to say, I'm not a fan of watching those boys defile you."

I fucking refuse to blush or think about him watching us, watching *me* during my most intimate moments. He could be bluffing. He's probably not but I hold onto that hope for now. "What would you like, Jackal? What are you really here for? Because I'm not going to leave with you. I'm content here and who shares my bed every night is no concern of yours."

He twitches. His little tick when he's trying not to attack someone coming out in full force. I've watched him torture, maim, humiliate, pulverize, and destroy a thousand times before and I know his every tick.

He wants to break me.

"You will leave here with me tonight. I've grown tired of our little game, Starbright. I was hoping to wait for you to be a little older, a little wiser, before I claimed you but you've pushed my hand."

I cross my arms. "Claim me? What are you, a fucking caveman? I'm not yours."

He leans forward, the gentleman mask melting away and leaving nothing but the sociopath behind. "You are mine. You've been mine from the second I saw you. I've fixed every single problem you've ever had. You owe me and there's no way I'm going to let some little rich cunts take what's mine."

I laugh at him, so clearly I've gone insane, but the haughty, arrogance of the boys fills me. I've had a steady diet of it for months and now I can breathe that same fire, even if it gets me killed. "You killed my mom. You destroyed my leg. You took my voice away. You murdered any person, man or woman, that tried to be my friend. You did everything you could to cut me off from any help that may have been offered to me. You're not a good man, Matteo. You never have been."

He laughs back at me, flicking a hand at me dismissively. "And you think Johnny is? He's far crueler than I am with his kills. He taught me half of his tricks, back before the French slut ruined everything."

I grit my teeth. "That's your problem; you don't want friends. You want to own people, and Illi and I have never been the type to bow down to your rules."

He drums his fingers against the table, glaring over at me and then nods at me like I've agreed with something he's said. "I can see you've been tainted here. I think your time at Hannaford is over, little Wolf. We need to go home and wipe you clean of all of these new ideas. Rich people can have dreams, and love, and free will. But we are not rich people. We are the lurking shadows."

I grip my knife and his eyes track the movement. I don't care that he knows, that he's watched me just as closely as I've watched him. I'm not going with him without a fight.

"You're a rich man now, Matteo. You may still stand in the shadows but you're richer and more powerful than god. Just not to me."

He stands and I see the gun in his hand, he's had it pointed at me the whole time. I knew it but seeing it pisses me off. Fine. We'll play this his way for a little longer. I just need to be patient.

"Let's go, Starbright. I'm looking forward to wiping you clean from all that this school has done to you."

I stand and keep my hand around my knife. He smirks at me and puts his gun away, motioning for Luca to get my arm. I force myself not to tense as his fingers wrap around my elbow but he's gentle enough with me that it's not so hard.

The moment the Jackal is no longer watching me, Luca drops his hand away and when I glance up at him he gives me a stern look. I frown.

The Jackal walks ahead of us, lazy and confident in his stride and he never sees it coming.

Luca wraps an arm around his neck and squeezes.

Holy fuck.

Holy. *Fuck.*

I stand there like an idiot as the Jackal scrambles against his most trusted and loyal supporter, a man who's been with him since the very beginning, but Luca is bigger and stronger than Matteo and holds firm, even when his arms begin to bleed from the deep gouges Matteo leaves.

The door to the dining hall bursts open and Ash storms through, gun drawn and wild looking, with Harley on his heels. I stare at them both, at the blood on Harley's hands, and then back to Luca who is now laying an unconscious Jackal down on the floor.

He's not dead, not yet.

"WHAT THE FUCK MOUNTY?!" Harley roars, and I blink at him.

I think my brain is a little broken.

Luca gives me a wry smirk and then shocks the shit out of me. "I've been waiting to do that to him for years, princess. It felt as good as I thought it would."

I turn to look at him but I can't get my head around his

words. He's never been anything but loyal to the Jackal and now he's standing over his prone body. I just... I can't figure this out.

He chuckles at me and I glance out the now open doors at the other flunkies but they're all on the floor, bleeding and groaning. Fuck, I forgot how good Harley and Ash are.

The sound of feet slapping on the wood floors has us all tense and then Blaise and Avery bolt through the door, looking frazzled and desperate.

"Good fucking use you two are!" Ash snarls at them both, but Avery ignores him, stumbling over to me and wrapping her arms around my waist. I've never seen her so shaken.

Luca plants a foot over the Jackal's throat in case he wakes up and says, "Atticus sends you his *personal* regards and would like you to know he's been watching you for a long time. Now he is sure Miss Beaumont is guarded by such a capable and competent friend he would like to assure you he will not hesitate to offer you any help necessary. That includes me."

Holy.

Sweet.

Lord.

He's a double agent. A spy. A fucking made man in the Jackal's den, spying on the psycho's every move, and I never would have guessed it. The Jackal clearly hasn't either. Luca has been trusted with *everything* since the very beginning of the Jackal's reign of terror in the Bay. Fuck.

Atticus is *good*.

"I GUESS he'll know now that you're a spy," I say, breaking the silence.

We all stare down at the Jackal and Luca shrugs. "Don't worry about it. I'll drop him home and head back to the Crow. I'm sick of watching the sick fuck hurt people anyway."

I nod and then pull away from Avery to hold my hand out to him. "Thanks for breaking your cover for me. I hope it was worth it."

He grins at me and tugs me into a hug. "Like I'd let him kill you, princess. Even if I wasn't on orders from the boss, I'd have figured a way out for you. It's time for me to go home, it's been too long."

Ash finally lowers his gun but he's still staring at Luca like he wants to shoot him. Harley shakes himself out of his stupor and stalks over to me, so fast I don't realize he's moving until he's pulling me away from Luca's arms and running his hands over me to check for blood and bruises.

"Are you okay? Did he touch you? Tell me he didn't touch you, babe. What the fuck were you thinking?!" He says, voice hoarse and panicked. I catch his wrists in my hands and pull away.

"I was thinking he wasn't leaving without seeing me and I needed to face him. He would've killed you if I had brought you guys. It's fine, I told Illi-"

"We know what you told Illi, who the fuck do you think called us?" Ash snaps, and I glance up to see him staring down at the Jackal, his eyes like black voids. Luca steps in front of the Jackal's prone form.

"You can't kill him. The Twelve will come after the Wolf if you do. There's a process that needs to be followed." He says, hands out placatingly.

Ash's gaze doesn't waver from his perusal of the Jackal.

"The Twelve are choosing sides as we speak and we have Atticus, don't we? Without this dickhead, we'll be able to take on the rest."

Luca shakes his head. "He's been recruiting. There are other members who have sided with him. They don't like the Crow cleaning things up. There's a lot of talk about the Vulture's business being disbanded. They're criminals for a reason, they don't have morals. Even the Bear isn't happy with the skin markets being gone. He used to sell in them as punishments to his followers. We have to let him go and do this the right way."

Ash sneers at him and I sigh, stepping in. "He's right. The Crow can't defend against nine other members."

Luca shrugs. "Five. The Jackal has five that have followed him. He's working on the Boar but he's very reluctant to side with him over you."

I startle. "Over me? Why the fuck would he side with me?"

Luca shrugs again, grabbing his phone and tapping out a text. "We can't figure that out either. The Jackal is going fucking insane over it, but the Crow can't find a reason why either. He just says it's a blood thing. Whatever the fuck that means. Bikers are a strange breed."

I groan. Will anything ever be straightforward and simple?!

"Fine. Take him and drop him off. I'll call the Crow later and we can... discuss plans."

Luca nods and grins at me again, swooping down to kiss my cheek and making Harley growl at him like a rabid fucking dog.

"I guess I'll have to carry him out myself now you've incapacitated my men, O'Cronin." Luca jokes and Harley snaps at him, "It's Arbour, dickhead."

WE HEAD BACK to the room for a debrief and Avery's handshakes in mine the whole walk back. I feel awful for not warning her and also a little shocked at how badly this has affected her. I mean, I've known all along we're family now but to know just how much she cares is still jarring.

Harley won't stop touching me, clutching at my hand if I move away from his arms, and I think I made a mistake in going down without telling them.

Avery makes us all tea, even though we all said no when she offered to make them, and I clear my throat in an attempt to move the lump in my throat. "I'm sorry I didn't wake anyone. I didn't know Luca was a plant. I thought I'd have a better chance getting him out of here if I wasn't worried about him killing one of you."

Blaise nods but he's staring at his feet, refusing to meet my eyes. Fuck.

Ash takes the cup Avery hands him but doesn't sip it. "There were a lot of options you had, Mounty. This won't work if you don't trust us. Not just the relationship, the whole fucking family won't work if you run off towards the threat to sacrifice yourself at every sign of danger."

I wince but nod. "I know that. I just... I don't want him touching any of you."

Harley's fingers flex in mine, a reminder of how close we got to losing him only weeks ago at the hands of the Jackal. Avery gives me a soft look, knowing exactly what I'm thinking.

"Don't be so harsh. Annabelle drugging Harley did a lot of damage. Lips is barely sleeping now, and she can't make perfect decisions every time something happens." She says and Ash snorts at her.

"I'm not asking for perfect, I'm asking for trust. We all trust you, Mounty. With our lives. Why can't you trust us with the same?"

Tears prick my eyes but I refuse to cry. "And if he'd killed you, Ash? What would I do with myself then? Knowing that he did it for me. He thinks I belong to him, even with me telling him it'll never happen, he doesn't give a fuck about what I want."

Ash slams the coffee cup on the table and stalks into the bathroom, closing the door quietly, though it sounds like a deafening bang in the silence of the room.

Harley squeezes my fingers again. "Just tell someone next time. I thought you were dead at the look on Ash's face when Illi called."

My gut squeezes again and I pull away, ready to grovel at the bathroom door until Ash forgives me.

The Jackal poisons fucking everything.

Harley stops me and directs me back to bed, undressing me and tucking me in as if I can't do it myself. It's only when I end up jammed between Harley and Blaise that I notice how badly I'm shaking. Maybe I wouldn't have managed undressing.

Avery climbs into her bed but the glow of her phone confirms she's not planning on getting any rest. We're all stuck in the limbo of what-ifs.

What if Luca wasn't a plant?

What if I had woken them up?

What if I died?

I startle awake hours later, having not even realized I'd fallen asleep, to Ash sleeping across the bottom of the bed. I'm penned in completely.

"I think he's worried you'll run off on him. He's asked me to put a GPS tracker on your phone." Avery murmurs, making me jump again.

I look over and find her tapping away on her phone again. "I think I fucked up, Aves. I'm really fucking sorry."

She nods and smiles at me. "I get it. I don't like it, but I get it. Ash will too, he's just... worried."

I fight back tears again and nod. When I'm sure I won't cry, I carefully pull out from between the bodies and crawl over to Ash, curling myself around him. His eyes fly open the second I touch him but he relaxes back once I'm plastered to him, his arms wrapping me up tight as he kisses the top of my head.

"I'd rather you hate me for going alone than being dead. I'm sorry I worried you but I'm not sure I'll make a different decision next time. In my mind, I will always be expendable because... I've survived it all before. I can survive it again. I can't face that stuff happening to you and he wouldn't torture you. He'd slit your throat and bleed you out in front of me. He told me that when he called me down to meet him."

Ash nods but doesn't speak. I don't think he's forgiven me, not even close, but I know we'll be okay. At least until something else happens.

"Sorry to interrupt your little make-up session, but Atticus just informed me that we've been summoned by Senior. He's told Atticus he knows about his... plans to keep us separated and he wants to meet with the Wolf." whispers Avery and I groan.

There are too many threats in our lives.

I need a week off.

CHAPTER THIRTY-SEVEN

Exams consume our every waking moment for two weeks.

It's a blessing really because no one has the chance to panic or argue about the Jackal's impromptu visit and Avery is so consumed by her studies that she trusts Atticus to put protective measures in place for our meeting with Senior, despite her rage at his deception.

Harley and Ash become so competitive that I ban them from talking about classwork around me. I can't cope with the snarking and arguing at all, especially not with Blaise looking green the second they start quoting random lines from our literature readings to out do each other.

I just need to get him through the exams.

He's ready. I know he is. We've worked too fucking hard this year, around all the fucking bullshit trying to kill us all, for him not to pass his exams now.

Avery refuses to let any of the guys sleep in our room for the week, claiming they're a distraction for me and bad for my sleep, and I don't have the heart to tell her I sleep better when I know they're all around me. I'm plagued by constant dreams of Jackal, and what would have happened if I hadn't snuck off by myself.

On the last day of exams, I am the first to finish our history exam and I spend ten minutes rereading my answers even though I know they're perfect. The teacher, still the substitute, takes a call and then gestures me to the front. Ash glares as his eyes follow me and I shrug at him.

"You've been called to the principal's office, Miss Anderson. If you're finished, you need to head there now."

What the actual fuck? Mr. Trevelen must be losing his damn mind.

I collect my bag from the front of the class, away from where we could sneak looks at our notes, and make my way to the office.

Something is up.

I slip my knife into my blazer pocket in case it's Joey or Senior, and I prepare my defense in my head if it's some skank running her mouth about me and the guys again to get me kicked out. I mean, Annabelle is taken care of and the cougar was fired so I should be finished with that bull-shit but Hannaford knows how to test my very will to fucking live sometimes.

I'm rehearsing the exact way I'll tell Mr. Trevelen to *fuck off* as I arrive to the office. The receptionist is missing and I frown, weaving my way through the partitions until I get to the principal's office, the door open for me.

I walk in only to find a gun aimed at my chest.

MISS VIVIENNE LOOKS FUCKING DERANGED as she holds the piece in her shaking hands. I stare at her, unblinking and unafraid. Well, I'm a little worried she's taking the safety off and she's going to shoot me by accident with all of the trembling she has going on, but one look into those big doe eyes of her tells me she has no real spine for murder.

"You just couldn't let him go, could you?" She hisses and I struggle to keep myself from rolling my eyes. Really, bitch? *Seriously?!*

"You're going to go to prison for killing me just so you have a chance at climbing on Harley's dick? I mean, he's good but is any dick really worth that?" I say, calmly. I'm waiting for the perfect opening to break the slut's arm. There, I said it; she's a dumb slut and I'm a hypocrite. Sue me.

"Like I give a fuck about that mobster's dick. I don't want to fuck him. I want him fucking dead. I want to deliver you to my love so we can be happy together finally. He can't focus now you've betrayed him. He's fucking gutted you've left the fold."

She continues rambling, on and fucking on, and it takes me a second to process her word.

The Jackal.

The fucking slut was sent here to kill Harley by the fucking Jackal.

I snap. My patience and her fucking arm. She screams so loudly the whole school will have heard it during the exams and fuck it if I care.

I hope Avery can clean it up for me. When I have her on the ground, her unbroken arm pinned behind her back with my knee and her own gun pressed against her skull, I lean down to question her.

"Are you so stupid that you believe Matteo's lies? What did he tell you, that I'm a defector? That I belong to him?"

She sobs and whimpers, not planning on answering, so I

grab a fistful of her hair and yank until her neck bows beautifully. "Answer me. I'm not a patient person."

"He loves me. He just needs you out of the way so we can be together. He found me, he saved me from my husband. Why wouldn't I help him catch you after what you've done?"

I shake my head and fish out my phone. I hesitate for a second and then text the group number. I have to trust them this time and contact them before I call Illi.

I fucking hope it's the right thing to do.

Ash texts back immediately. *On my way.*

I don't want him to see the mess I've made of Miss Vivienne, I don't want to risk it triggering some deep dark memory, but I have no way of cleaning her up a bit.

Fuck it.

When the door eases open and Ash steps through, barely three minutes later so he must've fucking ran here, the look on his face when he sees the gun is *bad*.

"That's not yours, is it?" He snaps, and I shake my head.

"I've just been chatting with the lovely cougar. It turns out we have a mutual friend. Would you like to tell Ash who it is you love so much that you were trying to kill Harley for him?"

She laughs, spitting blood on the floor from where I've broken her nose. "He'd be fucking dead if you hadn't sent the Butcher in. That dirty roofie would've done the job perfectly."

I freeze and Ash's eye flare.

"You gave Annabelle the roofie?" I say, my hand steady as I press the gun into the base on her neck.

The slut chokes on her own blood a little more as she gurgles out, "I drove her down to the Bay myself. We had struck up a lovely friendship before you ran her off. Now I have to answer to her parents, they blame me for not knowing where the fuck she went."

The door slips open again and my other two guys walk in. Blaise frowns at me for a second and then leans back against the door like he's holding it shut. I doubt anyone will disturb us if the scream hadn't sent them running but I guess I should've locked it by now.

Harley pulls up a chair and then helps me off of Miss Vivienne, peeling her off of the floor and dropping her into the chair. I can't look at him right now because all I'll see is the thick tube down his throat and black circles under his eyes that had been permanent while he was in the hospital.

Miss Vivienne is going to die.

She's going to die bloody.

"How about we call your little friend, hmm? How about we ring him and see if he wants to collect you." I say handing Harley the gun and directing the guys until Ash is guarding the door, Blaise is covering the cougar's mouth, and Harley's finger is steady on the trigger.

I lean forward until I'm right in her face. "I didn't defect from him. I'm the *fucking* Wolf of Mounts Bay, and that sadistic fuck sent you here against the Twelve to die for him."

She shakes her head, sobbing behind Blaise's hand and I hit dial.

I hear him breathing as he answers but he doesn't say a word.

"Your little girlfriend is dead."

Her eyes widen at me and she tries to shake free from Blaise but his hand is steady. I'm glad it's him holding her. His trust in me is so complete that he's willing to get blood on his hands because he knows I'll clean it up.

The Jackal's voice is the same one he uses when he's

trying to sweet talk me. "Like I give a fuck about some cougar pussy. I wouldn't put someone in that building with you, little Wolf, unless they were disposable to me and we both know every pussy I've ever had is disposable. Yours is the one I want to keep."

Pathetically, tears fill her eyes. I cannot understand what these women see in Matteo. How can they look at him and not see the monster under his skin?

"I told you I'm not interested."

"And I told you, you're *mine*. I'll kill every fucking man that touches you. You think the Butcher can keep them safe? The Crow and his *fucking* spies? Little girl, I was born in hell and I fought my way to the throne. If I want you, I'll fucking have you."

I stare over Ms. Vivienne's head to my guys and say, "Enjoy the throne for now. It'll be mine before this is all over."

I hang up to the sound of him laughing.

Ms. Vivienne is sobbing behind Blaise's hand now, big heaving gasps like she's heartbroken. I can't stand the sound of it. She's just as fucking weak as the rest of the rich skanks at this school, only she thought she could win over the Jackal.

He doesn't have a soul to win.

My phone pings and I jerk my head for Ash to answer the door, murmuring quietly with Avery until she hands my bag over. He shuts the door and drops the bag at my feet. Ms. Vivienne's eyes land on the bag and the sobs dry up in her throat.

"Let her go, Blaise. Go wait outside, all of you." I say, and I unzip the bag slowly, enjoying the way her eyes track that movement. I'm not a sociopath but fuck it if it doesn't feel satisfying to finally get rid of this bitch.

I dig around for the plastic sheeting, spreading it out with steady hands. It's much easier to be patient and prepared than to be rash and attempt to clean up evidence later.

Ms. Vivienne watches while I prepare for her death and the sobbing starts up again until she's fucking hysterical. Ash grimaces and grabs Blaise's arm, pulling him out the door until I'm left with Harley. I sigh at him which he totally ignores.

"Do you ever listen to me? I'm not trying to hide this from you, I just don't think you should have to watch it." I grumble, tugging my uniform off and then slipping the plastic jumpsuit over my lacy lingerie. I'll have to get Ash to pick me out some more.

Harley's eyes don't falter from where he's watching Ms. Vivienne. One wrong move and I think he'll break her neck. "Blaise is green and Ash has a history that makes killing women hard for him, even when they're treacherous sluts. I don't give a fuck. She pulled a gun on you, she's gotta go."

I grab her by the hair and lean down until I'm at eye level with her. The tears don't work on me, not at all. The second she told me she gave the dirty pills to Annabelle she'd sealed her fate.

"The second you climbed into bed with the Jackal you killed yourself. If I delivered you back to him, he'd cut you into pieces first just to hear you scream. I don't get off on that shit so I'll kill you first even though you deserve all the pain in the fucking world for what you've done. *You're welcome.*"

Then I get to work.

CHAPTER THIRTY-EIGHT

I T TAKES five hours to deal with the problem.

Once she's dead and her heart stops pumping I'm able to do what I need to with minimal mess. I send Blaise to go pick up a couple of black tubs while Avery runs interference so no one stumbles on us while I work. Harley and I argue when he tries to help and eventually he agrees to sit on a chair by the door and just watch. He niggles at me until I explain what I'm doing, and why I'm doing it, teaching him the optimal way to dismember a corpse for transportation and an easier cleanup.

There's still a fuck-tonne of blood.

The smell is fucking vile and once the body, plastic sheeting, and my suit are all sealed in the tubs we open all the windows and I scrub the floor with bleach, killing the smell and any leftover DNA that might have spilled over. Once that's over with Harley cracks the door and snaps at Blaise to grab a tub while he grabs the other one. Ash takes both of my bags and slings them over his shoulders. We head down to the staff carpark together to stash the tubs until we can hand them off to Illi in the morning.

"What the hell is in this thing to make it so fucking heavy?" Blaise grouses, and Harley shakes his head at him.

Ash snarks, "I've seen your exam marks, so I know you're not that fucking stupid."

Blaise blinks at him and then at me. I sigh. "We have to get rid of the... problem somehow. Rolling her up in a rug would have us all in juvie in a second."

Blaise scoffs. "Avery would never let that happen... fuck, is the cougar in here? Disgusting! How the fuck did you bend her into it?"

Harley bursts out laughing but it's more of an are-you-fucking-kidding-me sort of sound. "She didn't bend her. She hacked the cunt into pieces. You wanna fuck a member of the Twelve then you should know your girlfriend isn't scared of getting her hands dirty."

Blaise blinks. Then again. Then finally he looks are me and says, "With that tiny knife? Fuck, that seems like a lot of hard work."

Fuck me.

Is he for real?

"I have a bone saw. Can we just move this shit quietly and get this over with? Avery is going to have a fucking fit if we're not back soon." I say and they all grunt in agreement.

My leg is aching by the time we have both of the tubs loaded into the Maserati. It's a tight fit and when Harley starts bitching about the lack of space Blaise snaps back, "Well, I didn't pick it for its trunk size! How the fuck was I supposed to know we'd be moving... this shit. I'll buy a fucking truck for next year."

I groan. "I don't want to think about next year. Let's just get back to Avery."

Ash stops me and then slowly checks every inch of my skin for signs of the work I've just done. I'm thorough, so I'm not worried, but he turns me and pulls at my clothes until he's sure I'm blood-free.

I crack a joke in an attempt to lighten the mood. "I could just blame my period if I've missed a spot."

He glares at me and then slings his arm around my waist, helping me to walk with my sore leg. "You're so fucking strange, Mounty."

I scoff at him. "So the joke is strange but the work isn't? You're just as twisted as I am, Beaumont."

Avery is twitchy when we arrive in the dining hall for dinner. She scans my body, much like her brother had until she's satisfied I'm unharmed. I smile at her a little crookedly but I'm still mostly human. The new and improved Lips, the one who wears the skin of the Wolf even while I'm at school, she doesn't need to be coddled. She isn't wary of touch anymore.

I'm so fucking glad I have my family.

Blaise pulls a face when Ash asks him what he wants for dinner and I ignore their snarking. I can't eat now, not until tomorrow at least and for once they don't push me.

Harley eats just fine.

Blaise gags at the sight and I can't help but laugh at him, his moral lines as fucking blurred as the rest of us despite his dramatics.

When I go to bed that night, tucked between Harley and Ash and listening to Blaise soft snore from the couch, I sleep like a fucking baby.

No one goes after my family and survives.

THE END of year assembly is subdued this year compared to the last few years.

I'm not worried about anything and even the whispers have completely stopped around me. Every student at Hannaford has noticed the disappearance of anyone who crosses me and my little family.

They're all terrified.

I get the top of the class in every subject except choir, which Blaise wins by the smallest of margins. No hard feelings and the smug look on his face makes my chest hurt in the best way. Harley and Ash come second, Harley in more subject than Ash which I'm sure he'll crow about until classes start up again next year. I'm honestly a little terrified about it.

We spend two days packing our rooms and when it's time to leave Blaise is grumbling and pissy over how bad the smell in the Maserati will be thanks to the tubs being left in them for days. He's shocked to find them missing and I laugh at him.

"Did you really think I'd leave them laying around? Illi picked them up for us."

Blaise frowns and pops the trunk to sling our bags in. "How the fuck did he get into the car? The alarms on this thing are insane."

Harley chuckles at him. "The key. I gave him my set when he called. Why are you being so fucking precious over this thing? At least it's still in one piece."

Blaise cringes and nods. No one likes to bring up the 'stang.

I give Avery the front seat even though Blaise pouts about it and we head back to the Bay together. Avery starts telling us all about the renovations to her ranch and I make another mental note to call the Coyote for a security system upgrade. There's no way I'm calling the Crow, if Ash lays eyes on him he'll fucking skin him and the only help in that situation will be Harley holding the fuck down.

We stay at the same hotel, stupidly I should know better than to stick to a routine.

I walk with Avery, our arms tucked together as the boys trail behind us, bickering and arguing like idiots. Avery freezes at the door and I glance up to find a well-dressed thug in the hotel room.

I dart around her, shielding her even as Ash does the same, but his eyes don't look shocked. They look wary, knowing. Fuck, that's not a good sign.

"Your father has invited you to dinner. You will not be late. You will not decline. You will not invite any further guests. The Wolf and the Crow will both attend. If you know what is good for you, you'll track your brother down and bring him as well. Nine pm."

Then his lists off the name of a place I've never even driven past, it's so far uptown and walks out. Avery groans and slumps down, resting her forehead on my shoulder.

"I need a week off." She mumbles and I sigh. Don't we all.

Ash stalks to the bar, foregoing the glass entirely and taking deep swigs straight from the bottle. Blaise waves a blunt at him and they disappear out to the balcony. I narrow my eyes at them but Avery stomps over, cussing them out.

"There's hours left. He won't go down there without a clear head." Harley murmurs behind me and I nod. I don't like it but it's not my choice.

Hours of stewing on the couch in silence later, I climb into the shower and pray the hot water will give me the fucking answers on how to get through tonight without losing one of our family.

Avery sinks on the bathroom sink, wearing only a silk robe, and pouts. "I don't want to see Atticus. I'm so angry at him, I'm not sure I ever want to see him again."

I scrub at my hair and shrug. "Why? I mean, I know he didn't tell you who he was but... you know the real him."

She narrows her eyes at me. "Are you defending him? Ash will spit it at you."

I snort at her, such a lady. "No, I'm asking my best friend what the exact problem is so when this entire night goes to hell in a handbasket I know enough to pick the right battles."

Her eyes soften and she sighs, leaning back to bump her head against the mirror gently like she trying to knock some sense back into her brain. "He still sees me as some precious little girl that needs to be protected. I'm not angry he didn't tell me he's a member of the Twelve, I'm angry he came up to buy me from you like I'm... an object. That's exactly what Rory thought of me too, but Rory was a distraction not... Atticus."

There are tears rimming her eyes but the look on her face is fucking fierce. Oh boy, he's fucked up. He's fucked up so bad he may never dig himself out of this bullshit he's buried himself in.

"Well, maybe it's time we reminded him that you're Avery fucking Beaumont and you might have shown him your soft side because he meant something to you but that doesn't make you any less of a ruthless, cutthroat dictator. Beat him in his own game because Aves, he has no fucking clue who he's really dealing with."

She smiles at me and hands me a towel. "None of these stupid boys do."

CHAPTER THIRTY-NINE

I HATE the dress Avery has put me in but I have to admit, she knows her shit. I fit right in. The restaurant is flashy, overdone, and intimidating to stand in. If I didn't already know half the waiters I'd be uncomfortable as fuck, but Joseph Beaumont has underestimated my reach.

I nod at the maître d' and he tips his head at me respectfully. Ash scoffs at me. "Is there anyone you don't know in the Bay?"

I shrug and wait for him to take us to our seats. The Crow is already waiting for us in the lounge, sipping a malt whiskey, with Luca flanking him in a sharp suit. I sigh as Harley's fists clench at his sides.

"Wolf."

I shake my head at him and say, "Are we the Twelve today, or are friends? I don't make my friends call me the Wolf."

Harley glares at Atticus like he wants to beat him bloody for everything that has ever happened to Ash and Avery while this man stood by and let it, and I grab his wrist gently to try to remind him of our conversation.

We win nothing here by being obvious in our dislike of this man.

"Forgive me, I'm not accustomed to seeing you as anything but the Wolf." Atticus's eyes flick over to Avery and the slow perusal of her outfit is the last straw for Harley.

"I'm going to bathe in your blood, you manipulative, spineless *cunt*." He hisses and Blaise barely manages to grab him before he chokes the fucker out.

"HA! There it is! There's the impulsive Irishman in the kid. Can't say I blame him, I'd slit your throat any day of the week for the shit you've pulled on *our* family." says Illi, sauntering in behind us, looking as dangerous as ever in his suit.

I gape a little and then snap a photo on my phone, giggling at him like a little schoolgirl. I don't even care about the danger we're all facing in that second. Because Illi. In. A. Suit.

He smirks at me and shrugs. "You can't get in here without one and I didn't want to make a scene."

Ash quirks an eyebrow at me and I laugh, "He didn't even wear a suit to his wedding! It's ridiculous to see him in one now. What the fuck did Odie say when she saw it?"

Illi cackles and when he steps up alongside Ash, I'm shocked to see them exchange a knowing, and respectful, nod. They stand like a wall between Avery and Atticus like they've become best friends without me noticing. When the fuck did that happen?

Atticus looks straight through them, unconcerned with their clear threat. "Avery-"

Her voice is glacial. "No, thank you. I'm quite fine where I am. Lips, I'm happy to wait for our table here with Illi."

That's my girl. I smirk and Illi catches on quickly, slinging himself in the chair next to her and slinging an arm over the back of her chair.

Neither Ash or Harley tense up in any way but Atticus stares down at the Butcher of the Bay like he's planning on ripping that arm right the fuck off of him.

Illi winks at Atticus. "Odie has decided to embrace the polygamous lifestyle of our little club and she *loves* the little Ice Queen."

Blaise snickers under his breath. Harley elbows him in the ribs but the smirk on his face gives him away.

I wait, fully prepared to dive into the fray to get Avery out safely if Atticus loses his damn head. Illi's arms are loose and casual but I know he could tear Atticus in half in a split second without breaking a sweat.

The silence stretches on until finally, a waiter comes to direct us to our private table in the back. Illi jumps up and helps Avery to her feet like the perfect gentleman, guiding her over to walk with Ash behind me. Then he takes up the rear, watching everyone and ready to start swinging his cleaver the second things go south.

As we weave our way through the tables to the private area I glance back to Ash and raise an eyebrow at him. He knows what I'm asking and rolls his eyes at me.

"The night he called me to go find you, even after you told him not to, I decided he's not so bad."

I shake my head. "Not so bad?"

Blaise laughs, his fingers dancing along my arm. "Star, he's a part of our family now too. Maybe not our *immediate* family, but he's like a distant cousin we hang out with at family reunions because everyone else sucks ass."

Illi cackles at me, listen to our every word. "See kid? I'm the cool cousin you can't wait to drink with."

Harley snorts. "The cousin we call when we need a body to disappear. How useful."

Avery giggles and says, "I'm just glad Ash approves. It's nice that he's no longer snarling at my choice in men."

Atticus's shoulders tense so badly even his expensive suit can't hide it. To think I've been so wary of this man from the moment I met him and all along his weakness has been my dictator best friend with an icy gaze and a heart too fucking big for those she loves.

No matter what happens between them, I'll back her.

Even if we have to add him to the list of people hunting us.

The waiter ushers us into the back room where Joseph Beaumont Senior is already seated at the table waiting for us.

"Who would have thought a slum slut from Mounts Bay could look so good in a dress? From Joey's descriptions, I thought you must be hideous but I can see the appeal."

His voice makes my skin crawl.

How the fuck did he convince a young Alice Arbour that he was human? He sounds like a fucking monster.

Atticus steps up next to me and pulls out a chair, gesturing for me to sit. Harley cuts him a look, then takes a seat to my right and Avery sits to my left. One by one, everyone sits on my side of the table, except Illi who takes up watch by the door, a knife dancing back and forth between his hands.

I'm tempted to get him to throw the fucking thing right into Senior's throat.

"I don't appreciate being summoned." Says Atticus, taking a napkin and laying it across his lap like he's actually preparing to eat. There is no way I can stomach food right now. No fucking way.

"And why would I give a fuck what the useless third son of Crawford should want? Ah. But you've gone out and made a new name for yourself, haven't you? The peasants of Mounts Bay don't impress me and neither do their Kings."

I keep my mouth shut while I watch him.

Ash is right, he and Avery get their looks from this vile man. I suppose this is what Ash will look like in thirty years, but only if all of the humanity has been squeezed out of him. The difference between Ash and Senior is his soul, the same one he shares with Avery. I look at Senior and see nothing of his children in him. Not the twins anyway.

I see far too much of Joey.

I glance around, but the psycho fuck isn't anywhere to be seen. I glance at Avery and she gives me the slightest shake of her head. Fuck.

"I'm not here to speak to *the Crow*. I want to talk to the little girl who thinks she can take my children from me."

I glance back to Senior and stare him down, my gaze and my breathing as steady as always. He's a monster, but he's not the worst I've ever faced.

"I don't think I can take them, I *have* taken them. I'm only here so you know for sure that they're mine now. We can discuss terms, but nothing changes that fact."

Senior's eyes flick across my face and neck, the same way Joey's do like he's looking for my weak point. I don't rise to the bait.

He leans back in his chair, flicking a wrist to summon

himself a drink. "And what are you going to do if I don't agree to your terms? I have plans for them both."

I make a big show of staring down each of his bodyguards, all eight of them. "I'd put money on my men over yours. Honestly? I'd put money on the Butcher taking care of the whole lot of them without any help."

Senior raises his glass to his lips and smiles at me, chilling my blood with the cruel twist to his lips. "I own everyone. I own the police who will arrest you and the judge at your trial. I own the prison officers who will tuck you into bed every night and fondle you in the showers. I own your teachers and taxi drivers, and I own your friends. I think you're underestimating me, little girl."

I don't let the trickle of fear running down my spine show. He may have reach, it might be widespread and tangled up in our lives, but I know he isn't as powerful as he's making out. Why else would he try to deal with the Devil?

My voice doesn't waiver as I reply, "And I *know* you're underestimating me."

He lifts a shoulder at me and then fixes his gaze on Ash. The sadistic gleam to his eyes lights something in my blood and I damn near climb over the table and slit his throat myself.

"Where is your brother? I told you to bring him with you."

I mentally call dibs on killing him.

Ash stares at him, unflinching, and my heart nearly bursts with pride. "How should I know? He's not my responsibility."

Senior's eyes narrow a fraction. "Your time fucking slum pussy has made you forget yourself, boy."

Avery's leg tenses against mine and I tuck my hand in hers under the table.

"I will never set foot in your house again. I will never live by your rules again. I will never babysit Joey and cover for his deranged games again." Ash hisses, leaning forward slightly. Illi rumbles happily under his breath by the door, reminding us all that he's watching and prepared to spill blood.

Hmm, more than prepared. Itching to bleed them all out.

The anger leaks out of Senior's face as he replies, "You could be so much more than your brother. I look at you and see every inch of myself, all the bloodlust and rage. If only you weren't corrupted by the little cunt in the womb, maybe then you'd be a man."

I roll my eyes and clasp my hands in front of myself on the table, drawing his gaze back to me. I'm done with this little show of power. I want to go home and plan how I'm going to climb the walls of Beaumont Manor and gut this fuck in his sleep, nice and quietly, where none of his bought police force can save him.

"I'm leaving now. I was hoping for a more productive dinner meeting but if all we're going to do is boast about whose dick does more damage then I'm leaving."

Senior flicks his wrist again and the waiters start to bring out the first course of dinner. "You can leave if you want, little girl, but Avery isn't going anywhere. I've secured a buyer for her and the exchange is being made on her birthday."

Buyer?

Exchange?!

Over my dead fucking body.

I open my mouth to tell the sadistic fuck that when the

waiter moves to place my plate in front of me. Only it's not a plate.

It's a cardboard box.

With my full name on it.

No one at the table speaks. Harley hasn't noticed the box, he's too busy trying to contain the rage pumping through his bloodstream and clouding his brain. Avery's skin is beyond white, a thin sheen of sweat covering her forehead, but she's now looking at the box.

Why would Senior be giving me this?

Has he been sending the heads all along? Why? I look up at him but he's staring at the box with the smallest of lines between his brow. So not from him. Fuck.

The Crow doesn't look away from Senior either.

I pick up the steak knife and slit the box open. The smell is less putrid, the head clearly a far more recent kill than the last two.

I lift the flaps and find that for the first time there's a note sitting on top of the head. I grab it first, stupidly because I should grab gloves from Illi first in case we can lift some prints, but my brain isn't working properly at all. The words are written in large cursive letters and a chill races down my spine.

No one touches my blood.

Fuck. Who the hell else have I pissed off?! I think back over the people I've taken out but there's been too many to narrow it down at all. Fuck.

Avery stops breathing next to me, her lungs just ceasing to work.

I look down and my heart jumps into my throat as I stare down into the vacant, lifeless eyes of Joseph Beaumont Jr.

Joey is dead.

Fuck.

Lips, Avery, Harley, Ash, and Blaise will return for senior year.
Preorder your copy here:

Hannaford Prep Year Four

ACKNOWLEDGMENTS

This book was made possible by Laura Frazier.

She is my number one cheerleader, beta-reader, and dear friend. She holds my hand through all the tough shit and also tells me to suck it up when I'm being a sook. And to say thanks to her I strand her on chapters that end with heads in boxes and Harley being comatose in hospital. I can't actually thank you enough. Seriously, you're the best.

To Katy, who completes our Coven. Thank you for being such an amazing, loyal, kind, freaking perfect supporter and friend. I mean it when I say I'd do anything for our little Coven and someday I will write that M/M book for you! We've just got to convince Laura to read it!

Thank you to Laura Marrero for beta reading, cheerleading, swapping photos of hot guys, listening to me ramble, and being such a supportive member of the indie book community. I am so glad you reached out to me!

To everyone in my Facebook group, you all give me life and

make this whole journey so much fun. Thank you from the bottom of my black stained heart.

And thank you to my amazing readers who gave Hannaford Prep a chance. It's turning out to be a wild ride and I hope you come back for the final year.

ABOUT THE AUTHOR

J Bree is a dreamer, writer, mother, farmer, and cat-wrangler. The order of priorities changes daily.

She lives on a small farm in a tiny rural town in Australia that no one has ever heard of. She spends her days dreaming about all of her book boyfriends, listening to her partner moan about how the wine grapes are growing, and being a snack bitch to her two kids.

If you want to know when J's next book will come out, please visit her website at http://www.jbreeauthor.com, and sign up for the newsletter or join her group on Facebook at Breezie's Wolves

f

CONTINUE READING FOR A SNEAK
PEEK AT

To the End
Hannaford Prep Year Four

PROLOGUE

Blaise

Star looks down at the box and I don't have to be psychic to know whose head is in the fucking thing. She looks like it's the worst possible choice and her face is blank before her eyes flick back up to the deranged serial killer at the table.

Joey is dead.

I can't say I'm sorry to see that psychotic fuck go but as Senior's eyes bore into my girl I kinda wish Joey was still breathing. How the fuck do we get out of this?

Harley knocks my leg under the table and I dip my chin a fraction so he knows he's got my attention. He traces an 'A' on the table in front of him, an old signal we've used a million times before.

He's telling me to get Avery the hell out of here and for the first time I'm torn. She's not cut out for when shit goes south like this, not physically at least. Some day that girl is going to dance on a big stage and have pompous rich dickheads falling at her feet. She can't afford to be injured, but more than that, we can't afford for Ash to see his sister hurt.

I'm fairly certain Ash is more dangerous than Senior, one-on-one. It's the damn statement about the cops that has me worried. What the fuck is Star going to do?

It's only that I'm watching her so closely that I see her pass her phone to Avery under the table, and Floss' face stays carefully blank and her fingers move swiftly across the screen by memory alone.

"How much do you owe your buyer? Now that you can't deliver?" Lips says, her voice is so fucking flat and bored I'm impressed.

The serial killer just ignores her, cutting his steak up into tiny pieces with surgeon-like precision. He takes his time, waiting until he has a piece speared on his fork before answering her. "What's in the box, little girl? Who is delivering parcels to you during my time?"

She leans back in her chair, cool and calm. "Answer my question, Beaumont. The box is none of your concern."

He doesn't like that. Not one fucking bit.

His lip curls at her, slowly shifting into a cruel smirk that makes him look deranged. "He was very interested in her, I don't think even the *Wolf of Mounts Bay* could convince the Devil not to take what is his. Run along, go hide her. He'll only enjoy the chase."

The Devil.

Harley's fingers twitch and I bump his leg with mine, reminding him that we'll be fucking fine.

We've survived the kinds of hell people couldn't even dream.

Why not add *the Devil* to the mix?

Lips stands, smoothing her dress down like Avery does, and we all stand with her. Even that stupid fuck Atticus.

"I'd thank you for the meal, but your company has been... lacking." Lips says, tucking her hand into Harley's and tugging him away from the table. Avery looks up at me and I give her a curt nod.

Senior watches Lips' back like he's imagining all of the things he's going to carve into her skin and get off to and I can't fucking take it.

Apparently, neither can Ash.

"Here. Just so you know we did our best to get him here. He seems to be... otherwise occupied." Ash sneers, and pushes the box until Joey's head rolls out.

I could fucking vomit.

I hold it in, because no one else looks sick and I'll be fucked if I'm the only one puking over this shit, and I tug Avery away from the table.

Two of Senior's bodyguards jolt away from the far wall, ready to throw themselves at Ash and Lips, and I hesitate for a second.

I shouldn't bother.

Illi palms two meat cleavers and *throws them across the room.*

Avery makes a little noise in the back of her throat and I decide pretty fucking quick that I need to keep her walking. We stalk through the restaurant at a slow enough pace that no one notices us but still cutting through the building pretty fucking quick.

Avery hums under her breath, completely distracted by whatever-the-fuck-it-is she's piecing together in that evil genius brain of hers. I'm too busy trying to look out for more of Senior's men to question her.

When we get to the exit, there are cop cars everywhere and I curse viciously under my breath, but there's also more than a hundred motorcycles with scary-ass bikers on them, starting fights with the pigs and smashing up the cars.

Right.

Lips called in a favor.

There's a biker leaning against the wall of the restaurant, watching us both intensely. He's wearing a president patch so I figure out pretty quickly he's the Boar.

Avery stares right back at him, cataloging every fucking inch of the man until I bump her shoulder with mine to distract her. I don't need her accidentally starting shit with a member of the fucking Twelve while Lips isn't here.

"Does he look familiar to you?" She murmurs, and I shake my head.

"I don't exactly spend much time with dirty bikers, Floss."

She purses her lips at me, something she does when she thinks I'm being particularly stupid. I fucking hate it.

"I need to speak to Atticus. I need to look into Lips' background. We know nothing about who her family really is. Or her father."

I blink at her.

What the *fuck?*